SONGS OF WAR

Also by Kate Alexander

Fields of Battle
Friends and Enemies
Paths of Peace
Bright Tomorrows

Songs of War

Kate Alexander

Macdonald

A Macdonald Book

Copyright © Tilly Armstrong 1987

First published in Great Britain in 1987 by
Macdonald & Co (Publishers) Ltd
London & Sydney

British Library Cataloguing in Publication Data

Alexander, Kate
Songs of war.
Rn: Tilly Armstrong   I. Title
823'.914[F]   PR6051.L363

ISBN 0-356-14549-2

Photoset in North Wales by
Derek Doyle & Associates, Mold, Clwyd.
Printed in Great Britain by
Redwood Burn Limited, Trowbridge, Wiltshire.
Bound at the Dorstel Press.

Macdonald & Co (Publishers) Ltd
Greater London House
Hampstead Road
London NW1 7QX

A BPCC plc Company

Luke

The autumn afternoon was pleasant, but the Liverpool docks looked bleak. On the quayside a crowd of passengers waited to board the liner which would take them away from the European war. The mood was sombre, with an undercurrent of excitement. They had all heard the news: Germany had invaded Poland early the previous morning. There was still talk of negotiations; Hitler had spoken of his 'modest proposals'; but no one really believed that war could be averted.

The passengers were a mixture of nationalities – many British, predominantly women and children, with family connections on the other side of the Atlantic, who were being sent out of harm's way for the duration, Jewish refugees who had already fled once from Nazi persecution and who did not believe that the French and British would be able to hold Hitler at bay, some Germans, a scattering of Poles and Czechs, and a contingent of Americans, one of whom was, even at this late hour, still voicing her disgust at being sent away.

It was not the place to get into an argument and it was too late to do any good, but Prue Lindquist had to make one last protest while she still had her husband by her side.

'I don't *want* to go back to the States.'

'I know, honey, I know.'

Prue's temper began to rise.

'Don't talk to me in that soothing way when you know darn well you don't mean to let me stay.'

Luke Lindquist grinned and Prue sighed in defeat.

'If only I hadn't got pregnant,' she said.

'I'd still rather know that you're safely back home.'

'I thought my home was with you, no matter where your rotten job might take you.'

'That was before we knew about Junior.'

'If I get as seasick as I did last time I crossed the Atlantic,

Junior is going to have a bumpy ride. How about the damage that might do him ... or her?'

'I talked to the doctor and he said as long as you were sensible a sea voyage wouldn't be harmful. You know what to do if you feel queasy.'

There was a surge forward amongst the waiting crowd and Prue dropped the unequal argument until she was on the ship, her luggage stowed away and the parting was really on them. The woman with whom she was sharing the tiny cabin had gone up on deck. Prue and Luke clung together, both desperate at the things that had been left unsaid.

'It's going to be hell without you,' Luke muttered at last.

'Hell for me, too.'

'I wish I could have arranged for someone to meet you in Montreal ...'

'I guess I can manage to get myself on a train OK.'

'Make sure you get a porter. No lugging heavy luggage around.'

'I'll send you a cable as soon as I arrive.'

'You may find that difficult if war's broken out. Get the paper on to it and make them let me know you're all right.'

'I'll write as soon as I get to Boston.'

'Remember me to your Mom and Pop.'

'At least you've earned Mom's approval by sending me back.'

'The first thing I've done right since we got married,' Luke agreed.

Leaning against him, Prue said in a low voice, 'You'll look after yourself, won't you? Remember you're a family man – very nearly. The *New York Times* can survive without another world scoop from Luke Lindquist, but Junior is going to need his Dad.'

'I'll take care,' Luke promised.

Prue closed her eyes and hid her face against his shoulder so that he should not see the fear that racked her. She understood the worth of that promise too well. If Luke was on the track of a good story he would go after it, come hell or high water, and never mind the risks. She had known it when she married him, just as she had known for too long now that if there was war in Europe Luke was going to be right up front reporting it.

The passengers were sent ashore and Prue went on deck to wave goodbye. Luke, craning his neck to get a final glimpse of her, had to blink his eyes and swallow as he made out the figure of his wife, looking very small and far away, lonely in spite of being surrounded by her fellow passengers. At that distance her pregnancy was unnoticeable. She was wearing the good camelhair coat he had given her as a farewell present, swinging loosely open.

As he watched, Prue took off the green silk scarf she had twisted round her neck and waved it. The gay, brave little banner fluttered in the breeze and then a sudden gust of wind caught it and snatched it from her hand. Prue leaned over the railing until the scarf touched the water, then she looked towards Luke again, pantomiming her annoyance and regret. Luke, too, could see the scarf, no longer bright and attractive, but just a sodden rag.

The ship was moving away down the Mersey. He gave one final wave, but without that bright green speck he could no longer make out the figure of his wife.

They had been married five years and it was not the first time they had been parted by the demands of his job. They had married in a hurry when Luke had been posted to China. Prue had insisted on going with him, but she had always known that for a reporter of Luke's calibre there was no substitute for seeing events with his own eyes, and she had accepted that she would remain in Peking while he was in Chunking trying to get to grips with the fighting between the Chinese and the Japanese.

Before their marriage Prue had had a career of her own on the newspaper in New York and she had made up her mind to keep it up in some form or another. The steady trickle of departures from Peking of other foreign residents, as the war went badly for the Chinese, had left her even more isolated than she would otherwise have been and she had turned to writing fiction, both to keep herself occupied and to blot out her worries about Luke.

After a few small successes with short stories she had become more ambitious and written a novel. When Luke had returned to Peking in 1937 at the time of its occupation by the Japanese

Army, Prue had a completed manuscript to show him. She had some misgivings because *Eastern Windows* dealt with the experiences of a lonely wife trying to come to terms with life in a strange country, but although Luke admitted that there were passages in the book which made him feel uncomfortable, if not downright guilty, he had urged her to submit it for publication since he believed that with this new venture Prue had revealed an unexpected talent.

Eastern Windows had been accepted and published in America after Prue and Luke had left China, just before they sailed for Europe. It had sold in respectable numbers and had been noticed by critics whose opinion both Prue and Luke respected. Prue had been sufficiently encouraged to get down to writing a second book as soon as they had settled in England, and Luke thought that this more assured novel was going to be a real breakthrough for Prue.

'Nineteen-forty is going to be your year,' he said. 'A baby and a best-seller: there can't be many women who achieve both at the same time.'

Prue was taking the manuscript with her on her reluctant journey back to the United States. If it had not been for the coming baby nothing would have persuaded her to leave Luke, certainly not the war they both anticipated. Although she had argued that British women were going to go on having babies even in wartime, there had been just the tiniest doubt at the back of her mind about the wisdom of exposing herself and the unborn child to air raids and possible invasion. Luke had been quick to detect her fears and to use them to bolster his determination to get her away before hostilities broke out.

They both knew that this was likely to be a longer and more difficult separation than anything that had gone before. Luke had been in Germany recently and had been appalled by the evidence he had picked up of the country's readiness for war. The ordinary man in the street might say that he had no wish to fight the French and British, but in Luke's opinion the armed forces were panting for the opportunity and were sure of their ability to win a quick and easy victory.

It hardly bore thinking about, but he was none too sure that Nazi Germany could be defeated. What would happen if

France and Britain went down? Would the United States come to the rescue? On the morning of the day he saw Prue off, the British newspapers had reported President Roosevelt as saying that America would make every effort to keep out of it.

Luke got a train back to London, groped his way home in the blackout that had already been imposed, even though war was not yet declared, and reluctantly let himself into the flat he and Prue had rented in Kensington, hating it for being so spic and span. Prue had gone in for an orgy of cleaning and tidying before she had left. She had stocked up the refrigerator, but he had no appetite; all his socks were darned, all his buttons had been sewn on, the saucepans glittered, even the curtains were newly washed.

Luke understood that she had been both making a protest about being sent away from her home and expressing her love for him when she had chased after non-existent cobwebs and washed down the tiles in the bathroom. He tried to feel that her presence was still there, but the rooms seemed desolately empty, particularly since they had agreed that it was wiser for Prue to pack her cherished Chinese scrolls and porcelain vases and take them with her to the States. Her half of the wardrobe was empty; there was none of her usual clutter in the bathroom; in the morning her pillow would be undented.

Work was the one thing that would help. Luke went to the desk he had shared with Prue. Only the previous day she had been sitting there, typing furiously in an effort to get her amended manuscript ready for packing away in her trunk. The original pages, covered with scrawled alterations, had been bundled untidily into a cardboard box. Luke knew that Prue had intended him to throw the box away, but at that moment he could not bring himself to discard such a tangible reminder of her. He put it in the bottom drawer of the desk instead. He would write and tell Prue and she would tease him about it, but she would understand his sentimental gesture. Probably she would have done the same, if he had gone off leaving nothing of himself behind but an unpublished book.

Luke plunged into the story he was due to write on Britain's

9

last minute preparations for war, a cigarette smouldering forgotten in the ashtray by his side. The flat began to look more normal, especially after he had had some food, left the dishes in the sink to be washed later, and taken his cup of coffee back to his desk so that he could get on with his story.

By the next day Luke had got over the worst of it and had recovered his certainty that it was right for Prue to go back to her parents to bear the coming child.

He turned on the wireless in the middle of the morning and heard the expected news that Great Britain's ultimatum to Germany had received no response and the country was at war. Prue would know now that Luke had been right when he had insisted on booking the first available passage for her, even though it meant disembarking at Montreal. They had both seen the anxious Americans queuing outside shipping offices, trying to get home.

The sound of an air raid warning took him by surprise, though he should have been expecting it: most people thought that the bombardment from the air would start as soon as war broke out. It was a mournful noise, a horrible wail, and it had already come in for a lot of criticism. Luke smiled to himself in affectionate amusement. Only the British would take up space in their newspapers to suggest that their air raid warnings should be more cheerful.

He debated whether to go down to the shelter in the basement of the block of flats and decided against it. In the event he was right because nothing happened. The 'All Clear' sounded quite soon. Either the bombers had not got through or else it had been a false alarm.

Luke went out in the evening for a drink and a meal with some of his Fleet Street cronies to pick up any crumbs of information that might be floating around. As he had guessed, the air raid warning had merely been someone with a jittery finger on the buzzer.

He sat around, chatting idly, until midnight, reluctant to go home to the empty flat.

'Are you going over to France?' someone asked.

'Yeah, in the next couple of days. I wanted to go to Poland, but I was told to sit tight until the big balloon went up. At least I was able to see Prue off.'

'She did finally go?'

'Under protest!'

'So you're a bachelor boy again. Have another whisky.'

'No, thanks. I'll be on my way.'

He paused by the door for a word with a man who had just come in.

'Hi, Joe! What's new?'

'Don't ask me! Getting information out of the Brits is like getting blood out of a stone. There's some buzz on at the Admiralty, but the Silent Service is living up to its reputation and the Ministry of Information – so-called – knows nothing.'

Luke froze for a moment with his hand on the door, then he shrugged off the feeling of apprehension. It was pretty damned stupid to let his mind turn automatically to fears for Prue, sailing safely across the Atlantic in a civilian vessel, just because there was talk of action at sea. If there had been fighting it had probably been in the Channel, or perhaps the North Sea.

It was one o'clock before Luke got into bed. He had slept badly the night before, missing Prue, and because of his fatigue and the several whiskies he had drunk he fell asleep quickly and heavily.

He was woken up by his telephone ringing insistently. Luke groped for it and muttered, 'Hello', still half asleep.

'Luke? Can you come in to the office right away?'

Luke grunted and forced his eyes open enough to see the clock. It was barely seven o'clock.

'I suppose so,' he said, sitting up. 'What's up? An invasion?'

'No – not yet. Just get in here and I'll tell you when you arrive.'

Luke showered and shaved and made himself some coffee before he left and then, by great good fortune, picked up a stray taxi to take him to the City.

'Heard the news?' the taxi driver said. 'Bloody U-boats have started sinking ships in the Atlantic.'

In the Atlantic. All the uneasiness Luke had felt the previous

11

night came back in a rush. A U-boat, though; no U-boat would make the mistake of sinking a liner on that route, knowing it must be carrying neutral, civilian passengers. It was unthinkable.

There were more people in the office than Luke would have expected at that time in the morning.

'What's up?' he asked a colleague, who was typing busily with a telephone cradled against his ear.

'Some U-boat captain's gone off his head and sunk a passenger liner. A lot of Americans on board.'

Something about Luke's silence made the other man look up and ask, 'Something wrong?'

'Do you know the name of the ship?'

'Sure. The *Athenia*. One of the Donaldson Line, en route for Montreal. She was torpedoed about two hundred and fifty miles west of Donegal.'

'Survivors?'

'Being picked up by other ships. The U-boat didn't stay around to help, which is a direct contravention of the rules of submarine warfare.'

The words made no sense. Who cared about rules in wartime? Luke turned away, moving blindly for the door. He bumped into someone and looked at him without recognizing the head of the London Bureau.

'Thank God you're here,' he said, clutching Luke's arm. 'That ship ... I know Prue sailed on Saturday ... Was it ... ?'

'Prue was on board the *Athenia*.'

The grip on his arm tightened.

'A lot of people have been picked up, a hell of a lot. Casualties aren't heavy. No need to give up hope.'

'She was ... she's expecting a baby.'

'Yes, I know. Even so ... Prue's a tough, healthy girl. A lousy experience for her, but she'll rise above it, you'll see.'

Everyone tried to help him. They badgered the American Embassy, the British Admiralty, the authorities in Belfast and the shipping line for information, but although it was known that several ships in the vicinity had picked up survivors from the *Athenia*, no lists of names were available.

'Two destroyers are taking passengers to Clydeside and a

Norwegian steamer called the *Knute Nelson*, with four hundred survivors on board, is making for Galway,' Luke was told.

'I'll go to Glasgow,' he said.

The train was overcrowded and the occasional delays were not explained to the passengers, which made Luke guess that they were due to troop movements. He could find nothing better than a place in the corridor and stood leaning on the wooden bar across the window, staring out for as long as the light lasted at the English countryside rushing past, green, peaceful and untouched.

As darkness came, Luke wedged himself into a corner, sitting on the canvas bag that had been round the world with him. The dim blue lighting did not allow him even the distraction of reading. There was nothing he could do except sit and think, about Prue, about sinking ships and the grey, heaving sea.

It had been intended to land the survivors at Old Kirkpatrick, but there was thick mist on the Firth and the ships were diverted to Greenock.

'Everything's in confusion,' a man standing near Luke muttered, but it was a halfhearted grumble. They all knew nothing could be done about the weather.

'Who are you waiting for?' he asked Luke.

'My wife.'

'Me, too. And my son. He's eight years old. My sister's married to a Canadian, so I sent them off to her for the duration. Thought they'd be safe.'

Luke moved away, not wanting to talk. He saw the man later, when the passengers began to come ashore. A small boy in a seaman's jersey which reached his knees detached himself from a woman who seemed to be looking after him and looked round uncertainly. The man stepped forward.

'Bobby!'

'Hello, Dad.'

'Hello, Son.'

They looked at one another, beginning to smile, then the

13

boy's mouth trembled and the man caught him up in a fierce, awkward embrace.

When he let his son go he tried to sound normal.

'You've had a real adventure.'

'It was ever so exciting,' the boy agreed, without much conviction. 'Where's Mum?'

'Isn't she ... isn't she with you?'

'There was only room for one in the lifeboat, so she put me in and said she'd get in the next one. I couldn't find her anywhere on the ship that picked us up, but everyone said she'd be here when we arrived.'

Luke still did not want to get involved with anyone else, but he could not bear the sight of the child's desperate eyes.

'There's another ship docking,' he said. 'My wife wasn't on this one either, but I expect she's on the second one with your mother.'

He wished he had not spoken when he saw the look of satisfied trust on the boy's face. He stepped back, out of the throng. No use scanning faces any longer. Prue was definitely not amongst this lot of passengers. Not amongst those who had been carried ashore on stretchers either, and that was something to be thankful for.

The second ship came in. Another period of tension and waiting. A woman appeared in what had once been a smart black crêpe dress. It was stained with sea water and had shrunk up round her knees. She had no shoes. There was a livid scratch across one cheek.

'There's Mum!'

The woman caught sight of her husband and son. Luke had never seen such glory as that which spread across her face. That was the way Prue would look when they had their son.

He watched as the three of them met and stood clasped together in a triangular huddle. The boy detached himself first.

'You were right,' he said to Luke. 'She was on the other boat! Have you found your wife yet?'

Luke shook his head and the woman freed herself from her husband to look at him sympathetically.

'I suppose you wouldn't have seen her?' Luke asked. 'Prue Lindquist. American, blonde ... pregnant.'

14

'I'm sorry. I was looking after Bobby and barely had time to get acquainted with any other passengers. I don't remember seeing anyone like that.'

'There's still Galway,' Luke said. 'And, of course, we don't know that all the survivors have been picked up yet.'

'There seemed to be a lot of ships searching for us,' the woman said. 'I do hope ...'

'Yes. Thank you. Very glad you and the boy are all right.'

He rang the London office. A list of passengers who had landed at Galway had been sent through. Prue's name was not on it.

Everyone said the same thing: don't give up hope. Small ships without wireless might have taken people out of the water. There was still a chance that more survivors would straggle in. But in his heart Luke knew that the time for hope was past. Prue was lost.

Nesta

To Nesta Gordon the outbreak of war in September 1939 was a monstrous interruption to her career as an actress.

'Why did it have to happen *now*?' she demanded. 'Just when I had a chance of being taken seriously.'

Her mother went on cutting slices of bread for the family breakfast, unmoved by her youngest daughter's latest outburst.

'There'll be other opportunities,' she said.

'Not with the Mervyn Hall Company. You do realize, don't you, that I was going to play *Jessica*?'

'Yes, dear, so you said. Go and give your Dad another call, there's a love.'

Nesta went to the foot of the stairs and yelled, 'Dad! You'll miss your bus!'

She slouched back into the kitchen and collapsed on to a chair. She only roused herself from her gloom when her father came into the room a few minutes later and asked, 'What's the news?'

'They're closing the theatres!' Nesta said.

'I suppose that's only to be expected in case we start having air raids. Anyway, who's going to want to go out to a theatre in the blackout? I was asking whether there was any real news.'

'Nothing much. Everyone seems stunned that a war has actually started. I don't see how you can say that closing the theatres isn't real news. You're as bad as Mum. Neither of you understands how much it means to me.'

Mrs Gordon put down a plate in front of her husband with an irritated snap.

'That's quite enough, Nesta,' she said. 'You've had a disappointment, but at nineteen I don't think your life's been blighted. God knows, we all hoped this war would never come, but that man Hitler's got to be stopped somehow. Forget your troubles and give a thought to your sister, with a husband

17

likely to be called up and a baby on the way.'

'And think about the Goldsteins,' her father put in. 'Refugees in a foreign country, not knowing what's happening to the friends they left behind in Germany. They're part of your family too, and don't you forget it.'

Nesta hunched her shoulders and looked mutinous. At that moment it was difficult to imagine her as a promising young actress. She had hooked her heels over the rung of her chair and was leaning forward with her elbows on the table, her cup of tea cradled between her hands. She had dragged a comb through her black hair and it hung in a frizzled mass round her pale, bony face. When Nesta was in low spirits her whole body sagged and her skin took on a sallow tint. She looked plain beyond redemption, and yet if she became excited or if she was playing a part that demanded it, Nesta could assume beauty in a way which made her mother uneasy. It was as if another person looked out from behind the familiar façade of the girl who had always been stage-mad, and had given them no peace until she had been allowed to try her luck in the theatre.

The family was Jewish by origin, but had long since abandoned its roots. Nesta's great-grandfather had been called Aaron Goldstein. He had settled in London in the early part of the nineteenth century, married a good Jewish girl and produced two daughters and a son. The son had married a Gentile, changed his name to Gordon and let his religion lapse. Nesta's father had been the result of this marriage. Due to the breach between his father and grandfather, he had scarcely remembered that he had relations called Goldstein until the German branch of the family, desperate for a way to escape from the increasing persecution in Nazi Germany, had traced their British connections and appealed for help.

Mr Gordon had responded generously and had given his distant cousins what help he could do to establish themselves in England, but he had found them as alien as men from the moon and they had been offended by his lack of Jewishness. All the same, their arrival had brought home to Mr and Mrs Gordon the reality of the sufferings of the Jews in Germany and Mrs Gordon had spoken for both of them when she had told Nesta that Hitler 'had to be stopped'.

18

The fact that Nesta's appearance betrayed her Jewish blood had influenced her casting in the part of Jessica in a production of *The Merchant of Venice* which had been rehearsing when the crisis finally came. A famous character actor was to have played Shylock, his wife was to have been Portia, the rest of the cast — apart from Nesta — were experienced Shakespearian actors. She had been the promising beginner in a part she knew to be well within her capabilities. It had no great dramatic possibilities of the kind she yearned after, but it would have got her noticed and might have led to better things. She was sick with disappointment when all the theatres were closed by government decree. It was no use hoping that the production might continue later if things settled down. Several of the younger men were expecting to be called up, and Shylock had film commitments which would presumably go ahead.

The trouble was, none of Nesta's family understood the depth of her frustration. They had been pleased when she had been chosen for the part, but they did not appreciate the compulsion that drove her. Nesta knew that the reason she had been born was to be an actress and she burned for the world to recognize her qualities. She was special, she had it in her to be great; any disruption of her progress was a tragedy on the same level as the outbreak of war. Because of the force of this conviction it was galling to be treated as a silly girl who had had a disappointment.

'It's my whole life!' she cried in despair when her mother finally lost patience with her.

'Here, take a look at this,' Mrs Gordon said, slapping the morning paper down in front of her. 'They're starting up something called Entertainments National Service Association to give our boys a bit of amusement. Why don't you try to get into that?'

'Variety acts and chorus girls,' Nesta said in disgust.

'There's going to be a drama group as well.'

Mrs Gordon managed to keep quiet while Nesta read the article, knowing that it would be a mistake to urge her daughter too hard, but she breathed a sigh of relief when Nesta eventually said in a grudging way, 'I suppose I could go along to Drury Lane and find out what it's all about.'

If it did nothing else, it would get the girl out of the house for the morning and give Doris Gordon some peace. The way Nesta had been carrying on you would think she believed the government ought to have held up the war until she had had a chance to get herself launched on the stage.

Nesta approached the Drury Lane Theatre with some reluctance. Basil Dean, who was in charge of the organization of the Entertainments National Service Association, had a fearful reputation as a martinet who drove actors and actresses to the edge of their endurance, and Nesta was not at all sure that she wanted to get involved in any production he might have in hand.

There seemed to be a lot of people going in and out of the theatre, mostly with a purposeful air, as if they knew where to go, which she certainly did not. Nesta paused to look regretfully at the posters advertising Ivor Novello's *Dancing Years*. Not quite her line, but she was sorry she had not taken the chance to see it while it was still running.

As soon as she got inside Nesta realized that she need not have worried about meeting the man at the top, since the queues of hopeful entertainers were being dealt with by a team of harassed secretaries, using the corridors as offices.

'The NAAFI is responsible for the organization, control and finance of entertainments for the Forces,' Nesta was told in a way that showed that the words had been reeled off many times.

'What's the NAAFI?' she asked.

The girl who was interviewing her paused as if the interruption had jolted the needle off her gramophone record.

'The Navy, Army and Air Force Institutes,' she said. 'They run the canteens and that sort of thing.'

'Shouldn't have thought they'd know much about the stage,' Nesta said.

'That's why ENSA – er, the Entertainments National Service Association ...'

'I know *that*,' Nesta told her.

'That's why ENSA has been set up. We'll provide the entertainment that's asked for. Now, if I could have details of your experience ... unless you'd prefer to write in?'

20

She sounded hopeful, but Nesta was not going to be put off after making the effort to go along to offer her services. She gave the girl the details of her training and experience, galled that it came out sounding hopelessly inadequate.

'Mervyn Hall would speak for me,' she said in desperation. 'I was going to do Jessica in *The Merchant* with him if this damned war hadn't broken out.'

'Hard luck,' the secretary said perfunctorily. 'The thing is, we've hardly got the drama group organized yet. We're relying mostly on things like seaside variety shows. They're lively and popular and they're all set up with costumes and acts, ready to go off anywhere at a moment's notice, because they had to close down when the war started.'

Nesta wrinkled her nose distastefully. 'I don't fancy myself in a Pierrot show,' she said.

'What about singing and dancing? Can you offer anything in that line?'

'Not really. I'm an actress.'

She saw the secretary glance at the meagre lines of writing in front of her and guessed that only politeness stopped her from commenting that Nesta was not even much of an actress.

'I'm *good*,' Nesta insisted. 'I don't mind doing comedy, if I have to, but I really ought to be concentrating on serious drama.'

'What the army wants is a leg show,' the girl said out of the experience she had garnered in the last few weeks. 'Look, we've got you on file now; if anything suitable comes up you'll be contacted.'

'I know – "Don't call us, we'll call you",' Nesta quoted.

'That's the way it has to be. We're run off our feet, as you can see.'

Nesta was turning away, limp with disappointment, when a big, middle-aged man with a shock of white hair, followed by a shorter, round-faced man wearing glasses, came along the corridor.

'Mervyn!' Nesta exclaimed.

The white-haired man stopped, opening his arms expansively, and Nesta threw herself into his embrace.

'Nesta, my darling!' Mervyn Hall kissed her on both cheeks and then put her away from him so that he could see her scowling face. 'Something's troubling you?'

'Of course it is! I was sick, absolutely physically sick, when I heard our tour was cancelled.'

'It was hard on me, too, sweetie.'

'You've played Shylock before. I may never get another stab at Jessica – or anything else for that matter. No one takes me seriously. This stupid organization wants me to make a fool of myself waving my legs in the air.'

The other man frowned in vexation.

'There's a limited demand for Shakespeare ...' he began.

'Of course there is,' Mervyn Hall interrupted with a twinkle in his eye. 'Don't get into one of your states, Nesta. You and I know that you're going to be the greatest Shakespearian actress of the age ...'

'Am I?' Nesta demanded.

'I was joking, but that's not to say it might not be true. For the time being you have to accept that the Forces want light entertainment. Something suitable for your talent will come along in time, I promise you.'

'You're telling me to be patient,' Nesta said. 'Everyone says that to me. How can I be patient when my life is rushing by unused?'

The sentiment might have sounded comic if it had not been for the force of the conviction that shook Nesta's thin body. Looking at that intense, remarkable face, Mervyn Hall was not tempted to smile.

'I recognize your hunger,' he said. 'I know how you feel. I can only say that I'll mention your name around.'

He turned to the other man. 'Basil, I can commend Miss Gordon as an excellent actress.'

'Make a note of it on her record,' Basil Dean said impatiently. 'Mervyn, may I remind you that we're on our way to a most important meeting?'

'Just one moment,' Mervyn Hall said, unmoved by the other man's irascibility. 'Nesta, remember this – keep working! Read, read, read; do your voice exercises; keep fit.'

'I will,' Nesta assured him. 'Oh, I will!'

She watched anxiously to see what the secretary would write and was satisfied to see the words: 'Personally recommended to Mr Dean by Mervyn Hall.' That ought to do the trick.

22

Conrad

The German spy was looking at a photograph of his mother. It was beautifully posed and lighted. Conrad Aylmer smiled in affectionate amusement. Mama the socialite, every blonde hair in place, her thin eyebrows raised in delicate surprise, one long-fingered hand supporting her chin. The fine sapphire ring she wore had been his gift when he had landed his first starring role, and he knew that the way she displayed it was a message to him.

He placed the photograph inside the lid of the suitcase which held his supply of stage make up. Amongst the sticks of greasepaint, liners and powder, were the chemicals for producing the invisible ink with which he communicated with his masters.

Conrad sighed as he snapped shut the lid of the case and then he pulled himself up with a frown. It would be a long time before he saw his elegant mother again, but there must be no regrets. She knew the course he had chosen and she approved of it. Her belief in the destiny of Germany was as fervent as his own. Indeed, it was because of her teaching that he had arrived at a true understanding of National Socialism and all it stood for in the resurgence of Germany's greatness.

Almost the only mistake Wanda von Lynden had made in her life had been to marry an Englishman. It had been in the summer of 1912 when she was just eighteen, lovely, spirited, wealthy and irrevocably set on having her own way. James Aylmer had been ten years older and completely swept away by her combination of high spirits, blonde beauty and aristocratic disregard for the obstacles both their families tried to put in their way.

Two years later, by the time Conrad was born, Great Britain and Germany were at war. Conrad had no recollection of that first conflict. He only knew what his mother had told him of her

23

sufferings at the hands of her English relations. She had been an alien, for all her status as the wife of a serving British officer. Her regrets for the fate of her German relations had been disregarded, her natural patriotism derided.

Conrad's father survived the war, but not for long. By 1920 he had coughed away the tattered remnants of the lungs which had been destroyed by German gas. By that time his marriage was in ruins and the will he left reflected the worry he felt about the upbringing of his six year old son. Conrad's natural guardian was his bereaved mother, but his financial affairs were in the hands of British trustees. He was to be educated at his father's old school, restrictive clauses tied up his father's estate, and he would lose the bulk of his inheritance if he chose to discard his British nationality.

Wanda had raged at the terms of her husband's will, but she was too shrewd to attempt to challenge it. Besides, conditions in post-war Germany were not such as to make life there an attractive proposition. It was not until the nineteen-thirties that she began making prolonged visits to her old home and finding it very much to her taste.

Conrad adored his mother. He had only the vaguest recollection of his father. There had once been a thin man with a persistent cough, who had thrown a red ball to him on a beach, that was all he remembered. He had no difficulty in believing Wanda's stories of the unfeeling treatment she had received at the hands of his father's family. It was they who had condemned Conrad to a school he had hated, and his uncle Bertram had been appalled by Conrad's wish to become an actor. Every possible difficulty had been placed in his way, while his mother – by that time living permanently in Germany – had applauded his ambitions and given him encouragement.

As he grew older, Conrad recognized that Wanda had her faults, but he found them loveable and human. She was a woman of violent affections and enthusiasms and at first he had looked upon her allegiance to the Führer as one of Mama's passing crazes. Then he had met the man himself, had felt the force of his magnetism and, almost against his will, had been converted to a belief that in Adolph Hitler Germany had found the leader who would take her into her rightful place in the world.

24

Once Conrad's enthusiasm had been kindled he had burned to throw up his British nationality and become a proper German, but neither Wanda nor, surprisingly, the Führer himself had been in favour of this idea. It had been put to Conrad that he was uniquely placed to serve the country of his heart. He was British by right, he had a modest fortune in England; because of his education and family connections, reinforced by a growing awareness of his acting ability, he was accepted in the highest circles. He was to stay put and apply himself to helping Germany in secret in the struggle against the British Empire which must surely come, little as the Führer wanted it. The only false step he had taken had been a brief involvement with the British Fascist Party under Oswald Mosley, but he had dropped out in response to a vehement rebuke from Berlin, and it had almost been forgotten. After all, full-blooded Englishmen had made the same mistake and been forgiven for it.

All the same, Conrad's association with the Fascist Movement had been well publicised and his mistake had to be paid for. His close relationship with his mother had had to be broken off, since her views were too well established to make a change of heart believable. Since 1937 there had been no open communication between them and Conrad had made his home exclusively in England.

He had already shown himself adept at collecting information. He was a cultured young man, at ease wherever he went, socially acceptable, charming and becoming known as an actor. The fact that he employed his talent to hide the contempt he felt for most of his acquaintances was not something that was likely to occur to them.

Conrad sometimes thought, with secret amusement, that he would have made a good burglar. To creep through a house in the dark, to steal not money but secrets, filled him with excitement. His audacity was unbounded. He had once come close to being found out when he had been spending a weekend in the home of a Cabinet minister whose son had been at school with Conrad. Another guest, visiting the bathroom after everyone had gone to bed, had made the lavatory cistern overflow and had burst into Conrad's room to ask for help, only to find it empty and the bed unused. This was a titbit of scandal Conrad's fellow guest had not been able to keep to himself. Conrad had been vexed at being quizzed the next morning, but he had refused to explain and his silence and enigmatic smile had given rise to some interested guesswork as to whose bed he had been visiting. It occurred to no one that he had been downstairs in his host's study, photographing his private correspondence.

To Conrad's regret he had not inherited his mother's fair colouring, but he had her fine bone structure and her blue eyes. His height and athleticism he got from his father, though he would have been loath to admit it. Conrad was a natural games player. His eye for the ball and beautiful co-ordination had made him a first class cricketer, he was a pleasure to watch on the tennis court and he swam like a fish. When he discovered at school that his prowess made him popular he exploited it to the full, but he did not greatly care for the winter games and refused to exert himself when it came to playing football or going for muddy cross-country runs. His passion in the winter was for ski-ing, which was not a sport available in England except to the wealthy few who escaped each year to snowy slopes on the Continent.

Because it came so easily to him, Conrad did not greatly value his sporting ability, except insofar as it won him privileges at school and invitations to agreeable houses where he was expected to play village cricket and make up a four on the tennis court. He liked to win, but if he thought it necessary, in order to endear himself where liking would be useful, he was prepared to lose with grace and generosity, accepting suggestions that he was 'a little off form' with a deprecating shrug.

Apart from his allegiance to Germany and his love for his mother, the only thing he took seriously was his acting. He had announced his intention of going on the stage at an early age, and had stood by it in spite of his uncle's old-fashioned insistence that it was no life for a man. He had gone up to Cambridge and done the minimum amount of work, although he had somehow managed to scrape through with a moderately satisfactory degree, and had devoted every spare moment to college theatricals.

This had been the period when he came most heavily under

the influence of his mother. Wanda had discovered an extraordinary pleasure in the devotion of her newly adult, sophisticated, handsome son. Conrad, flashing over the ski slopes like a swooping bird, or hauling himself out of the swimming pool, his sleek brown body running with water, laughing at her with eyes like sapphires in his tanned face, made Wanda's bones melt in adoration.

She knew about his sexual conquests and laughed at the girls for being so susceptible, secure in the knowledge that none of them touched his heart. They were both special people and had a right to their privileges. In Wanda's philosophy, other people existed to serve her and her wonderful son and, by implication, similar choice spirits of the German nation.

It was only very occasionally that Conrad had qualms about the deception he was practising, and even Conrad did not realize that his uneasiness had started in the two years since he had been cut off from Wanda's influence.

As an undergraduate he had believed he was doing the right thing. He had seen his allegiance to Nazism as a necessary protest against the left wing tendencies of many of his contemporaries. His visits to Germany, prolonged as they had been, were holidays. He had mixed with young people of his own kind, bronzed, fit, living in the open air, frankly amoral, in spite of the Führer's puritanical streak. It was not difficult to believe that the world belonged to them.

The darker side of the Nazi regime had scarcely touched him, at least not at that time. As he grew older he was sometimes uneasy, knowing with half his mind that not all the persecution stories could be dismissed as foreign propaganda, but still unwilling to believe that the splendid young men and women he knew could be involved in anything malignant.

Left to himself, Conrad would have come out in the open as soon as he was of age, renounced his British citizenship and applied for German nationality, but when he talked it over with Wanda he began to see the difficulties that would arise.

'Losing the money would be tiresome, I admit,' he had said impatiently. 'But I could earn a living in Germany, surely? I'm a *very* good actor, darling!'

'You're quite wonderful and I adore you,' Wanda said. 'Of

course, if you're determined to throw everything away – which I must say I think is entirely unnecessary and foolish – then I'll do my best to economize. Naughty boy, you shouldn't have encouraged me to be extravagant if you meant to cut me off without a pfennig!'

It had silenced Conrad. Wanda owed the greater part of her income to his generosity. She certainly could not support her agreeable life from her own resources and it might take him time to get established on the German stage. At that time he had only just begun to get a foothold in England.

'I could live in Germany without giving up my British passport,' he suggested.

'Darling, such an uncomfortable arrangement! Do let's be practical. The work you are doing for the Reich is of immense importance and very much appreciated. My own standing is enormously enhanced because I'm Conrad Aylmer's mother. I can't tell you how proud it makes me that of all the young men who serve him the Führer knows *you* personally, and sometimes compliments me on my splendid son. In private, of course; he's totally discreet. It would be a little difficult to explain that you wanted to give up your work, just on a whim.'

At that time he had still taken a pride in his skill in extracting information. The actual mechanics of his secret trade fascinated him and he still enjoyed the excitement of deceiving everybody. Four years later, as a man of twenty-five who was established in his chosen profession, Conrad was more impatient of the details of his undercover work.

Conrad had hoped that war between Great Britain and Germany could be avoided. The Munich Agreement had been a far greater reprieve to him than it had been to most Englishmen, welcome though it had generally been. A year later, when he saw that war was inevitable, he had struck a bargain with his German masters: he would go on with his vital work for an adequate recompense, which was to be paid entirely to Wanda.

Since his special talents would be more useful in the civilian area, he had been told to avoid armed service for as long as possible. It was his own decision to offer his services to ENSA. With any luck this would take him to army camps, naval bases and air force fields, possibly also to important munitions factories. He would not indulge in any acts of sabotage, but would pick up all the information he could, drop his poisoned hints of secret disasters, spread his dark rumours and pass on his way, smiling at the psychological havoc he left behind.

The war would, of course, be short. The rest of Europe was no match for the might of the German Reich. The splendid young men who had been his friends would be triumphant, and with England under German domination Conrad's nationality would no longer be important. It was an incentive to continue his role. The declaration of war, dreaded in anticipation, had had the effects of clearing his mind. Now he felt he could regard himself as a soldier under orders and every report he dispatched would bring peace nearer.

Stephanie

There was fog in the Atlantic, as there usually was in late October. A thin, cold mist hung around the *SS Washington*, en route from New York to Britain. There was no horizon: grey sea and grey sky were one, so that the ship might have been moving inside a glassy bubble, shut off from the world outside – if there was a world outside. The waves heaved and fell with a sluggish, monotonous motion. At three o'clock in the afternoon the sun was reduced to a flat red disc giving out a diffused, uncertain light.

Luke Lindquist turned up the collar of his jacket and put his hands in his pockets as he stepped out into the chill air. He thought at first that the deck was deserted, which was not surprising when the prospect around them was so dreary, then he saw that he was mistaken: a solitary woman was leaning against the rail with her back to him. She was wearing a camelhair coat with a long green scarf tossed carelessly round her neck. A wisp of mist drifted round her, almost hiding her from view. For one moment every pulse in Luke's body stopped, then the mist thinned, she turned her head and he recognized her.

That profile had been on too many billboards not to be known immediately – the pretty, straight nose, the wide, curling mouth, the winged brows above sea green eyes, the long mane of dark chestnut hair. Stephanie Bartram, Hollywood's latest golden girl, who had thrown it all up to go back to Britain to fight for King and Country, a well-publicised gesture that had aroused nothing but scepticism in Luke Lindquist.

She had gone back to gazing over the sea and did not look round as he drew level with her, until he said, 'What are you thinking about, Queen Christina?'

Stephanie turned to face him, leaning against the rail with both her elbows propped against it.

31

'Someone asked Garbo that, you know,' she said. 'And she said "Nothing". Extraordinary, the way that shot at the end of the film conveys such desolation if her mind was really empty.'

It was a more articulate reply than Luke had expected and she had seized on his reference straight away, without having to ask what he meant, which surprised him.

'Are you in films, too?' Stephanie asked.

'No, I'm a reporter.'

He sensed her wary withdrawal and went on, 'You can relax. Show business is not my line and I'm not going to interview you.'

'Just as well, because I've said everything I'm going to say.'

'I'm Luke Lindquist. I'm with the *New York Times* and I'm on my way to report the war in Europe – when they get it started.'

He was slightly, very slightly, drunk. Not offensively, but she could smell the whisky on his breath, and his speech was too precise because he was taking care not to slur his words.

'I think the war has started,' Stephanie said. 'You asked me what I was thinking: I was looking at all that empty water and wondering just how empty it really was.'

'U-boats?' Luke asked evenly.

'Mm. To me, there's something particularly repulsive about them, creeping along under the surface out of sight.'

'Scared?'

'To be honest, yes.' Stephanie smiled in a rueful attempt to make light of her fears. 'It's a mistake to know your Shakespeare too well,' she said. ' "Lord, Lord! methought what pain it was to drown ..." '.

'Shut up!'

Stephanie stared at him, shocked by the way he had spoken. He was leaning over the rail as if he were going to vomit. After a minute, he said, 'My wife went down with the *Athenia*.'

'Dear God! I'm sorry, so terribly sorry.'

Stephanie took her hand out of her pocket and clasped it over his. It felt warm against his cold fingers.

'You said the sea was empty. It's not, you know. Prue is out there somewhere. Prue and all the other poor devils, washing to and fro in the tide.'

'I'm heartbroken for you,' Stephanie said, and because she sounded as if she meant it, Luke went on talking.

'I've never found anyone who remembered seeing her. I don't know what happened, whether she was killed straight off by the explosion, or got into a boat that capsized, or just floundered around in the water, hoping to be picked up. She was a strong swimmer. That's what haunts me, the thought of her swimming, swimming, keeping going. Prue was a fighter, she wouldn't have given up. And then, losing hope, alone ...'

'No! It couldn't have been like that. There were too many ships looking for survivors. She would have been seen. Besides, in this cold water ... forgive me, but no one could stay alive for very long.'

'Perhaps you're right.'

The clasp on his hand was still warm; some tiny measure of consolation had got through to him. In a low voice he said, 'She was expecting our first child. That's why I sent her home.'

'Oh, my dear!'

Surprised, Luke looked at Stephanie and saw that tears were streaming unchecked down her lovely face. Above them the ship's foghorn sounded a long, melancholy note.

'I've upset you,' Luke said. 'I don't know why I unloaded it all on you. Something about this mist, a feeling of drifting in limbo – and I've shifted half a bottle of whisky since lunchtime.'

'Does that help?'

'Not much,' he admitted. 'I don't make a habit of it. Prue would *not* have approved. I'm nerving myself to do something I don't want to do and I hit the bottle to get myself over it.'

Stephanie's silence encouraged him to go on.

'I've just come from a visit to Prue's parents. My paper sent me on leave and, of course, I had to go and see them.'

'Trying for you.'

'Very. Prue's Mom ... she's given me a wreath. She asked me to cast it on the water, you know, at an appropriate spot and, bloody hell, I just can't bring myself to do it.'

He expected sympathy, but Stephanie said, 'I think you should do it. In fact, you must.'

'I know, I know. I have to be able to write and say truthfully that I did what was expected of me. It will comfort her, God knows why.'

'That wasn't what I meant, but let it go. When are you going to do it?'

'I thought tonight, when everyone's at dinner. That's when ... when the torpedo struck. About a day's sailing out of Ireland, which we are now, so it will be the right spot. Not that it makes any difference.'

'Do you want to be alone?'

'I believe Prue's Mom thought I could arrange some sort of ceremony, but that's the last thing I want. Officers saluting and prayers for the dead and people staring. I'll just come up and chuck the thing in the water. It's horrible. Dried flowers and evergreens. Prue would have hated it.'

'I'd like to be with you. Would you allow that?'

Luke stared at her. The whisky was beginning to evaporate and he was ashamed of the impulse that had led him to unburden himself.

'I can't stop you coming on deck,' he said roughly. 'Just so long as you don't blow the Last Post or say anything about those in peril on the sea.'

The wind had freshened when Luke stepped out into the darkness that evening. The mist had cleared, there was a gleam of moonlight and some ragged clouds chasing along overhead. He had managed to bring the wreath up out of his cabin concealed in a large paper bag. He took it out, hating the dry feel of the everlasting flowers, and stepped up to the rail. A figure came forward out of the shadows. Stephanie, wrapped in a long velvet evening cloak.

'Not here,' she said. 'Come to the stern.'

Luke followed her to the lower deck, to the point where they could look out at the long white wake, faintly visible in the fitful moonlight.

They stood in silence for a moment and then Luke lifted the wreath and sent it skimming out over the water. He saw it fall, settle on the white foam and float.

When Stephanie began to speak he had a flash of blind anger, then the extreme simplicity of the quiet words reached him and he listened until she had finished.

'O God of Love; O King of peace,
'Make wars throughout the world to cease;
'The wrath of sinful man restrain,
'Give peace, O God, give peace again.'

He heard the soft movement of her velvet cloak and realized
she was leaving him. In blind and desperate need Luke reached
out and grabbed her arm.

'Don't leave me alone,' he said.

When Luke woke up the next morning he could hardly believe
what had happened. He remembered being bitterly cold, so cold
that he had clenched his teeth together to stop them chattering,
so cold that long rigors had shaken his body from head to foot.
He remembered Stephanie having to support him as he
stumbled from the deck to his cabin.

After that the sequence of events was confused. It had been
Stephanie who had made him get undressed and into his bunk.
She must have helped him because he doubted whether he
would have been capable of coping for himself. Delayed shock,
he told himself; delayed shock, that was what it was.

Thinking about that, taking time to tell himself what had
gone before was just a way of putting off recalling what had
really happened. Luke sat up abruptly and hit his head on the
bunk overhead. Thank God it was empty and he had no one
sharing with him who might have come back and interrupted
them last night.

He felt sick when he remembered the way he had clutched at
her. Her arms had been warm and soft as she held him. He had
turned his head against her breast, seeking comfort, and like a
thunderbolt desire had struck him. This woman, any woman,
who would accommodate his body and free him from his
haunted dreams.

He remembered a voice saying, 'Gently, my dear, gently;
there's no need to force me. Let me go free for a minute and I'll
come back to you.'

He had held her naked in his arms and she had been kind
and clever and infinitely generous. He had plundered her body

like a miser let loose in a treasure house. It was as well that the details escaped him, but even what remained, the memory of a hot, blind plunging, without consideration for her or restraint for himself, filled him with misery.

So soon. Prue, Prue ... my dear love, forgive me.

Luke sat for a long time with his head in his hands. And he still had to face Stephanie herself.

They met in the bar just before lunch. It was obvious that Stephanie had been on deck again. There was fresh colour in her cheeks and a sparkle of damp on her hair. She was dressed in slacks and an emerald green jacket. Before sitting down she slipped off the jacket. Underneath she was wearing a white sweater. Luke averted his eyes from the full breasts outlined under the thin cashmere.

'I don't know what to say to you,' he said heavily.

'Say nothing. You were in a bad way. I was there ... and not unwilling. Try to think of me kindly. I meant well.'

'You! It's myself I can't forgive.'

'But you must.' Stephanie looked at him thoughtfully. 'Do you expect to stay faithful to the memory of your wife for the rest of your life?'

Luke did not reply. It was not going to be possible, he knew the urgency of his own body too well not to realize that.

'It was bound to happen and with me there are no strings attached,' Stephanie said, reading his silence correctly. 'Prue is dead, Luke, and you're alive. Sooner or later you're going to have to accept that.'

'I seem to have fallen sooner rather than later,' Luke said. 'I'm sorry, I'm being rather less than grateful ...'

'Gratitude is something I definitely don't want. Forget it. Talk about something else.'

With an effort Luke wrenched his mind away from his corroding sense of guilt.

'That thing you said last night, up on deck,' he said abruptly. 'What was it?'

'The first verse of a hymn. Would you like me to write it out for you?'

'Would you? I thought I'd send a note to Prue's Mom, saying the ceremony had taken place, quoting that. If she likes to believe the bugles were blowing and the ship's company lined up at the rail she can.'

'Of course. There are four verses. I think I can remember all of them.'

'I must say you've surprised me.'

As soon as the words were out Luke thought they might be misinterpreted and hurried on, 'I mean, one doesn't associate your average film star with hymn singing.'

Stephanie gave him a curious, sideway look and decided to confide in him. Perhaps then he would stop sitting there with his jaw set in that obstinate way, refusing to look at her, blaming her even while he pretended to take the blame on himself. At least it would give him something to think about, perhaps give him a different perspective on her.

'I was left alone for a long time in a room where there was nothing to divert my mind but the prayer book I had been expected to carry to my wedding,' she said. 'There arc hymns in the back of the book and when I came across those verses I was struck by their appropriateness. It was at the time of the Munich crisis, you see.'

'And you kept them in your mind all this time?'

'I'm a pro. If I tell my memory to hold on to something it obeys me. Besides, the concentration helped me to shut out the knowledge that my bridegroom had run out on me.'

She saw that she had disconcerted Luke and was glad that his reaction was so spontaneous.

'Don't tell me the story's new to you?' she asked. 'I thought it had been printed in every newspaper in the world.'

'I told you show business isn't my line. I was in Germany at that time and my attention was fixed on the coming war.'

'That'll teach me not to imagine that my tawdry little life is of importance to anyone outside my own small circle.'

'Don't talk like that. Tawdry you are not.'

'Sure about that?' Stephanie asked.

'Very sure. If I've said or, even worse, done anything to make you think otherwise then I really am ashamed of myself.'

Luke was relieved when she looked satisfied.

37

'Are you going to tell me what happened?' he asked.

'If you'll keep the details to yourself. A lot of people suspected the truth, but I don't want to drag poor Dwight in the dirt more than is necessary.'

'Dwight David?'

'Mm. My first Hollywood leading man. Divinely handsome – you must have seen him, that cleft chin, the dimple in one cheek, all that boyish charm, and he was great fun, too. The thing about Dwight is that he's terribly *nice*. Only, unfortunately, he doesn't like women.'

'And you didn't know?'

'He kept up a terrific front and, of course, the studio helped. Looking back, I can see that they were terrified of a breach of their precious moral code. It was a real bonus when their difficult boy and the new star from England took to one another. I'd made a couple of films in England and I'd got a small reputation, but *Flowers by the River* was my first American picture. I was a new discovery, the best thing that had happened to movies since Garbo, more beautiful than Vivien Leigh, sexier than Marlene Dietrich. Ask for the moon, Stephanie, and we'll give it to you. The romance with Dwight was one big publicity stunt. We went everywhere together – first nights, parties, golf, tennis, swimming. There were endless articles in the film magazines; we were photographed wherever we went.'

'But you must have been suspicious if there was a lack of ...'

'Sexual overtures? Dwight's an actor. He made it look good – up to a point. He treated me like some precious flower, to be guarded and cherished. You've no idea how thrilling I found that. I thought he was a real gentleman, and I hadn't met many of them in my career up to that point.'

'How did you get him to propose marriage?'

'That was part of a deal the studio did with him. Dwight had been compensating for all this good behaviour with me by getting involved in a particularly sordid affair with a Mexican boy. The studio got it hushed up, but they gave him an ultimatum – he was to get married or they'd drop him.'

'But didn't anyone advise you ... warn you?'

'The only person who had my interests at heart was my

38

mother, and the fact that she was against the marriage only made me the more determined to go through with it. I thought she opposed it because she wanted to keep control of me – which was true, of course. She didn't dislike Dwight, and she was all for the deluge of publicity that surrounded our 'romance', but she certainly didn't like the idea of my getting married before my twenty-first birthday ...'

'Your *what*?'

'I was twenty-one in March. You sound surprised.'

'I thought you were older,' Luke admitted.

'I've been around a long time. I made my first film when I was seventeen. You'd have thought I would have been more knowing, but I was quite deceived.'

Stephanie's mind went back to that lovely autumn day which was to have been her wedding day. It had seemed strange to both Stephanie and her mother that the ceremony was to take place in a private house instead of a church, but everyone told them it was the usual thing, and certainly the mansion loaned by the studio head could not have been more impressive.

Stephanie had arrived early at the house, smiling sweetly and blindly at the waiting photographers. The truth was that now that the day had arrived she was sick with nerves. She had had her hair done, her face made up, her nails painted and all the time she had fought the feeling that she was merely preparing to go on the set and play a scene before the cameras. She had a moment of rebellion when she thought to herself that she and Dwight would have done better to have slipped across the border for a private ceremony, but when the white slipper satin gown – cut on the cross to make the most of her lovely figure – had been lowered over her head, when the crown of orange blossom and the chiffon veil had been adjusted on her hair, she had to admit that she had never looked better.

After a few carefully posed pictures had been taken by the official photographer, Stephanie had been left on her own to compose herself. Afterwards she remembered that the people who had hovered around during that photographic session had been slightly abstracted, but that was with the benefit of hindsight, when she had realized that they must even then have been uneasy about the failure of the bridegroom to put in an appearance.

Stephanie had waited ... twenty minutes, half an hour ... and then she had been visited by a sweating official from Invincible Studios who had told her that Dwight had been delayed, that everything was all right, that she was to be good and patient and they would call her when she was 'on'. At the time she had smiled at his use of the studio floor term. She had stopped smiling when she had discovered that he had locked her in and that no one answered the telephone by the side of the bed. Something was terribly wrong and no one was telling her what it was.

Perhaps at that moment some slight inkling of the truth had begun to dawn on Stephanie. Instead of pounding on the door or shouting out of the window, she had sat down, very sedate, very collected, very controlled, and waited. She had been going to carry a white prayer book. It was the only thing available to distract her mind. She avoided looking at the Marriage Service and leafed through it until she discovered the plea for peace, which seemed appropriate reading.

It had been her mother who had been sent to tell her the truth, and that had been hard to take. Officially, the bridegroom's failure to put in an appearance was explained on the grounds of 'sudden illness', which was true enough. Dwight, unable to face keeping his bargain, had drugged himself into a stupor which had required a stomach pump to save his life. The story put out by the studio was that he had appendicitis.

Gritting her teeth, Stephanie allowed herself to be seen visiting the nursing home carrying bunches of red roses, but once inside the building she had refused to go anywhere near Dwight's bedside. The full story had never been printed, but there had been plenty of speculation and it had not gone unremarked that the disrupted wedding had never taken place.

'The only good thing about it was that it certainly made the studio more co-operative when I said I wanted to return to England,' Stephanie said to Luke with a lightness that was not quite convincing.

Looking at her he saw what he had not realized earlier, when he had been taken up with his own grief: how young she was and, under the surface gloss, how vulnerable.

'You poor kid,' he said gently.

40

Stephanie straightened her shoulders and even smiled.

'I weathered it,' she said. 'I told you, I'm a professional – an old trouper. A setback in my love life wasn't going to stop my career, but I thought I was better out of Hollywood and the war was a perfect excuse. I patched things up with Dwight. God knows I felt sorry for him when I understood. We did the rounds of first nights, promoting *Flowers by the River*.'

'Which was a great success.'

'A riotous success! I nearly split my face open smiling about it. Even so, the studio breathed a sigh of relief when I decided to leave. They explained my patriotic decision as the reason for my break with Dwight – heartbroken star puts country before love. Now I'm going to find myself something useful to do.'

Luke saw her look past him towards the door.

'Don't look round,' she said. 'My mother has just come in and she's sizing you up. There are three things she'll want to know: are you rich, are you influential and can you help my career?'

'No, to all three.'

'Then I'll spare you an introduction. There'll be a million things to do before we dock and we may not meet again so I'll say goodbye, Luke.'

They both stood up and Stephanie held out her hand. As Luke took it he said helplessly, 'What does a man say to a woman who's been as generous to him as you've been to me?'

'Say thank you and goodbye. Since Dwight I've been pretty wild. I've taken almost any man who asked me, looking for reassurance, I suppose, that I was a woman men wanted. I think last night exorcised that for me. Your need was so desperate and I suddenly realized how small my loss was compared to yours. Give yourself a chance to recover. Don't let this episode prey on your mind. Good luck, and look after yourself, Luke.'

'You, too, Stephanie.'

Vera Bartram's first question was exactly what Stephanie had expected.

'Who was that man you were talking to?'

41

'A newspaper man called Luke Lindquist.'

It was a touch of malice that had made her mention Luke's profession. She was ashamed when she saw her mother's quick alarm.

'I hope you were careful what you said.'

'He's a war correspondent, not interested in film actresses.'

'If you made any remarks worth quoting he'd pass them on. You know what they're like.'

She had, in fact, been outrageously indiscreet, but then the circumstances had been unusual. Besides, something about Luke inspired trust, which was probably one of his assets as a reporter. He was a big man, tall, with long bones and large hands and feet, but he moved quietly and easily – the sort of man who slipped through a crowd without difficulty, in spite of his size. Nothing remarkable about him, and perhaps that was an asset too. Hair which was too dark to be called fair and too light to be called brown, straight and flat against his head like wet straw. His eyes were grey, with a darker line round the iris. High cheekbones, a thin, straight nose, a bony jaw. A very Nordic-looking face. Lindquist ... his forebears had probably been Scandinavian. She would remember him, perhaps long after his own horrified recollection of their night together had faded.

'I don't know why you have to waste your time on a man who can't be of any possible use to you,' Vera said, and the remark was so predictable that it made Stephanie smile.

She decided not to tell her mother about Prue Lindquist's death. It was a story that Vera would love and it would immediately transform her opinion of Luke, but Stephanie found that she could not bear the way Vera would mull it over, worrying away at it until she had extracted every scrap of sensation.

'We were talking about my decision to go back to England,' Stephanie said.

'I suppose he was patting you on the back, encouraging you just like everyone else who doesn't have your real interests at heart.'

'He seemed to think I was doing the right thing.'

'Much he knows about it! When I think what you're giving up ...'

42

'The chance to build up my reputation as a sex symbol in another second-rate film,' Stephanie said evenly, knowing that it was unwise to get into the old argument, but unable to stop herself.

'The audiences *loved* you in *Flowers by the River*.'

'I didn't love myself. I can do better than that.'

'You're too choosy by half, my girl. It's not so long since you were kicking your heels in the second line of the chorus. Who pushed you into taking a film test?'

'You did.'

When I think of all I've done for you ...

'It was all my doing. When I think of what I've done for you ...'

The sacrifices I've made ...

'The things I've had to give up, the sacrifices I've made ...'

Scraping and saving ...

'Hundreds of pounds I've spent on you, first and last. And it didn't come easy, never forget that! Scrape and save, a penny here, a penny there. Dancing lessons, singing lessons, elocution ...'

'I was earning most of the time,' Stephanie put in.

'And me! What about those times I came on tour in the pantomime with you and worked as a dancer myself?'

'You enjoyed it.'

But it was impossible to win an argument with Vera. Quick as a flash, she pounced.

'If I did, it was because I could have had a career of my own if it hadn't been cut short when I married your Dad.'

Instead of which, she had concentrated all her ambition on her daughter. Stephanie braced herself, knowing what was coming next.

If I hadn't thrown myself away ...

'It would all have been different if I hadn't thrown myself away on a man who had no sympathy for my talent ...'

'Mum, he's been dead for the last eight years!'

'Too late! My freedom came too late!' Vera said triumphantly.

'All right, Mum: game, set and match to you,' Stephanie said wearily.

43

'I don't know what you're talking about, but there! you've become a mystery to me since you started getting so independent. A swollen head, that's what you've got, Stephanie Bartram.'

'I don't think so,' Stephanie said, pretending to consider the possibility dispassionately. 'I know *Flowers* made a stir, but I don't admire myself for what I did in it.'

'You're *famous*! You made a mint of money ...'

'And spent almost as much. It was a very expensive life.'

'You had to look good, be seen in the right places ...'

'Why? What did being seen at The Coconut Grove have to do with my acting ability?'

'It was part of the glamour, the ... the ...'

'Falsehood. Lovely Stephanie Bartram escorted by heart-throb Dwight David.'

'I know you were upset about Dwight,' Vera admitted. 'Well, I was myself. But if you'd taken my advice it would never have happened.'

'You didn't want me to marry, but your reasons were the wrong ones. You were as deceived as I was.'

'It ought not to have been such a shock. We both knew there were men like that who ... who didn't have any time for women,' Vera said, persuading herself into broadmindedness.

'Knowing is one thing; finding yourself engaged to a homosexual so afraid of spoiling his career that he almost persuades himself into going through a form of marriage is different altogether. I don't know which hurt most, the thought of the people who believed I knew and was going along with it for the sake of the publicity, or those who laughed at me behind my back because I was ignorant of his real bent.'

'Well, of course you were taken in,' Vera said swiftly. 'Being a nicely brought up young girl ...'

'Mum, I've been on the stage since I was seven. I lost my virginity when I was fifteen ...'

'Stephanie!'

'Oh, come on, Mum, you knew. And you didn't care much, so long as I didn't get pregnant. I ought to have recognized that there was something wrong about my relationship with Dwight, and I would have done if we hadn't been handled as if we were

44

a fairytale prince and princess. I was dazzled ... bamboozled. I haven't got over feeling bitter about it, but now I'm going to start something new, make a fresh reputation for myself, and help the war effort as well.'

FIRST ACT

One

The rehearsal hall was dusty, echoing and cold. As Stephanie pushed open the door the rest of the cast of *Arms and the Man* turned to look at her.

'I hope I haven't kept you waiting,' she said. 'When I got off the bus I turned the wrong way and walked smartly down the road in the opposite direction. Incredibly stupid of me.'

She felt them beginning to warm towards her. She had come by bus; they all registered that. And she was dressed for work. Slacks and a sweater, her hair tied back with a green chiffon scarf. In the church tower next door the clock began to strike eleven o'clock.

'You couldn't be more punctual,' Peter Branden, the director, said.

He realized he was holding his watch in his hand and snapped it shut, trying to look as if he had not been checking up on the time.

'What a beautiful watch,' Stephanie exclaimed. 'May I see?'

'It belonged to my grandfather,' Peter said.

The watch was silver, with a delicate pattern scrolled over the outer case.

'He was Bill Branden, the comedian, wasn't he?' Stephanie asked as she examined the watch.

'That's done it – she's got Peter hooked,' Nesta Gordon murmured to Thelma Montagu.

Nesta folded her arms and pushed her hands into her sleeves, hugging herself against the cold. Charm, that was what it was, and whether or not it was consciously exercised, it was remarkably effective, judging by Peter's pink, pleased face.

All the same, the woman was better than she had expected. Not, as Nesta had feared, a spoilt film actress with little to offer but her name. She had presence, something that lifted the atmosphere of that dreary hall. Star quality. Whatever you

49

thought about her work, you had to admit she had it.

Peter was beginning to run through the introductions.

'Duncan Lomas, who is playing your father.'

'Duncan and I have worked together before,' Stephanie said. 'In my first British film.'

'A bit part – and most of it left on the cutting room floor,' Duncan said. He sounded offhand, but like Peter he was gratified by her recognition.

Score two to me, Stephanie thought, with wry amusement. I wonder if it will occur to any of them that I got my agent to do some homework for me beforehand.

'Thelma Montagu, who will be your mother, and Nesta Gordon, who is Louka, the maid.'

'No use pretending we've met before because this is my first London engagement – if you can call it that,' Nesta said.

'It was desperately hard luck on you that *The Merchant* never opened,' Stephanie said sympathetically.

Nesta felt herself beginning to gape in astonishment and pulled herself up. Damn it, the woman was too good to be true. She knew all about them, she was saying all the right things, it was impossible not to feel pleased, which was presumably exactly the effect Stephanie wanted to create.

'Murray Andrews, who is Sergius; Claud More, who will be doubling the part of the Russian officer who appears briefly in the first act, and Nicola, the servant, who doesn't appear until the second; and, finally – and I suppose I should have introduced him first as he's your leading man – Conrad Aylmer, who is Bluntschli.'

Stephanie turned her friendly smile towards the man who had been standing at the back of the group watching her, and held out her hand.

'I know your name, of course,' she said. 'But I've never managed to catch one of your plays.'

Conrad took her hand and bowed over it, raising it to his lips in Continental fashion. At that moment it was difficult to see him as Bluntschli, the blunt, disillusioned soldier.

Stephanie took the chair Peter brought forward for her and opened her book, glad to have got the first hurdle over. A scratch lot, but she had known that when she had agreed to join up with them. Duncan, Claud and Thelma were well-tried professionals, not in the top rank, but competent and reliable. Nesta was an unknown quantity and looked as if she might have a chip on her shoulder. Murray Andrews was too handsome for his own good, a golden-haired boy, stiff with consciousness of his own beauty. He might be superb as Sergius if he could be coaxed into softening up in his scenes with Louka. Peter was an inexperienced director, but there was not a lot he could do to muck up *Arms and the Man*, considering that it contained some of Bernard Shaw's most amusing writing. The contrast between a romantic girl's idea of war, as represented by the role Stephanie was to play, and the reality typified by Bluntschli, the Swiss mercenary who avoided the fighting whenever possible and concentrated on survival, would strike a topical note, and Stephanie foresaw guffaws from the troops when he was discovered to be carrying chocolates rather than bullets.

Conrad Aylmer was on the young side for Bluntschli, who was supposed to be thirty-four, but it would not be difficult to age him. A touch of grey at the temples perhaps, a slight accentuation of the lines which ran from nose to mouth, a stiffening of the supple grace with which he moved, and it would be done.

As they began their first read-through, always difficult with a group of actors who had not worked together before, Stephanie began to form an opinion of them.

Peter was patently unsure of himself, agonizingly sensitive and not likely to accept even the most sensible suggestion as anything but a criticism. Still, he did seem to understand the play, and if he could be lulled into a sense of security he might take on the authority that was needed to weld them into a team.

Nesta was a surprise. She might be inexperienced, but she was going to be good. A lovely sense of timing, and she seemed to be able to rise above her unpromising appearance. She was too thin, but she had two assets: a good speaking voice and huge dark eyes, full of expression.

As for Conrad, he obviously meant to play Bluntschli with a world-weary cynicism that was perversely attractive. Women in

51

the audience would sigh over the golden beauty of Murray Andrews, but they would understand why Raina ditched him for the Swiss soldier of fortune.

'Stephanie, darling, I want you to try for the utmost simplicity,' Peter said. 'Raina is full of feminine wiles, but totally unsophisticated ...'

'While believing herself to be quite knowing?' Stephanie suggested.

'Precisely. I knew you'd understand.'

Nesta hooked her heels over the rung of her chair and hunched her shoulders, scowling down at her book. All this deference and gratitude because a half-baked film star said something so obvious that it leapt out of the page. And Murray Andrews was going to be a damned awful Sergius, stiff as a wooden doll. Still, it was better than weekly rep, it was a chance to extend her range. Any experience, she told herself fiercely, anything at all, just so that I keep working. One day I'll get to the top and then I'll choose the roles I play.

They broke off for coffee and sandwiches, brought in from outside, and then carried on. The light began to fade early in the February afternoon.

'Better do the blackout before we put a light on, I suppose,' Peter said. 'Duncan, could you and Claud ...? Ghastly black paper shutters on wooden frames they've got here, absolute hell to lift into place.'

There were six tall windows. By the time three of them had been covered it was impossible to see to read.

'Have you heard yet where we're taking this production?' Thelma asked Peter.

'To some army camp up north first,' he said. 'Since we're working for ENSA we have to go where we're sent, but I think there's a chance you might go on to France or Belgium after that. If things stay as static as they have been, that is.'

'The war that never began,' Nesta remarked. 'Surely something must happen soon?'

'Don't wish for action,' Conrad said. 'The fighting will start soon enough and it will be terrible.'

As he spoke the last of the shutters slipped into place and they were in total darkness. Stephanie shivered. In the sudden

gloom the word 'terrible' echoed round the empty hall. For the
first time since coming back to England she felt afraid of what
the future might hold.

'For God's sake put some lights on,' Thelma said, and the
irritability with which she spoke made Stephanie suspect that
she, too, had been affected by Conrad's words.

They worked on for another hour and then Peter stopped
them.

'I think we've done enough for the first day,' he said. 'I don't
know about anyone else, but I'm cold right through to the
bone.'

'There's a café down the road where we could get a cup of
tea,' Nesta suggested.

They all trooped down to the café with the exception of
Conrad and Murray. Murray said with self-conscious
vagueness that he had to meet 'a friend' and Conrad merely
said that he preferred to go straight home.

'Have they gone off together, do you think?' Nesta asked,
peering into the darkness.

'Oh, I don't think so,' Thelma said. 'Poles apart, I would
have thought. Besides, Murray's got himself fixed up with a
rich widow.'

'You know all about it, do you?' Nesta asked.

'I always do, dear,' Thelma said with simple pride. 'Ask
anyone, I always know what's going on.'

It was a lorry driver's café, warm and brightly lit once they
got inside the heavy curtain covering the door, and smelling of
chips and hot fat.

Stephanie cupped her hands gratefully round the cup of dark
brown tea.

'Tell me about Conrad,' she said to Peter. 'He's half
German, isn't he?'

'English father, German mother,' Peter said rapidly.
'Educated in this country, of course. Well, you can tell, can't
you? Not the trace of an accent.'

'It's rather tragic actually,' Thelma put in. 'The father died
donkey's years ago and the mother lives in Germany. Conrad
split with her because she supported Hitler – at least, that's
what I've been told.'

'He's going to be an asset,' Peter said seriously. 'There's something about him ...'

'A whiff of brimstone, dear,' Thelma said. 'He can't be more than twenty-five, but he looks as if he's seen everything and done everything and doesn't much care what comes next. Sends a delicious cold shiver down your back.'

They all laughed, but there was something in what she said. Quite apart from his acting ability Conrad was infinitely attractive. He was tall, which was going to be a joy for Stephanie after playing in films with men who had to stand on boxes to make love to her. His head was beautifully modelled and his eyes were astonishing. Stephanie had never seen such a piercing blue before. His voice was good, too, as good as Nesta's, a fine flexible instrument over which he had complete control.

As the rehearsals progressed they all began to realize that they were on the verge of achieving something better than might have been expected from a hastily thrown together production destined for garrison theatres in out-of-the-way places. Peter glowed with pride, though the truth was that their success had been brought about by an alchemy outside his command.

Nesta was playing Louka with a fire that threatened to overshadow the lighter approach of the rest of the cast. Conrad ventured to drop a hint about it, with one eye on Peter in case he took offence.

'Perhaps a shade less revolutionary fervour?' he suggested.

'Louka is a downtrodden maid sticking up for her rights,' Nesta pointed out.

'But you're playing her as an ardent young partisan in the People's Army!'

'Conrad's right,' Peter joined in. 'I've been meaning to tell you to tone it down a bit, Nesta. Let's take your scene with Sergius again.'

Nesta glowered, but managed to keep back the protest she longed to make.

Conrad dropped into a chair by Stephanie's side and made an expressive grimace at her.

54

'I've offended our Louka,' he murmured.

'You were right. Louka's outburst is important, but Nesta was upsetting the balance of the play.'

They watched as Nesta and Murray ran through the crucial scene.

'She's a Jew, isn't she?' Conrad asked abruptly.

The question took Stephanie by surprise.

'I've no idea. Why don't you ask her?'

The innocence of that question jolted Conrad. In Germany it would have been unthinkable to ask someone in cold blood to admit to being Jewish. Watching Nesta he thought that his suspicion was correct. The girl was good, possibly even potentially great. It was a pity she had that tainted blood.

He thought it as well to make some other remark, to divert attention from a question he might have done better not to ask.

'Does it strike you that this is a curious choice of play to tour army camps?' he said. 'To me it seems almost subversive in the way it preaches against war.'

'That's what makes it so funny,' Stephanie pointed out. 'The soldiers will love it, especially some of your speeches.'

They were interrupted by Peter, querulous because Stephanie had missed a cue.

'Sorry, darling,' she said lightly. 'I was talking to our fascinating Bluntschli.'

In the shadows which they tolerated because they all hated the chore of fitting the blackout into place, Duncan murmured to Thelma, 'Have we got a romance on our hands?'

'Stephanie and Conrad? I don't think so, at least not yet. She's interested and perhaps piqued because he doesn't fall down and worship.'

'She's not conceited, at least not so that it shows, not in a film-starish kind of way.'

'No, but she's used to men being bowled over without her having to make much of an effort. Come on, duckie, I've seen you smirking yourself because Stephanie threw you a kind word.'

'She's difficult to resist, even at my age,' Duncan admitted, with all the self-confidence of an exceptionally well preserved fifty-five. 'But Conrad ...?'

55

'The complete lone wolf. It'll be interesting to see if he keeps it up when we're on tour.'

The tour was to take them to Yorkshire, to an army camp and an RAF camp, and then on to the north of Scotland to entertain the navy.

'And then, my dears, you are going overseas!' Peter announced triumphantly. 'You'll be playing for a week in Arras, a second week in Lille and finally a one-off show right up near the front line at Rheims.'

'Is that wise?' Conrad asked. 'So near the fighting? We might be overrun.'

'You're a proper worry boots,' Thelma said. 'What makes you think the Germans are going to advance?'

'Their record so far,' he retorted.

'We'll get plenty of warning,' Duncan said impatiently.

'I must say the notion of being interned by the Huns is definitely unenticing,' Murray remarked with a lightness that did not conceal his uneasiness.

'You should have thought of that before you joined us,' Nesta said.

'Well, of course, one longs to do one's bit and I've loved working with all you dear people. I just hope we're going to be properly looked after, that's all. I mean, in the short time it's been operating ENSA has *not* become famous for its efficiency, has it?'

'Considering the way it's all had to be thrown together from scratch, I think the organization's done wonders,' Peter said in a hurt way, as if he took the criticism personally.

'I'm sure the army will pack us off home if there's the slightest chance of our being caught up in a German advance,' Stephanie said. 'They'll be only too keen to get shot of us.'

'Darling, don't say "shot",' Murray begged.

'Spruce up!' Thelma said briskly. 'You're supposed to be our valiant soldier, remember?'

'On stage, darling, only on stage! If anyone points a gun at me I shall die of shock.'

After that the journey to Yorkshire could only be an anti-climax. Cold, draughty trains, overcrowded and without any of the facilities of peacetime, blacked out stations and few porters.

'A decent hotel,' Thelma pleaded, stamping her cold feet on the platform at York. 'Please God, let there be a decent hotel.'

It was not bad. At least there was hot water and an appetizing meal. They settled in, grumbling and laughing, knowing themselves to be larger than life and a source of wonder to local people and visiting wives, and sometimes exaggerating their behaviour to conform to what was expected of them.

The biggest drawback was the places in which they were expected to perform.

'Converted riding schools and hangars! All the decent garrison theatres have been turned into cinemas,' Duncan grumbled. 'You and I should have stuck to films, Stephanie. Live actors have become the poor relations.'

'Doesn't it strike you as odd that there should be a hangar available for use as a theatre?' Conrad asked. 'In wartime surely one would expect them to be fully occupied?'

'We haven't got into our stride yet,' Thelma said comfortably. 'Besides, most of our planes are in France, I expect.'

'What fills me with horror is nothing to do with the war, but the fact that so many of the men who come to see us seem to have no idea what the theatre is about,' Nesta said.

'I told you – we're the poor relations,' Duncan said.

'If you'd lived in the country with no theatre nearby then you might never have seen a play before either,' Stephanie pointed out. 'They're enthusiastic enough when they've grasped that there are three acts and the story isn't over until the end of the last one, and *Arms and the Man* is a popular choice.'

She kept to herself the remarks she had collected from some of the autograph hunters, who crowded round her and made no bones about their puzzlement over her change of direction.

'It were real nice and I got a laugh out of it,' one soldier told her. 'But I thought it would be a bit more spicy-like. You were a fair sizzler in *Flowers by the River*.'

'Pity there weren't a chance for you to give us a song,' his mate added. 'Tell you what, why don't you come back some time with some music and give us a sing-song? We'd like that.'

Stephanie was wryly amused by this reception of her efforts to be taken seriously on the legitimate stage. What the boys really wanted, it seemed, was a sight of her legs and some popular songs.

It was April before they finally embarked for France.

'I hope you're being half German doesn't cause any difficulties,' Thelma remarked to Conrad.

'Don't worry, that's been taken care of,' he replied.

There had, in fact, been doubts about sending him abroad, but Conrad had anticipated this and had made careful enquiries about the channels through which his papers would proceed. A word in the right ear about his anxiety to be allowed to make his contribution towards keeping up the morale of the British forces and all difficulties had disappeared.

The note of caution against his name was treated with scorn.

'Conrad Aylmer? Good Lord, he was at my old school; up at Cambridge with my young brother; plays cricket like an angel. I know all about his German mother. Conrad broke with her because of her Nazi views. Damn difficult thing to do. He's all right. A thorough-going Englishman. His father fought in the last do and conked out early as a result. Conrad was brought up by Bertram Aylmer, and you couldn't get a more dyed-in-the wool patriot than old Bert. Of course Conrad must be allowed to go abroad with his outfit. I dare say when he's got that out of his system he'll join up and make a damned good soldier.'

They crossed from Dover to Calais and were glad that the voyage was short since the sea was decidedly choppy.

'The things I suffer for England,' Thelma grumbled. 'Another ten minutes and my poor old stomach would have let me down. How much longer are they going to keep us hanging about on this horrid little boat?'

'Patience, darling,' Claud More counselled her. 'It's soldiers first and ladies last in wartime.'

At last they were able to disembark and the two skips containing their costumes were swung down on to the dockside. Their scenery was to be of the simplest and they were carrying only their smaller props, relying on local suppliers for larger pieces, such as Raina's bed in the first act.

'I thought we'd be met, and where's our transport?' Murray demanded.

'There's a little man waving over there and I think he's trying to attract our attention,' Stephanie pointed out.

He was a breathless young man in spectacles, clutching a sheaf of papers.

'Frightfully sorry everyone, should have been here an hour ago,' he apologized. 'Got held up on the road. I'll just check your names off on the list, get you through the controls, clear your luggage and we'll be on our way.'

They bore with him, grumbling good-humouredly under their breath, but when they were still kept hanging about Conrad wandered away and had to be recalled when at last they were free to leave.

'Conrad, where's Conrad?' Duncan demanded.

The breathless young man darted away and brought the truant back.

'Does he remind you of a sheepdog rounding up a stray from the flock?' Nesta murmured to Duncan.

'Conrad's a nuisance. He's always going missing when we're about to leave,' Murray said in an injured way.

Jealous, Nesta diagnosed. As well he might be. Conrad was the great success of this production. It was a pleasure to work with him; a painful pleasure sometimes because as well as being a fine actor, which was what she really admired him for, of course, he was also a devastatingly attractive man.

'Sorry, people,' Conrad apologized. 'I knew the port so well in peacetime that I was curious to see it tricked out for war. My God, is that our transport?'

'Think yourselves lucky,' the young man from ENSA told them grimly. 'Some of our people have had to travel in open lorries. You've got two good vans. One will take your luggage and one passenger in front with the driver, the other is fitted up with seats for the rest of you.' They looked in disbelief at the bench seats in the back of the second van, but managed to refrain from comment. With a lot of protesting and laughter they fitted themselves in.

'Can't your make-up case go with the other luggage, Conrad?' Claud asked.

'I'm superstitious about keeping it in my own hands,' Conrad said. 'I'll put it on the floor and it won't be in your way.'

'Funny thing, superstition,' Murray said in a way that made Nesta suspect that he was trying to make amends for his ill-humour on the quayside. 'I feel absolutely *sick* if my rabbit's foot isn't on my dressing table.'

'You'll be lucky to have a dressing table on this trip,' Duncan told him.

It was not as bad as they had feared once they had recovered from that first long, bumpy ride. They opened in Arras, where ENSA had established its French headquarters.

'You'll be based in Lille next week and then we're sending you on to Rheims,' the organizer told them. 'Of course, the difficulty with a production like yours is finding somewhere suitable for you to present it.'

'You don't have to tell us,' Duncan murmured.

'Oh, quite. I know you've had a lot to put up with, but we've got some very good portable stages now and I'll make sure that you at least have something to stand on.'

'Good of you,' Conrad said with a gentle sarcasm that was lost on their organizer.

By the end of the first week in May they were in Rheims.

'Three performances and a rest day,' Stephanie said, looking at their schedule. 'I must say, that will be welcome.'

'Do you ever regret Hollywood?' Nesta asked curiously.

'I do when I look at my hair,' Stephanie said. 'When I think that I used to be able to have it shampooed and set *every day*! I must wash it before tonight's performance, I really must.'

'Better do it while the hot water lasts,' Nesta said. 'If this hotel is anything like the last there'll be nothing but cold at exactly the time when everyone wants to wash.'

They were sharing a room, an arrangement that Stephanie accepted with an equanimity that surprised Nesta.

'You know, you haven't turned out to be a bit like I expected,' she said abruptly that afternoon.

Stephanie was bending over the washbasin, her head a mass of soapsuds.

'You thought I'd swan around in silver fox, travel with my

own maid and demand caviare for breakfast?' she suggested indistinctly.

'Something like that,' Nesta admitted with a reluctant grin.

'I'm an old trouper,' Stephanie said. 'I've been on the road since I was seven.'

'Lucky you. I had to fight like anything to get my family to let me go on the stage.'

'I wouldn't call myself lucky. When I was a child I felt I was missing something, always being sent off to dancing lessons or rehearsals when the other kids were out playing.'

'That would have suited me down to the ground. I could never see the sense of chasing a ball round the playground. I wouldn't have minded doing ballet.'

'You've got a one-track mind,' Stephanie said. 'Be an angel and rinse me off, would you?'

Obligingly, Nesta picked up the jug of water and began pouring it through Stephanie's hair.

'I envy you, being so sure about what you want to do,' Stephanie said, her words half obscured by the towel she was holding up to her face. 'I sometimes think I only go on acting because I don't know how to do anything else.'

'You could give it up and go into the Forces,' Nesta suggested.

'I may yet come to that decision. And yet ... it seems such a waste of all those years of learning.'

'A chartered accountant might think the same thing.'

'At least he could go into the Pay Corps,' Stephanie retorted. 'Thanks, my hair will do now. I'll give it a good rub and twist it up into a few pins. Thank goodness for a bit of natural curl.'

'My horrible mop just frizzes up when it's washed. I'll wait and follow your good example tomorrow.'

'You do know that we're invited to the Officers' Mess tonight, don't you?'

'Ah! So that's why we're working on our glamorous image!'

Stephanie grinned. 'All those lovely men,' she said. 'Surely there must be one for me somewhere?'

'Actually, Stephanie, have you made love to a lot of men?'

Stephanie gave a quick, shrewd look at Nesta, sitting cross-legged at the end of the bed, her face intent, but she answered readily, 'I was a terribly good little girl apart from a bit of naughtiness when I was very young – under the age of consent, in fact, God help me – because it seemed like a lark and terribly daring, and I wanted to know what it was all about. It was a mistake and I shied away from a real, grown up affair until after I'd had a bit of a setback in my love life and I suppose I was looking for reassurance. I packed a lot of experience into my last few months in Hollywood, but none of it meant much – to me or to the men involved.'

'What about Dwight David? Weren't you going to marry him?'

'We decided we weren't suited,' Stephanie said with careful lightness.

Fortunately, Nesta was not really interested in Stephanie's past.

'What I really want to know is, do you think it's a necessary part of an actress's development to have a deep emotional experience?' she asked earnestly.

'It probably helps,' Stephanie said with only the faintest tremor in her voice. 'Do you have anyone particular in mind?'

'Claud is rather keen,' Nesta admitted. 'He's kissed me once or twice and I quite liked it.'

'Quiet old Claud? Who would have thought it!'

'He's only thirty.'

'He does rather sink into the background, doesn't he? Now, if you'd said it was our wicked Bluntschli …'

'Conrad doesn't take the slightest interest in me, not in that way.'

'But you wish he would?' Stephanie asked.

'Oh, hell!' Nesta said. 'Does it show?'

'We all watch him. You're no different from the rest of us in that respect. I don't think anyone else has realized that it goes deeper with you.'

'It's not likely to come to anything. If anyone catches Conrad's eye it'll be you rather than me. I'm … I'm desperately jealous of you sometimes.'

That frank, shamefaced admission touched Stephanie. There was scarcely two years' difference in their ages, and yet she felt immeasurably older than the other girl.

'Conrad thinks you will become a fine, classical actress,' she said. 'That's what he really admires.'

'It's what I want more than anything else in the world!' Nesta exclaimed, her face lighting up in the way that transformed her.

'More than making love to Conrad?'

'I'd like that, too,' Nesta admitted, but this time she was able to laugh about it.

The performance went well that night. The theatre was more acceptable than some they had played in and the audience was quick off the mark, particularly delighting in Bluntschli's remarks about carrying chocolate instead of bullets. The cast had suddenly realized that unless they received fresh instructions when they returned to Arras, this was likely to be their last performance and they put something a little extra into it.

For the party afterwards the girls discarded the nondescript khaki which they wore for travelling and blossomed out in party dresses. Stephanie, in a short, full-skirted gown of stiff black taffeta, her newly washed hair gleaming, was the centre of attraction. She was surrounded by a crowd of eager young men, vying for a chance to catch her eye.

She had just surrendered her glass to a triumphant young lieutenant who had offered to fetch her another drink when there was a touch on her arm. Stephanie turned her head to find a tall man wearing the armband of a war correspondent behind her.

'Luke! How lovely to see you again!'

It sounded too effusive, but for all her sophistication Stephanie was disconcerted to see Luke so unexpectedly, and all the more so because her talk with Nesta that afternoon had brought him into her mind.

'I was in the audience and wangled an invitation to the party,' Luke said. 'I enjoyed the play.'

'How nice of you to say so. How are you, Luke?'

'I'm in great form.'

With a significance that only Stephanie appreciated he added, 'I've come a long way since we crossed the Atlantic together.'

'I'm glad. What are you doing here?'

'It'd be rather more to the point if I asked you that. Rather close to the front line, isn't it?'

'Yes, isn't it exciting? I've been teasing Captain Buller to take me to see the Maginot Line that we've all heard so much about.'

'I hope he resists you,' Luke said with a dryness that arose from a feeling of irritation at the bright, careless attitude she seemed to have adopted. 'There has been some skirmishing, you know.'

'I know. Captain Buller says it's the only place where there's been a shot fired in anger.'

'Apart from Finland, Denmark and Norway.'

Stephanie remembered that she had thought that his family had probably originated from Scandinavia and felt contrite.

'I'm sorry, Luke. Have you got relations in that part of the world?'

'Only very distant connections – and in Sweden, which seems safe at the moment. How much longer are you going to be in this area?'

'We leave in the morning. I'm afraid there's not much chance of seeing you again after tonight.'

'I'm not angling for a date, honey. I'm moving on myself tomorrow. No, what I was thinking was that the German spring offensive must surely open soon and it might be better for you and your company to be further west.'

'Don't listen to him, Miss Bartram,' the perspiring lieutenant said, handing her the drink he had battled through the crowd to fetch for her. 'We won't let the horrible Huns capture our favourite film star.'

'I'm sure I'm in good hands,' Stephanie said, looking at him over the rim of her glass in a way that turned him scarlet with pleasure. 'Luke is as much of a gloom merchant as our Bluntschli.'

Conrad was standing close by and heard that remark.

'I'm not gloomy,' he protested. 'The only thing I said was that the speech in the play about the cavalry charging the guns made my blood run cold because that was what the Poles did – and got massacred as a result.'

64

'Don't worry,' the young lieutenant said. 'We've got something better to use than horse soldiers.'

'Your lot are equipped with the six-inch howitzer, aren't they?' Conrad asked in an interested way.

'That's right. Old-fashioned, but reliable.'

'All right for longer range work, but what about tanks?'

'We're getting a few two-pounders for the anti-tank gunners. Deliveries have been slow coming through, but there's a train in a siding now waiting to be unloaded. Think of me tomorrow, Miss Bartram, supervising the fatigue party.'

'I'll think about you, all of you,' Stephanie promised. 'But only if you'll stop being so formal. Stephanie – please.'

Luke turned away. There was going to be no chance of any further conversation with Stephanie and, in any case, she was not his reason for being at the party.

Like Stephanie, but more seriously, Luke wanted to get up to the so-called front line, where the Allied troops, predominantly French but with some British manning the outposts, were facing the enemy. He was bored with the long, drawn out 'phoney war' and profoundly dissatisfied because he had not been assigned to the Scandinavian area where something was happening.

Denmark had capitulated. Norway was fighting on, but Luke saw little hope of the resistance being successful. Neutrality was no protection in this war. He had visited The Hague and had found the Dutch on edge. No one would admit that they expected an invasion, but Luke knew that plans were in hand to open the dykes and flood the country if the worst happened.

Luke was privately dismayed by the lack of initiative shown by the Allied armies. He knew from his own observation that they were ill-equipped to fight a major war, but it seemed to him that a firm display of strength on the western front while the Germans were still heavily engaged in the north might be just the deterrent that was needed to dissuade Hitler from invading the Low Countries.

He had tried to say as much in his reports, only to have them cut so severely by the censor that they were hardly worth sending. He knew better than to get into an argument about it that evening. Most of the soldiers present would have agreed with him; there was no lack of eagerness to fight amongst the rank and file. It was in the upper echelons that there seemed to be a reluctance to go on the offensive.

He secured a promise of transport up to the French front line the next morning and left the party satisfied, without saying goodbye to Stephanie.

Stephanie woke up the next morning with what she had to admit was a hangover. With champagne available at bargain prices their hosts had seen no reason to stint themselves and their hospitality had been lavish. She winced as she raised her head from the pillow. It was much earlier than she usually woke up and the light was still pale. There was a strange booming noise in the air, which must have been what had roused her. In the next bed Nesta also stirred.

'What's that row?' she asked sleepily.

'I think … perhaps guns,' Stephanie said doubtfully.

'No!'

Nesta sat up, immediately awake and enviably immune to the effects of the previous night's party.

'I say, do you think we're going to see a battle?' she asked.

'I hope not, but I have a nasty feeling we may get caught in an air raid.'

Stephanie slipped out of bed and went over to the window. As she looked down a small car drew up with a screech of brakes and Luke jumped out. Stephanie siezed her dressing gown and pulled it round her.

'Luke Lindquist, that American war correspondent, who was at the party last night,' she explained to Nesta. 'I'm going down to see if he has any news.'

She met Luke on the stairs.

'I was on my way to see you,' he said. 'The Germans have invaded Holland and Belgium and it looks as if they're making a push through the Ardennes. You said you were leaving today? My advice is to make it snappy.'

'But they won't get past the Maginot Line,' Stephanie protested.

'Oh, won't they? Like a hot knife through butter, if you ask me. The French army isn't ready to fight and the British are going to have their hands full in Belgium. Get your people together and make for the coast.'

'We're supposed to return to Arras,' Stephanie said. 'I'll talk it over with the others and see what they want to do.'

'You'd all do better to get back to England. France is going to be a battlefield and a party of play actors can only be in the way.'

'You really think the Germans are going to get over the frontier?'

'Yes, Stephanie, I really do,' Luke said in a quiet exasperation. 'I can't stop to organize you. I need to get as far forward as I can to find out what's happening and I'm keeping my transport waiting.'

'It was good of you to come and warn me,' Stephanie said.

'I owed you that much. That night, on the ship ... after that I started to get back my sanity.'

'You're all right now?'

'More or less. I still feel lopsided when I remember Prue isn't waiting for me to finish my job and go home, but I'm not haunted the way I was then.'

'I'm glad. Goodbye, Luke, and look after yourself.' Stephanie smiled. 'I seem to remember I said that before.'

She moved forward until she was standing very close to him and lifted her face. There was a tiny pause and then Luke put his arms round her and kissed her. Stephanie could feel the warmth of his hands on her back through the thin dressing gown. He let her go, a little too quickly, and turned to leave. At the bottom of the stairs he looked back. Stephanie was leaning over the banister watching him. He raised his hand in salute and farewell and she did the same.

Stephanie lingered a minute or two before she went back to her room. The unexpected meeting with Luke had been difficult. They had been stiff with one another; he because he still felt guilty about betraying his dead wife, and Stephanie because she was afraid she had left Luke with the impression that she was a promiscuous woman to be had for the asking. She treasured the fact that he had cared enough to come that morning to warn her of danger. Had it been a mistake to kiss him? She had wanted it and so had he. Something still lingered between them; a trace of sensuality, a hint of remembered passion, enough to keep her loitering regretfully out in the passageway when she ought to be passing on Luke's warning to the others.

Stephanie gave Luke's message to the rest of the company as soon as they were all together for breakfast and found that they were as sceptical as she had been about the need to return immediately to England. The only exception was Conrad, who thought they should drive straight for the nearest port.

'You're a defeatist,' Thelma told him scornfully. 'You have been right from the beginning, always making remarks about how good the Germans are.'

'I'm a realist,' Conrad said. 'However, if I'm over-ruled ...'

He was in a dilemma. His own belief was that the German forces would be swiftly victorious, in which case France would be overrun, but even Conrad did not think that anything so dramatic could happen in the short time it would take them to return to Arras, get fresh instructions and make their way to Calais or Boulogne. All the same, it would be annoying if he were captured. Provided he could convince the German army of his credentials he would be assured of first-class treatment, but his undercover role would be exposed and his usefulness would be at an end. Far better for him to return safely to England and carry on his work.

Presumably all the information he had been amassing in the last few days would now be superfluous. He felt irritated, which was not a bad thing because his preoccupation with the waste of his time served to mask his inward exultation at the way the Germans had stolen a march on their opponents. He felt vindicated. He had made the right choice. It would be a quick war, and as soon as it was over he could drop his deception and assume his place in the new order. Nevertheless it was important not to make his relief apparent. Thelma's remark about him being a defeatist had shown that his attitude was already slightly suspect.

In the end their discussion about where they should go was solved when their two drivers refused to take them anywhere but Arras. That was where they had been ordered to drive their party, and that was the only destination they would consider.

The cast took their time packing up and getting ready to leave. After all, there was no performance that evening and without that incentive none of them could bring themselves to rush into their singularly uncomfortable transport. The drivers, their part done once the skips and scenery had been loaded, leaned against the bonnets of their vans, smoking and exchanging pithy comments about the vagaries of actors.

What the company, with their scant understanding of war, had not anticipated was that progress would be far slower than normal because the roads were congested with military traffic. Nor had they realized that they would have to stop if there was an air raid warning.

'It's not as if there's anything happening,' Nesta said in exasperation, looking up at the empty sky.

'No chance of getting through to Arras now,' the driver of her van said. 'Where do you want to stay the night?'

They were forced to put up in two separate village inns and were shocked to discover that in both villages families were packing up and preparing to move south, because they believed the Germans would be on them in the next few days.

'It can't be true,' Stephanie said. 'I mean, we're miles and miles inside the frontier and surely the main attack is in the north, in Belgium?'

'If it is, we're going towards it,' Duncan pointed out. 'I'll tell you something, Stephanie: I'll be glad to get back home. The atmosphere here makes me uneasy.'

They were tired, grubby, hungry and disgruntled when they eventually arrived in Arras. They were also, although they hid it, rather frightened.

'If this is war, I don't like it,' Nesta remarked thoughtfully.

She got a laugh, but it was perfunctory. None of them liked it, especially since they had encountered their first parties of Belgian refugees on the road outside Arras.

'You should have been here yesterday,' their organizer scolded them.

'We couldn't get through,' Stephanie said, suppressing the fact that it had been partly their own fault. 'You've got a billet for us, I hope?'

'Oh, there's plenty of room,' he said. 'People are moving out.

69

You may find service in the hotel is a bit wanting. I'll try to get you away tomorrow, but you may have to wait about in Calais until there's room on a boat to take you across the Channel.'

Although they stood by, ready to depart at a moment's notice, it was another twenty-four hours before the company were told that they would leave at first light the next morning.

'And I mean that,' the organizer said severely. 'Crack of dawn, my children. You're to be on the road by six o'clock and you can stop on the way for breakfast. You'll be making straight for Calais and I've been promised accommodation for you on a ferry tomorrow evening, which is why you *must* get away early.'

As he finished speaking the air raid warning sounded again and this time they did not argue about whether the explosions they heard were caused by bombs or not; it was all too obvious that they were. They sat uncomfortably in the cellar of their hotel and the wine bottles rattled in the racks as the building shook all round them.

After it was over Stephanie stood up and stretched.

'I must go out,' she said. 'I hate being cooped up like this, not knowing what's happening outside.'

'I'd just as soon not know,' Murray said, but Nesta and Conrad agreed with Stephanie and went with her.

As soon as they left the hotel they could see that buildings nearby had been damaged. Broken glass crunched under their feet and there was a smell of smoke in the air although they could not see any fires. They turned the corner into the Place outside the station and stopped.

The railway had been hit, apparently several times. The station was burning fiercely. There were bodies scattered near the entrance, grotesque in the way they had been thrown sprawling across the cobblestones.

'No ...! Oh, no!' Stephanie said in a sick whisper. 'Nesta, they're *children*!'

It was Conrad who walked forward, very slowly, as if hypnotized. He knelt down by the first of the pitiful little bundles of blood-spattered clothes. It was a girl, perhaps ten years old, her face a pale, pure oval. She was still alive. She seemed to look at him as he bent over her, but her eyes were already remote, unseeing. Her lips parted, as if she was trying to speak, and then a thin stream of blood ran from her open mouth and the light faded from her eyes.

Conrad walked back to the waiting girls.

'There's nothing we can do here,' he said. 'Get back to the hotel.'

At another time perhaps Stephanie, and certainly Nesta, would have resented the sharp, almost dictatorial way he spoke to them, but they were too shocked to do anything but turn and walk meekly back the way they had come.

Stealing a sideways look at him Stephanie thought that Conrad looked ill. She felt shaken herself, but it would not have surprised her if Conrad had keeled over at any moment.

He caught her looking at him and said, as if to explain his revulsion, 'She had such blue eyes ...'

In spite of their early start the next day, they made slow progress on the road to Calais. There was military traffic travelling towards them and a lot of cars on the road out of Arras. Later in the day they began to come across groups of people on foot, their belongings piled on carts, sometimes pulled by a horse, sometimes by the refugees themselves.

Of them all, it was Conrad who showed the most impatience, although he tried to control it. He was ashamed of the weakness he had shown the previous day. For one moment he had been sickened by the death of a little girl, but since then he had told himself that Arras was a legitimate military target; it was the fact that the British General Headquarters was housed there that had exposed the unfortunate child to danger. Atrocities against women and children were no part of the German design for the better management of decadent Europe. If anything, his experiences in the last couple of days had renewed his dedication to his mission. Hastening the end of the fighting would eventually be seen as conferring a benefit on friends and enemies alike. If that meant continuing with his spying activities then he would be obedient.

71

Two

'I don't know why you're not in the army!'

Bertram Aylmer eyed his nephew with mingled disgust and puzzlement.

'Considering the fix we're in I would have thought that you and every other able bodied man would want to join up.'

'My call-up was deferred because I was entertaining the troops in France,' Conrad pointed out.

'Well, that's over. Lucky you got out when you did. What are you going to do now? You'll choose the army, I suppose?'

'I'm not sure.'

'Damn it, Conrad, what's the matter with you? You're not a coward; you can't be, with your sporting record. I could put in a word in the right quarter, perhaps get you into your father's old outfit.'

'There might be a difficulty about giving a commission to someone who's half German and I don't feel any urge to serve in the ranks.'

'Lot of poppycock! You're as English as I am,' his uncle said, but he sounded less certain than his words implied.

'Has it occurred to you that I might feel a qualm about killing my mother's people – possibly my own cousins and friends?'

'I can't imagine anyone having an objection to killing a Hun,' Bertram said frankly.

'I think I could be more useful in a noncombatant role.'

'Doing what? Play acting again?'

'Broadcasting perhaps. I'm completely bilingual. Or I might be of use as an interpreter.'

'Propaganda,' Bertram said distastefully.

'And Intelligence,' Conrad suggested. 'Interrogating prisoners-of-war, for instance – if we manage to capture any.'

He watched the effect of this statement on his uncle, and after a carefully judged interval went on, 'If you know anyone who might be interested in making use of me in that capacity I would be glad of your help.'

'I'll put out a feeler or two,' Bertram said reluctantly. 'Personally I'd rather fight with a gun in my hand, but I suppose if you have a special talent it's only sense to make use of it.'

He shifted uncomfortably in his seat and then asked, 'Do you ever get any news of your mother?'

'We manage to exchange an occasional letter through friends in the neutral embassies. She is well.'

'Thank God she's living in Germany this time. Damn fool woman. I'm sorry, Conrad, I know you're as besotted by her as your poor father was when they were first married, but I had to live through the first war with her and, believe me, it was a trying experience.'

'Some allowance might have been made for her anxiety about her family in Germany,' Conrad said stiffly.

'She could have had all the sympathy she needed if she would only have been a bit more tactful. I remember the Christmas of 1916. We were all at your grandparents' house, as many as could get leave, and that didn't include your father. Wanda was there, and you, though you won't remember, and she caused a scene at the end of our Christmas lunch when your grandfather proposed a toast to 'Victory and an early peace'. Wanda stalked out of the room as if she'd been mortally insulted.'

'It seems to me that Mama was not the only person lacking in tact.'

'Poor old Dad, he meant it for the best. He was thunderstruck by her attitude. But it was all of a piece. People gave up inviting her to public functions because she refused to stand up for the National Anthem. Considering she was married to a serving British officer I would have thought she could have brought herself to do that.'

A vision of his mother, beautiful and defiant, exalted by her convictions, came into Conrad's mind and he suppressed a smile. The last time he had seen her looking like that she had been standing rigidly to attention with her arm raised in the Nazi salute. Everyone had been impressed by her fervour, even the Führer, who was used to the effect he had on his followers. When the Party came to power in England there would be a very special place for Wanda von Lynden – and her son.

Conrad left his uncle and went out into the July sunshine. He was reasonably pleased with the way their conversation had gone. He had put the idea of a job in Intelligence into Bertram's mind and he thought that something might come of it. Bertram, as Conrad very well knew, was by no means the blundering old Colonel Blimp he pretended to be. He was shrewd, apart from a fortunate blindness about his nephew's allegiance, and he had some extremely useful contacts.

It amused Conrad to think that he might penetrate the British Intelligence operation, and it would certainly impress his own superiors if he could unmask the British Secret Service operatives when the invasion took place.

After the brilliant success of the breakthrough in France, Conrad had assumed that one of two things would happen: the Allies would sue for peace or, failing that, England would be invaded and swiftly defeated. Neither event had taken place. The British army made an ignominious retreat from Dunkirk – which the British insisted on regarding as a victory – France fell, and the German army, instead of keeping up the momentum of its advance with a surge across the Channel, was kept kicking its heels and looking longingly towards the white cliffs, so tantalizingly near.

On his way to meet his uncle Conrad had already handed over to a contact in the Spanish embassy what purported to be a letter to his mother, but between the widely spaced lines there was another message, written in secret ink. It was a good report, packed with solid facts which he had verified with his own eyes. The British were incorrigible gossips and admonitions about 'careless talk' stopped nobody from talking to someone as personable and charming as Conrad.

The details he had been asked to supply on morale were not going to give as much satisfaction. The fall of France appeared to have had a cheering effect on his unpredictable fellow countrymen. They formed fire fighting teams, joined the Home Guard, put air raid shelters into their gardens and used them for storing vegetables, tightened their belts and accepted rationing, and were apparently prepared to sit out a long war.

The spirit shown by the British had surprised Conrad. He felt disgruntled by it because it upset all his calculations. He had known that there would be fighting, death, destruction of property, even civilian casualties, but he had expected the ill-effects to be limited by the short duration of the war. It was beginning to look as if he might have been wrong and his position was being made difficult by the general assumption that he would be joining up. This had never been his plan, and he was casting around for a way of avoiding it which would not damage his credibility. It was trying to have the reputation of being a daredevil with almost reckless courage, and yet to avoid the risk of having to kill anyone on what he thought of as his own side, particularly since Conrad suspected that he would have been a good soldier.

Conrad walked quickly from St James's Street to Charing Cross Station and bought a ticket for Greenwich. He was on his way to a meeting which he had only agreed to with extreme reluctance.

Since the return of the *Arms and the Man* company he had cultivated Stephanie because she was part of a plan he had formed to do some useful tours around the country. What he had not expected was that this had also entailed keeping in touch with Nesta, because the two girls had become firm friends.

The last time he had met Stephanie she had given him a message from Nesta, and because he had seen that it would damage his image in Stephanie's eyes if he refused, he had reluctantly agreed to meet Nesta's German-Jewish relations.

Nesta had spoken to him about them more than once.

'They're trying to learn English, but they don't seem to make much progress,' she said. 'It would be heaven for them to meet someone like you, Conrad, who not only speaks the language, but also knows the country. They still think of Germany as home, you know, in spite of the way they've been treated.'

Nesta was waiting for him at Greenwich Station. She looked pale and tired, and thinner than ever, but her eyes still blazed with the intense inner fire which stirred Conrad to reluctant admiration. He felt a curious, exasperated affection for her. She was enormously talented and she was burning herself up, trying to make a misguided attempt to help the war effort and to keep up her acting career at the same time.

'I suppose you still have your silly job at the munitions factory?' he greeted her. 'Serving cups of tea and hot pies in a canteen! What good do you think you're doing?'

'It's a sop to my conscience,' Nesta said. 'I know perfectly well I ought to go into the ATS or something.'

'You look worn out.'

Nesta smiled and shook her head, trying not to show the pleasure his concern gave her, but she could not keep back the extra colour in her cheeks and her shoulders, which had been drooping with fatigue, straightened because of the effect of his words on her. It was damned stupid, and she scolded herself fiercely for it, but there was something about Conrad that made her go weak at the knees every time she set eyes on him. Love, she thought gloomily; or, at any rate, infatuation. The heroine of one of Trollope's novels had described it exactly: 'Stricken to the very bone' because of the way a man looked. But there was more to Conrad than his good looks. He was a fine actor and he ought not to be wasting his time lounging around London, any more than she should have been working the night shift in a factory canteen.

'I suggested you came to Greenwich Station so that we could walk across the park,' she said. 'We go up the hill, cut across diagonally behind the Queen's House and out through a side gate.'

'It's a fine collection of buildings,' Conrad said. 'Is that the Naval College on the waterfront?'

'Yes. Isn't it magnificent? I do hope it doesn't get bombed,' Nesta said.

Conrad felt the familiar tweak of divided allegiance. He would hate to see a historical building damaged, and yet ... a Naval College?

'If only the war would end,' he said out loud, and it was a symptom of his anxiety that he allowed the words to escape him.

'I think it'll go on for years,' Nesta said wearily. 'I'd better tell you about the Goldsteins before you meet them. They're

77

quite distant relations. Dad's second cousins, I think, and proper, religious Jews, which Dad's side of the family have long since given up. Dad and Mum were married in the Church of England and my sister and I were christened. The Goldsteins nearly died when they discovered that. Unfortunately for them, the members of the family who stayed in the Jewish religion have long since got dispersed all over the world, so they're stuck with us. So although our lack of orthodoxy pains them, they've been grateful for the help we've been able to give.'

'It doesn't sound as if I'm going to have a lot in common with them,' Conrad said, which was an understatement only he was capable of appreciating.

'More than you might think, quite apart from speaking German, which will be a pleasure to them, poor things. I've made them sound bigoted, which they're not. I think they're clinging tightly to their religion because it's the one familiar thing in a strange land.'

'That's very shrewd of you.'

'I do try to understand people. I mean, quite apart from being sympathetic, you never know when it will come in useful, do you? I still regret not having played Jessica.'

' "My daughter and my ducats",' Conrad quoted flippantly. 'Is that the way your cousins talk?'

'No, of course not! They're very cultured people and they understand the importance of the theatre far better than my own family.'

'How long have they been in England?'

'They got out just after Munich. They won't tell even us how it was managed, but it cost every penny they had.'

'Bribery,' Conrad said distastefully.

'Thank goodness there are people who can be bribed, when they come down on the side of humanity,' Nesta retorted.

She led him out of the park and across the road towards a row of pleasant, nineteenth-century houses.

'Have you always lived here?' Conrad asked.

'Yes, always! The house belonged to my grandfather and we lived with him and Granny until they both died, and then Dad inherited the house. It's old-fashioned, but we like it, except that Mum grumbles about the kitchen.'

'You haven't told me how many of these Goldsteins there are.'

'There's Joachim and Helga, who are in their forties, and Joachim's mother, Wilhelmina, who's getting on for seventy, and their two children, Erich and Zarah.'

'Quite a tribe.'

'Yes.' Nesta sighed slightly. 'A bit of a strain on Dad's resources, to be honest, although the Jewish community have been wonderful about helping the refugees.'

'Is that why you've taken your ridiculous job?' Conrad asked quietly.

'I have to support myself. It's simply not fair to sit at home and do nothing. Of course, I'm keeping an eye open for acting opportunities as well.'

The Goldsteins were not what Conrad had expected. Helga, in particular, slim, dark and elegant, her sleek black hair just touched with silver, her dark eyes as intense as Nesta's, was a woman who could hold her own in any society in the world. It was no effort to remember his manners and to bow over her hand in a way that brought a momentary sparkle to her sombre face. She wore black, as did her mother-in-law, and neither woman wore any ornaments, not even a wedding ring.

The rest of the family lacked Helga's distinction, but they were all pleasing people, or would have been if it had not been for the air of tragedy that hung about them.

It was obviously a relief for them to be able to speak German with someone who understood every nuance of what they were saying.

'We have spent the last year learning English and the children, in particular, have made great progress,' Joachim said.

He looked with affectionate pride at the boy and girl, who were making painstaking conversation with Nesta's parents.

Helga and Joachim spoke with quiet despair of the decision to leave their native country.

'We always felt ourselves to be German,' Helga said. 'Even after Hitler came to power we believed that if we lived quietly and got into no trouble we would be able to survive. Jews are used to keeping their heads down, you understand.'

She glanced quickly at her mother-in-law, but Wilhelmina was absorbed in trying to follow her grandchildren's conversation.

'After my husband's father was killed we knew we must go, and quickly,' Helga said.

'How did he die?' Conrad asked.

He had heard stories, and had been sickened by them, and yet he had been able to rationalize the atrocities by measuring them against his acceptance of the ideal of a superior race of people who would rule wisely and well and, above all, fight against the menace of communism. It was something different to sit in a suburban sitting room with this quiet woman and listen while she said, 'He was beaten to death in the street.'

'Had he done something to ... to offend ...' Conrad asked helplessly.

'It was a cold day. He was wearing an overcoat which concealed the yellow star on his jacket. You know, of course, that Jews in Germany have to wear the yellow star? He was recognized, accused of trying to conceal his race and, when he tried to explain, knocked to the ground and beaten with truncheons.'

There was nothing Conrad could say. He tried to tell himself that the man had committed a technical breach of the rules, but it was not easy to believe that what had happened had been right.

'But we must talk of happier things,' Helga Goldstein said. 'You are an actor. Nesta admires your work. Tell me, what is your opinion of her own ability?'

'She has it in her to be very good indeed,' Conrad said. 'I've only seen a glimpse of what she might do. If it were not for the war ...'

'Ah, yes, everything comes back to that. My daughter, Zarah, is, we believe, a musician of real talent. We have managed to get a violin for her – to Zarah, you understand, a violin is one of the necessities of life – but it is a poor thing and she suffers.'

'Zarah sold her violin to help raise the money to bribe our way out of the country,' Joachim explained.

'If she could obtain employment she could afford to pay for

lessons,' Helga said with a sigh. 'As it is ... Joachim earns a little, repairing watches.'

'A trade I learnt in my father's workshop as a boy,' Joachim said with a smile. 'When I think how I rebelled against it ... but, looking back, I see that those were happy days.'

His wife's hand covered his for a moment. 'We are not to look back,' she said. 'Instead, we will trespass on Mr Aylmer's kindness by saying that if he should hear of any opening for a violinist – anything, even the orchestra pit in a theatre, then we will be grateful from the bottom of our hearts if he will remember Zarah.'

Zarah played for them later that afternoon. Conrad did not consider himself an expert, but it was obvious that the girl had great technical skill, even though she cast the violin away from her when she had finished and complained that it was like playing on a shoe box.

'If I hear of any opportunities for you, I'll let you know,' Conrad promised.

He felt jarred and faintly irritated. He was being drawn into a circle that challenged all his beliefs and he wanted to be free of it. He would keep his word and mention Zarah Goldstein's name to a few musical acquaintances. Having done that he could bow out gracefully.

'Was that the reason I was asked?' he said to Nesta when she insisted on walking down the hill to the station with him.

'No, truly. I never thought of them wanting your help with Zarah. I'm sorry. They do push their luck a bit sometimes. I suppose because they're too desperate to have any pride.'

She felt uneasy about Conrad's mood, even though on the surface the meeting had gone off well. He had been charming to the Goldstein family and her own mother was completely bowled over by him, and yet something had gone wrong. It was more than the mild irritation of being asked to find a job for Zarah. Indeed, Nesta had been conscious of a troubling undercurrent before that incident.

'Was it ... did it upset you, talking German?' she asked.

Her voice was gruff because she was afraid of probing too deeply and alienating him, just when they had achieved something more than the offhand friendship of the ENSA tour.

'It brought back memories,' Conrad admitted.

'It must be terribly difficult for you, having relations on both sides.'

'There are times when I feel torn in two,' Conrad said with a desperate weariness that alarmed Nesta. 'I'm expecting my call up any day, you know.'

'And you don't want to fight?' she said slowly.

'Would you?'

She did not answer him as his uncle had done, though she might with equal truth have said that she could not envisage not wanting to do battle against the Nazis. Instead, Nesta put her quick, surprisingly practical imagination to work and suggested, 'Couldn't you volunteer for ARP work? Doesn't that give deferment?'

'Men between twenty-five and thirty can be taken on the strength of certain services unless they're wanted for military service. I don't know whether I'm wanted or not.'

'I thought of ARP because Stephanie has volunteered to be an ambulance driver.'

'Has she?' Conrad frowned. That was something that did not fit in with his plans for Stephanie. 'I was hoping to fix up an act with her to go on tour again.'

'Just the two of you?'

'And a pianist. A song and dance act.'

'It's a terrible waste of your talent,' Nesta said severely, but some of her disapproval came from a dismal feeling of being shut out.

'That's my dedicated actress speaking!' Conrad said.

He was not, like some of Nesta's theatrical friends, very much given to affectionate gestures, but when his train came in he bent and gave her a kiss on the cheek. He saw her quick flush and the way she put up her hand to touch the place where his lips had brushed her cheek and he was amused and touched because her feelings were so obvious. She was in love with him, as so many other women had been, but any close involvement with Nesta was out of the question.

Bertram Aylmer did not like having a nephew who appeared to

82

be doing nothing to help the war effort. As soon as he had spoken to Conrad he made a point of looking up an acquaintance at the War Office who might be able to solve Conrad's dilemma.

His friend was sympathetic and made vague promises about putting Conrad's name forward for some special service where his knowledge of German, both the language and the country, might be useful, but once he had got rid of Bertram he went off to see a colleague more closely tied to Intelligence than he was himself.

'Conrad Aylmer,' the other man said thoughtfully. 'Yes, his name's been mentioned to me before. I'll get an up to date report on him.'

It would have shaken Conrad if he had known who was consulted about his reliability. Claud More – quiet, unobtrusive Claud, who said little and saw a great deal.

'I was with him on the tour of *Arms and the Man*,' he said. 'I disliked him, but that was partly personal. The girl I fancied had eyes only for Conrad.'

'Anything else?'

'He went on smiling, but his muscles stiffened when anyone criticized Germany.'

'His mother is a Nazi sympathizer, and so was he at one time,' the other man said thoughtfully. 'The story is that he broke with his mother when his opinions changed.'

'He was one of Mosley's supporters,' Claud pointed out.

'But dropped out after a few months.'

'Very suddenly, after a visit to Berlin.'

'A put up job?'

'Possibly. I'm not easy in my mind about Conrad. I even suggested putting a watch on him, but because I had nothing concrete to go on and we were undermanned at the time, nothing came of it.'

'Perhaps we should revive the idea, with the excuse that we're thinking of using him for confidential work.'

'I hope we're not!'

Claud spoke so sharply that his chief looked at him thoughtfully.

'You must have some reason for being so much against the idea.'

'Nothing specific. When we were on tour it struck me that he was better at picking up information than was really healthy. Everyone talks to Conrad, including people who ought to keep their mouths shut. He's a very charming fellow.'

'You do dislike him, don't you?'

'It may have biased my judgement. Another thing I noticed was the way he had of coming out with the one remark that was guaranteed to depress everyone. It was all done by way of being clearsighted and realistic, but one of our party accused him, quite rightly, of being a gloom merchant.'

'As you say, nothing concrete. All the same, a bit disquieting, given his background. We'll put a watch on him, but no matter what excuse I may use, we won't take him into Intelligence, and if he wants his military service deferred I'll see no fuss is made about it. He'll have to do *something* of course.'

'He's made enquiries about joining Civil Defence.'

'Very suitable. He can't do much harm guarding the home front.'

The uneasy lull between the fall of France and what Conrad expected to be the invasion of Britain came to an end as Germany began to fight for air supremacy over its one remaining enemy. From early July there were air raids every day and on a large scale. In the southern counties of England the sky was criss-crossed by vapour trails as the Luftwaffe and the RAF zoomed and soared, manoeuvring for position in the single combats that were called dog fights. The outcome was not as decisive as Conrad would have liked. The RAF proved unexpectedly resilient and the people in the fields and towns below began to accept air raids and to carry on their lives with dogged determination not to be put out by 'that Hitler'.

Conrad volunteered to become a member of a Civil Defence Rescue Squad. He started to learn first aid, attended lectures on gas and demolition and went on duty at a post in the East End where he was accepted with tolerant contempt as 'one of them actor fellers'. He spoke very openly about his half German nationality which, as he had expected, earned him more sympathy than suspicion. It was generally felt that the war was

84

hard on people like him, that he was doing his bit and ought not to be expected to go out and kill his own relations, even though they were on the wrong side, that he was on the whole a good sort and vaguely 'all right'.

His call up papers arrived, but Conrad appealed for deferment and it was granted with just a little doubt and fuss, designed, if Conrad had but known it, to dispel any suspicions he might feel if he were dealt with too leniently. With the same aim in view he was asked to do a broadcast to Germany, which he agreed to without a qualm since he doubted whether many people would hear it. He took the precaution of mentioning it in one of the reports that seemed still to be going through smoothly, and asked particularly that his mother should be reassured that he had not changed his allegiance, even though it might look that way to the uninformed.

Because he was feeling confident and pleased with the way things were going – except for the long drawn out Battle of Britain – he also took time to look for work for Zarah Goldstein. When he got the promise of an audition for her he dropped a note to Nesta to give her the details. It brought her to his doorstep in a state of incoherent rage.

'They've been *interned*!' she said as soon as he opened the door.

'Come in,' Conrad said. 'Are you talking about the Goldsteins?'

'Of course! Who else? It's so *stupid*! More than that, it's downright wicked! They're *refugees*, for God's sake!'

'I suppose it's a sensible precaution,' Conrad said. 'They're German, they appeared out of the blue not long before war was declared, and the government must be worried in case they've let in Fifth Columnists who might be a liability when the invasion comes.'

'Oh, don't be so reasonable! And don't talk about "when" the invasion comes – it may never happen.'

'A slip of the tongue,' Conrad said.

Nesta felt for her handkerchief and blew her nose. She was shaking with the force of her feelings.

'I'm so angry,' she muttered.

'I can see you are,' Conrad agreed.

Her enormous dark eyes were full of tragedy and tears were not far away. Conrad put his arm round her shoulders and made her sit down beside him on the sofa. The thinness of her body and the way her inner tension came to him through the fine trembling that ran through her affected Conrad with a curious, reluctant compassion. It was as if he were trying to soothe a wild, nervous animal, and because of this he used the same tactics as he might have done with a highly bred horse, making gentle murmuring sounds that meant nothing and smoothing his hand over her hair and down her back, until Nesta sat quietly under his touch, her anguish receding into the background.

'Feeling better?' Conrad asked softly.

'Yes. Thank you. I didn't expect you to be kind like this.'

'Why not? I'm sorry for your unfortunate relatives, even though I see more clearly than you do that security had to be tightened up.'

'It's the injustice of it that upsets me. Just as they had settled down and begun to feel secure they had the knock on the door and the imprisonment they had run away from. I thought we treated people better than that.'

'They ought to have been held and properly investigated when they first arrived,' Conrad agreed.

'That wasn't quite what I meant, though I suppose you're right. They would have understood it then, but now they are bewildered – almost broken. Helga, of course, was marvellous, but old Mrs Goldstein ... I think it will be the death of her. She didn't understand – thought the Nazis had come for her ... oh, God, it was awful!'

All the comfort that Conrad had given her was driven away by the memory. Nesta put her hands over her eyes while he looked at her helplessly, then he put his arms round her again and pulled her hands down, forcing her to look at him.

'Nesta, you're being self-indulgent. Giving yourself an emotional lashing won't help the Goldsteins. There will be things you can do – practical things – comforts to be provided, visits to be made; they may even be released. Pull yourself together.'

The tiny shake he gave her brought an unexpected, twisted

smile to Nesta's face.

'I know you're right,' she admitted. 'I can't help it, you know. I do feel things and something like this hurts me all over.'

'If I say "artistic temperament" will you hit me?'

'Probably.'

Because they were both beginning to smile, because he understood the anguish that racked her, because he was a little off his guard, Conrad bent his head and kissed her.

Her mouth was soft and warm and her lips were slightly parted. Conrad heard the startled sound she made, no more than a catch in the throat, and then she gave herself up to him with an abandonment that carried him far beyond the casual caress he had intended. He was leaning over her, pushing her back against the cushions and he could feel beneath him the smallness of her body, the young, hard breasts and the jutting pelvic bones.

Nesta had wound both her arms round his neck. When Conrad moved away he had to detach the tight clasp of her hands from behind his head.

As he looked down at her he saw that Nesta was transformed. Her pale face was full of colour, her eyes were luminous, the pupils dilated, her lips looked fuller and very red. She smiled and he saw how small and white and even her teeth were. Nesta stretched against the cushions, sinuous as a cat, and held out her arms to him.

'I love you,' she said. 'I know you don't feel the same, but I think that you want me. Make love to me, Conrad.'

It was true that he wanted her. She had fallen to him as easily as any other woman he had pursued, but this was a conquest he had never intended and for once he hesitated.

Nesta took his hand and held it to her breast.

'Feel how my heart beats for you,' she said. 'I've never had any other man, never longed for love as I do now. Don't send me away empty handed.'

Against all the warnings that shrieked unheeded at the back of his head, Conrad took her into his arms, kissing her with a roughness that he thought might deter her. But Nesta only laughed, low and deep, throwing back her head as his lips moved down to her throat.

'Yes,' she said. 'Oh, yes! Anything! Anything, my darling.'

With the practised strength of his stage training, Conrad swung her up and carried her into the bedroom. All the time Nesta laughed, raining kisses on any part of his face that she could reach, but Conrad did not speak.

He had understood her capacity for feeling when it was applied to the anger and sorrow she felt for the Goldsteins, but he had not considered how it would affect both of them when Nesta shuddered with passion in his arms. She was like no other woman he had ever had before, neither in the torrent of emotion she poured out for him in the heat of their union, nor in her tenderness afterwards.

He lay beside her, spent and motionless, and it was Nesta who gathered him to her with an almost maternal gentleness and cradled his head against her breast.

'If the world ended tonight I should die happy!' she whispered. 'You love me! You really do! I can't believe it.'

He had not said it, but he found it was impossible to tell her she was wrong, even though he still refused to admit to himself that she meant anything more than the means of satisfying a passing lust. He was frowning as he lay still, trying in his mind to explain away the experience they had just passed through. Nesta twisted away to look down at him and smoothed the frown away with one finger.

'Do you know you speak German when you make love?' she asked.

No, he had not been conscious of speaking at all.

'It's the language of my childhood and of my first love,' Conrad said. 'I suppose because of that German endearments come more easily to me.'

His first love ... Conrad was perfectly aware that all through his adolescence the woman he had been in love with was his mother. Some trace of that romantic attachment still lingered, but it had never stopped him forming physical relationships with other women. His first girl had been a vigorous blonde Bavarian with strong brown legs on which she strode up and down mountains, when she was not flat on her back on the grass with her young lover on top of her. Her no nonsense approach had been just what he had needed to shake his mind free of guilty dreams. He thought of her far more kindly than he did of any of the women who had succeeded her, the ones who had asked for a commitment he was not prepared to give, just as Nesta was asking, except that this time he had been taken out of himself in a way that was quite new.

He would have to be careful not to let their liaison get out of hand. Even thinking that was an admission that this was not a once only affair. It was unthinkable that he should deny himself while he still wanted her so fiercely. The reluctant compassion he had felt for her, the way her ardour and the immaturity of her body had stirred him, would have to be subdued. He would have to be strong, admit her physical appeal, exploit it until he was sated with her and then discard her, because when the invasion came it would be impossible for him to be discovered harbouring a mistress who was a Jew.

Three

'Hitler isn't having much luck with his spying system,' Claud's superior remarked. 'A radio operator was dropped in Norfolk by parachute last night and picked up within the hour and, what's more, with his radio intact.'

'Is he talking?' Claud asked.

'Singing like a bird. He's not a young man and he was totally unnerved by the parachute jump and by being captured so swiftly.'

'What's his cover story?'

'He's supposed to be an out-of-work waiter, Austrian by birth, but a naturalized Briton. He was to apply for a job as a man servant which is advertised in – would you believe – *The Lady.*'

Claud grinned. 'A nice touch,' he said. 'Are people really still advertising for servants?'

'They are, but most of them are for places in the country to help with houses full of evacuees or hostels for land girls, that sort of thing. This one is in London.'

'Can we turn the radio operator round and get him to work for us?'

'Too risky. He was to have lived in the same house as his master. We couldn't risk the chance of Grossmeyer revealing the deception the minute they were alone. On the other hand, it seems a pity to waste such a heaven-sent opportunity to intercept the messages and substitute our own.'

'What are you going to do? Get a false servant to apply for the job and see who his employer turns out to be?'

'We already know who placed the advertisement. Conrad Aylmer.'

'So I was right,' Claud said heavily.

'You were right,' his chief agreed. 'We think he's been sending out information through diplomatic channels. That's a slow way of sending messages. A radio set, located in his own house, would be faster and more convenient.'

'Risky.'

'The Germans don't seem to have caught on to the fact that we've located their transmitters with the greatest of ease.'

'Will you have Conrad arrested?' Claud asked.

'That's why I've called you in. I want your opinion on whether Aylmer himself could be turned round.'

'I doubt it. He's not in it for the money and he's not a professional. He's the worst thing of all, a dedicated amateur. I suspect Conrad would go to the stake for his beliefs.'

'He may do just that,' his chief said drily. 'Or at any rate, hang. He's a British national and what he's doing is treason. There's only one penalty for treason.'

'Death.'

'Exactly.' The other man sat in thought again, frowning heavily.

'I'm reluctant to bring Aylmer to trial because of the sensation it would cause,' he admitted. 'He's well known, popular, a bit of an idol. Bad for morale for a figure like that to turn out to be a traitor. Something we could do without at this point in the war. Your idea of a false Anton Grossmeyer might be better.'

'I only thought of that as a means of trapping the London contact,' Claud said, startled. 'To foist an imposter on Conrad as an inmate in his house, that would be very difficult.'

'The two men have never met. The real Anton is talking freely. We can probably get enough out of him to make our substitute convincing.'

'You can't get his individual touch on the transmission keys, nor can you be sure he won't withhold any secret signal he's supposed to send to confirm his identity,' Claud pointed out.

'The real Anton is shivering in his shoes. I think he'll tell us everything we need to know. It's worth a try, in my opinion.'

The man who presented himself to Conrad was around forty, a quiet, soft-spoken man with an obsequious manner. To the deception unit's amusement he really was an Austrian waiter, but he was not a naturalized Briton, not yet. That was a prize that had been promised to him when the war was over. Before hostilities had broken out he had already offered his services to do anything, anything at all, that would help to destroy the Nazi regime. His background had been investigated and found to be authentic. His family had suffered in the *anschluss* when Austria was annexed to Germany. He had the best of reasons for wanting revenge. He had been trained as a radio operator, but the opportunity of infiltrating him into Germany had been missed. He had been standing by for a possible mission in France when the idea of making him the substitute Anton Grossmeyer had come up.

Conrad was cautious at first, but all the answers he got from his new employee were satisfactory and he began to relax. All the same, he made it clear that he was the master and Anton the servant, not only in their fictitious roles, but in actuality.

The reports Conrad compiled in the next few weeks were specific, especially after Hitler's offer of peace terms in July had been rejected. Conrad addressed himself with singleminded thoroughness to finding out everything he could about the success of the German air tactics. There was no doubt at all that the attacks on the airfields were having an overwhelming effect and should be continued, even stepped up if possible. In the hands of the deception unit exactly the opposite view was transmitted. Early in September the attacks on the RAF slackened off, but London and the other industrial cities paid a heavy price: the Luftwaffe's attacks were switched to them.

The beginning of the *blitzkrieg* on London brought unwelcome fame to Stephanie. There had already been some raids in August on the fringes of London, with bombs falling on Croydon Airport and in Harrow, and then came a haphazard, isolated raid on the East End of London on 24 August and Stephanie went into action with her ambulance for the first time. The following day Luke turned up to see her.

She had not known he was in London. Perhaps it was because she was unprepared that seeing him again was a disturbing experience. She had been conscious of the same frisson when they had met in France and now she was even more shaken by the sight of his tall, rangy body and

93

straw-coloured hair in her own familiar surroundings. In their first brief encounter they had achieved an intimacy, not only physical, which Stephanie had rarely known with any other man. And yet they were strangers. She would have been hard pressed to describe him accurately until he turned up at her door, but when she set eyes on him again he seemed acutely familiar.

'Hi!' he said. 'Wash your face, sweetie, and perk yourself up. I'm taking you out to dinner.'

Stephanie recognized the same false jauntiness that had been behind their meeting in France and felt her spontaneous pleasure at seeing him wither.

'I've been in show business too long not to be wary when a reporter offers me a free meal,' she said. 'What do you want, Luke?'

Quite apart from her uneasiness about his attitude towards her she was worn out, both physically and emotionally. She had planned to have a scratch meal and put her feet up for the rest of the evening.

'A little gaiety won't do you any harm,' Luke said more gently. 'I'll bring you home early, I promise.'

'You'll have to! If I stay out late I may fall asleep at the table. You still haven't told me what you're after.'

'A happy evening with a beautiful woman.' In the face of her scepticism he smiled and admitted, 'And a story.'

'I knew it!'

'All I want is the lowdown on what it's like to drive an ambulance in an air raid.'

'I can tell you that in one word: nasty!' Stephanie said. 'I'm stationed in Stepney, where most of the bombs fell, you know.'

'So I heard. That's why I looked you up.'

Luke seemed to realize that he might have phrased that more tactfully, but Stephanie only laughed.

'I'll take you out with me one day so that you can find out for yourself how we operate.'

'Great! That's what I'd like to do. Of course, there'd have to be a raid on at the time.'

'We all take it for granted that it's going to come.'

'If the RAF start bombing Berlin, which Hitler promised

94

would never happen, then the Luftwaffe is certainly going to retaliate.'

'What a delightful prospect,' Stephanie said with a sigh.

'So let's have dinner together while we can,' Luke urged. 'I've got a table booked at the Ritz.'

'Wow!'

'I hoped that would impress you,' he admitted.

Stephanie let herself be persuaded and, in spite of the fatigue that still lingered from the previous night's nerve-racking work, it was relaxing to feel herself cherished, to sip a drink slowly and to eat a proper meal, even if it was not what it would have been in peacetime. She had changed into a simple, clinging gown of sapphire blue and brushed out her lovely hair from the neat roll in which she wore it while she was on duty.

'I feel like a film star again,' she remarked when the *maître d'hôtel* recognized her and murmured that he was pleased to see her.

'You look like one,' Luke said. 'A million dollar girl. And you're driving an ambulance. You must admit it's a good story.'

'I knew it was going to be a "beautiful star in mercy dash" story,' Stephanie said with resignation. 'Must you really have me in it, Luke? There are hundreds of girls who will be doing as much, and more, as I am.'

'But you're news,' he pointed out. 'I know you don't like it and it's to your credit that you feel that way, but your country can do with all the favourable propaganda it can get, and Stephanie Bartram is still well known enough to get the story read by the ordinary man in the street back home in the United States.'

'There's one nasty little word you used unconsciously in that speech,' Stephanie said. 'I'm "still" well known, but I won't be for long unless I make another film. My sort of fame fades quickly.'

'Any plans to do more filming?'

'I've had one or two approaches,' Stephanie admitted. 'I've been rehearsing an act with Conrad – Conrad Aylmer, you know – which we hope to take around the country, but that depends on how the bombing develops. If it's as bad as we all fear I'll have to stay with the job I've taken on. I'd need special permission to take leave to make a film, and I'd hardly like to ask for it if things got sticky.'

She was beginning to feel more at ease with him now that Luke had stopped looking away every time their eyes met. Obviously he was never going to speak about the night they had spent together, nor would Stephanie have wished him to do so, since it was clear that it was a guilty memory for him. She wondered, cynically and with a degree of hurt that surprised her, just who had thought of approaching her for this particular story. She would have been prepared to gamble that it had not been Luke's own idea.

She was right about that. Luke had said as much as he ever intended to say about that episode on the last occasion when they had met, when he had warned her to get out of Rheims and had brought himself to acknowledge that it had been Stephanie who had jerked him out of his downward spiral of self-pity and back into life again. He had done his best to obliterate from his mind the memory of a warm naked body entwined with his on a narrow bunk, and he had not wanted to meet the girl involved again. He had tried to avoid the assignment, but now, talking to Stephanie, cool, friendly and undeniably glamorous, he saw that it was going to be a good story.

To Luke's frustration, although the authorities were willing, even eager, for him to have a chance to do a firsthand report on the work of the ambulance service, the expected raids did not materialize. He met Stephanie several times and dug out background information, but there was no excitement for him to report.

'Stop wishing for action,' Stephanie said to him severely. 'People get killed in air raids, Luke Lindquist. They're not firework displays laid on to give your readers a thrill.'

'I know, and I feel guilty when I catch myself looking round for something to write about,' Luke admitted.

'You're not the only one. The people on stand-by at my post are grumbling about being bored! Conrad and I have been doing the rounds of fire stations and ARP posts giving them a performance of the act we've put together. No piano, of course, but he unearthed an old man with an accordion and it works very well.'

'Say no more! You've given me the beginning of my story.'

It made a good lead in, the lighthearted songs performed by the two well known names, and the old busker who had discovered a new role in wartime. And within days Luke was seeing all the action he wanted – and more.

On 7 September, on a fine, clear Saturday, the bombs began falling on dockland and the fires that were lit in the daytime guided the waves of bombers to their target all through the night.

Even Luke, who had been under fire before, was shaken by the devastation. He was afraid of the effect it would have on the people who crowded nervously into the shelters, knowing that there had been panic and hysteria in the first raids, even though it had gone unreported; but not for the first time he had cause to wonder at the resilience of human beings. The Eastenders began to settle down to endure their ordeal, even to take a pride in the number of bombs that fell in their own neighbourhood.

At the end of the first week of nightly air raids Luke went and joined Stephanie at her ambulance post.

'Our night together at last,' he said, and then could have bitten his tongue out, but Stephanie appeared unaware of any double meaning. She merely smiled and offered him a cup of the strong brown tea which appeared to fuel the British in every emergency.

Luke had seen her in battledress before and had complimented her on her workmanlike appearance. That night he remembered that there had been a touch of mockery behind his compliment and Stephanie had frowned and then laughed it off. As the night wore on Luke became more and more ashamed, because in his heart he had not taken her work seriously.

It began quietly enough. The horrible wail of the siren sounded and everyone stopped talking to listen for a second or two. Then the chatter started again, the knitting needles began to clack, a couple of the men who were playing pontoon slapped their cards down with an appearance of unconcern.

Luke put on his tin hat and went outside. It was a moonlit night. Bomber's moon, he thought, remembering the phrase he

97

had heard everywhere. Searchlights were sending long beams of light across the sky, somewhere in the distance he heard the crump of heavy guns, and then a steady drone of aircraft advancing towards the city. The first whistle of the bombs sent him cowering instinctively against the nearest wall, but the explosions were nowhere near where he was standing.

He went back inside the ambulance post. Nothing seemed to have changed except that the tension was more obvious. More bombs were falling. There were three explosions in rapid succession and the last one shook the building.

'Getting nearer,' someone remarked.

A bell sounded and they all looked up.

'Incident in Stepney Way,' the report came through. 'Ambulance requested immediately, but avoid Jamaica Street because of incendiary bombs.'

'That's us,' Stephanie said. 'Come on, Luke.'

He had never seen a woman drive as Stephanie drove that night. Indeed, to his shame, he had not thought a woman capable of handling a vehicle in such a way. Where was the girl who had sat opposite him at the Ritz with the light gleaming on her hair? Where was the film actress? Stephanie had become two steady hands, eyes so sharp that they seemed to see in the dark, and reflexes acute enough to hurtle them time and time again round obstacles Luke had barely registered.

There were shattered buildings all round them and debris all over the road. Even so, Stephanie kept up a speed that had Luke gritting his teeth. Suddenly she put on the brakes, so precipitately that Luke was thrown forward.

'Sorry,' Stephanie said. 'Now, how are we going to get round that?'

Peering through the dust and smoke in the diminished light of her shielded headlights, Luke saw an enormous bomb crater in front of them.

'Would you get out and see if there's enough room for me to get past?' Stephanie said, as if it were the most ordinary thing in the world.

Luke climbed out. The raid was still going on. Fragments of shell were falling like rain in the street outside. He heard a bomb coming and once again he ducked, but it came down a street or two away. He thought Stephanie might squeeze round the hole by going up on the pavement, though he did not much like the look of the crumbling edge of the crater.

'You'd better guide me,' Stephanie said. She grinned suddenly, a wicked, mocking smile. 'The trained man I've got in the back is too valuable to risk: war correspondents are expendable.'

The wheels of the ambulance grazed the edge of the crater. Luke, standing a few yards ahead, held his breath, but in the nick of time Stephanie slewed the vehicle round and it lurched past and on to firmer ground.

'Not far now,' she said as Luke climbed back in the front seat with her. 'Getting past that saved us a long detour.'

At the end of the road they were flagged down by a policeman and pointed in the direction where they were needed. A tenement block had received a direct hit. To Luke it looked like nothing but a pile of rubble, with one crazy wall left standing, exposing a patchwork of different wallpapers, then he saw that men were clambering over the piles of bricks and shattered concrete and that some of them were carrying stretchers.

'Don't wander away,' Stephanie said. 'As soon as we've loaded up we'll leave and I shan't wait for you.'

The return journey was slower because Stephanie was mindful of the injured patients in the back of the ambulance, and now that the vehicle was heavier she did not risk the narrow passage round the bomb crater.

When they arrived back at the hospital Stephanie got out and stretched and Luke joined her. The injured were unloaded and he was struck by the quiet, offhand efficiency with which they were handled.

'Right, back we go,' Stephanie said as the doors were slammed shut.

'Again?' Luke said.

'Of course. Until everyone has been brought in who needs to be brought in. I thought you understood that. Of course, there's no need for you to come if you don't want to.'

'I'm with you for the night,' Luke said. 'Where you go, I go.'

'Quite biblical,' Stephanie remarked.

They set out again and this time he managed not to grit his teeth quite so often until, just as they reached a stretch of straight, untouched road where Stephanie could put on speed, something whistled over their heads. There were no loud explosions, but ahead of them a string of fires broke out along the road.

'A stick of incendiary bombs,' Stephanie said. She craned her neck out of the driving cab. 'Behind us as well. We were lucky not to be hit. Oh, well, it's no use taking this slowly. Damn it, why couldn't they drop them in a straight line?'

To Luke's horror she began to drive in a crazy slalom, veering from side to side to avoid the small, fierce fires burning in the road.

'All right, you can open your eyes now,' she said as they left the fires behind them.

'As an accredited war correspondent I keep observation at all times,' Luke said severely. 'Of course, my hair has turned white and I've mislaid my stomach, but I deny shutting my eyes.'

The casualties they picked up this time had only just been dug out. They were in deep shock, silent and smudged with dust and soot. One of them was a young woman, cradling a baby to her breast. Bending over her, Luke saw that the child was dead.

He straightened up and caught Stephanie's eye.

'Yes, I know,' she said. 'Let her go on holding it until she gets to the hospital.'

This time, when they descended from the ambulance, Stephanie led him back to the ambulance post.

'We get a break now,' she said. 'Would you like a cup of tea?'

The light was bright when they got inside. After the dark, littered streets, the sinister fires and shattered buildings, the pitiful, broken bodies they had rescued, this oasis of warmth and normality had a welcoming air, but there was little of the cheerful talk Luke had heard earlier in the evening. The few people inside were quiet and tired. Luke saw the signs of strain on their faces and held back the questions he would have liked to have asked.

'Dirty night,' the woman at the tea urn commented.

'Fairly rough,' Stephanie agreed.

She and Luke sat in a corner, sipping the hot, strong tea.

'I hope Hitler never realizes that the British will definitely lose the war if their supply of tea is cut off,' Luke remarked.

'Actually, what I really miss is the lovely coffee you make in America,' Stephanie said.

'Next time I get a parcel from home, you shall have the coffee,' Luke promised.

'Luke, really? What a treat!'

He took hold of the hand that had been nervously playing with her teaspoon and held it between both of his.

'Honey, after tonight I'd give you the Victoria Cross, the Congressional Medal of Honour and the Crown Jewels.'

'Keep something in reserve,' Stephanie said. 'The night's not over yet.'

Twenty minutes later they were out again.

'Different sector,' Stephanie remarked. 'We may see Conrad. This is where he operates.'

'Different, but no less hair-raising,' Luke said as they lurched round a corner. 'Have you ever thought of driving at Le Mans?'

Stephanie laughed. 'I've always been a good driver,' she said.

Luke felt sick with anger as he saw the row of little houses that had been reduced to rubble. The stretcher cases were soon loaded up, but one obstinate old woman was causing difficulties. She sat herself down on the remains of a garden wall and refused to budge. On her ample lap she was holding a wire cage with a yellow canary in it.

'I'm not going nowhere without me bird,' she said.

There was a rough bandage round her head, soaked in blood, but she seemed to have all her wits about her.

'Of course you can keep your canary,' Stephanie said. 'When we get to the hospital I'll take him into the canteen until you've been patched up. What's his name?'

'Joey.'

The old woman allowed herself to be helped to her feet, but Luke noticed that she leaned heavily on Stephanie as she was guided towards the ambulance. The little bird hopped nervously from the floor of his cage on to the perch and made a small twittering sound.

101

'Listen to him! Still singing!' the old woman said proudly. 'He's a proper Cockney, aren't you, Joey me lad? Old Hitler won't get him down.'

'Contrary old devil,' the ARP warden remarked to Luke. 'I told her I'd see her blasted bird was looked after, but nothing would do but for her to take it with her. You have to admire her spirit, though. We didn't dig her out until a quarter of an hour ago. There she was, sitting in the cellar when Mr Aylmer got through to her, complaining about the time he'd taken.'

'Conrad Aylmer?' Luke asked quickly. 'I'd like to see him. Is he around?'

'Over the other side of the street — or what was the street,' the warden said.

'Stephanie, I'll make my own way home,' Luke said. 'It's beginning to get light; I guess I can manage under my own steam. I'd like to finish off with a glimpse of what Conrad's doing.'

She smiled and nodded and he saw that most of her attention was being given to the casualties being loaded into the ambulance.

Luke found Conrad, with three other men, moving bricks one by one with a caution that Luke did not understand at first. Conrad seemed to sense Luke's approach and looked round with a frown.

'Don't come any closer,' he called out. 'The ground's unstable and we've heard a movement down here.'

Luke stayed where he was, impressed by the delicacy with which they were working. One of the men shifted his foot incautiously and swore as it broke through the weak structure on which they were standing. For a moment they all froze, then he pulled his foot free, the rubble shifted slightly and they went on with their work.

A hole was cleared and Conrad lowered himself down into it. Luke saw his arm come up and something like a crowbar was handed down to him. Again they waited, and then he saw that Conrad was handing out pieces of broken plaster and brick. He must have made the hole larger, because a second man went down to join him. The other two moved away and came back with a light stretcher which they lowered into the hole.

102

A few minutes later a survivor, strapped to the stretcher, was levered into the open air. The light was growing stronger, the pale, grey light before the true dawn, and everything had a ghostly air.

Luke stood around, growing colder by the minute, until Conrad came to join him.

'Three,' he said. 'All alive, though one of them looks bad.' He looked round with a frown. 'Isn't there an ambulance?'

'It filled up and went,' Luke said. 'Stephanie was driving. I guess she'll be back.'

The All Clear began to sound. People looked up and the atmosphere seemed to lighten.

'It's been quite a night,' Luke said. 'I'm full of admiration for the work you're doing, Aylmer. And as for Stephanie ... well, that was a revelation!'

'It can't be wrong, to save life,' Conrad said, under his breath. 'No, it must be right.'

'Well ... of course,' Luke said. 'Are you all right?'

Conrad put up his hand to touch a livid bruise on his cheek.

'I got slightly knocked about when a bit of roof caved in,' he said. 'Nothing serious. I'll go home now and get cleaned up and have a rest.'

'On duty again tonight?'

'Oh, yes.'

'I'll tell you something,' Luke said as they picked their way across the broken ground. 'I've started to believe that the British are going to win this war. I had my doubts when you were fighting in France and in the first few days of the bombing when everything seemed chaotic, but now ... nothing's going to break these people, especially not Adolph Hitler.'

He got no reply at first. Glancing at Conrad he saw him frown and then smile in a peculiar, twisted way, like an involuntary spasm of his facial muscles.

'Sometimes I almost think you're right,' he said, with what Luke took to be deliberately exaggerated understatement, by way of a British-style joke.

'It was one of the best stories I ever wrote,' Luke said. 'They

103

loved it back in the States. I even had a cable from the editor saying "Congrats raid story why no pix Stephanie?" '

Stephanie wrinkled her nose in the way he had come to recognize and look for.

'You made it too personal,' she said. 'You know I didn't want that.'

He was giving her lunch, a late lunch because Stephanie slept as far into the day as she could.

'The cable also said "Proceed soonest Cairo report Western Desert",' Luke said.

'So this is a farewell lunch?'

'I may be around for a little while yet. Depends how soon I can fix up a passage.'

He waited for her to say something, but Stephanie was silent, so he asked, 'Will you miss me?'

'Yes, of course,' Stephanie said.

They had spent a lot of time together since Luke had made his first contact, to begin with because Luke saw it as a duty, but now increasingly because they enjoyed one another's company. Stephanie had seen Luke's wary manner alter into something easier and more friendly, but the most profound change had come since the night when he had joined her in the ambulance. Stephanie had earned his respect and because of that Luke had relaxed and allowed himself to admit that he was very much attracted to her. On the last two occasions when they had met they had kissed on parting and Stephanie had sensed how unwilling Luke had been to let her go, just as she had moved away from his arms with real reluctance. And now he was going away. It seemed miserably unfair, just when something worthwhile was beginning to grow between them.

'You'll be carrying on with your ambulance driving?' Luke asked, and Stephanie came out of her regretful thoughts with a start.

'Conrad wants me to press for leave to go on tour round the country with him. I don't see how I can unless the raids ease off.'

'You and Conrad,' Luke said carefully.

He was wondering how to go on when Stephanie smiled and shook her head.

'No,' she said. 'It's a professional partnership, nothing more.'

She had wondered once or twice why that was so. Conrad was an attractive man and Stephanie was well aware of her own appeal. They were thrown together and they were both free, unless she counted this new attachment to Luke as a tie. It was the sort of situation in which she had come to expect the tentative approach, almost as a matter of course, and yet Conrad made no move towards her. There must be someone else. She would have liked to have thought that it might be Nesta, but it was a long time since Stephanie and Nesta had met, and since Conrad never mentioned her Stephanie assumed that he did not see her either.

'It's over a year since Prue died,' Luke said, apparently at random, but Stephanie guessed the direction in which he was moving.

'I thought of you on the anniversary of the day war broke out,' she said gently.

'It's not a date I'm ever likely to overlook,' Luke agreed. 'I haven't forgotten her, but as far as one ever can get over such a loss, I have picked up the pieces and put them together again.'

'I'm glad,' Stephanie said, waiting for him to come to the point.

'I thought I'd never be able to look at another woman.' Luke avoided looking at Stephanie as he went on, 'That night on the ship ... I told myself it was a once only lapse, the result of strain and desperation.'

He had felt that he had broken faith, and in his heart Luke had blamed Stephanie for making herself available to him. He believed he had put that unworthy thought behind him, but there was still something he had to make clear.

'I'm not ready for a formal, settled relationship.'

Luke looked up and caught Stephanie's eye and smiled a rueful, guilty smile. 'Oh, heck, Stephanie, I'm making one hell of a mess of telling you this.'

'I understand. You've discovered that you're still a man, even though the wife you loved is dead. You like me, you admire me and you desire me. You're about to go off to the Middle East, and before you bury yourself in the sand you'd like to make love to me.'

'You certainly believe in spelling things out! You've left out one thing, though, and that's the very deep affection I've developed for you.'

'Affection? I think I like that. On the whole I'd rather you didn't pretend to be fathoms deep in love with me.'

'I'm not sure I'll ever love anyone the way I loved Prue. She was my other half, in every sense of the word. That doesn't come easily, not a second time.'

He could not see Stephanie's expression because her head was bent.

'Prue was a very lucky woman,' she said in a low voice.

'I do care for you,' Luke said.

Looking at his worried face, at the tense lines of his long body and the big-boned, restless hands, sensing how much he wanted to touch her, Stephanie felt regret and the stirring of something more than the excitement of a new affair, the sort of game she had played after Dwight had wounded her so badly. She could have loved Luke, as much as Prue had loved him, if he had wanted anything more from her than the brief satisfaction of a sexual encounter. He did like her, and he did think of her as a real person − which was more than the other men who had lusted after her had done. If they had had time they might have worked out a truly satisfactory relationship. If they had had time.

'This war,' Stephanie said. 'There must be thousands of people like us, rushing into bed together and then having to say goodbye. Luke, the answer is yes.'

His hand flew out and caught hold of hers.

'But not today, not now,' Stephanie said. 'I'm off duty this weekend. Will you take me away somewhere? A quiet place where we can find some peace together.'

'I'll have to keep in touch with the office in case my passage to the Middle East comes through,' he warned her. 'Apart from that − yes, of course; a wonderful idea. Two nights?'

'Saturday and Sunday.' Stephanie looked suddenly mischievous. 'Can you wait that long?'

'With difficulty!'

'I must go,' Stephanie said. 'I'm on duty tonight and I have several things I want to do before then.'

He took her back to her flat and stepped inside without being asked, taking her in his arms for a long kiss. Stephanie clung to him, suddenly wanting him as urgently as he had desired her. Why not this afternoon? she thought, and then, as Luke's arms slackened, No, don't rush it; the weekend, when I'm not so darned tired, then it will be wonderful.

The thought of the coming weekend stayed with her all that night and the next, and helped her through harrowing scenes of injury and destruction, but when she arrived home in the early hours of Saturday morning there was a note waiting for her from Luke.

Stephanie, my dear girl, we should have remembered old Herrick: 'Gather ye rosebuds ...' and all that. I'm flying to Lisbon at dawn to link up with a ship to Alexandria. Blast, damn and every other curse you can think of. There's nothing in the world I want more than to be with you this weekend, but I'm under orders and I have to go. I'll write. Forgive me. Take care of yourself. Bless you. Luke.

She wept slow, difficult tears of hurt and frustration. In spite of the way Luke had spoken about his feelings for her, even though she had understood his warning that she took second place to his dead wife, Stephanie had not been able to stop herself from hoping that this time she had found the right one, the man who would love her for something more than her beautiful body. Luke had qualities she valued, more than any she had found in the men she had known in the past.

As she dried her eyes, Stephanie thought about Prue Lindquist. With a flash of insight she knew that Prue, too, had cried, many times and in the same way for this man who made himself dear to his women and then left them behind while he pursued a bright new story on the other side of the world.

Four

'You're losing all your looks!' Vera Bartram complained.

'I know,' Stephanie said, with the equable patience that never failed to infuriate her mother. 'I've lost half a stone in weight, my hair's falling out in handfuls and my complexion looks like mud.'

'Then why don't you do something about it?'

'I am. I'm taking a holiday here with you.'

At the very beginning of the bombing Stephanie had persuaded Vera to go and live in a village in Devon. Vera loathed it and never stopped complaining, but she had heard enough about conditions in London to keep her out of the capital until it finally seemed as if the raids were becoming less frequent.

'I ought to come back and look after you,' she said.

Stephanie recognized this for what it was, a kite flown to see what her reaction would be.

'You can come up and stay in the flat while I'm away if you like,' she said. 'I'm going on tour with Conrad next month.'

'Wasting your time! You ought to be making another film.'

'I may do that.'

'Oh?' Vera sat up, looking alert. 'Who with? Is it a good script? How much are they paying you?'

'It's rather vague at the moment. The idea is that Conrad will be my co-star.'

'Make sure they put your name above his. You're an international star. He's only known in Britain.'

'I can't be bothered with details like that.'

'Like I said before, you need me to look after you.'

The news had put fresh life into Vera. After all the dreary months of boring country life she was going to be back in the thick of things once more. She would be able to talk about 'my daughter, the film star' without getting blank looks. She could visit the set, chat to the dressers, keep an eye on Stephanie's publicity – which, goodness knows, the girl was incapable of doing for herself.

'I'm not sure living together again would work, for either of us,' Stephanie said.

Because of the keenness of her disappointment Vera spoke with deliberate sharpness.

'I suppose that means you're up to something you don't want me to know about. Some man, no doubt. Or men.'

'No man. No men,' Stephanie said. 'The only one I was at all keen on went off to the Middle East without a backward glance. I had a Christmas card from him, which arrived in the middle of January. Apart from that – nothing.'

'What about this Conrad? You keep on the right side of him, I presume? Going off touring alone, which you can't expect me to approve of.'

'Oh, Mum! You wouldn't care if I slept with Conrad provided we were accompanied by a full chorus and orchestra. It's not the immorality you dislike, it's the lack of razzle-dazzle.'

'That's no way to talk to me. Of course I care whether you're being a good girl or not. It nearly turned my hair white, the way you carried on in Hollywood ...'

'That was just a phase I went through,' Stephanie said wearily. 'You know why. I needed reassurance. I'm over that now. I'm a stronger person, and not because of any man, but because I know that I'm capable of facing up to danger and worse than danger, the dreary unending slog of turning out day after day, night after night, putting up with the dullness as well as the excitement, and the horrible conditions, and the way people aren't always grateful when you help them.'

'You don't have to tell me that,' Vera said with emphasis.

Stephanie smiled with more affection than she had shown her mother in the past.

'I never win an argument with you,' she said. 'Come back to London if you must; it seems quiet enough at the moment. Don't imagine you're coming to a glamorous life, though. I'm flat broke and this ENSA tour I'm going on only pays £10 a week. More than I'm getting as an ambulance driver, of course, but it won't keep two of us in pre-war comfort.'

110

When Stephanie returned to London at the end of May, rested and with a better colour in her cheeks, her mother went with her. She settled into the little semi-basement flat in Kensington, grumbling about the lack of light and drawing unwelcome comparisons with the villa that had been provided for her daughter in Hollywood, but proving unexpectedly amenable about being left on her own while Stephanie and Conrad set out on their tour of factories, army camps and hospitals.

'It's not what I want for you, but it's better than wasting yourself driving an ambulance, which anyone can do,' she said.

'Conrad and I are only on leave from our Civil Defence posts,' Stephanie warned her. 'Like it or not, I'm still on call, and if I'm really needed I'll drop the tour and come back.'

It was a simple act that she and Conrad had put together and they had already performed most of it at various times in shelters and ARP posts when the air raids permitted. Because of their experience in these limited spaces, and because they had heard horror stories from other people about the pianos available, they were taking an accordionist with them to provide an accompaniment, not the elderly man they had used in London, but a weedy young man exempted from military service because of his poor medical history, who handled his unwieldy instrument with a touch of genius. Conrad had unexpectedly produced a pleasant baritone and although he was not an expert dancer, he moved well enough to partner Stephanie when she needed him. They did two solo songs each, two duets, Stephanie danced – mainly as an excuse to show off her legs, which proved wildly popular even with the sick men in hospital – and the accordionist performed a virtuoso piece, after which the performance usually became a 'sing-song'.

The first night they spent in a quiet country town near a military hospital and Conrad slept as if he had been knocked on the head. He woke up the next morning with a new sense of purpose. At last he was free to get on with the work he ought to be doing to help Germany towards victory and, quite apart from that, he was not sorry to be away from Nesta.

She was fiercely opposed to his tour and to the proposed film with Stephanie.

'If you can get time off from being a rescue worker then you ought to use it to do something worthwhile,' she insisted.

'By which you mean the classics ... Shakespeare ... and so on?'

'Of course I do! Darling, you're capable of such great things. I can't bear to see you wasting yourself on the sort of trivialities Stephanie will drag you into.'

'Jealous?'

'No!' Nesta pulled herself up and grinned, reluctantly. 'Yes. I don't agree with what you're doing, but at least it's show business. I can't get into anything except a works canteen!'

'Actually, I meant are you jealous of my being with another woman,' Conrad said, amused.

'Oh, that! No, not really. What we've got is special. If you spoil it by doing something daft like going to bed with Stephanie then I'll despise you and if I do that I shan't want you any more.'

'Do you think so? Oh, my inexperienced infant! You might find out I had feet of clay and make excuses for me and still go on loving me and that, let me tell you, is the uttermost depths of hell.'

'So behave yourself while you're away,' Nesta said flippantly, but the way she looked at him was searching and very shrewd. 'Have you been to the depths of hell, my darling?' she asked gently.

' "Why this is hell, nor am I out of it",' Conrad quoted.

'Mephistophilis,' Nesta said. 'Poor old Mephistophilis, I always felt rather sorry for him. Now there's a part you could play.'

'I could, indeed I could!'

Conrad threw back his head and laughed. 'Dear Nesta! Do you ever think about anything but the stage?'

'I think about you. You don't feel you're sliding into hell when I'm with you, do you?'

'You help,' Conrad admitted.

'Is it your mother you worry about?' Nesta asked, diffidently, because this was not a subject on which Conrad encouraged discussion.

With a familiar switch of the mind Conrad remembered that he was supposed to have broken with his mother.

'We quarrelled, but naturally I think about her,' he said stiffly. 'Berlin has been bombed as well as London, you know. Seeing the damage here, I can't help wondering how good the German defences are.'

It served as an excuse to Nesta to explain his unwary reference to being in hell, but the truth was that he was tormented less by his fears for his mother than by doubts about his own position.

The alliance between Germany and Russia had always bothered him, but he had explained it away in 1939 as a matter of expediency. It was less easy to accept the renewal of the pact in January 1941. One reason Conrad had supported Hitler was because he believed he would take a strong line against communism. If Conrad was wrong about that, could he be wrong about other things as well?

The internment of the Goldstein family had been something of a relief because it proved that Britain, too, could be callous towards harmless Jews. All the same, Conrad knew in his heart that he was not likely to see the sort of brutality that had killed Joseph Goldstein in an English street, and he could not really condone that death even if, as he argued obstinately, there had been provocation.

The bombing, too, had been worse than he had expected. He had been shaken by the death of the children in Arras; since then he had become hardened to sights that would have shocked him to the core a year earlier. It was civilians who were being killed. No matter how often he told himself that the London Docks were a legitimate military target, he could not disguise the fact that bombs fell indiscriminately on the old and the young, the fighting men and the harmless clerks.

He had been pleased at having his own radio operator and it had certainly expanded the scope of his work, but the constant presence of Anton in his house, even though the man was useful and added to his comfort, rubbed on Conrad's raw nerves. He was often rude to Anton, which Anton accepted with a meekness that exasperated Conrad still further. Worst of all, Anton doubtlessly knew about his affair with Nesta, and to

Conrad's heightened imagination it seemed all too likely that Anton reported on it to Berlin. He had to give her up before she became a total obsession, but from day to day he put off making the break.

Conrad had always believed that he had the nerve to carry on his deception for as long as was necessary, but he had not expected to be worked to dropping point salvaging the victims of Germany's fight for a dominant position in the world. He raged at the postponement of the invasion of Britain, which in Conrad's view would have brought a quick end to the war. He even put unwisely strong remonstrances into the communiques he compiled for, as he supposed, transmission to Germany.

'I think our boy is beginning to crack,' the man at MI5 remarked thoughtfully. 'If the messages he's sending to the Führer got through he'd be given a real flea in his ear.'

'Still harping on about the invasion?' Claud asked.

'Almost hysterical about it. Read this.'

Claud took the deciphered message and scanned it with interest.

'The thing we mustn't forget about Conrad is that he's an artist,' he remarked thoughtfully. 'He's highly emotional, sensitive ...'

'Is it possible to be sensitive and a Nazi?'

'I doubt whether the Nazi philosophy has ever impinged on Conrad very profoundly. He's in love with Germany – or his idea of Germany. He's swallowed all that stuff about how badly Germany was treated under the Treaty of Versailles. To him this war is a romantic crusade and he is on the side of the Knights of the Cross, even though the cross is crooked. It's tied up with his devotion to his mother. He identifies the country with the woman.'

'I'll take your word for it,' his superior said doubtfully. 'I suppose we're right to keep on running him?'

'What choice do we have unless we admit we know Conrad's a spy and arrest him? We have to intercept his messages and it's been useful to interpose our own stuff instead. We can't eliminate Conrad and carry on the deception without him because he's too well known. Some travelling neutral might notice his disappearance and mention it in the wrong place.'

'It'd be a pity not to carry on sending the fake messages,' his superior agreed. 'They seem to have been quite successful so far.' He laughed suddenly. 'If he did but know it, Conrad Aylmer has got us in a cleft stick.'

'I doubt if that's the way Conrad would see it,' Claud commented. 'Poor devil, I sometimes feel almost sorry for him. He's going to be shattered come the end of the war when he finds out he's been helping our side all the time.'

'Provided, of course, that we win. Things aren't exactly going our way, are they? Our gains in Libya have been thrown away and we haven't made much of a showing in Greece.'

'Ah, but if Hitler's plans to invade Russia materialize then the tide may turn,' Claud pointed out.

'Can he really be such a fool?' his chief murmured. 'No, don't answer that – of course he can. The man's mad.'

The news of the German invasion of Russia came on a day in June when Conrad and Stephanie were due to give an afternoon concert in a hospital in Yorkshire. The hospital was housed in a beautiful mansion which had been handed over to the Forces and the concert took place in the former ballroom, a vast apartment with a white and gold ceiling and long windows looking out over what had once been sweeping lawns and were now vegetable plots.

There was a small dais at the far end of the room where an orchestra had played in days gone by, creating a far better stage than most on which Stephanie and Conrad had performed recently. Rows of chairs were set out in the middle of the room, but all along the sides the patients who were unable to leave their beds had been wheeled in to enjoy the treat.

'Lovely setting,' Stephanie said, peering through a crack in the swing door to see whether the audience was ready for them.

'Splendid!' Conrad agreed.

He was in high spirits, quite different from the morose companion Stephanie had had to put up with for the last two weeks. He hummed a tune to himself as they waited, even shuffled a few steps of their dance routine.

'What's happened to cheer you up?' Stephanie asked.

'I'm pleased about the invasion of Russia,' Conrad admitted.

'I suppose it's something to have the Russians on our side,' Stephanie said. 'Though for someone as anti-communist as you are I would have thought that wouldn't have been such good news. Still, I'm grateful for anything that makes you less of a misery than you have been lately.'

She was even more conscious of Conrad's change of mood when they danced together. It was exhilarating, in a way that it had never been before. She almost expected to see sparks fly when their hands met, so vivid was the impression of excitement tingling in his veins. Stephanie was breathless and laughing when Conrad sent her into a final twirling pirouette and the men in their invalid chairs were clapping wildly.

The nurse who had opened the doors for them stopped Conrad as he and Stephanie made their final exit.

'It was wonderful!' she said with simple fervour. 'I've always been a fan of yours, Mr Aylmer. Please, I am right in thinking that you're partly German, aren't I?'

Conrad's charming smile slipped a bit.

'Yes,' he agreed.

'And you speak the language?'

'Of course.'

'Then could I persuade you to go and speak to a German airman we have in here? He wouldn't come to the show. In fact, he won't talk to anyone very much, not even the doctor we've got who can make himself understood.'

'Is he badly hurt?' Conrad asked, playing for time while he considered what line he should take.

'Lost both his legs, poor lamb. We did our best to save one of them, but it was hopeless.'

They were already walking along the corridor. It was quite impossible for him to refuse the distasteful task. The nurse opened the door of a side ward where the German airman lay in bed on his own.

'*Guten tag*, Hans,' she said with a brightness that showed she was pleased with herself for having learnt that small phrase. 'We call him 'Hans' because his other name is such a mouthful,' she explained to Conrad.

Glancing at the airman Conrad saw how offensive that familiarity was to him. He was, or had been, a splendid young man, fair-haired and pink-skinned, with a faint golden down on his cheeks. He looked at Conrad with undisguised animosity, especially when Conrad began to speak to him in flawless German.

'Are you a doctor?' he interrupted.

'No, just a chance visitor. I'm here as an entertainer.'

'Really?' He drawled it out, with a glance that was a sneer. 'I suppose the truth is you've come to interrogate me.'

'Nothing of the sort! I didn't ask to come and talk to you, it was the nurse's idea.'

'Interfering bitch. You talk the language as if you were one of us.'

'My mother is German.'

'Pity you ended up on the wrong side. Why aren't you in the army?'

'I've been excused. I work in Civil Defence.'

Hans leaned back against his pillows with a derisive smile on his lips. 'I knock them down and you pick them up,' he suggested.

'More or less,' Conrad agreed. 'Is there anything I can do for you? Any message I can pass on to the hospital authorities which you haven't been able to get across?'

'Ask them to give me back my legs,' the boy said with a bitterness that sickened Conrad. 'They've cut them off, you know. Sadistic swine.'

'I was told your legs were beyond saving.'

'They would say that, wouldn't they? And you and your sort believe them. All they really care about is making sure a Luftwaffe pilot doesn't get into the air again. If I could have coaxed the Dornier home ... but I couldn't do it. We crashed and all the others died – Karl and Erich ...'

As he spoke, his weakness betrayed him. He turned his head away and closed his eyes, but the tears gathered and ran down his cheeks. With an exclamation of distress the nurse hurried forward. Hans opened his eyes and looked up as she bent over him, then he spat in her face.

Outside in the corridor Conrad passed a shaking hand over his forehead.

'Don't let it worry you,' the nurse said. 'He does it nearly

117

every day. Poor boy, he's taken the second amputation very hard. I thought talking to you might help, but obviously I was wrong.'

'He thinks his legs were taken off unnecessarily.'

'I know. Silly boy, as if we'd do a thing like that! Perhaps he'll believe we want to help him when he gets his artificial legs.'

As soon as Stephanie saw Conrad again she realized that his earlier gaiety had disappeared.

'I thought I'd lost you to that pretty nurse,' she said.

'She took me to see a German pilot who's lost his legs. It was distressing,' Conrad said, trying to subdue the black despondency that had fallen on him.

'I've been going round some of the beds, too,' Stephanie said with a sigh. 'Their spirit is wonderful, but the braver they are the more I want to cry.'

'Let's get out of here. We've done our bit for one day.'

Stephanie and Conrad had been booked into a hotel which was obviously suffering from wartime shortages. Their accordionist was luckier because he had relatives in the town and was going to stay with them.

'See you in the morning, George,' Stephanie said. 'And don't be late!'

She watched his thin figure out of sight. 'Horrible of me to say so,' she remarked. 'But it's a relief not to have to spend another evening with George.'

'I can stand everything except the way he picks his teeth,' Conrad agreed.

'I think we both need a stiff drink,' Stephanie said. 'Come up to my room and I'll give you some bourbon whisky.'

'Where did you get that?' Conrad asked.

'Do you remember Luke Lindquist, the American war correspondent? He got one of his friends to bring me a parcel. A pound of coffee, a whole pound! And this whisky and one or two other things, like silk stockings and a box of chocolates!'

It was difficult to say why this parcel had been faintly unwelcome. Luke had meant it as a treat and, of course, it was, but it had not been accompanied by any message, except a verbal one to say that it was from him. Stephanie could not suppress a feeling that she had been paid off. He had never written. He had no real feelings for her. If they had spent their weekend together no doubt it would have been a pleasant memory, but she had wanted it to be more than that. She felt discarded, almost as unwelcome as when Dwight had run out on her. Conrad was not the only one who needed cheering up.

She kicked off her shoes and sat on her bed while Conrad lounged in the only armchair, sipping his drink out of a tooth glass.

'Just like every other second-rate tour,' Stephanie said. 'Now, what about this film we've been offered? Do you want to do it?'

'I've seen the script. It's just straightforward propaganda.'

'None the worse for that,' Stephanie pointed out. 'Don't you like the idea of playing an intrepid airman?'

Conrad thought of the young Luftwaffe pilot and his cor-roding bitterness.

'Not particularly,' he said. He drained his glass. 'Can I have another drink?'

'Help yourself. The thing is, it would compensate both of us for not taking a more active part in fighting the war.'

'Wouldn't you call this winter active?'

Stephanie thought back to the nights filled with noise and danger and shuddered.

'I would, but I know I really ought to have gone into one of the Women's Forces. I *must* make this film, Conrad, just to justify staying a civilian, and I'd rather have you as my leading man than anyone.'

'Nice of you.'

Conrad glanced at her as she sprawled on the bed, her legs carelessly exposed.

'What a beauty you are!' he remarked.

'Oi! How much of my whisky have you had?' Stephanie demanded.

She did not object when he came over and sat on the edge of the bed, nor when he clasped his hand over one slim ankle. A thrill of uneasy excitement ran through her as his hand moved slowly up from her ankle to her calf. Oh, corks, here I go again, she thought. I must not, I really must not get in a state over Conrad. One kiss and I'll send him packing.

119

The kiss was long and slow and expert, but behind it Stephanie sensed a desperation that tugged at something more in her than the sensuality Conrad was trying to exploit.

'I didn't mean this to happen,' she said in a whisper.

'Liar!' Conrad said. 'You've been thinking about it ever since we first met, just as I have.'

'You're an interesting devil,' Stephanie admitted. 'OK, I've wondered what you might be like as a lover, but thinking is one thing and doing is another. I'm not sure it's a good idea to let it go any further.'

Conrad closed his eyes and kissed her again, but all the time their lips were engaged he was realizing with total surprise that what he really wanted was to have Nesta in his arms. Stephanie would do, but she was second best. And how would our lovely sex symbol react if she knew that, he wondered sardonically as his hands wandered over the fastenings at the back of Stephanie's dress. Second best to a whippet thin, black haired young Jewess, who had the power to take him right out of this world and into a place set apart.

'Mm,' Stephanie breathed voluptuously. 'Damn you, Conrad. Another couple of minutes and I'm not going to be able to say no. Let me go.'

'After hearing that?' There was a laughing note in his voice, teasing her because they both knew that if she really wanted to, she could break free.

His lips moved down to the hollow at the base of her throat, his hands were caressing her spine.

'N-no,' Stephanie said.

'Sh ... this is what we both want. Let's stop pretending.'

Luke ... Stephanie thought; if this had happened with Luke she would have had no doubts; but Luke was far away and not thinking about her.

She arched her back and moaned faintly as Conrad's lips fastened on her breast, turning her head from side to side in an effort to break free from the spell he was weaving round her. She heard his breathing change and knew that for him, too, it was too late now to turn back. She wrapped her arms round him, holding him close, but even as she went down into a whirlpool of excitement a small voice echoed and re-echoed inside her mind – this is the wrong man; even though I want him madly, now, this minute, he is still the wrong man, the wrong man.

Five

'Cut!'

Stephanie relaxed and rubbed the back of her aching neck.

'Splendid, Stephie, darling. Lovely,' the director said. 'Just one more time, sweetie, and give me more shock – almost horror – on the line "You *know* Karl Eiermann?" '

If there was one thing Stephanie loathed it was being called 'Stephie', but he was a good director and this was only the fourth take of a particularly difficult scene. She shook back her hair, took a deep breath and turned slowly once more to confront Conrad, wearing RAF uniform.

They had been shooting *Wings of Courage* for three weeks and it was going well. Stephanie relished her part, infinitely more dramatic than anything she had attempted before. This was the film that was going to make her name, she was sure of it, and it was going to surprise everyone who had seen her two earlier British comedies and the torrid sex story that had come out of Hollywood.

Conrad, too, was giving an outstanding performance in a part that was putting something of a strain on him. Someone had come up with the idea of capitalizing on his dual nationality and he was playing two roles, a U-boat captain and a bomber pilot in the RAF, with a family link between them to account for the strong resemblance they bore to one another.

Stephanie was the girl who had loved the German before the war and was initially drawn to the British pilot because of his likeness to her lost lover. She appeared not only in the contemporary story but also in dream sequences and flashbacks to pre-war Berlin. She had to switch from being a careless, frivolous girl to playing a deeply suffering woman and the demands of the part taxed her ability to the utmost. All the same, she was getting there; she felt it, she was sure of it. The despair she had sometimes felt the previous winter, driving her

123

ambulance through the Blitz, could be drawn on to give depth to her understanding of the role.

As for Conrad, he might be acting magnificently, but he was being thoroughly unsatisfactory in every other way. Stephanie felt both exasperated and disappointed. While they had been touring she had thought that Conrad was really in love with her. Certainly he had shown no scruples about getting her into bed whenever there was an opportunity. She had always known that their affair was based more on the physical excitement they awoke in one another than on any romantic ideal, but for all that she had hoped that it was a real relationship and that it would last longer than it had.

She had sensed that Conrad wanted something more from her than brief moments of intense sensation, and because of this unexpressed need she had given him her body with warmth and generosity. She had expected the same response from him, but Conrad remained aloof. Even in their most intimate moments he eluded her. He had a way of turning away from her after they had made love that struck coldly at Stephanie.

'Turn round and face me,' she demanded fiercely on one occasion. 'Don't make me feel like something that's been used and put on one side.'

Obediently Conrad turned and took her in his arms again, but when Stephanie whispered, 'What is it you want that I'm not giving you?' she got no reply but his hands tightening on her once more, and a kiss that broke the skin on her upper lip. She lay, tasting blood in her mouth, and wondering at the frenzy that possessed him, but for the first time not feeling a part of it.

It was never the same after that. They still made love, but there was a curious element of showing off in their lovemaking. Physically, they were brilliantly well matched. Their quick reactions and highly-tuned nerves gave them exquisite pleasure, but it seemed to Stephanie that as their beautiful, disciplined bodies strove together they were each silently exerting a skill that was intended to subdue the other. When she cried out at the height of Conrad's assault on her, it was a defeat; when she heard him give a long sigh as he slackened and fell away from her she exulted because she had driven him to the point where he could do no more.

124

The trouble was that when they returned to London and saw less of one another, Stephanie still wanted him. It startled her, the intense physical need she began to experience. It had never been like that before. Her escapades in Hollywood had been a despairing attempt to drive away the memory of her humiliating experience with Dwight. She had shrugged them off, with shame and regret, and had thought that she would never behave so foolishly again. She would have made love to Luke, with warmth and kindness and real affection, but although she had been miserable when he had gone out of her life she had never lain awake at night with every nerve straining with longing for him as she now did for Conrad.

Once they started filming the affair flagged. The early rising, the long, tiring hours under the camera made for an exhausting routine. Twice they went away for weekends together, ostensibly to rest, but in reality to indulge in long, frenzied bouts of lovemaking that almost frightened Stephanie by their intensity.

Stephanie saw no sense in hiding the affair. She told her mother where she was going, and although Vera pursed her lips and tried to look disapproving, she had seen enough of the film to know that Conrad was going to rank as a star on an equal footing with the big names, and being associated with him could do her daughter no harm at all from a career point of view.

For the time being Stephanie and Conrad were excused from Civil Defence duties. Stephanie was uneasy about it, but Conrad shrugged it off.

'We're doing our bit,' he pointed out. 'All this blatant propaganda, it ought to count as service.'

'The story's not entirely one-sided,' Stephanie protested. 'The German is a sympathetic character, in spite of being a U-boat captain. That's what makes it interesting.'

'But, of course, being German, he has to be defeated and drowned,' Conrad drawled sarcastically.

'Of course. That's what we hope will happen to all of them. Our shipping losses have been horrendous. All those poor men – and not only men.'

She was remembering Luke as she spoke. Luke and his wife,

Prue. The memory filled her with sadness. Conrad was the man in her life now, but still she could not shake off the treacherous feeling that the change was not for the better.

A month into the filming one of the minor characters fell ill with appendicitis.

'Thank God we hadn't reached her scenes,' the director said. 'Stephie, darling, I've had to re-arrange the schedule and you'll be on the set all day tomorrow. Sorry about that.'

He was not sorry at all. He did not care if she dropped with fatigue, as long as she did it off camera, as Stephanie very well knew. She accepted the change philosophically, but when the question of re-casting the part came up she exploited his sense of obligation to her to press the claims of someone she knew.

'Nesta Gordon,' she said. 'Have you ever seen her? She toured in *Arms and the Man* with me. A very good actress and she looks the part.'

The director was dubious, especially since the departed actress's agent was pressing another of his clients on him, but he agreed to give Nesta a test.

As Stephanie had anticipated, Nesta's waiflike looks were ideal for the role of a young Czechoslovakian refugee.

'An interesting face,' the director said thoughtfully. 'She'll have to tone down her approach for the screen, of course. Her acting owes everything to the stage. Still ... it's a small part, and she looks right, and she's a friend of yours, Stephie dear, so I'll take a chance on her.'

When she was told that she had got the part, Nesta turned so white that Stephanie thought she might faint. To be acting, even though it was in a film and not on the stage, to be in the same cast as Conrad, it was an ecstacy that shook her thin, ardent body with a force that Stephanie saw, smiled at, and totally misunderstood.

'Dear Nesta,' she said affectionately to Conrad. 'She couldn't be in more of a state if she'd been asked to play, Juliet, Camille and Lady Macbeth!'

His smile was perfunctory and Stephanie let the subject drop. It was not as if he knew Nesta well, not as well as Stephanie had come to know her, and he could not be expected to take the same interest in Nesta's ambitions.

126

Nesta, too, was disappointed by Conrad's reaction when he heard that she had a part in the film.

'I thought you'd be delighted for me,' she said.

She did not mean to sound aggrieved, but her face and voice were too expressive for her feelings not to come through.

'I'm pleased, of course,' Conrad said. 'It might be a little awkward if it became known that there was any connection between us.'

'I don't see why. It was Stephanie who mentioned my name. No one worries because I'm a friend of hers.'

When she got no reply she went on, 'I suppose you're thinking that there's a difference between a friend and a lover?'

She had done something she rarely did, gone to his house without being invited. He had seemed surprised at first, but now she was curled up beside him on the sofa in his living room, her feet tucked up, his arm round her, in bliss as she always was when she was with Conrad.

'Why do we have to keep it a secret that we're in love?' Nesta persisted. 'Other actors and actresses have affairs and it's taken very calmly.' In a small, gruff voice she added, 'It's not because I'm a bit player and you're a star, is it?'

'Of course not! I prefer to keep my private life private, that's all.'

He took his arm away and got up. 'Come on, I'll take you out to dinner to celebrate your first film part.'

'I'm hardly dressed for an evening out,' Nesta said.

'A quiet little restaurant. There are still a few where you can get a meal that's worth eating, in spite of the restrictions.'

'I'd rather have a sandwich and stay here with you on our own,' Nesta said.

'I want to go out,' Conrad said. 'Go and comb your hair, scaramouche.'

While Nesta was tidying herself he managed to have a word with Anton.

'Miss Bartram may call,' he said. 'Please tell her I've had to go out unexpectedly and I'll see her on the set tomorrow. Give her my apologies, of course.'

When they were alone together Anton sometimes dropped the obsequious manner he adopted in front of other people.

127

This was one of the occasions when he spoke more as the master than the servant.

'You haven't forgotten that you've got work to do?'

'Send the code for "Nothing to report",' Conrad said.

He spoke impatiently, trying to suppress the unease he felt because he had not yet obtained answers to a long list of questions which had been fed to him, but Anton's disapproving expression did nothing to make him feel better.

Stephanie arrived half an hour after Conrad and Nesta had gone out. When Anton opened the door she smiled at him with the delightful friendliness that made people warm to her.

'Hello, Anton! Mr Aylmer is expecting me,' she said.

She had recovered all her looks. Her hair had been expertly cut and waved, the colour was back in her cheeks, in spite of the clothing shortages she was elegantly dressed, and she had gained an added poise from the knowledge that she had advanced in her profession. There was a particular sparkle in her eyes that evening because she thought that Conrad was waiting for her, that in a few minutes she would be in his arms.

Anton let her into the hall, but he did not take her coat. He recognized the excitement she tried to conceal and once again resentment welled up in him. Two women, and both of them hot after the man who called himself Anton's master. This one had the looks and the other had the temperament – Anton knew a *grande amoureuse* when he saw one. Conrad was running them in tandem, which was disgusting in itself, but what drove Anton mad was that they were throwing themselves at a filthy Nazi spy.

'Mr Aylmer had to go out,' he said, delivering his message in a flat voice that successfully concealed his turmoil.

'How disappointing!' Stephanie exclaimed. 'Did he leave me any message? A note perhaps?'

'Just his apologies.'

'Tiresome of him. Now I don't know what to do with myself for the rest of the evening and I've sent my taxi away, too. Have you any idea how long Mr Aylmer will be? Perhaps I could wait for him.'

Anton gave a little laugh. When he spoke it was with spiteful relish.

'I don't think Mr Aylmer would like to find you here when he brings the other young lady back.'

At first Stephanie looked no more than puzzled and then, as his words sank in, she said slowly, 'The *other* young lady ...?'

'Miss Gordon. Nesta Gordon. She's been visiting Mr Aylmer for a long time, longer than you, in fact, Miss Bartram.'

Nesta and Conrad. Conrad and Nesta. It made no sense and yet the inference behind Anton's words was clear. He knew that Stephanie and Conrad were lovers. She had stayed the night too often for him not to know. If he suggested that Nesta was on the same terms with his master then he was probably right. Nesta. Nesta and Conrad. She had been in love with him, she had admitted as much, but that was a long time ago. There had never been any hint that her love had been returned.

Anton was watching her. To Stephanie it seemed that he was gloating over the sensation his words had caused. If he thought that he was going to see Stephanie make a scene, then he was very much mistaken.

She said, with a dignity that even to Anton had a touching quality about it, 'Miss Gordon, Mr Aylmer and I are all old friends. She has just started working on our film and I'm delighted to hear that Mr Aylmer has taken her out to celebrate.'

As she turned to go, Anton realized what he had done. If Stephanie told Conrad that she had discovered his double dealing through his man servant then Conrad was all too likely to send an arrogant demand to Berlin to be relieved of Anton's presence. All Anton's work, all the long months of subservience to a man he hated, all the benefit of the confidence his despatches had inspired in Berlin would be wasted.

He caught hold of Stephanie's arm, his words tumbling over themselves in his anxiety to undo some of the harm.

'I oughtn't to have spoken the way I did. I meant nothing by it. Please don't tell Mr Aylmer, Fraulein. It'll cost me my place.'

'There's nothing to tell,' Stephanie said coldly. 'You mentioned that Mr Aylmer had gone out with Miss Gordon and I said I was glad. You may tell him that yourself when he comes home.'

Stephanie walked blindly along the street, stumbling over unfamiliar paving stones in the blackout. Conrad and Nesta. The trouble was, she had immediately believed it. Why? She had scarcely seen them together since they had been in France and yet the idea of them as lovers fitted like a long known truth. Conrad had only turned to Stephanie when they were on tour together, he had shown signs of wanting to drop her when they returned to London. He had been irritated to hear that Nesta was to appear in the film. Well, it must be trying for a man with two mistresses to have them both working with him.

Nesta was the one he preferred. That, too, came to Stephanie out of some deep, unacknowledged disappointment with the way her affair with Conrad had progressed. He had enjoyed making love to her, but if she had been really truthful with herself she would have admitted that he had mounted her as he might have ridden a spirited horse, for the excitement, for the pleasure of his mastery over her, for the exercise, damn him.

She was hurt, but more than anything else, she was angry, and with herself as much as with Conrad. She had been an easy conquest in spite of putting up a show of resistance at first. Worse than that, she had sought him out when he showed signs of cooling off. And all the time she had been a second best choice for Conrad, just as, if she were to be really honest, he had been for her.

By the time she found a taxi Stephanie had calmed herself down. She would finish the film and then break with Conrad, but not too obviously. There would be no more lovemaking, which presumably would not worry him, not if he had Nesta to console him. Stephanie would just cool off and drift away, never letting him know that she had found out about the other girl.

I'll go abroad, Stephanie thought. Under my own steam, if ENSA won't send me. Just me and a pianist. Or I'll join a concert party. I bet the boys in the desert would be pleased to see me. The film company won't like it, but to hell with them. I'm my own woman. I am, in spite of a weakness for no-good, two-timing men. I can rise above a second-rate love affair. Conrad, you swine, you're not going to see this girl breaking her heart for you.

SECOND ACT

One

Luke Lindquist ran his hand over his forehead and then swore softly at the resulting sludge of sand and sweat. They were three days into the battle which was supposed to defeat the Axis forces in Libya and relieve Tobruk, the coastal town which had been left isolated by the great German sweep forward in the spring of 1941.

That had been a setback the British did not care to dwell upon. Their campaign in the desert had started well, with the Italian army being routed. The Allied forces then had had certain advantages: the Italian tanks were lightweight affairs which had been knocked out with comparative ease, the Italians had no great desire to fight, and they had made themselves too comfortable; they had dug in, made permanent bases, enjoyed comforts unimaginable to the hardbitten British soldiers, who had learned to live with the desert. The mobility of the British and Commonwealth troops had been one of the decisive factors of the campaign, that and their willingness to make do with rationed water and bully beef, while the Italians, to the Britons' incredulous disbelief, when they took possession of the Italian camps and villages, had been provided with wine and tinned food, pasta and tomato sauce, freshly baked bread, jam, coffee and chocolate. It had all added up to something of a joke, especially when watching the long lines of dispirited Italian prisoners trailing by, but the laughter had turned sour when the German forces arrived and went on the attack.

The victorious Commonwealth army which had pushed as far west as Benghazi was worn out and its lines of supply were dangerously extended, while at the same time, unknown to the men in the field, a decision was being taken to divert troops for the invasion of Greece. The Empire forces began to withdraw. At Tobruk they halted. The Australians and British, with their backs to the sea, fought with desperate courage. Month after

133

month they held out while Rommel threw against the beleaguered garrison the full power of his Stukas, Heinkels and Messerschmitts in a thousand heavy air raids.

At the end of three months the raids abated, the Germans dug themselves in and began shelling the town. Still the garrison held out, even retaliating with a series of daring night sorties. They were still in touch with Army Headquarters through the ships braving the German aircraft to creep into the port, and which returned to base with stories of the individual courage and ingenuity with which Tobruk was defended.

The invasion of Greece had been a failure and a midsummer attempt to sweep the German army out of the Western Desert had also been unsuccessful. Luke understood, as did all the men engaged in the fighting, that the November offensive which he was now witnessing was an all out attempt at a decisive blow against the Afrika Korps.

Some of the war correspondents, tolerated but not exactly welcome, had remained in the concentration area, relying on communiqués from Army HQ for the stories they would send home. That might be the way to obtain an overall view of the progress of the campaign, but Luke believed in getting onto the battlefield. What he lost in understanding of the higher strategy he gained in the minute human details which gave life to a newspaper report.

There were four in his party: himself, Ed, a fellow American, Jock, a Scot, and a Canadian known as Red. They had picked up a driver and a conducting officer and set out in a Morris truck to find the action.

Two regiments of the 7th Armoured Brigade had captured the enemy airfield on top of the escarpment at Sidi Rezegh, only twelve miles from the Tobruk perimeter. Jolting over the desert, Luke and his companions were on their way to Sidi Rezegh to see the fight for themselves.

A tank lumbered up out of the midday haze. There was a hole in its side and its guns were twisted upwards at a grotesque angle. Luke managed to snatch a brief word with the crew as they drew level with one another.

'Orders have come through to make a push for Tobruk and the garrison there is to start its breakout. God knows how it'll go – the German anti-tank guns are giving us hell. This tank's taken a knock and we've had to withdraw. With any luck the fitters will put us back into action by tomorrow, so we may still get into Tobruk.'

As the reporters drew nearer the battlefield they saw other maimed and burnt out tanks and armoured cars. A truck like their own lay on its side, wheels in the air, two limp bodies sprawled across it in the untidy abandonment of sudden death. Flies rose in a cloud from the putrefying flesh. Luke was glad when their driver accelerated to get away.

They joined the protective laager of the 7th Armoured Brigade that night, the vehicles drawn together in a way that always reminded Luke of the wagon circles of the American trek west, and saw for themselves the toll which the days of fighting had begun to take on soldiers who had been in the thick of it. Short of sleep, exhausted and hungry, there were few men who wanted to be troubled to answer questions from curious newspaper reporters.

'It's not that we haven't got any food, if you like bully beef for every meal,' one gunner complained. 'But we've not had time all day to swallow more than a few bites. I couldn't half do with a plateful of my old Mum's steak and kidney pie.'

'And a pint of bitter,' his navigator said yearningly. 'Never mind, Nobby, I've brewed up. Have a nice mug o' desert tea. Full of chlorine, just the thing to keep your belly cleaned up.'

Luke got a more detailed picture of the way the battle was going when the tank commander was able to spare time for a word with him.

'Two of the British armoured units from Sidi Rezegh have been diverted to meet a German advance. I don't have any details, but I don't think things have been going too well for some of our side, particularly the 7th Hussars. We're expecting the 22nd Armoured Brigade to join up with us, but that move's been delayed because they've gone to the aid of the 4th Armoured Brigade. On the whole, I'd recommend you chaps to move back to the rear. We'll probably come under strong attack tomorrow.'

'What about Tobruk?' Ed asked.

'The garrison joined up with New Zealand forces, but for the time being the breakout is suspended.'

135

He either had nothing more to say or, as Luke suspected, was unwilling to enlarge upon what he knew. Left to themselves, the four war correspondents looked at one another, each trying to gauge the reaction of the others.

'I think I'll take the man's advice and head for home in the morning,' Jock said. 'I'll do the rounds tonight, pick up what I can from anyone who's willing to talk, and get out as soon as it's light enough to move.'

'I'm for that, too,' Red agreed. 'How about you two Yanks?'

'I'm staying put,' Ed said. 'I'm the new boy, remember. You've all seen tank battles before, but it's new to me and I want to be in on the fighting. Besides, Luke and I are neutrals, so if we get captured we can demand to be set free.'

'I hope the Jerries see it that way,' Jock said drily. 'You're liable to get shot before you've had time to show them your press card.'

It would have been more prudent to withdraw: Luke smelt danger. All the same, he agreed to stay with Ed, partly because he thought the other man might be glad of a companion and partly because of his own devouring need to be at the scene of the action.

They used what was left of the light to write despatches which Jock and Red promised to get away for them. Once the sun had gone down the air chilled rapidly and by dawn a nasty searching little wind had sprung up. Luke had slept poorly. The cold had got into his bones and he had twisted about uneasily, trying to hitch his blankets round him to keep warm.

'Bloody desert,' Ed said.

It was his standard greeting to every day, but this morning he went on, 'Why did I say I'd stay? Why don't I go back to Cairo and report the war in comfort?'

'Because if Tobruk's going to be relieved you want to be there – and so do I,' Luke said, sitting up and running his hand over the uncomfortable stubble on his chin.

'True, true. The eyewitness account, the human interest, the front line reporting – and we'll be damned lucky if we can get the story back to our papers in time for it to be of any use to them.'

Since this was true, and well known to all of them, Luke did not bother to reply. He was watching Jock boiling up water for a hot drink before he and Red left. Coffee was what Luke longed for, but tea was what he was going to get.

He took the steaming mug with a muttered word of thanks, pulled his blanket round his shoulders once more and sat, huddled and comatose, but gradually becoming more human as the hot liquid ran down his throat and into his stomach.

All around them the men of the 7th Armoured Brigade stirred into similar life and so, too, it seemed, did the Afrika Korps, because they had barely had time to get into battle formation before the guns started firing.

Just after midday Ed crawled towards Luke, putting his head down close to speak to him. They were both lying full length in a shallow trench they had scraped out of the sand, to give them some protection from the shrapnel and bullets that whistled around their unprotected heads.

'What wouldn't I give for a well armoured tank to crawl into,' Ed said fervently.

His eyes were red-rimmed from peering through the heat haze, his face was scoured by the sand which was blowing over them. Luke noticed that his hands shook as he lit the last of his cigarettes.

'So what do you think of a tank battle now that you've seen one?' Luke enquired.

'Bloody hell – and I'm not swearing,' Ed said. 'How do they keep it up?'

'What I ask myself is not "how" but "why",' Luke said. 'A few miles of empty desert and all these lives being thrown away so that one general can claim he's got the advantage over another.'

'Who's going to win?'

'Depends what you're talking about. I'd guess our side will be told to withdraw from this position – they've got no real answer to the German heavy guns – and that's a loss. We're too close to this little section to know how the battle as a whole is going, but in the end I suspect it'll be inconclusive. Whichever side pushes ahead will eventually have to withdraw because the supply lines are too long. Eventually one side or the other will build up sufficient forces to be able to push the other into the sea, and now that Hitler is committed to fighting in Russia I think it'll be the British who'll take over the Middle East.'

There was a momentary lull and Ed sat up.

'Keep your head down,' Luke warned.

'I've got a dose of gyppy tummy. Guts like water. No help for it, I'll have to take a stroll. Back in a minute.'

He began to walk away, then bent double as a high velocity shell whistled overhead. It burst some fifty yards away from Ed, sending up a cloud of sand and pebbles. Ed picked himself up and turned to give Luke a thumbs-up sign to show that he was all right. A second shell caught him as he crouched over the makeshift latrine he had scraped in the sand.

Luke crawled out of his inadequate shelter and wriggled towards the shell hole. Ed's legs were a tangled mess of torn flesh and splintered bone. He lay flat on his back with his eyes wide open and his mouth stretched in the last agonized shout that had been wrenched out of him. His blood was still seeping into the hungry sand.

Luke felt the remains of his last scanty meal rise up in his stomach. He turned aside to retch, but nothing came up but sour tasting liquid. He spat it out and wiped his mouth, then he went back to Ed's body and made himself feel in the dead man's pockets for any personal papers or possessions that his family might want. There was a wallet, which he took, and an identity tag, but Luke left him that in case it was wanted when he was buried. *If* he was buried. From the way the tanks were beginning to lumber past him, Luke guessed that this body might have to be left behind for the Germans to deal with.

The officer who had been given the job of conducting the war correspondents to the battle zone came to join Luke in his scraped out trench.

'Your colleagues got away safely,' he reported. 'I only wish I'd made you go with them. Where's your other man?'

'A shell caught him.'

'Dead? Oh, hell!'

To Luke it sounded more like he was worried that he might be reprimanded than an expression of regret.

'We're going to have to make a dash for it,' the officer went on. 'I've agreed to give a lift to a couple of chaps who are wounded. You'd better look lively if you don't want to miss the truck.'

Bent double in the instinctive protective crouch adopted by men under fire they raced towards a truck which already had its engine running.

The driver had a field dressing on his forehead.

'Just a scrape,' he said cheerfully in answer to Luke's question. 'Cor, what a set out! Hang on to your seat, sir. We're going to have to drive hell for leather if we're to keep out of Jerry's hands.'

The other two occupants of the truck were both wounded, one more seriously than the other. Luke saw him grit his teeth as the truck jolted over the rough ground and swerved to avoid a burnt out tank. He caught Luke watching him and grinned in helpless resignation.

'One step forward and two steps back, same as usual,' he commented. 'The bloody Jerries threw all they'd got at us – two whole Panzer Divisions. Couldn't be expected to hold out against that, could we?'

They lurched into a hole and out the other side. The driver swore under his breath. 'Didn't see it in time,' he excused himself.

The unexpected jolt had thrown them off the hard track. In spite of the frantic way he dragged at the wheel the truck ploughed into another cavity which had filled up with drifting sand. The wheels spun helplessly, finding no purchase, and the truck came to a halt. The driver swore again, more forcefully.

'Spades and wheel tracks,' the officer said.

Luke pressed the more severely wounded soldier back into his seat.

'I'll do your stint,' he said.

'But you're an officer, sir,' the man protested.

'Only nominally. I don't command anything but a typewriter.'

'We'll all give a hand, if necessary,' the conducting officer said impatiently.

It took no more than ten minutes to get the portable metal tracks in place, but the sweat was running off Luke in rivulets as he paused and leaned on his spade. The driver revved up his engine, the wheels gripped on the runners they had placed underneath the vehicle and he coaxed it forward, back on to the track.

They stumbled after it and climbed on board. This time the driver set out more cautiously, until they came to one of those mysterious spots in the middle of the desert which constituted a sort of crossroads. Rough signposts painted with regimental names and jumbles of letters pointed towards apparently empty space. It struck Luke as they drove on that their little truck was remarkably isolated.

A couple of minutes later he glanced back and then swivelled round in his seat and felt for his binoculars.

'Don't look now, but I think we're being followed,' he said.

'By one of theirs, do you mean?' the conducting officer asked in alarm.

'That's what it looks like to me.'

'Blimey, they must think we're a blooming staff car, or something. That's what comes of looking so classy,' the driver remarked.

A machine gun chattered behind them and they all ducked.

'What a nasty man,' one of the wounded soldiers said reproachfully.

They all knew that there was little hope of escaping, but the driver did his best, putting on speed and swerving from side to side. There was another burst of firing and they came to a skidding halt.

'Bloody hell, we've been hit,' the driver said in disgust. 'Pile out everyone, the petrol's pouring out of the tank. Sorry an' all that. It's prisoner-of-war camp for us – if they don't decide to shoot us to get us out of the way.'

The conducting officer and the soldiers were sent to the rear of the column, but Luke, repeating with monotonous vigour, *'Ich bin Amerikana'* eventually found himself in a tent which had been put up for the night for the benefit of the commander of this Panzer Division.

The leather satchel in which he carried his possessions had been removed from him and Luke saw that all its contents had been spilled out on a small trestle table. Prue had given him that satchel. They had joked about it being his handbag. Luke

140

waited for the familiar pain to strike and was vaguely surprised when he felt nothing more than a dull regret. Ed's death was closer to him now – Ed and all the other young men whose lives he had seen destroyed.

His papers were being examined by a trim young officer in the grey-green uniform of the Afrika Korps, the very epitome of the Aryan type, tall, well built, blond and blue eyed – and arrogant as hell, Luke thought disgustedly.

'*Sprechen Sie Englisch?*' he asked. It seemed a reasonable assumption since the young devil appeared to be reading what was in front of him.

'I speak very good English,' the officer said.

He stood up and clicked his heels like the hero of a romantic operetta.

'Allow me to introduce myself. Ernst von Lynden. And you are Mr Luke Lindquist – or are you Mr Edward Hopper? You appear to have two sets of papers.'

'I'm Lindquist. I took the other papers from a colleague who got killed.'

'Ah, yes,' Ernst von Lynden said, looking with distaste at the stained documents. 'That explains the blood. So, Mr Lindquist, you are reporting the war in the desert from the British point of view, and now you find yourself visiting the other side. If you care to write about our side of the battle you will doubtless be given every facility. We always like to have our victories fully covered.'

He was turning over the pages of a week-old Cairo newspaper as he spoke. Luke had stuffed it into the satchel on the day he set out for the front and had forgotten it was there. There was a picture in it which had interested him and now it seemed that the same photograph had caught Ernst von Lynden's eye.

'How unexpected! How strange!' he exclaimed. 'News of my wicked cousin Conrad.'

It was a publicity shot of Stephanie and Conrad from the film they had made together. For Luke the interesting thing about it had been that the caption suggested that Stephanie would be making a Middle Eastern tour, but it was the picture of her companion which held the German officer riveted.

141

Luke's news gathering antennae twitched. There might be a story in this coincidental meeting on the battlefield with a relation of a well known actor.

'If you mean Conrad Aylmer, I know him,' he said.

'You do? I see he is still able to acquire beautiful women. Stephanie Bartram ... you know her too? You are a fortunate man, Mr Lindquist.'

'You said he was your cousin,' Luke probed.

'Correctly speaking it is our mothers who are cousins. I call his mother Tante Wanda, which is not strictly correct and does not please her, since she prefers young men to treat her less respectfully. As for Conrad, there was a time when we were good friends. I visited him in England to perfect my English ...'

'You speak it very well.'

'Thank you. Conrad also was often the guest of my family in Germany. He is a little older than me, I admired him, "looked up to him" is the expression, I believe. In those days he was one of us, you understand. A good Nazi, or so I thought. Now, if we met, I would spit in his face. I would not have believed it, that Conrad could have turned traitor, rejected his German inheritance – and for what? – for money, Mr Lindquist, to secure his father's British bank balance. It is despicable. Tante Wanda, of course, excuses him. She hints at some wonderful secret mission which Conrad fulfils for the Führer, but me, I think he has no motive but greed.'

'He's not actually taking part in any fighting,' Luke said.

He wanted to keep this conversation going. It was interesting, more than interesting, disturbing in a way he could not quite analyze.

'I wrote an article about him, as a matter of fact. He did some good work rescuing civilians who were trapped in the Blitz on London.'

'I would respect him more if he joined the army and fought. He made a broadcast, did you know that? A filthy propaganda exercise. And this film – you see that he wears the uniform of the RAF? No doubt that, too, is full of propaganda lies.'

He crumpled up the paper in futile rage, then he smoothed it out again.

'I'm sorry, this is your property,' he said stiffly.

'I've no further use for it,' Luke said. 'But I'm interested in what you say about your cousin Conrad. Maybe I'll see him soon. You may not think much of him, but I guess he'd be glad to have news of his mother. Have you seen Mrs Aylmer lately?'

'Mrs ...? Oh, she has dropped that name long since! No, I have no message to send to Conrad, unless you care to tell him that when we have conquered England I will see that he is dealt with as he deserves.'

'He is, after all, a British citizen,' Luke pointed out.

'He was *German*,' Ernst von Lynden insisted, but at that moment his superior officer came into the tent. He snapped to attention, the correct young officer once more, instead of the angry boy who had been disappointed in a childhood hero.

Luke was treated very correctly. He resisted, with smiling politeness, all attempts to question him about the British position and eventually he was sent back behind the lines. The fighting soldiers, he was given to understand, were not interested in holding on to him. As far as he could see he was in a sort of limbo, not exactly a prisoner-of-war, but by no means free. He managed to get himself sent to Tripoli and set up a vigorous campaign to get himself out of North Africa.

While he was hanging around Luke had plenty of time to think. His conversation with Ernst von Lynden kept knocking at the back of his mind. Conrad, for years before the war, had been a 'good German'. More than that, Ernst had believed his cousin to be a committed Nazi. Conrad's mother had hinted at a secret mission. Perhaps, as Ernst thought, it was her way of excusing her son's defection — or was it an unwary boast about something that should not have been revealed?

Luke had a reporter's memory for past conversations. He remembered a party in France, right up by the Maginot Line, and an interested voice asking, 'You're equipped with six-inch howitzers, aren't you?' He remembered the way people talked to Conrad, his charm, the way he encouraged their confidences, and something else — an admiring comment from Stephanie that on their tour of army camps and factories Conrad had

143

always made a point of getting down amongst the audience and talking to them.

It was the beginning of December before Luke was handed his passport and told that he was free to travel on a Portuguese ship which would creep round the coast. Eventually – provided he was not torpedoed, mined or bombed – he would arrive in Lisbon, from where he could make his own travel arrangements.

The *Princesa dos Mares* was a grimy little vessel and the accommodation that was offered to Luke was no more than a cot on the floor of the second mate's cabin, which Luke suspected he would be sharing with a tribe of cockroaches, but it was his transport to freedom and Luke was not going to complain.

He slept on board on the night before they were due to sail on the morning tide because he had a nervous dread of missing the boat. His misgivings about the livestock were well founded and he was kept awake for the first part of the night, falling into a heavy sleep in the early hours of the morning.

He was disturbed by a hand pulling at his shoulder and a voice urging him to wake up. Luke turned over and blinked. In the sunshine filtering into his dark little cabin he saw the figure of a Swedish journalist who had been a good friend to him since Luke had arrived in Tripoli.

'It is most urgent that I speak with you,' the Swede said. 'Are you awake?'

'Just about,' Luke said, sitting up. 'What's wrong? If the Germans want me back they can go take a running jump. I'm not leaving this ship.'

'That is what I wish to say to you. You *must* not leave this ship. Japan has attacked the American Fleet at Pearl Harbour. It is inevitable that the United States will enter the war. Your status has changed, Mr Lindquist. You are no longer a neutral. On board the *Princesa dos Mares* you are safe, I think, but you must not set foot ashore at any port or perhaps you will be interned.'

It was a long, slow, boring voyage to Lisbon and Luke's impatience to find out what had happened at Pearl Harbour made it seem endless. He had only the skimpiest details, but even from what he knew it had obviously been an appalling disaster. Luke had never liked the Japanese, not since his time in China. Treacherous little devils. All those American ships, all those men. It hardly bore thinking about, especially if you were a frustrated reporter pottering about the Mediterranean in a foreign cargo boat.

The *Princesa dos Mares* edged along the North African coast, wallowing in the swell and sending out clouds of evil-smelling smoke. There were alarms when air raids threatened, but they finally scuttled across to the European shore and crawled unscathed into Lisbon.

'Good trip, eh?' the captain asked Luke. It was one of his half dozen English phrases.

Luke scratched thoughtfully at the flea bites on his arms, then he grinned.

'First class,' he said.

There was one thing to be said for being a long-time overseas correspondent: he had a string of contacts all round the world. He had only a few escudas, but on his second telephone call he struck lucky and found an old acquaintance who was able to give him a bed.

Lisbon was the most civilized place Luke had seen in months. The shops were full of luxuries, there were throngs of wealthy, cosmopolitan people in all the restaurants and bars, the streets glittered with lights, there was music and theatre and art exhibitions, beaches to visit, and the casino at Estoril which was the preserve of the British and avoided by the Germans. It all seemed very agreeable, but Luke was too old a hand not to pick up the currents of intrigue below the surface.

'Spies, spies, spies,' his host agreed when Luke mentioned his suspicions. 'We're surrounded by them. Lisbon is the clearing house for espionage. Hasn't anyone invited you to make a detailed statement about your interesting stay in German hands? I'm surprised! The Brits must be slipping.'

'If anyone did contact me, how would I know he was genuine?' Luke asked.

'If he's a real spy he's probably serving both sides anyway. If you've got anything to tell why not spill it to one of our own embassy boys?'

145

'This is for the British – a domestic matter.'

'I'll introduce you to a man called Malcolm Morley.'

Malcolm Morley was a middle-aged man wearing pebble glasses, a vague expression and a tussore suit which looked as if it had been tailored in an Indian bazaar.

He blinked mildly at Luke, who struggled to conceal his disbelief in this unlikely intelligence agent.

'You have something to tell me,' he said and then, as Luke hesitated, he added encouragingly, 'You were taken prisoner by the Germans, I understand?'

'Yes, but it's not connected with that, not directly,' Luke said.

In a few sentences he spilled out his story of the encounter with young Ernst von Lynden, the way he had spoken about Conrad, the suspicions that had been aroused in Luke's mind.

'It may be nothing, but I couldn't be easy in my mind until I'd mentioned it to someone,' he concluded. 'Will you pass it on to London, for what it's worth?'

'I'll do that,' Malcolm Morley agreed. 'It's a strange coincidence, but Conrad Aylmer's new film will be shown in the cinema here next week. I shall make a point of going to see it.'

'So will I, if I'm still here,' Luke said.

'You won't talk about your encounter with the German cousin to anyone else, will you?'

'Not if you want me to keep quiet,' Luke said obligingly.

Knowing that his recent captivity had been less than popular back in New York, Luke cabled his newspaper, with little hope of getting the go ahead, to suggest that he should be transferred to the Pacific theatre of war. To his disgust the reply came back: 'Congrats release nix Pacific assignment return Cairo soonest.'

'Damn,' Luke said. 'I want to get into an area where our own troops are fighting.'

'Building up your readership back home?' his friend enquired.

'Do you know any reader who looks at the name of the correspondent on the by-line? No, that's not what's in my mind.

146

I've been finding the British ideas on censorship irksome, to say the least. I've been going along with it since war broke out and I'd like to get back to our own more open system of reporting.'

The other reporter's gloomy cynicism seemed to deepen.

'Oh, boy, are you in for a shock if that's what you think! How much do you know about Pearl Harbour?'

'Not much,' Luke admitted. 'I was on board the *Princesa* when the news broke. I couldn't get off at any of the ports we called at until I arrived here in Lisbon.'

'Well, don't bother to read the newspapers to catch up on the facts. The truth is a lot worse than anyone has been allowed to say. There are people here in Lisbon who can quote you eyewitness accounts; the Japs know how many ships they sank; so who's being kept in the dark? The great American public, that's who.'

'You're shaking my faith in the power of the press,' Luke said, only half joking.

'Come on, little boy, you must have had doubts when you were reporting in China?'

'You're darn right I did!'

Luke didn't enlarge on it, but the memory made him pensive. He had suspected, with how much truth he never knew, that one reason he had been switched to his European assignment had been because of his lack of enthusiasm for the regime of Generalissimo Chiang Kai-shek. He had not argued about his posting at the time because it had suited him very well to be sent to England. Now he wondered whether he should have gone into it more fully, instead of thinking only that the new job would allow him a period of home life with Prue.

After that Luke mooched round Lisbon in a mood of disenchanted gloom. It was all very well for the newspaper to demand his swift return to Cairo, but transport was difficult to come by and he had to take his turn. He thought of turning his experiences on the *Princesa* into an article. It might earn him a few dollars. When he put a sheet of paper into his typewriter and got started he was surprised how much there was to say. And it was funny. Horrific at the time, but funny in retrospect. With growing enthusiasm Luke made a fresh start, outlining his reasons for being in the desert, recounting some of his

147

experiences during the fighting which had not gone into his newspaper reports, describing Cairo in wartime and the contrast with the stark conditions at the front, and leading up to his capture.

At the back of his mind he had always had an ambition to become what Prue had referred to caustically as 'a proper writer'. She had encouraged him and had been disappointed when the attempt he had made to write up his experiences in China had come to nothing. It would be ironic if this semi-humorous account of his recent experiences actually got somewhere, when a serious bid to write an account of China had eluded him.

He took one evening off from his typewriter to see *Wings of Courage*, but it only raised more questions in his mind. It was weird to watch Conrad in his dual roles and to wonder whether it was the German one that he would have liked to play in real life. It was a gripping performance – two performances, really. Stephanie was good, too. She had matured, become more of an actress than she had been before. Was she really going to visit Cairo? If so, it seemed that they would be meeting again.

Luke wished, now that it was too late, that he had done something more to keep in touch. She had not deserved the casual treatment he had handed out. Stephanie was something more than a pick up girl to be dismissed from the mind when she was out of sight. Still, no point in having regrets now. What he had to concentrate on was finding some way of getting himself back to Cairo.

Two

The great P & O liner moved slowly out of Cape Town harbour, as she had done so many times in earlier years, but now the ship had been converted to wartime use and was carrying more passengers than its peacetime crew would have believed possible.

Stephanie hung over the rails to wave goodbye to the new acquaintances who had come down to see her off. Cape Town had been heaven, apart from one or two drawbacks: she had found the flat, nasal Afrikaans voices unattractive, especially when combined with a patronizing attitude that implied that the British were, yet again, making a mess of the war they insisted on fighting, and the rigid demarcation between black and white had made her uneasy. There had been plenty of compensations: the crystalline air, the perfect climate, beautiful houses, smiling black servants, overwhelming hospitality. She was saying goodbye with real regret.

It was a lovely morning, even Table Mountain was without its trailing veil of cloud. Stephanie turned away with a sigh, knowing that she had to go below and stow away her luggage in the tiny cabin she was sharing with three other girls.

She was part of a concert party en route for Cairo and apart from a few high spots, like Cape Town, the voyage had been no holiday cruise. They were overcrowded, none too well fed, freezing with cold in the northern waters and sizzling in heat when they reached the sun. On top of that, they had lived for weeks with the knowledge that the convoy was in constant danger. They had known what it was to be woken from uneasy sleep to stand by in their life jackets because a U-boat was in the vicinity, and they had heard the dull thud of depth charges as the navy tried to knock the enemy out of the water.

Stephanie had arrived at the Cape feeling tired and nervy, now she stretched her arms above her head, glorying in her recovered fitness and admiring the splendid suntan she had acquired on the beach while they were waiting to continue their voyage.

They were rounding the Cape and going through the Suez Canal. That would be another interesting experience. And then Cairo, the desert, the pyramids, the sphinx and, of course, the hard work of entertaining the troops.

The concert party was called 'Hello, Boys'. They had a four-piece band, four dancers – very young – a tenor and a comedian – both middle-aged – and Stephanie, who was the star of the show and did a bit of everything, duets with the tenor, dancing with the troupe and feed to the comedian, as well as her own solo spots.

Her mother had been annoyed about this departure.

'Just got yourself accepted as a straight actress – which I always understood was your ambition – and you throw it up and disappear to the other side of the world as a glorified chorus girl!'

Stephanie smiled at the memory as she went below. Good old Mum, always predictable. And, of course, she was right. It was a mistake to switch her career about. She ought to have stayed in England and consolidated her position by making another film after the success of *Wings of Courage*. The authorities would have been sympathetic and looked upon it as a worthwhile war effort. However, it would have meant working with Conrad, and that was something Stephanie did not want to contemplate for the time being.

Bloody men. She had gone off them in a big way – except for a delightful flirtation with a naval lieutenant which had whiled away the days she had spent in Cape Town. He had been a darling and he had taken it reasonably well when she had refused him anything more than a few kisses and a lot of lighthearted repartee. No more lovers, no more wretched physical dependence on men who were either neglectful or doubledealers. She had quite made up her mind about it and if a small, cynical voice at the back of her mind whispered 'Until the next time', Stephanie was refusing to acknowledge that there would be a next time.

Cairo, when they reached it, was not as unpleasantly hot as

150

Stephanie had feared, but the air felt heavier than it had in Cape Town. When she explored the old town the narrow alleys seemed to admit neither light nor any movement of air, the white buildings glittered under the unremitting sun; there were too many smells, too many sleazy bars, too many over-eager men in loose robes with ever-ready palms offering their services, their manner insinuating and their eyes insolent.

The company was reasonably well housed in a hotel on Sharia Talaat Harb, but Cairo was crowded and even for the star of the show there was no possibility of a room to herself. Three of the young dancers shared a room and the fourth went in with Stephanie. Since they had already been forced into close proximity in the cabins they had shared on the ship they all accepted this with cheerful resignation.

'The beds look clean, the fan in the ceiling works and we've got hot and cold water,' Stephanie remarked. 'What more do we need?'

She twitched aside the blind covering the window and wrinkled her nose distastefully at the sight of the littered back alley below.

'Not a scenic view,' she admitted.

The first performance was to take place at the Cairo Opera House on the day after they arrived. They had a quick run through in the early morning before the day hotted up, but they needed little rehearsing because they had spent a lot of time on their routines whenever they could get up on deck during the seven week voyage.

The reception they got on their first night startled them.

'Makes you realize how welcome a bit of live entertainment is,' the comedian whispered to Stephanie. 'We're not that good!'

'If they feel like this in Cairo, where there are cinemas and other amusements, what's it going to be like when we get out into the field?' Stephanie wondered.

There were flowers waiting for her when she arrived at the theatre the following evening, and a note: 'I caught the performance last night and it was great. Congratulations. I'll stop by the stage door tonight in the hope of seeing you when the show is over. Luke.'

Stephanie propped the note against her looking glass and thought about it. In the end she came to much the same conclusion as Luke: she would have to see him; it would look odd to refuse; but there was no going back to the relationship they had achieved – or nearly achieved – in London.

She greeted him coolly when he was shown into the dressing room.

'Hello, Luke. Nice to see you again. How have you been keeping?'

He looked much the same as she remembered him, big and quiet, with the controlled movements of a man who was in charge of his body. There was a touch of grey in his nondescript hair which had not been there before. His face was deeply tanned, with lighter lines at the corners of his eyes where he had screwed them up against the sun. A little thinner perhaps, which made his nose seem sharper and the lines of his jaw more clearly defined.

'I'm OK, thanks,' Luke replied. 'You're looking wonderful, more beautiful than ever. You've been doing great things since we last met. I saw your film. It was good.'

He was nervous. Why the hell should he be nervous? This was just a girl. A beautiful girl, and he'd fancied her once, but it had been a passing thing. No reason for his stomach to get tied up in knots.

'I thought maybe you'd come out to supper with me?' he suggested tentatively.

'How kind. Yes, I could do that,' Stephanie said, and it rankled that she made it sound as if she were doing him a favour.

She had already changed out of the striking evening gown she wore for the finale of the show. She was wearing a plain white sleeveless dress, caught in at the waist with a gold mesh belt, a dress she had managed to buy in Cape Town. Her arms and legs were smooth and brown against the white sharkskin. She picked up a long white chiffon scarf and draped it over her head and round her neck with the ends floating out behind.

'I'm ready. Shall we go?'

Luke had taken the precaution of booking a table at the fashionable Gezirah Club. As they went in Stephanie pushed back the scarf from her head and let it drop down to hang loosely from her elbows. She had the beautiful carriage and assured manner of an established celebrity, turning her head neither to right nor left as she walked across the crowded room. Luke caught the soft hissing of sibilants as her name was repeated.

'Stephanie Bartram ... film star ... Stephanie ... Stephanie ...'

'How do you come to terms with your fame?' he asked as they sat down at their table.

'By pretending to ignore it,' Stephanie said.

He liked the frankness of that 'pretending', that was like the girl he had known in London. She accepted a drink and Luke made another attempt to get the conversation going.

'I had my own moment of fame recently,' he said. 'Got myself captured by the Germans.'

He had certainly caught her attention.

'Really? And they let you go?'

'It took time, but it was before Pearl Harbour, so officially we were still neutral. At one time I thought they were just going to file me away and forget about me, but fortunately I had an influential Swede on my side and he helped me to get a passage to Lisbon. In fact, I've not long been back in Cairo. I got a bit of a write up in my paper. "Our intrepid reporter", you know – but on the whole they were fairly disgusted with me because I missed the best of the fighting.'

'What was it like, being held by the Germans? I mean ... the people we're fighting against, who are they?'

'Men like any other men, except ...' Luke paused, frowning, trying to sum up the impression Rommel's Afrika Korps had made on him. 'They're so damn sure they're right,' he said at last. 'It's frightening, that absolute certainty.'

'It's what makes them dangerous, and perhaps what makes them good soldiers,' Stephanie suggested.

She had lost that cool British manner he found so offputting, but the shutters came down again at his next question.

'Stephanie, you know Conrad Aylmer as well as anyone, I guess. If you had to make a snap judgement what would you say was his chief characteristic?'

153

'Treachery.'

The reply was so close to Luke's suspicions that his hand jerked, spilling his drink on the table.

Stephanie watched him mopping up the liquid with his napkin.

'I'm not the best person to give you a disinterested verdict on Conrad,' she said deliberately. 'The reason I didn't invite him along on this trip was that I discovered he was two-timing me with Nesta. Or rather the other way round. She came first, I was just the follow on.'

She had told him on purpose, because she wanted Luke to know that she had not sat around pining for him when he had disappeared. Luke recognized that, even while he was taking in what she had said.

'You and Conrad,' he repeated mechanically.

'Did you expect me to stay true to your memory, dear Luke? Our affair never came to anything, did it? You forgot, so did I.'

'I felt badly about leaving you, but I had no choice,' Luke protested.

'I accept that you had to go, but I've always suspected that if you'd really made the effort you could have seen me to say goodbye. Still, that's all past and over now. Thank you for the food parcel – and the postcard of the Nile.'

'I guess I ought to have written,' Luke said.

'You might have done that,' Stephanie agreed. 'Even a few words would have been welcome, just to show that I was more to you than a tumble you didn't manage to have.'

'I came nearer to loving you than any woman since Prue.'

'You told me that before. It gives me a very poor idea of the quality of your marriage.'

She knew she had gone too far when Luke turned white.

'That's unforgiveable,' he said.

'Yes, you're right, it is,' Stephanie agreed miserably. 'Damn. I didn't mean to quarrel with you. I was annoyed by the calm way you walked back into my life after dropping out for so long, and then you brought up Conrad and I remembered the way he'd treated me, too. I'm sorry. Do you want me to go?'

'Oh, let's put the past behind us. I behaved like a heel. You were right to bawl me out. Fresh start?'

He held out his hand, palm upwards, and after a moment's hesitation Stephanie put her hand into it.

'I still think you're a wonderful girl,' Luke said quietly.

Stephanie took her hand away.

'What made you ask about Conrad?' she enquired, making an effort to speak without constraint.

'While I was in German hands I ran across a relation of his.'

'No! How extraordinary! Was he like Conrad?'

'Not really, except that he was a good-looking youngster. He was very bitter about the way he thought Conrad had changed sides.'

Luke was watching Stephanie, but as far as he could see the words meant nothing to her.

'Poor Conrad. Where women are concerned he's a swine of the first order, but I do feel sorry for him. I was with him once when he was asked to visit a badly wounded Luftwaffe pilot in one of our hospitals. It made him ill – literally ill. It must be awful to be torn in two like that.'

Or forced to act a part which was sometimes difficult to sustain. More than ever Luke was glad that he had talked to Malcolm Morley. There was nothing more he could do. He ought to put it out of his mind instead of worrying away at it like a dog with a meaty bone.

'Are you planning on visiting the pyramids while you're here?' he asked.

'Oh, I must! I want to have a ride on a camel and do all the touristy things, as far as time will allow.'

'Maybe I could take you? I've got transport,' Luke said cautiously.

'Thank you, I'd like that. I'll be free all day on Sunday. Is that possible for you?'

'I'll make it possible.'

'Don't put yourself out.'

It came out with a snap that made Stephanie pull herself up with a rueful smile.

'Something amuses you?' Luke asked and he, too, recognized a sarcasm behind his words that was not pleasant.

'I sounded exactly like my mother – ungracious, grudging, suspicious, looking for the motive behind a favour.'

'No ulterior motive. I'd like us to be friends.'

'That's what I want, too,' Stephanie said. 'Friends.'

By the time they left the restaurant the temperature had dropped. Stephanie shivered and wrapped the long chiffon scarf round her shoulders.

'You're lucky to be here at this time of year,' Luke said. 'The daytime temperature is rarely above seventy degrees and the nights are cool.'

'Cooler than I expected,' Stephanie admitted.

'Cairo rarely gets much rain, but the winter weather has been causing havoc on the front. The local people say they've never known so much rain in Cyrenaica. Everything's bogged down, supplies can't get through – and neither can war correspondents!'

'Is that why we did so badly? It was a defeat, wasn't it?'

'The winter offensive didn't go as planned,' Luke admitted. 'At the moment we've got stalemate. Rommel has withdrawn from the Egyptian border because he had the same difficulty as our side did in maintaining a long supply line. A lot of men have lost their lives, a lot of equipment has been destroyed – and I'm talking about both sides ... and it's all to be done again as soon as the losses have been recouped.'

'It makes me wonder what I'm doing here,' Stephanie said in a low voice.

'Keeping up morale. Now that the fighting's died down for the time being, a lot of men are being given leave. Seeing people like you and your party who've come out from home to be with them gives them a real kick.'

'I feel I'm not doing enough. Perhaps I ought to throw it all up and join the ATS.'

'You'd only be drafted into a concert party. I know how you feel. I've had the same doubts myself, especially now the US is in the war. Should I join the fighting army? I've been told I'm doing a job no one else could do. It may be true. If American troops land in these parts and I can report on them for their folks back home I'll feel better about it. Whatever happens, I've got to get back to the front line. Come hell or high water, I'm off to the desert on Monday.'

They had been strolling along as they talked. The streets

156

were still full of people, servicemen on a night out, and other, more mysterious figures, flitting by in veils and long robes.

'You must try to see the sky by night out in the desert,' Luke said. 'Deep dark blue with stars like Christmas tree baubles.'

'If things go right I'll be sleeping under it,' Stephanie told him. 'We go to Alexandria next week and after that we're touring round with a portable stage, visiting hospitals and camp sites and, I hope, real outposts where the boys don't see many entertainers.'

As they drew near Stephanie's hotel their steps slowed, almost as if they were reluctant to part from one another, but at the door Stephanie held out a cool, slim hand and said sedately, 'Thank you, Luke. I'll look forward to our trip on Sunday.'

'Yeah. OK. Sunday,' Luke agreed.

When he picked her up on Sunday Stephanie was wearing a long, loose cotton galabiyya she had picked up in one of the bazaars. She had covered her hair with a blue cotton scarf and put a wide brimmed hat over the top. Her feet were bare in flatheeled, strong leather sandals.

'How do you manage to wear the same clothes as one of the fellahin and look glamorous?' Luke demanded.

'Do I? I ought to be wearing uniform really, but I decided to give myself a day off. This is cool, comfortable and the long sleeves will shield my arms from the sun.'

The road they took was the usual tourist route. For anyone else Luke would not have visited the pyramids again since he privately considered them boring constructions, but Stephanie's glee at seeing them was almost childlike and he found himself smiling all day at her uninhibited delight.

'If only we didn't both have other commitments we could have taken a cruise on the Nile,' he said. 'And Karnak – I'd have liked to have shown you Karnak.'

'Don't make me regret what I can't see. This is enough to be going on with. The sphinx, the actual real sphinx, and the pyramids and the desert, just like the picture books.'

'You'll see more than enough of the desert before you've finished,' Luke commented.

Stephanie turned towards him, her face solemn but her eyes sparkling with mischief as she recited:

The Walrus and the Carpenter,
Were walking close at hand;
They wept like anything to see
Such quantities of sand:
'If this were only cleared away',
They said, 'it would be grand'.

'My sentiments exactly,' Luke agreed. 'Quotations are your speciality.'

'My stock in trade.'

'I've still got that hymn you wrote out for me.'

'Have you?' Stephanie turned to him again, her face a picture of surprise, eyebrows raised, lovely lips parted. ' "Make wars throughout the world to cease",' she said. 'Just for this one day I'd almost forgotten the war. Not entirely, of course, because there are so many uniforms around, but killing seems remote from this timeless place.'

The pedlars had surrounded a group of servicemen. Stephanie saw some postcards being passed from hand to hand and heard the shouts of raucous laughter.

'Feelthy pictures?' she enquired.

'I shouldn't be surprised.'

Her amused scrutiny attracted the notice of the soldiers. Stephanie saw the way their heads swivelled, the consultation between them, the way one perspiring man was pushed towards her, and guessed what was coming.

'Excuse me, miss, are you Stephanie Bartram?'

'Yes, I am.'

That appeared to be the end of the conversation as far as he was concerned, but once they were sure of her identity the other men crowded round.

'We saw your show last night – smashing!' one of them told her.

'I'm glad you liked it. Are you on leave?'

'Yeah, that's right. Only a couple o' days left.'

'I'm leaving Cairo myself tomorrow, going to Alexandria and

then visiting some of the units in the desert. You never know, I may see you again.'

'Can we have your autograph?'

'If you've got something for me to write on.'

She scribbled her name on half a dozen views of the pyramids, always with a personal message: 'All the best, Stan', 'Good luck, Ben', 'Best wishes, Joe', while Luke stood on the fringe of the little group.

Stephanie gave him a quick, shrewd look when she eventually got away.

'You didn't like it, did you?' she said.

'It's a pretty meaningless exercise. Still, it gave them pleasure and you did it very nicely.'

Stephanie said nothing in reply to that, but she felt jarred by his impatience.

As they drove back to Cairo the light was fading.

'Sunset over the Nile,' Luke remarked. 'One of the great cliches of travel, but it *is* beautiful. You'll have dinner with me?'

'Take me back to my hotel and give me half an hour for a wash and change. I feel sticky and sandy.'

They went to a restaurant in Sharia Qasr el Nil, not far from Stephanie's hotel. Something of their earlier constraint had descended on them again.

'Did I remember to thank you for a lovely day?' Stephanie asked towards the end of the meal. 'It was a real dream come true for me. I've always been fascinated by the idea of Egypt. I'd love to play Cleopatra.'

'Perhaps you will.'

'I doubt it. I don't think anyone is ever going to take me seriously as a classical actress.'

They fell silent again as the coffee arrived, dark and bitter in tiny cups.

'I wish this didn't have to end tonight,' Luke said abruptly.

'It does seem a pity when we've just got reacquainted,' Stephanie agreed.

She knew what was in his mind, just as she had known when they had had this same conversation in London, but this time she was armoured against him. No more men. She had held by

159

that decision ever since she had discovered Conrad's deception, and it was going to take more than a large American with a slow smile and a nice way of looking at her to make her change her mind.

They walked back to her hotel, slowly, as they had on their first evening together. In a patch of dark shadow Luke stopped and pulled Stephanie towards him. She went willingly enough and her lips parted under the insistent pressure of his mouth. He shifted his arms to hold her more closely and Stephanie fitted herself against him, admitting that it felt good even while she was deciding that it was going no further.

When Stephanie drew away she said, with an ironic intonation in her voice, reminding him of the decision they had taken only a few days earlier, 'Friends?'

'Mm, friends,' Luke agreed, although his body was telling him that what he wanted went a long way the other side of friendship.

He tried to stop her moving away, but Stephanie lifted his importunate hands, first one and then the other, and dropped them away from her.

'That's all there's going to be, Luke,' she said. 'We're going different ways tomorrow. We might never meet again. I'll be returning to England eventually and you ... who knows where you may be sent? Something you said sounded as if you'd be reluctant to spend the rest of the war in the Middle East.'

'I asked for a transfer to the Pacific and was turned down,' Luke admitted.

'There'll be other opportunities, other countries, other fights. In a few weeks' time we could be on opposite sides of the world. I can live with a mild feeling of regret at parting from you like this. I don't want any heartbreaks.'

He pulled her back into his arms and held her tightly against him. Stephanie stood passively for a moment and then she struggled to get free.

'I said no, and I meant it. Goodbye, Luke.'

Three

The one thing the 'Hello, Boys' concert party prayed for before every performance was a firm base on which their portable stage could be erected. To their surprise, the desert did not consist of sand dunes, but was mostly hard rock, the top two feet of which had been eroded into fine grit. The trick was to find a spot where the sand covered an area of level rock.

'All very well for the band to say it looks all right to them,' one of the dancers commented bitterly. 'They're sitting safely on the ground. By the time we'd finished last night there was a six inch dip to one side. I nearly landed up in the colonel's lap!'

'That would have been popular,' another girl remarked. 'What are you grumbling about? He was a bit of all right, that colonel.'

'Oh, well, it's a hospital today, so we should have a decent floor.'

Stephanie, who had been listening to this exchange, laughed at this remark.

'Wait until you see what sort of hospital it is!' she said.

As they travelled out into the desert the dancers looked round in disbelief.

'Is there really a hospital out here?' one of the girls asked.

'A hospital for sick tanks,' Stephanie told them. 'We're doing our stuff at a repair depot.'

It was a joke that had to be repeated to their audience. The men had probably heard it before, but they laughed and cheered. At least that day the concert party had plenty of experts on hand to see that the platform was stable.

It was like working in an oven. The portable stage had a canvas canopy and sides and although these provided welcome shade they also trapped the hot air underneath. The audience sat on the ground, eager brown faces turned towards the performers. The girls wore abbreviated kilts and matching

161

pantees in vivid blue sateen, with white tops and coloured bows in their hair. They began the show with a bright song and a tap dance. When they came off the perspiration was running down their faces.

The comedian was acting as compere, telling a few jokes every time he went on, achieving his effect more by timing and innuendo than by the originality of his material. He was apt to throw in an unpleasantly blue joke if he thought he could get away with it.

Stephanie kept an ear open for what he was saying and slapped him down after the show if she thought he had gone too far. Surprisingly, jokes with a strong sexual undertone were not popular. The men were all too aware of their deprivations. Neither was it tactful to make references to infidelity or to the foreign troops back home in England. Communications were poor, letters were slow in arriving, the imagination did not need a lot of stirring up to interpret a missed post as a more serious betrayal.

Stephanie was very well received. Most of the men had either seen her films or were at least familiar with her picture in the popular press, so that they felt as if they knew her. She had a sweet, nostalgic voice, not powerful but big enough for these conditions, and she stirred sentiments in the men so far from home. At her best she could hold her audience in total silence in even the most adverse conditions.

The trouble that day was that work on the broken down tanks and trucks was continuing in the background. They were to give two performances, both in the daytime because lights would attract the notice of the Luftwaffe, and the shift who were still working would be coming along for the second house, with only a short interval in between.

Stephanie wound up the first part of her performance by whipping off the bouffant skirt of her glamorous evening gown to reveal that the top was, in fact, a sequinned leotard which left her long legs completely bare. Amidst wolf whistles and cat calls she whirled into a lively dance, the girls came on to join her and they ended with high kicks and splits.

Stephanie and the girls hurried behind the canvas screen that had been put up for them. Stephanie stripped off her

162

costume, rubbed herself with a towel and struggled to pull her second evening gown up over her sweat-damp skin. It was a romantic, pale pink gown with a halter neck. Stephanie knew that by the end of the day it would be dark with perspiration and the hair she was combing out would be laid against her head in limp waves.

They had brought water with them. Between the two performances they were allowed a pint of water each with which to wash and freshen up.

'Once upon a time I lived in a house which had its own swimming pool,' Stephanie remarked to no one in particular.

'Sounds like the beginning of a fairy story,' one of the girls remarked. 'To think I used to grumble about washing in the kitchen sink at home!'

Their day did not end with the performance. Hospitality had been offered and had to be accepted. It was one of their duties, unstated but understood, to sit around and talk to any man who happened to be off duty. They were pathetically anxious to be reassured about conditions in England. Even the fact that any news the concert party had was already many weeks out of date made no difference.

'You sound like a Londoner,' one of the soldiers said diffidently to the girl who led the little dance troupe.

'Almost. I come from Croydon.'

'Not far from my home. I've lived in Sutton all my life.'

'Get away! My Aunt Meg, my Mum's sister, lives in Sutton. The times I've been to Sutton! She lives in Collingwood Road.'

'Well, I'll be … my house is in Crown Road.'

'Is that the road that runs down by the side of the gas works, the one with the pub on the corner?'

'That's right, and the school about halfway down. That's where I went to school, and a rotten scholar I was, too! I was football mad.'

'Did you used to play in the Collingwood Road recreation ground?'

'That's right! Cor, I can't get over it! Fancy you knowing the old rec!'

It meant nothing really. At one time in their lives they had both walked over the same suburban pavements. And yet

163

Stephanie saw that it had enormous importance for the soldier involved. His identity had been restored. He was not just a name and a number, an anonymous unit flung down in an empty desert; he was a man with a place of his own, a background which someone else recognized, a family who were still living in their familiar surroundings.

'They've had a few bombs,' he said in an offhand way.

'Last time I heard from Auntie Meg she said they were still fine,' the dancer told him. 'No real damage.'

She was a kind girl. Stephanie guessed that she had not had a letter from her aunt for months, but her quick improvisation had given one man the reassurance he desperately needed.

Stephanie liked the informality of these desert gatherings, the way the officers and men seemed to have struck a balance between discipline and cameraderie, the way the men crowded round, their lively curiosity, their friendliness and decency, the effort they made to subdue their language in front of the girls, their delight in talking to a woman – it was not a matter of crude sexual desire, but a much more subtle yearning for a feminine side of life which was totally absent from their present existence.

At one of their stops Stephanie had been struggling with a bolt on the tailboard of the truck which contained their costumes when a burly sergeant had come to her aid. The bolt which had been too stiff for her slid along easily under his strong fingers. As she had thanked him he took one of her hands in his and looked at it curiously. Stephanie stood, amused and patient, until he suddenly realized what he was doing and hurriedly let go of her hand.

'Sorry, miss,' he apologized. 'I'd forgotten how small women's hands are. You're different ... quite different from us.'

'As the French say, long live the difference,' Stephanie said gravely.

'Too right!' he agreed fervently, with an expression he had picked up from the Australians.

That visit to the repair unit was a far cry from their next call, when Stephanie was entertained in the officers' mess of a famous regiment. She was escorted back to her quarters by two

164

cheerful young lieutenants.

'On our own we're not to be trusted,' one of them informed her. 'But I'll keep an eye on old Bertie ...'

'And Bertie will keep an eye on you, old son,' the other lieutenant promised.

Stephanie gave them both a quick, competent kiss and sent them off into the night loudly protesting that they were '*slain with love, Stephanie, darling.*'

'I'm slain, too,' Stephanie muttered to the girl in the camp bed next to hers. 'My feet are killing me!'

They were back in Cairo the next day, a long, wearisome, boneshaking journey. It came as no great surprise to find that no one had any clear idea of what was to happen next.

The war news could hardly have been worse. Singapore had fallen to the Japanese and then Rangoon. The Russians had re-occupied some of the territory wrested from them by the Germans, but there were signs that Hitler planned a spring offensive which would renew the intense fighting.

In the desert all the hard-won autumn advance had been eroded and the Germans held the line at Gazala. Both sides were racing to build up reinforcements and the Germans and Italians, who could ship new guns, tanks and ammunition into North Africa within a month of their manufacture, had the advantage over the British, who needed three months or more to bring up the equivalent supplies, and longer if the equipment was shipped from America.

In the circumstances, it was a battle to keep up morale and Stephanie raged when her little troupe sat around in disconsolate idleness.

'If I hadn't thought I was going to be fully occupied I would never have come,' she said, goaded into exasperation by the ineffectual ditherings of the organizing officer.

'The Opera House is occupied this week and anyway you've already given your show there once,' he pointed out.

'Surely you must have requests for entertainment?'

'Plenty of those,' he admitted. 'The trouble is, you've got girls in your party.'

'You say that as if they were some strange species never seen in these parts before.'

'We're not allowed to send girls beyond the Canal Zone,' he explained.

'I never heard such nonsense! We'd be as safe in the desert as in Cairo – safer probably!'

'Enemy action ...'

'A few months ago I was driving an ambulance through the London Blitz! Why weren't we told about this restriction before?'

'I should have thought your own commonsense would tell you that you wouldn't be welcome in a battle area,' he retorted.

'I'm not suggesting we should go anywhere where we would be a nuisance. Of course I understand that wouldn't be fair. But just at the moment when there's a lull in the fighting, when there must be men out there crazy with boredom, I do think that a few hours' entertainment would be of real benefit to them.'

She fought doggedly to get her way, even when the comedian of the party remarked acidly, 'I suppose it hasn't occurred to you, Stephanie dear, that not all of us want to make martyrs of ourselves?'

'You need not come if you're afraid,' Stephanie said shortly.

'It's not that I'm *afraid*, but I don't think it's *wise* to go against the advice we've been given.'

In the end she got her way. They would not be allowed anywhere near the ill-defined front line, but they were to do a short tour further west than they had ever ventured before.

'Stephanie, the sun must have got to your brain,' one of the dancers complained as they jolted over the pebble-strewn waste. 'Look at it! Not a soul in sight, just us and a cloud of dust.'

They had difficulty in tracking down their first contact and were an hour late arriving.

'Nearly gave you up,' the major in charge of the unit said. 'Jolly good of you to come all this way. Can we get cracking straight away? The men are waiting.'

'Give us a chance to get changed,' Stephanie said.

They had to use the inside of the truck as a changing room. It was hot and crowded and tempers were frayed, but the enthusiastic response of the men who had been waiting for them all day more than made up for their discomfort.

'We're sleeping on the road and doing a couple of anti-aircraft positions tomorrow,' Stephanie told the major.

'Jolly good! I expect they'll have sent out word and gathered in a few extra people. I say, do you know all the film stars?'

'Quite a lot,' Stephanie admitted. 'Are you a film fan?'

'Used to be! Not much chance out here!'

He had been right about the extra men who had gathered to watch the show the next day. It was difficult to get away to fulfil their second engagement. They drove through the heat of the day and arrived in the late afternoon when it should have been marginally cooler, but to Stephanie the air still seemed like a breath out of hell. She had not merely volunteered to do this, she reminded herself, she had begged and pleaded to be allowed to come to this devil's hole.

'Good job you're doing the show today,' the officer in charge said with a knowing glance at the sky. 'I don't like the feel of the weather. Shouldn't be surprised if we weren't in for a khamsin. Have you been in the desert when the khamsin is blowing? The worst wind in the world. Frankly, if it's blowing hard in the morning I'll have to order you to stay put. I can't take the responsibility of letting you drive off in the sort of visibility we get when the sand is in the air.'

With the thought of a possible sandstorm in her head Stephanie took no notice of the fact that the guns remained manned all the time they were going through their routine. She was in her green sequinned leotard, concluding the first half hour, when there was a sudden warning.

'Enemy aircraft approaching, take cover!'

There had been alarms before and the cast had practised their drill of cowering in the sand until the danger had passed, but whereas before the enemy aeroplanes had either been a vague hum in the distance or had been seen off by the RAF, this time three Stukas came hurtling down out of the sky, machine guns rattling, while the guns on the ground went into ear splitting action.

Stephanie, crouching in a slit trench with two other girls, put her head down on her knees. There was no room for the three of them to lie down, but she noticed that they were all making themselves as small as possible. In between the gunfire she heard a great whoop of delight go up. She raised her head to see what was happening and something small, red hot and sharp whizzed past her cheek and bit into her bare shoulder.

Silence fell. Somewhere in the distance there was a dull explosion. The noise of aircraft engines had faded.

'I think it's all clear,' the gunnery officer said. 'Great show! You brought us luck. We got one of the blighters.'

'One of the blighters got *me*,' Stephanie said faintly.

She took her hand away from her shoulder. A fragment of shell, thin, sharp and hot, had buried itself in the flesh just below her shoulder bone. When she stopped pressing the wound with her fingers the bright blood spurted out of it.

'We'll have to get you to a doctor,' the officer exclaimed in distress.

'I don't think it's terribly bad, though it's bleeding such a lot,' Stephanie said. 'We've got a first-aid kit with us and I've seen enough air raid injuries to know what to do.'

Her wound was cleaned and a big sterile dressing put over it. Apart from feeling slightly dizzy Stephanie insisted that she was in no need of further treatment for the time being.

'You'll feel it tonight,' she was told. 'Better have a couple of pills and go and see a proper doctor as soon as you get back to civilization.'

'I will,' she promised. 'Shall we carry on now?'

'You're going to do the rest of the show?'

'Of course.'

The other members of the cast had been shaken, as much by Stephanie's injury as by the air raid itself, but as soon as they realized that Stephanie was taking it for granted that they would carry on they rallied and trooped back to the stage. The girls' voices wavered at first, but the applause they got from the men put fresh heart into them.

Stephanie struggled into her pink evening gown. There was no disguising the unsightly dressing on her arm, so she left it exposed. When she went back on stage she said to the small, eager audience, 'Well, boys, as you can see, I've put up my first stripe.'

They stood up and cheered her. It was the most heartwarming thing that had ever happened to her. She smiled shakily and signalled to the band to start playing. If she stayed up there without performing she was either going to fall down or burst into tears.

They camped within sight of the anti-aircraft unit that night and were woken before day had fairly broken by an anxious officer.

'Start now and keep driving east,' he said. 'The khamsin is certainly coming, but if you set out immediately without stopping for breakfast or anything, and keep going steadily, you should avoid the worst of it. Your drivers are experienced; they'll know when it's not safe to continue.'

When the sun came up it illuminated an eerily changed landscape. The vast distances on which mirages had danced and beckoned had disappeared. To the west there was no horizon, just a yellow haze which shivered and changed colour as the light intensified. To the east, the way they were travelling, the air was clearer, but by the time they had been driving for an hour the fringe of the sandstorm had caught up with them.

They sat huddled in the backs of the lorries with the flaps down, but the wind lifted the canvas and drove the fine, stinging sand into every crevice. Stephanie, her arm throbbing painfully and with an uneasy feeling that she was running a temperature, tied the long white chiffon scarf which had once charmed Luke right over her head, shrouding her face like an Arab woman. Most of the others followed her example with anything they could lay their hands on. The wind shrieked round them with a strange low whistling noise, infinitely melancholy. They could hear the constant thud and patter of small pebbles flung against the sides of the trucks.

Stephanie ran her tongue over her sore lips and drew it back in disgust as she realized that the fine dust had penetrated her gauzy covering and coated her face. She tried to wipe it away from her mouth and made her discomfort worse because her hands were also covered in sand and sweat. There was nothing to do but sit and endure it in misery.

From the back of the truck a small, defiant voice began to sing, 'I didn't want to join the army, I didn't want to go to war ...'

There was a muffled laugh, two more voices joined in and a croaking chorus filled the small hot place in which they were enclosed. Stephanie was past singing. She put her head down on her bent knees, tears stinging the back of her eyes. They were such dears. Cheerful and resilient in conditions which would try the hardiest spirit. At that moment she loved them.

When they finally reached Cairo they looked at the wide, slow river and the jacaranda trees in bloom with dazed, disbelieving eyes.

'A different world,' the tenor murmured. 'I'll never play a seaside town again, not if it's got a sandy beach.'

They climbed down from the lorries, stiff and exhausted. Stephanie looked at the long drop, from which she usually swung down in one lithe movement, and said apologetically, 'I'm afraid I'll need some help.'

They were all overcome with concern when they realized that she could scarcely stand without support. Stephanie wished they would stop hanging around and chattering and let her get inside. All she needed was a nice cool room where she could lie down, then she would soon be all right.

She managed to get rid of all her anxious well-wishers except two of the dancers who helped her upstairs. After a thin palliasse in the back of a lorry, the bed looked infinitely inviting. The girls helped her to undress and bathed her face. They twittered, just like birds, Stephanie thought, giving herself up to their inexpert ministrations with resignation. She had just managed to get them to go away and leave her alone with the shutters closed to make a pleasant gloom when the doctor arrived, summoned by the other members of the company.

'You've got yourself a nasty little flesh wound, but it won't kill you,' he said with misplaced heartiness after he had examined Stephanie's arm. 'It's inflamed, but I don't think there's any serious infection. Of course, we have to keep an eye on these things in this part of the world. You're suffering from shock, fatigue, loss of blood, dehydration and a raised temperature.'

'I could have told you that,' Stephanie said. 'How soon will I be fit again?'

'A couple of days in bed should do the trick. Though, as I say, the arm must be dressed every day and a close watch kept on it.'

'Will I have a scar – a permanent one, I mean?'

'Possibly. Nothing to worry about, nothing unsightly.'

'It'll be a nuisance in front of a film camera,' Stephanie said.

'Can't make omelettes without breaking eggs. You chose to go into the desert, I'm told. Can't complain now about a little war wound.'

'Your bedside manner leaves a lot to be desired,' Stephanie told him.

He laughed as he scribbled on his prescription pad.

'I didn't get much chance to work on it before the army snapped me up. I'll have to polish my manners before I go back to Harley Street. I'll see you get something to make you sleep tonight ...'

'You must be joking! I could sleep for a week!'

'You may find it more difficult when you lie down and close your eyes. I know a nurse who works privately and I'll get her to come in tomorrow and change your dressing. Unless she calls me I won't see you again.'

'Were you really in Harley Street?' Stephanie asked curiously.

'No, but I had ambitions that way. Believe it or not, I intended to specialize in gynaecology.' He looked at her wistfully. 'I suppose you haven't any complaints in that direction?'

'Certainly not! Go away and leave me and my womb in peace. I may as well tell you that I intend starting work again no later than Friday.'

'You'll regret it if you try to do too much too soon.'

Stephanie passed an uneasy night, in spite of the pills the doctor had prescribed for her, but she did feel better the next day, until her room was invaded by as many of the concert party as could crowd into it.

'Bolt from the blue, darling!' the tenor cried. 'ENSA want us to go to Palestine!'

'At a moment's notice, Steph, would you believe,' the bandleader said crossly.

'I'd believe anything of our organizers,' Stephanie said, struggling to sit up. 'When you say at a moment's notice, what do you actually mean?'

'This afternoon! Well, I'm not going, for one,' the comedian said. 'I'm going back to England as soon as I can get out of this hellhole.'

'This afternoon?' Stephanie repeated incredulously. 'But why? We've still got commitments here.'

They all tried to tell her at once. A second concert party was due to arrive in Cairo, and since they would be new faces and new acts it was not unreasonable to suggest passing the first arrivals on to another venue.

'Except that nothing was ever said about going to Palestine,' one of the dancers grumbled.

'They must have known the fresh party was due to arrive,' Stephanie said, still not properly understanding.

'Only got news of it while we were away this week,' the bandleader said. 'Typical! Absolutely typical!'

'Are we being given any choice?' Stephanie asked.

'If we stay together we can be assured of an eventual passage home,' one of the girls said.

'No one has actually said that anyone who doesn't choose to go may spend the rest of the war hanging around Cairo with no work, but that's what I read into the way it was put to us,' another one said. 'The Palestine engagement is only for a couple of months. I'm quite keen to go.'

'Not me. I'm going back to England,' the comedian repeated obstinately.

'One man might get an air passage – possibly. Four girls and a band haven't a hope.'

'OK, next stop Jerusalem,' Stephanie said. 'I'd better get up.'

'You'll come with us? Oh, good!'

Stephanie was surprised by their pleasure, but once she was on her feet she did wish that she had had another twenty-four hours before being forced to set out on an arduous journey. After one glance at her pale face she reached for her stage make up and applied it liberally. It seemed to have little effect on the ENSA organizer.

'Sorry, Stephanie,' he said. 'You're only allowed on this trip if you can produce a doctor's certificate saying you're fit.'

'For goodness sake! I collected a trivial little scratch and ran a slight temperature. I'm as fit as a fiddle.'

She might have spared her breath, he was immoveable. With one desperate eye on the clock, Stephanie flung her belongings into a suitcase, sat on it to close it and set out to find the doctor who had visited her. By the time she had tracked him down she was hardly looking her best. Perspiration had trickled down the heavy make up she had applied to her face and yet she felt strangely chilly.

'You have a temperature of 100.4 and your wound is suppurating,' he said. 'Can you afford to pay for a private clinic? Because I think you should book yourself in for a week's rest and medical care.'

She felt so weak and despondent that tears began to run down her face, adding to the havoc on her foundation.

'I'm going to Palestine with my friends,' she said.

'Not with my blessing you're not. I agree you're not desperately ill — otherwise I'd find a corner in a hospital for you, though God knows where — but you're in no fit state to go on a long journey. Now be a dear sensible girl and do as I advise.'

She cried steadily all the afternoon as the disconsolate party trooped in to say goodbye to her, but once they had disappeared, Stephanie dried her eyes and let herself be taken off to a small, quiet, fearsomely expensive clinic where she had a room to herself, a high, soft bed, clean linen and all the luxuries she had almost forgotten existed.

Just as well her earnings from *Wings of Courage* had been high, she thought sourly as she drifted off to sleep, but this was not the way she had intended spending the money.

All the same, it was worth being in Cairo when the mail from home reached her there. Stephanie lay back against her plump, cool pillows and caught up with the news. Not that it was very up to date, since the letters had taken the same roundabout route she had had to follow herself. Still, they were a voice from England and the fact that they were so welcome brought home to her once again the deprivation the soldiers suffered when they did not receive their mail.

She skimmed through a letter from her mother. It consisted mainly of repeats of the favourable reviews of *Wings* coupled with complaints about Stephanie's shortsightedness in going away when she had just become a celebrity. Stephanie tossed it to one side and picked up a letter from Nesta which contained more dramatic news.

I've been called up. I'm going into the women's army, the Auxiliary Territorial Service. God knows what the ATS will find me useful for, but I can tell you one thing, if there's anything going in the entertainment line I'm putting myself forward as a topnotch experienced actress!
It's a great pity my call up has come just at this time because Conrad is not at all well. I don't have to tell you about me and Conrad, do I? You must have guessed. I don't suppose we'll ever get married, but I'm nuts about the man and always have been. I've been worried about him for a long time, but he's not a man you can fuss over. Anyway, it turns out that he's got a duodenal ulcer. Ironic, really, because I gather the army has been getting rid of some of its unsuitable soldiers from the acting profession with that excuse, but Conrad's ulcer is all too real and has been causing him agony, poor darling. I don't know what's going to happen when I'm not around to bully him into sticking to his diet – incredibly difficult in wartime, as you can guess. I don't trust that man of his. In fact, I don't like Anton at all.

You and me both, Nesta, Stephanie thought, remembering that it had been Anton's malicious gossip which had told her that she was Conrad's number two mistress.
Obviously Nesta still had no idea that she had ever had a rival in Stephanie. More than ever Stephanie was thankful that she had clung on to her pride and refrained from letting either Conrad or Nesta know how badly hurt she had been. She returned to the letter:

I almost wish I'd persuaded Conrad to come to Egypt with you. Though I went down on my knees and prayed he

174

wouldn't when I first heard you were leaving England. Selfish of me when I think how much good the sunshine and better food would have done him.

Stephanie, her arm throbbing, her head swimming, looked round the narrow, expensive room in which she lay, with the fierce bars of light lying on the floor from the half-shuttered window, and choked with silent laughter. Obviously Nesta thought that this was some sort of rest cure.

She found that she could think about Conrad quite dispassionately now. Poor Conrad, with his double anxieties as his two countries fought one another. That was what was tearing him apart and it would take more than fresh oranges and a glaring sun to put him right. Strange that she should have had news of his family from Luke so recently. Should she mention it when she wrote home or would it be better to keep it to herself?

Stephanie leaned back to think about it, closed her eyes and fell into a light doze.

Four

'You'd think, having been taken prisoner in one withdrawal, I might have had the luck to avoid a second retreat,' Luke grumbled to Jock Gulliver.

'Stop grousing. While you were enjoying a Mediterranean cruise the rest of us were chasing backwards and forwards like bloody yo-yos.'

'Some cruise! You should have been on that ship! Did I tell you ...'

The other three reporters answered with one voice, 'Yes!'

Luke subsided with a grin. It was good to be back with the old crowd. Without Ed, though, poor devil. They had made a bivouac for themselves and were crouched under it enjoying, if that was what it could be called, the luxury of bully beef stew and tinned fruit. A despatch rider had raced up to them only a few minutes earlier and taken away their stories for censoring and transmission to their newspapers. They were at leisure, except that they were all on edge, waiting for the anticipated orders to pull out once again.

The next move would take them back over the Egyptian border. Yet again Rommel had succeeded in turning the Allied advance into a rout. Individually the mixed nationalities which formed the British, French and Commonwealth army had fought magnificently; collectively they had failed to hold the Afrika Korps at bay. It was the same old story: the Germans had superior firing power and as they were forced back towards their base their supply position improved, while the British ability to bring up men, machines, ammunition, food and water diminished.

'We'll be sleeping in Cairo tomorrow night,' Jock prophesied, but although the prospect of a bath, a bed and clean sheets was enticing he sounded gloomy.

'Is your girl friend still in town?' Red Graham asked Luke.

'I didn't know I'd got a girl friend,' Luke answered.

'Oh, come on! In between getting back from his holiday in Portugal and rejoining our little circle our courageous reporter was seen escorting the lovely Stephanie Bartram – and not for the first time either.'

'She's probably got herself shipped out,' Jock said idly before Luke could reply. 'She's joined the ranks of the brave, too, didn't you know? Got herself wounded.'

Up to that moment Luke had preserved an air of cool, amused detachment, but Jock's remark took him by surprise and he said sharply, 'Wounded? I didn't know that. Was it serious?'

'The story I heard was that lovely Stephanie Bartram had got a piece of shrapnel in the shoulder,' Jock said. 'Doesn't sound particularly lethal.'

'How did it happen?'

'Shot up by a Stuka while performing in a forward position. Like I said ... one of the intrepid.'

'They shouldn't allow those girls to run themselves into danger,' Luke said.

He caught the meaningful wink Jock gave Red and subsided. He was letting himself show too much interest. They would only pull his leg about it. He shrugged it away and managed to turn the talk to something else, but after they had bedded down for the night the thought of Stephanie, wounded and in pain, came back to haunt him.

All the next day as they joined the rush back across the frontier he was conscious of anxiety at the back of his mind. At first he could not understand why it was a familiar sensation, then he recognized it. It was the same feeling as he had known when Prue had first told him she was pregnant. He had been pleased, of course, mainly because of her delight, but he had carried around with him, especially when they were parted, a constant worry in case something should go wrong. And now he felt the same anxiety for Stephanie – the same loving anxiety. He wanted to see her, to touch her, to make sure that she was all right. It was maddening to have such scanty news of something that touched him so closely.

When he saw her again he would tell her ... what would he

tell her? That he loved her. He tested the idea in his mind and found that it was true. This was not the hungry desire she had aroused in him in London, this was something that had got into his bones, his very marrow.

God knows how they would work it out in wartime, but somehow he had got to be in a position to get reliable news of her, to know that she was safe, if possible to have a chance of looking after her. He thought of the girl who had driven an ambulance through the hell of the London Blitz, the girl who had apparently insisted on running herself into danger to give pleasure to the desert army, and admitted ruefully that Stephanie might not take kindly to the idea of being protected.

She was hurt. The lousy Jerries had wounded the smooth golden flesh of his woman. Thinking about the politeness he had used on his captors, Luke was filled with vindictive rage. If he could have got his hands on Ernst von Lynden he would have throttled him. She *was* his woman, he had no doubt about that now. Somehow he had got to find her and tell her.

'Smoke over the British embassy,' Jock remarked as they drove into Cairo. 'That looks ominous. They must be burning their papers.'

There was no difficulty about finding a hotel room in Cairo at the end of June 1942. There was a sense of panic in the air. Women were being sent out of the capital. Stephanie might already have left. When he called at her hotel Luke could get no news of her. By greasing a few palms he managed to gather that Stephanie had been 'much sick, in hospital', but there was a marked vagueness about which hospital.

Luke went round to the ENSA office in the Sharia Kasr el Nil. There, too, there was a mood of quiet desperation which made it difficult to get hold of anyone who was prepared to talk to him.

'The "Hello, Boys" concert party? Oh, they went to Palestine,' he was told eventually.

Palestine! Well, at least she should be safe, but it was a bitter disappointment.

'All of them?' he asked.

'Except for the comedian chappie, who got himself back to England and, of course, Stephanie Bartram.'

179

'What happened to her?'

'She got a scratch on the shoulder and disappeared into a private clinic. Coming the leading lady, if you ask me.'

Luke bit back the indignant words that came to his lips.

'Can you give me the name of the clinic?' he asked patiently.

'Not right at this moment. Look, we're surrounded by all sorts of problems. Come back tomorrow.'

Another man standing by was more helpful.

'Didn't Stephanie Bartram volunteer to go on tour to Paiforce?'

'Oh, Lord, of course she did! You see what a state I'm in. It had quite slipped my mind. We might even have a copy of her itinerary somewhere, but not at this moment, dear chap, please.'

'An address?' Luke asked hopelessly.

'By the time the letter reached it she'd probably be in England.'

'Yes, of course.'

He had missed her. While he had been in the desert Stephanie had recovered from her wound – and he still did not know how serious it had been – and taken off for somewhere else. She must be all right or she would not have volunteered for the rigours of a visit to the units based in Persia and Iraq.

It niggled Luke that he was unable to imagine her whereabouts. She might be in Baghdad, Basra or Bahrain. Wherever she was two things were certain: the heat would be fearsome and she would get a tremendous welcome. Luke had heard some of the grouses about Paiforce being a forgotten army, out of the action, out of the limelight, but still enduring hardship and, above all, boredom. Stephanie, with her lovely warmth, her generous response to anyone needing sympathy, would become the idol of the men she visited. Lucky devils.

As the ENSA official had said, any letter addressed to her in that part of the world might chase around several places before catching up with her, if it ever did. He had her London address: he could write to her there.

Luke put a sheet of paper into his typewriter and sat looking at it helplessly, more at a loss for words than he had ever been in his life before. In the end he wrote that he had heard she had

180

been hurt and hoped that she had recovered. He said a little about his latest dash across the desert, but that had to be kept to a minimum because the letter would be censored. It all sounded very stilted, like a schoolboy essay, not at all the sort of thing he really wanted to write. After reading it through he added, not very hopefully, 'If you want to write to me a letter c/o my London bureau would always reach me.'

On an impulse he turned back to the beginning of the letter and numbered it 'Letter Number 1'. That would tell her that he meant to write again. Somehow he had to keep in touch with her. He took the letter out of the typewriter and then, before signing it, added in the rapid difficult scrawl of a man who always used a machine for writing, 'I have discovered that you are very precious to me. Look after yourself.'

'What I need is a piano and an accompanist,' Stephanie said patiently. 'Yes, I know it would have been better to bring someone with me, but I left Cairo at very short notice after my own concert party had gone to augment another one in Palestine. I know you've been kept desperately short of entertainment ...'

'Indeed we have,' the Paiforce Welfare Officer agreed.

'So I thought it might help if *someone* came, even if it's only me.'

'It was good of you to volunteer,' the officer said, but he sounded doubtful about it. 'As you say, anyone is welcome.'

'So what about my music?' Stephanie asked briskly. 'You must have someone who can play the piano, even if he – or she – is an amateur?'

'We have been running a few army concert parties,' he admitted. 'I dare say someone could be detached from duty to go on tour with you.'

'Splendid! I'll need forty-eight hours to get the act together, then we'll set out.'

'As soon as that?'

'Certainly. I'm only here for one month. After that I've got to return to England. I'm determined not to waste time hanging about doing nothing.'

181

She was puzzled by the look of derision on his face as he repeated, 'A month?'

'I know it's not long enough,' Stephanie said. 'But I honestly don't think I can manage to go on giving one-woman shows for longer than that. It requires a lot of stamina, you know.'

He seemed to struggle with himself and then burst out, 'To tell the truth, I doubt whether you'll stick it for longer than a week.'

'Oh, won't I! Stickability is my second name!'

Her accompanist arrived that afternoon, a diffident corporal with a heavy handed but accurate touch on the keyboard.

'Do you mind doing this tour with me?' Stephanie asked.

'Orders is orders,' he said. 'Besides, anything's better than sitting around doing nothing.'

He twisted his cap nervously between his hands and said, 'Miss ... ma'am ... I've got a pal who's a conjuror. I mean, he does it properly. His Dad's in the profession and Larry was going in with him before he got called up. The thing is, he's a driver. If we could get him to drive our lorry ...'

'We'd have the makings of a good little show. Wonderful idea! When can I see him?'

'He's off duty this evening.'

Private Larry Okehampton and Stephanie took one look at one another and each recognized in the other a fellow professional. He was a stocky little Geordie with wonderfully dextrous hands.

'When I saw how little amusement there was for us out here I sent for my gear,' he explained to Stephanie. 'It's taken all this time to reach me, so my act hasn't been seen before. I did what I could with anything that came to hand – the chaps know I can juggle and so on – but you can't do illusions without the props.'

'You've kept in practice?'

'I try to do at least an hour a day.'

They smiled at one another, both understanding the dedication needed to keep up the standards they set themselves in their different ways.

'I've been racking my brains for a way to introduce a bit of variety into the act,' Stephanie said with satisfaction. 'I'm going to do a few songs, a dramatic reading – while I was in hospital recently I worked up a couple of scenes from Dickens which ought to go down well – perhaps a dance if conditions allow ...'

'You'll be performing on the back of a lorry most of the time and the heat is fearsome.'

'So I've noticed! I'll try it out and see how it works. With your act and perhaps a sing-song at the end I reckon we ought to have an hour's show.'

'Would you be prepared to act as my assistant?' Larry Okehampton asked.

'Rather! You'll have to rehearse me.'

'Of course, that's assuming you can get permission for me to join you,' he said.

'Leave it to me,' Stephanie said.

By the end of the week they had already given the show four times in Baghdad and were out on the road.

'I'd feel happier if you had another woman with you,' the Welfare Officer said.

'Don't be silly,' Stephanie said. 'My two boys are the best watchdogs I could have.'

For the first time a gleam of humour lit up his face.

'Lieutenant Bartram, you're not supposed to tell a senior officer not to be silly,' he said.

'Oh, well, you know I'm not properly speaking in the army,' Stephanie excused herself. 'By the way, I've stuck out the first week. Do you believe now that I'll stay my full month?'

'I'm beginning to believe you might,' he admitted. 'But wait until you discover the conditions you'll be experiencing outside the city!'

At the end of their first gruelling day Stephanie caught her two companions watching her anxiously.

'Did you say you'd been in hospital recently,' Corporal Tidy asked, trying to sound casual.

'It was nothing. I got a bit of shrapnel in my arm.'

They looked at her with a solemn respect she found touching.

'You've seen more action than we have,' Larry Okehampton remarked. 'We was just thinking you looked a bit tired.'

183

'Four shows in one day and a total drive of two hundred miles – I'm entitled to look tired!' Stephanie protested. 'Where's this gunsite where we're supposed to be spending the night?'

'Another fifty miles and, of course, they'll be expecting some sort of show when we arrive.'

'Naturally. It's hard on you, Larry, doing all the driving and then having to get your hands supple enough to do conjuring tricks.'

'I can cope.'

They all learned to manage, working out ways of dealing with the debilitating effect of the heat as they went along. Stephanie stood by in her green leotard ready to hand Larry a damp cloth so that his fingers would not slip on the coloured balls, which disappeared and reappeared as if he were truly performing magic. Joe Tidy thumped vigorously on the piano when Stephanie signalled that she was hoarse and would have to rest her voice. The two men watched over Stephanie with an anxious care that moved her almost to tears. As for the places they visited, they ranged from an air force base at Habbaniyah to tiny oil pumping stations identified by nothing more than a map reference and guarded by a few soldiers.

Back in Baghdad Stephanie found that she was being treated with considerably more respect than she had received when she had first arrived.

'I've got to hand it to you,' the army Welfare Officer said. 'You said you'd stick it out and you did. We're grateful to you.'

'I'll spread the word around when I get home,' Stephanie said. 'With a bit of urging I'm sure other entertainers will pay you a visit.'

'Noel Coward has promised the same thing. I believe one of the people he's talking to is Joyce Grenfell.'

'She'd be marvellous! You wouldn't need a team to back her up because she can create a whole village with those monologues of hers. A lovely performer and a thoroughly nice person, too.'

Her parting from Joe Tidy and Larry Okehampton was as nearly emotional as those two stolid men would allow.

'First time I've ever been kissed by a lieutenant,' Corporal

184

Tidy said, his face brick red.

'What's going to happen to you now, Larry?' Stephanie asked her other helper. 'Will you go on entertaining?'

'Seems I've got a new posting. Weird – I can't understand it. I'm off to Cairo and they particularly asked for me because I was about to become a member of the Magic Circle before I was called up. Do you think they want me to teach them about camouflage?'

'Sounds like a waste of your talent,' Stephanie said in disgust.

'It's a bit hush-hush – shouldn't have told you, really,' he warned her. 'Better not say anything to Dad, if you do manage to see him when you get home.'

'I certainly mean to see him, and Joe's family, too.'

'Tell my Mum all those piano lessons weren't wasted after all,' Joe said. 'She always had me down for a concert pianist, but I was too hamfisted for that.'

England looked small, crowded and shabby, but the air was sweet. Dampness, Stephanie thought, looking up fondly at the pale sky where a weak sun peeped out reluctantly between the clouds. A lovely wet English summer. I'll never, never grumble about our climate again.

She had to endure a press interview at the airport. Her agent had arranged that, urged on, Stephanie guessed, by her mother. Stephanie parried the questions with a skill that was second nature to her. She had had a wonderful time entertaining 'our boys', conditions had been hard at times, the heat had been trying; yes, it was true that she had been wounded, but it was only a scratch; morale among the troops was high – and would be higher if more stars could be persuaded to visit the out-of-the-way spots; yes, she had heard criticisms of ENSA policy, but she would suggest that the critics went out and tried to do better themselves, given the difficult terrain and lack of amenities. Future plans? That was something she would be discussing after she had had a short rest.

She perched on the edge of a desk, her skirt obligingly raised, her cap worn at a jaunty angle, smiled into half a dozen cameras and then called a halt.

'That's enough, boys,' she said. 'Have a heart. I'm dead on my feet. All I want is a bath and a bed.'

'Willing to join you in either of them,' a voice from the back of the group offered.

It got a laugh and Stephanie managed to keep smiling, but at the back of her mind was the thought that they wouldn't have spoken like that to an actress they took seriously.

There was a car waiting for her, a car with cushioned seats and inflated tyres which ran smoothly along a macadamed road.

'I was expecting to slip back quietly without any fuss,' she said, leaning back against the blissful comfort.

'Not with me to look after your interests,' Vera said.

Stephanie slipped her hand into her mother's and clasped it tightly. 'It's good to be home,' she said.

'I hope you think so when you've had time to settle down! Things haven't got any easier while you've been away, you know. One thing I have got, thank goodness, and that's a supply of face cream. I started hoarding it as soon as you wrote about being out in all that sun. I knew you'd come back with a complexion like an old boot and I see I was right.'

'I'll start using it tonight,' Stephanie promised.

Her agent was riding in front. He twisted round to say, 'I've got one or two projects lined up for you, Stephanie. Perhaps another film.'

'I can't settle anything until I've reported to ENSA,' Stephanie said.

'You'll not go abroad again,' her mother stated. 'You've done your bit.'

'Probably not,' Stephanie said, which was a reply that committed her to nothing.

Stephanie called at Drury Lane and reported back on her experiences overseas. For once Basil Dean seemed disposed to be pleased with the efforts of one of his ENSA artistes, although he deprecated the way the 'Hello, Boys' concert party had been split up.

'It wasn't my doing,' Stephanie pointed out. 'If I'd been considered fit to travel I would have gone to Palestine with the rest of the company. Are they home yet?'

'They're on their way. Will you be available to join up with them when they arrive back in England?'

'No. I'm not doing any more variety. I'll go on working for ENSA, of course, but I want to join the drama group.'

There was a little grumbling about 'chopping and changing', but it had to be acknowledged that Stephanie was really known as an actress and when she left Drury Lane she had secured a promise that her next assignment would be a straight play.

'I know that will please you,' she said to Vera when she got home.

'If it means you taking your proper place on the stage again it must be a good move, though you know I think you'd do better in films. There's some letters for you, by the way. You were too tired to look at them last night and I forgot to give them to you this morning.'

One of the envelopes was from Cairo and it was marked 'Letter Number 1'. It was from Luke. So he had taken to heart her rebuke because he had not written when they had been parted before. Stephanie was amused and surprised. She had not expected to hear from him. After all, there was less between them now than there had been when he left London.

It was an odd letter, written in a way that seemed strangely stilted, considering he was a man who used words for a living. And then she came to the final message – 'I have discovered that you are very precious to me'. That one badly written sentence was worth all the rest of the letter put together. That was why he had written; that was the message he wanted to convey. Since he had taken the trouble to number his letter he meant to go on writing to her. She would reply, certainly she would reply, but if he was looking for any closer involvement between them, that would have to wait until they could meet again.

187

THIRD ACT

One

'I feel as if I've been away for years and completely lost touch with everything that's going on,' Stephanie said. 'Conrad, that was an absolutely delicious meal. How do you manage it?'

'Kind friends who live in the country and, of course, Anton contrives.'

'He's still with you?'

'Of course. Why not?'

'He's a funny character,' Stephanie said.

They had been brought together again by a well meaning producer who thought they should team up once more. Stephanie had accepted Conrad's invitation to dinner with an outward smile and inward reservations, but having got over the first hurdle she was surprised to discover how little it mattered that they had once been lovers and he had, as she saw it, betrayed her.

'I was sorry to hear that you'd been ill,' she said.

'A tiresome complaint, but I'm keeping it at bay,' Conrad said, as if it were something of no great importance.

He was thinner and to Stephanie it seemed that his face was more drawn than it had been, but he still had his fluid grace of movement, his startling eyes, the flexible long-fingered hands which had once given her such delight.

After they had eaten and were sitting together in front of the wood fire which Stephanie found welcome, Conrad slipped his arm carelessly round her shoulders and Stephanie's muscles tightened at his touch.

She bent forward to put her coffee cup down on the table in front of them and then she took Conrad's arm and moved it away from the back of the couch on which they were sitting.

'No, Conrad,' she said. 'Nothing like that.'

'What a pity,' he said lightly. 'You're looking more beautiful than ever, Stephanie darling. That rich golden sun tan suits you. Did you find a new man to love among the desert rats?'

'I made some good friends, but I was in no mood for lovers. We may as well have it out in the open, especially if we're going to work together again, and then perhaps you'll stop trying to use your damned charm on me. I never said anything, but before I went away I found out about you and Nesta. I was upset and fairly disgusted. I could never trust you in the same way again.'

'I see. I thought you cooled off rather rapidly considering ...'

'That I'd been flinging myself at you,' Stephanie said bitterly.

'We spent some memorable nights together. I refuse to pretend that I regret making love to you.'

'No, the only thing you're sorry about is that your double dealing was found out,' Stephanie retorted. 'Have you *no* shame, Conrad?'

'None at all. A beautiful woman let me see that she was willing to be my lover. I took her with, I thought, mutual pleasure.'

'You make it sound so ... so logical,' Stephanie said. 'But you wouldn't have liked Nesta to have known.'

'Nesta is different,' Conrad said stiffly. 'She hasn't your sophistication – or what I believed to be your sophistication – and she's capable of being very deeply hurt.'

'Do you think I'm not? No, don't bother to answer that. I'll admit that Nesta loves you in a way I never did. What I can't understand is that you were prepared to throw away that love for the sake of a bit of animal satisfaction.'

'No animal ever aspired to the refinement of our lovemaking, my sweet. Have you forgotten so soon?'

'You're a magnificent lover. Clever – perhaps too clever – subtle, overwhelming. But when I heard about Nesta I felt a revulsion I can never get over.'

'How did you find out?' Conrad asked. 'I didn't think Nesta would tell you.'

'She didn't, not at that time, and, of course, I never told her how you'd let her down. As you say, for Nesta it would be a real tragedy. We've talked about it enough, Conrad. Let it go. But please remember that as far as you are concerned, I'm very definitely not available.'

To her relief he did not press her to tell him how she had

discovered his liaison with Nesta, but she sensed by the very way he let the subject drop and started an abrupt conversation about something completely different that he was not pleased by her frank speaking. He would have taken up where they had left off if she had allowed it, not because of any real love for her, but merely to gratify his senses. He had accepted her rebuff with smiling carelessness, but Stephanie suspected that somewhere underneath that urbane exterior Conrad was angry, because a fleeting desire for her, aroused by seeing her again after a long parting, had been frustrated. If an affair was to be broken off Conrad liked to be the one who did it. She had seen him too clearly and had let him know that she did not like what she had seen. A complicated man. A fallen angel.

'What are you smiling about?' Conrad asked.

'You're one of Lucifer's own, aren't you, you devil?' Stephanie said.

'Of course, darling! That's my fascination! Now tell me about your future plans and let's forget about the past.'

'I want to do a play,' Stephanie said. 'I've said I'll be available to go anywhere within reason between now and the New Year, as long as it's a straight play. I simply must get away from singing and dancing and handing props to conjurers.'

'Is that what you've been doing? Not really?'

'Truly. He was a lovely man and clever as a wagonload of monkeys. The most extraordinary thing, he's been recruited to work in the desert. Whatever can they want with a conjuror there?'

'What indeed? You mean he's doing something besides entertaining the troops?'

'So I gather. He thought it might be something to do with camouflage, but I would have thought by this time we'd have plenty of experts to deal with that.'

'Camouflage and illusion,' Conrad said thoughtfully. 'How very interesting. Where was he being sent?'

'I've no idea, except that he had to report to Cairo. Perhaps I've been indiscreet in mentioning it. He did say it was hush-hush. Conrad, there's something else I want to tell you. I'm not sure whether it will be welcome news or not.'

'Tell me and find out,' he invited.

'Do you remember Luke Lindquist, the war correspondent? You must have met him with me?'

'The American?'

'That's right. He was in German hands for a time, but eventually managed to get released. He said that when he was captured he met a relation of yours.'

Conrad seemed to go very still. 'How extraordinary,' he said in an even voice.

'His name was Ernst von Lynden.'

'Young Ernst? A very distant relation. Some sort of second cousin.'

'I thought perhaps you'd like to know that at least one of your family is alive and well – or he was when Luke met him, which is some time ago now.'

'Did they talk about me?'

'Apparently they did. Luke was carrying a newspaper which had an item in it about *Wings of Courage*. That's how it came up.'

'Oh, I see.' Conrad seemed to relax. 'I don't imagine young Ernst had anything good to say about me.'

'Luke called him an arrogant young devil,' Stephanie said, avoiding answering that question.

'He wasn't arrogant with me,' Conrad said and something about the way he smiled to himself made Stephanie shiver and then hurry on to talk about something else.

'I've heard from Luke since I came home,' she said. 'In fact, I had another letter yesterday. He's been transferred to join the American forces in North Africa.'

'Our great American allies,' Conrad said. 'They mean well, but they're untried troops. It remains to be seen how successful they'll be.'

Two days later Claud More tossed Conrad's latest despatch to Berlin down in front of his superior in disgust.

'Bloody Conrad Aylmer has caught on to the deception campaign in the desert,' he said. 'Nothing very much, but enough to alert the Germans that we're up to something.'

'It's of no great importance, since the report won't be

194

transmitted,' the other man pointed out.

'It irks me that he's picked up something that's happening so far away and which we thought we'd been successful in concealing. He's a clever devil. I suspect he got it from Stephanie Bartram. She's been in that part of the world recently and they're seeing one another again now she's back, so Anton says. And that's another thing: Aylmer has accused Anton of making trouble between him and his lady friends.'

'And has he?'

'Probably. The relationship between those two troubles me. Between Aylmer and Anton, I mean.'

'I thought Anton hated his master's guts.'

'He does, of course,' Claud agreed. 'We wouldn't have let him take on such a dangerous role if we hadn't been sure he was virulently anti-Nazi. And yet ... there's a sort of jealousy in Anton's attitude when he speaks about Conrad's women. The tie between them may be hatred, but Conrad belongs to *him* and he resents anyone coming between them.'

'We can't let the deception fail now. When the planning for the invasion starts we'll need to have Anton and your friend Conrad working flat out sending misleading reports to Berlin.'

'There weren't any repercussions from the report that filtered through via Lisbon from that American war correspondent?'

'No, we sat on that hard. As far as we're concerned, Conrad Aylmer is above suspicion, in spite of his unfortunate family connections.'

To Nesta's despair she had been posted to an army camp on the north-east coast. 'Miles from a theatre,' she complained. Stephanie, conscientiously doing the rounds of the families she had promised to visit while working with their sons and husbands overseas, managed to meet her for one brief evening.

'You're looking marvellous,' Nesta said enviously. 'Did you enjoy Egypt?'

'Enjoy isn't the word,' Stephanie said. 'Part of the time, yes, it was a wonderful experience, but it was also extremely hard work under the most trying conditions you can imagine, and the trip I made to Paiforce was gruelling.'

She would not have admitted it, but she was just a little incensed that Nesta should have fallen in with the common assumption that she had been having a good time abroad, while people still in England were getting on with the mundane business of winning the war.

Nesta did not seem to notice that she had offended.

'I'm sorry you didn't get to Palestine,' she said. 'I'm becoming more and more convinced that the only answer to the Jewish question is to allow a proper state of Israel to be set up. In fact, I'm almost a Zionist!'

'All right as long as other people don't have to be pushed out,' Stephanie said. 'But it'll have to wait until after the war.'

Nesta looked as if she was about to embark on a long argument in favour of her latest enthusiasm, but Stephanie went on hurriedly, 'Tell me about yourself. How are you liking being in the ATS?'

'I'm browned off,' Nesta said.

She had had her frizzy hair cut short, which suited her, but she could not be described as having a smart military appearance. Her uniform was not a good fit for her thin, angular body and she wore it carelessly. The khaki colour was not kind to her sallow skin and, as always when she was in despair, Nesta's whole body sagged despondently. By her side, Stephanie was a glowing golden goddess.

'Have you seen Conrad?' Nesta asked abruptly. 'Was he looking well?'

'I've seen him a couple of times. He seemed to be in reasonable health. Thinner than I remembered, but apart from that I could see no change in him. He gave me a delicious dinner at his house and he seemed to be eating quite normally, so I suppose his ulcer is under control.'

Nesta scowled horribly. 'Black market,' she said. 'I do wish he wouldn't, even though I want him to have good food and keep well. I haven't set eyes on him for eleven weeks.'

It was typical of Nesta that she should know exactly how long it was since she and Conrad had met. Stephanie could only be thankful that Nesta had no inkling of the overtures Conrad had tried to make to her.

'I wanted him to marry me,' Nesta said. 'I might have been

196

able to keep out of the Forces and look after him properly if he had, but he made silly excuses about it not being fair to me. As if I cared about that.'

Stephanie could think of nothing to say. Conrad a married man? She could not see it somehow, nor was she entirely convinced of his commitment to Nesta. Perhaps Nesta, too, had doubts and that was why she was so obviously unhappy.

'I suppose you're going to be acting together again?' Nesta asked.

'Probably,' Stephanie admitted. 'I believe Noël is going to let us do a production of *Private Lives*.'

'A bit of a change from your last epic tear-jerker,' Nesta commented.

'What about you? Are you doing anything?'

'I'm producing an amateur version of *Love from a Stranger*. None of the cast can act for toffees – and they all think they can. They don't believe me when I tell them how wooden they are.'

'You must be popular,' Stephanie commented, with an amused realization of what it would be like to be rehearsed by Nesta. 'I've never quite understood why you were called up. Why didn't you go on working for ENSA?'

'I wouldn't agree to go abroad because of leaving Conrad,' Nesta admitted, shamefaced.

'Oh, Nesta!'

'It caused all sorts of reactions and they wouldn't support my application for deferment when it came up. Of course, I realize now that I was an idiot, but I wouldn't have wanted to get involved in the sort of song and dance show you've been doing.'

She seemed to realize that this sounded belittling and added hurriedly, 'I mean, I haven't your wide talent. My singing voice is nothing to write home about and although I've done the usual rhythmic movement stuff, I'm not a trained dancer.'

She looked at Stephanie wistfully. 'If there's ever anything you can do ...' she said, not very hopefully. 'I'll never forget that it was you who got me that part in your film.'

Stephanie felt herself to be in a quandary. The one thing she wanted to avoid was having to act in the same production as Conrad and Nesta again, and yet Nesta was so manifestly unhappy.

197

'I'll keep it in mind,' she said, knowing that it would be difficult to get Nesta released from the ATS without using considerable pressure. 'You haven't told me what you do apart from producing your amateur actors. How is the ATS employing you?'

'I'm a gunner,' Nesta said. For the first time a look of animation lit up her face.

'A *what*?'

'I help man an anti-aircraft gun.'

It was the last thing Stephanie had expected.

'I haven't any talent for anything else,' Nesta explained. 'I can't drive, I certainly can't cook, I never learned shorthand or typing. It seemed to me that if I was going to be in the army I might as well take an active part, so I took a gunnery course.'

'It doesn't worry you ... the shooting?' Stephanie asked.

'Kill or be killed. No, it doesn't worry me, not when I think about the Goldsteins and all the other people who have suffered under the Nazis.'

As Nesta spoke Stephanie recognized the same ruthless determination that she brought to her pursuit of the acting profession. Nesta wanted the war over quickly and she would do anything in her power to achieve that.

'I have to admire you,' Stephanie said.

'Even though you can't see yourself doing the same thing? To my way of thinking you can't afford to be sentimental about waging war. I bet the men you met in the desert would agree with me.'

'Perhaps. I suppose it's the spirit that will win us the war in the end.'

The tour of *Private Lives* went ahead and was a huge success. The only thing that marred it for Stephanie was the realization that Conrad had embarked on an affair with the actress who was playing his wife. Stephanie, drifting elegantly through the role of Amanda, had no difficulty at all in delivering her sardonic lines with real bite.

The letters from Luke continued to arrive. They followed no regular pattern, but Stephanie began to feel disappointed if, after she had been away from home for a long period, there was no letter waiting for her on her return. She replied, keeping him up to date with her professional engagements, but never mentioning her emotional life, so that Luke, scanning the pages for some hint that she understood his reasons for writing, was left uncertain about her relationship with Conrad. They were being thrown together and Conrad had a fascination for women. Luke could not help wondering whether Stephanie had overcome the revulsion she had felt when she discovered Conrad's affair with Nesta. He understood now, only too well, the worries of the soldiers posted overseas for long periods and separated from their wives and girl friends.

'Great news,' he wrote early in the New Year. 'My book has been accepted for publication. It should be out sometime in the spring. I'll see you get a copy.'

By the time she received *Intrepid Reporter* in the spring of 1943 Stephanie had embarked on another film with Conrad. She took the book to the studio with her and whiled away the boring hours of sitting around waiting for her scenes to be shot reading it.

It was lively, amusing and not, on the surface, a book about anything but one man's offbeat experiences, but Luke had slipped in a few observations which Stephanie, who had been on the spot, even though it was in a noncombatant role, found true and even penetrating. He had dedicated it to 'Prue, who wanted me to be a proper writer'.

It was only to be expected that he would want the book to carry this memorial to his dead wife, but Stephanie was surprised by the jealous pang she felt on reading those words. She did not know, because Luke could not bring himself to put it into a letter, that he saw the dedication as his farewell to Prue. The memory of her was still dear, but he was a living man and he needed a warm-blooded, loving companion.

The film was an even greater success than *Wings of Courage*. Conrad was magnificent. The story called on him to die in a blaze of glory and, as Nesta reported when she came on leave and saw it, 'there wasn't a dry eye in the house'.

'You didn't like it,' Stephanie diagnosed.

Nesta had the grace to look ashamed. 'You know I think

199

Conrad ought to stick to the classics,' she excused herself. 'It was a good film in its way. I mean, as a piece of entertainment it works all right.'

Fortunately, Stephanie's sense of humour allowed her to accept this grudging approval with a laugh.

'I daren't ask for an opinion of my performance,' she said.

'Oh, you were good, but then it's your sort of thing. I think you're far better as a film actress than on the stage.'

'Thank you,' Stephanie murmured.

'Stephanie, that's not a criticism – it's meant to be praise! You convey quite subtle emotions without apparently moving a muscle. My own approach is too broad. If I were to go into films seriously I'd need to learn a new technique.'

'And you would,' Stephanie said. 'Given the chance there's nothing you couldn't learn.'

It was a generous tribute and Nesta acknowledged as much.

'There aren't many famous actresses who would talk like that to an unknown, unemployed, unsuccessful bit player.'

Perhaps because she was moved she went on abruptly, 'Which of the girls in the film is Conrad sleeping with?'

'No one, to my knowledge,' Stephanie said untruthfully.

'Oh, come on, Stephanie! I don't have any illusions about my lovely wicked Conrad, not any more. Once I thought I'd die if he was unfaithful to me, but after we'd had our conversation about marriage I understood that he wanted to be free to go his own way. He can't resist the occasional conquest. I ... I've learned to live with it. He always comes back to me.'

'He saw quite a lot of the little blonde girl who played his sister,' Stephanie admitted.

'Kinky!'

Nesta tried to laugh, but Stephanie saw the pain behind her offhand manner and wished that she had not allowed herself to say even that much.

'Do you think the war will ever end?' Nesta asked and Stephanie had no difficulty in following her train of thought, her desperate desire to be free to love Conrad, to keep him away from other women, to pursue the career she longed for.

'I think the tide has turned in our favour,' she said quickly. 'I've been thrilled by the way the Eighth Army has pushed the

Afrika Korps back across the desert. Because I was there I think of them as my friends. The Russians, too, have been doing marvels. If only we can get the Second Front started, I'm sure we can clear up Europe.'

That conversation with Nesta weighed on Stephanie's mind. When *was* it going to end – the endless killing, the heartache, the miserable separations? In spite of her own optimistic words Stephanie felt low spirited and when her door bell rang that evening she went to answer it reluctantly.

She opened the door cautiously, careful to show no chink of light, even though there had been no air raids for so long that the violent days of the Blitz now seemed like something unreal. The caller was a tall man in uniform. It was too dark to make out his face, but when he spoke she knew him immediately, even before he said his name.

'Hello, Stephanie; it's Luke.'

All Stephanie's depression disappeared in a rush of happiness. Taking hold of his hand she led him into the living room.

She was going to tell him how pleased she was to see him, but instead, looking up into his face, she exclaimed, 'Luke, you've been ill!'

'Dysentery,' Luke said. 'I've had a bad bout of it.'

They stood looking at one another, hands still loosely linked, neither of them quite sure of the next move. Surely he was going to kiss her? After all those letters, Stephanie had expected their meeting to be warmer than this. Tentatively, she reached up with her free hand and touched Luke on his cheek, noting with concern the thinness of his face and the new lines drawn on it by hardship and illness.

Luke took her hand and turned it against his lips, kissing the palm, and with that encouragement Stephanie moved forward and his arms slipped round her. They kissed gently, without passion, exploring one another, remembering their past closeness.

When Stephanie drew away she was smiling.

'Dear Luke,' she said. 'I'm so very glad to see you. Are you back in England for good?'

'No, I'm only here to convalesce.'

'Not the place I would have chosen for sick leave,' Stephanie commented. 'Couldn't they find somewhere better than poor old England?'

'Nowhere that offered the chance of seeing you.'

'That's nice!' Stephanie said. 'Come and sit down and tell me what you've been doing. I haven't heard from you lately.'

'That's because I moved out of the desert and into Sicily and, of course, I've been suffering from acute griping of the guts.'

'Poor Luke! I've loved getting your letters.'

'Did you understand what I was trying to say?' Luke asked, looking at her intently.

'I think so,' Stephanie said, but when Luke would have continued she laid her fingers over his mouth again. 'Let's take it slowly. Writing to one another is one thing, being together again is different. Perhaps this time we can manage to stay in step with one another, if we don't rush at it. How long do you expect to be in England?'

'Difficult to say, but I'm hoping to be around for at least a month.'

'In London?'

'Most of the time, yes. Before I went abroad I sub-let the flat Prue and I rented in London. The tenants have just moved out so I'm going to make use of it while I'm here.'

His words were matter of fact, but Stephanie sensed Luke's reluctance to go back to the flat he had shared with Prue.

'I'd ask you to stay here,' she said. 'But Mum is still living with me and it would hardly be practicable.'

'It's kind of you to think of it, but I'll be all right,' Luke said. 'I did think ... perhaps we might take that trip into the country we once promised ourselves?'

'Let's see how things work out,' Stephanie said. 'I'm not working at the moment – not acting, I mean – but because of that I've gone back to manning the Ambulance Post, so I'm not entirely free.'

'I thought the air raids had died down?'

'We still have to turn up for duty, just in case there's an unexpected raid.' Stephanie sighed. 'It's deadly dull,' she admitted.

'Can't you apply for leave?'

202

'No ... no, I can't do that. I've taken such a lot of time off for my trips abroad and filming, which people envy as a glamorous kind of war service. It's only fair to take my turn at doing the boring bits.'

'You're too conscientious by half!'

Stephanie thought that he was not entirely pleased. She was tempted to point out that she had to obey orders, but it seemed too trivial a matter to argue about when they had only just come together again.

'Will you try to re-let your flat?' she asked.

'Probably. I've still got quite a long lease on it. I don't want to give it up in case I need a base in England again.'

Luke lapsed into silence and Stephanie thought it was because of his memories of living with Prue in that flat to which he had now returned. It seemed that she was right when Luke said abruptly, 'Prue wrote a book before she died.'

'I know. I read it,' Stephanie said.

She did not need to tell him that she had made a point of finding a copy of *Eastern Windows*: Luke understood that without having it spelled out. She hoped he was not going to ask her what she had thought of it because, although Stephanie had admired the novel very much, she had also found it disturbing, and more revealing than perhaps Luke realized.

'I don't mean the Chinese book,' Luke said. 'Prue had finished another novel before she left for the States. She was taking the manuscript back with her for publication and, of course, it went down with the ship.'

Stephanie reached out and clasped her hand over his, but she said nothing.

'I kept the rough draft she left behind,' Luke said. 'At the time it seemed no more than a sentimental gesture, something we would laugh about when we were together again. Later, I couldn't bear to look at it. Her publishers wrote asking about it and I never replied. I'm going to take this opportunity to get it out, have it typed and submit it for publication.'

Stephanie was shocked and ashamed by the jealous pang that went through her.

'It's as much a part of Prue as the baby would have been,' Luke was saying. 'I've come to think it would be wrong to deny her that much of a memorial.'

'What is it called?' Stephanie asked, trying to sound enthusiastic.

'*Drifting Islands*. It's about a young American woman living in England in the period just after Munich.'

'Biographical?'

'I hope not! My recollection is that she has a very sad time.'

'I'll look forward to reading it,' Stephanie said.

Was it her imagination or was there something reluctant about the way Luke said, 'Yes ... of course.'

He drew her into his arms and once again their lips met in a long, slow kiss. It worried Stephanie that they were being so careful with one another. There was none of the excitement she had known with Conrad. Instead, being back in Luke's arms felt like a homecoming. It was a warm, delightful experience, but was that all there was going to be?

'Why the frown?' Luke asked.

'Just wondering whether we can really pick up where we left off,' Stephanie admitted.

'I think we can, if we do what you always wanted and get away by ourselves for a time.'

When Stephanie did not reply he said, more urgently, 'You'll do what you can to arrange some free time, won't you?'

'I'm sure I can fix the duty roster,' Stephanie said.

If Luke had pressed it she could probably have arranged to be available to go away with him the following weekend, but when he seemed satisfied with her vague reply she did not suggest it. After all, they had only just met after a long separation, and she was the one who had said they should move slowly towards resuming the relationship between them that had never had a chance to blossom in the past.

When Luke eventually left it was with an unwillingness that was only partly due to his reluctance to part with Stephanie. The truth was, he did not want to go back to the flat he had once shared with Prue. So far he had done no more than drop his bags off there. Now he had to go and face a night there alone. He almost asked Stephanie to go with him, but that would have been an unworthy motive for getting her to spend the night with him. Besides, he was far from restored to health, he had had a long and tiring journey, and he was none too sure that he would have been able to do justice to the vibrant beauty he had just been holding in his arms.

He hinted as much to Stephanie and she laughed and stroked his cheek, as she had done when he had arrived.

'Poor Luke! Never mind, darling. A breath of country air and you'll be romping in the hay like all the other Yanks. Your countrymen have got themselves a shocking reputation with the girls.'

'So I've heard! "Over-paid, over-sexed and over here!" Is that the way you think of me?'

'Of course not! Go home and get a good night's sleep. I can see you're dead on your feet.'

The flat had only been empty for a couple of weeks, but already it smelt musty. There was a film of dust over everything and the furniture seemed distinctly shabbier than when Luke had moved out. It all looked very impersonal. There was nothing to remind him of Prue, not until he unlocked the cupboard in which, by agreement, he had stored some of his personal possessions – then she came back with a rush.

There was the sewing basket she had left behind because she had had to cut down on some of the things she was packing, and a wedding photograph in a silver frame which Luke had not been able to take abroad with him. Above all, there was the manuscript of her novel, the pages covered with notes and alterations in Prue's small, clear handwriting. Strange, that looking at her writing should bring back the sound of her voice.

Luke bowed his head over the untidy pages. He was deadly tired, as Stephanie had realized, and his long, debilitating illness had left him vulnerable to emotion. He told himself that it was this weakness that brought the tears to his eyes, but as he brushed them away with an impatient movement he knew that it was more than that. Even now, after all this time, after having believed that he had got over it, he still felt an aching regret for his loss.

'Prue,' he said out loud. 'Oh, Prue, my dear girl ...'

If he could have felt her near him it would not have been so

205

bad, but there was nothing there, no response but the rustle of a sheet of paper as it slipped from his grasp.

Luke picked it up and began to read. Before he had finished the first chapter he knew that this was a book that had to be published. He had always thought well of it, but now after having stood back from it for so long he was astonished by the strength of Prue's writing and her insight into the England of the pre-war period.

He had told Stephanie that Prue deserved this memorial and it was true. He would do everything he could to get her novel published. After that, he must and he would put her memory away from him.

Stephanie ... she was so lovely and, when he was in a fitter state than at the moment, so exciting. He wanted her, in spite of his nostalgia for Prue.

'I can't live alone,' he said into the silence.

Prue would have understood that. Surely she would have understood? If the situation had been reversed he would not have expected her to shut herself off from other men for the rest of her life, would he? Ruefully, Luke admitted to himself that the idea of Prue falling in love and remarrying after his demise was not at all welcome.

He got slowly and stiffly to his feet. There were things he had to do, such as finding bedclothes and making up his solitary bed. Tomorrow he would find a typist to make sense of this jumbled manuscript. After that he would see whether any British publishing house was interested in it, in spite of the chronic paper shortage, and he would take advice about sending a copy off to the States. If he could keep occupied he would be able to put these sad thoughts out of his mind.

There was the promised weekend with Stephanie to come. A long, slow rediscovery of the pleasure they had once taken in one another. A strange relationship, consummated before it had begun, and then put on ice. He had been right to revive it, right to come home to her now. Stephanie had a quality which he found himself thinking of as loving kindness. She was what he needed, not only now but perhaps in the future as well.

It was Stephanie who took some practical steps to make him more comfortable in the flat. She telephoned the next morning and said, 'I don't know whether you're a terribly domesticated person; I suspect that, like me, you're not. I have a very good charlady who's with me this morning and she says she'd be happy to come and "do" for you while you're in London. Are you interested?'

'I certainly am,' Luke said. 'I'm great at looking after myself at the back of beyond, but I'm not so good at sweeping and dusting in more civilized surroundings.'

'I'm hopeless,' Stephanie said. 'And don't think I'm not ashamed of it, because I am, but having been on the stage since I was a child I've never got used to ordinary domestic chores. I can cook sardines on toast over a gas ring in a theatrical lodging house, and I know all about underclothes pinned to a bit of string to drip into the bath, but I've never scrubbed a floor or cleaned a window in my life.'

Luke had a sudden recollection of the orgy of cleaning Prue had indulged in before she had left him for the last time. For the first time it occurred to him that she had probably suffered more than he had realized by not having a proper home. Their quarters in China had been pleasant, but Prue had had to defer to custom and employ Chinese servants. This flat was the nearest she had come to running her home herself.

'Are you still there?' Stephanie asked. 'Have my shortcomings shocked you so much that you can't speak?'

'I'm as bad,' Luke said. 'We're a couple of gypsies. Would you share a baked hedgehog with me this lunchtime?'

'Don't joke about it,' Stephanie said. 'You may find yourself eating hedgehog, or something equally bizarre. Luke, I'd love to see you. I woke up this morning not quite believing that you were really here last night. I'll bring my Mrs Bakewell round to see you and then we can go on to lunch.'

She arrived with a diminutive Cockney woman who sniffed disparagingly when she looked at the kitchen floor and inspected the inside of the bath, but as far as Luke could make out, Mrs Bakewell relished the idea of putting the place to rights.

The meal Luke and Stephanie ate together was not quite as grim as Stephanie had prophesied, but the menu was very restricted. It hardly mattered because what was important was that they had both relaxed after their first difficult meeting and were at ease with one another.

They lingered at the table, reluctant to part, but Luke had already realized that Stephanie was in uniform.

'Does that mean you're on duty?' he asked.

'I'm afraid so,' she said. She glanced at her watch and grimaced. 'I mustn't be late. Will you walk to the bus stop with me?'

'Stay another ten minutes and take a taxi,' Luke suggested.

'If I can get one! The American troops have a monopoly on them.'

All the same, she did not hurry and when they left the restaurant they sauntered slowly down the road together.

'Flowers!' Stephanie exclaimed, peering into the window of a florist's shop. 'You can't always get them because so much land has been dug up for vegetables. I'll buy you a bunch of those lovely roses to cheer up the flat. I thought it looked a bit bleak when I saw it this morning.'

'Hey, that's the wrong way round!' Luke protested. 'I'm supposed to give you flowers.'

'A homecoming present,' Stephanie said. 'Can you find a vase to put them in?'

'We had some fine Chinese porcelain vases,' Luke said. 'Prue was taking them home with her for fear of having them broken in an air raid and, of course ...'

'They were lost,' Stephanie said. 'Poor Luke, I'm so very sorry.'

She handed him an armful of golden roses and kissed him on the cheek.

'A taxi! I must fly!'

Luke found a glass jug for his roses and watched them unfold in the days that followed.

'They remind me of you,' he told Stephanie. 'Warm and scented, with a lovely golden heart.'

'Thank you kindly, sir.'

She smiled at him over the rim of the glass she was holding and suddenly Luke was possessed by a sense of urgency. Time

208

was rushing past and they were getting nowhere.

'Stephanie, this meeting for drinks and meals, kissing in taxis and parting, it's not enough. Have you thought any more about getting away for a while?'

Dear Luke, if only you knew! Stephanie thought with a touch of irony. I think about nothing else.

'I was waiting for you to ask again,' she said. 'Luke, if you really want it, I can be free next weekend from Friday to Monday morning.'

'That's nearly a week to wait,' he complained, but in spite of his impatience he still did not suggest taking her back to the flat. It was swept and dusted and as sparkling clean as Mrs Bakewell could make it; he told himself over and over again that there was nothing of Prue left in it; but still he could not bring himself to make love to Stephanie in the same room, on the same bed, as he had shared with his wife.

Stephanie glanced at him, seeing the shadow that had fallen across his face, and knew what he was thinking. The sooner she could get him away and into surroundings which held no reminders of the past the better it would be. All the same, she valued the time they spent together like this, talking rather than making love, getting to know one another, building a relationship that she hoped was going to be founded on something more substantial than the physical pull that had always been there between them.

It was all working out so well. Stephanie felt quite dazed with happiness. Luke was getting over his illness, feeling stronger every day; even the way he kissed and held her betrayed that. She wanted him quite desperately. Just touching his hand by accident sent a shock through her.

'Where shall we go?' she asked.

'I've heard of a small country hotel in Warwickshire which sounds ideal,' Luke said.

'Shakespeare country,' Stephanie said. 'Lovely!'

Even in wartime the little hotel, buried in green countryside in the heart of England, was an idyllic spot. Stephanie had been worried in case some embarrassment arose because of their

209

unmarried state, worried too in case she was recognized, but no comment was made when Luke signed the hotel register.

'I provided my own wedding ring,' she said to Luke and then wished she had not said it in case he thought it was a reproach.

'I never thought of that,' he admitted.

'That gives me a very poor idea of the morals of America,' Stephanie said in mock horror. 'Don't the hotels expect their guests to be married? In England they're frightfully narrowminded.'

'Even in wartime?'

'No, perhaps not. I must say this is a *very* nice place. You couldn't have chosen better.'

In the small, low-ceilinged bedroom Luke looked very large and somehow more foreign than usual.

He glanced at Stephanie with a slight smile.

'Feeling strange?' he asked.

'As jittery as a virgin bride,' she admitted.

Luke drew her close for a long kiss.

'Does that make you feel better?' he asked.

'A lot! Luke, I do love you, you know.'

'I know,' Luke said, with his lips touching her soft chestnut hair. 'And I love you, too.'

After a moment Stephanie moved away from him. 'Let's keep our heads,' she said. 'Unpack, go out for a short stroll before dinner, which something tells me is going to be good, and then ...'

'It's the "and then" I'm particularly looking forward to,' Luke said.

They got in one another's way in that small room as they unpacked and every time they blundered into one another the excitement between them mounted.

'Must we go out for a healthy walk?' Luke asked plaintively.

'Yes! Luke, a quick tumble before the gong goes isn't what I want, not when we've waited so long.'

There was a stream at the bottom of the garden. They walked along it, arm in arm. The sun was going down and the sky was shaded from pink to gold and then from a piercing green to soft blue. The grass beneath their feet was uneven and damp. A willow hung over the water, its leaves just touched

210

with yellow. In a distant group of elms rooks were tumbling in the air before settling for the night.

In the shadow of the willow tree Luke turned Stephanie to face him and they kissed once before sauntering back the way they had come. In front of them the old hotel buildings were silhouetted against the sky.

'No lights,' Stephanie said. 'It's sad, isn't it? I would have liked to have seen lights in the windows. The blackout reminds me of the war and I'd almost forgotten about it.'

They had a drink in the bar and Luke noticed that Stephanie collected some curious glances. He wondered whether she realized how striking her looks were in those surroundings. She had seemed to know all about her fame when they had met in Cairo, but since he had been back in England he had not thought about it. For the first time the same thought that had been in Stephanie's mind occurred to him: it might prove embarrassing if she were recognized.

'What's making you frown?' Stephanie asked.

'The difficulty of spending a weekend with a famous film star.'

'Oh, that! Don't let it worry you. The hotel people said nothing when they saw my identity card and ration book, so it looks as if they're prepared to turn a blind eye as long as the other guests are deceived. As for the newspapers, they are much too short of space to bother with an item about me.'

Since she dismissed it so easily Luke did put it out of his mind, but just for a moment he had thought that Stephanie's smile had seemed stiff, and somewhere at the back of his mind it occurred to him that she might have been expecting him to ask her to marry him.

In spite of wartime restrictions the meal was good enough for them to linger over it appreciatively.

'Simple food, well cooked,' Stephanie said. 'What could be better?'

'It's great for me to be able to eat my food and enjoy it again,' Luke said.

'You've got over that unfortunate weakness you hinted at the first night you got back?' Stephanie asked.

'Don't tempt me!' Luke warned her. 'I'm liable to throw you over my shoulder and carry you off upstairs, just to show you.'

'That would be nice, but it might put the colonel and his wife off their rhubarb crumble. Darling Luke, have I mentioned that I love you?'

She could feel her happiness surging through her in a way that must surely be visible to all the other sedate diners. She leaned back in her chair and tried to avoid catching Luke's eye again, because she knew that every time she looked at him she betrayed the longing that was becoming too intense to bear.

'Stephanie,' Luke said softly.

As their eyes met Stephanie smiled, silently acknowledging the need that burned inside her.

'Bed?' Luke asked.

'Please.'

They strolled out of the dining room and across the darkened hall, and then Luke caught Stephanie's hand in his and pulled her helter-skelter up the stairs and into their room, where they collapsed on the bed in breathless laughter.

'Idiot!' Stephanie said. 'I was trying to behave like a staid old married woman. Luke, do you realize it's only nine o'clock?'

'I've asked for a late breakfast,' Luke said. 'Twelve hours should be long enough.'

Not twelve hours, not even twelve times twelve, Stephanie thought in a delirium of pleasure as their limbs twined together and parted, as Luke's fingertips drifted over her body and his lips importuned her again out of the dreaming trance she had fallen into after the rapture of their first union. She heard the breath sobbing at the back of her throat and she thought that she spoke his name over and over, until the moment came when it was no longer possible to speak and she could only hold him and strive with all the force that was in her to give back to him what he was giving her.

'You wonder,' Luke breathed as he reluctantly slid away from her. 'Oh, you wonder! What did I ever do to deserve this?'

Still speechless, Stephanie turned her lips against his bare shoulder, nuzzling at him until Luke gathered her close once more and they fell into deep, untroubled sleep.

She discovered another pleasure the next morning, the delight of laughter shared in bed between two lovers who had visited the heights of love together and were ready to indulge in lighthearted teasing. It was something Stephanie had not known before, not that and not the companionship that made their days together as harmonious as their nights were exciting.

It was all too short, but by Monday morning when they had to leave Stephanie believed that they were welded together in a way that would be indissoluble.

She felt so confident that when they got back to London she said, 'Darling, does it really make sense for you to go to your flat and me to go to mine?'

'I guess not,' Luke admitted. 'Will you move in with me for the rest of my leave?'

'Of course I will, but I'll have to go home first to get some more clothes.'

And to tell her mother where she was going – but Stephanie thought it more tactful not to mention that to Luke.

As Stephanie had expected, Vera's reaction was disapproving.

'I don't know why you have to get tangled up with a man who can do nothing for you,' she said.

'I wouldn't say that,' Stephanie murmured as she tossed clean underclothes into her suitcase.

Vera sniffed. 'He'll be gone back to the other side of the world before you can turn round. Have you thought about that?'

'I'm trying not to. It's no more than thousands of other women are suffering because their husbands have gone off to the war.'

'You're not thinking of marrying him, I hope!'

Stephanie shut her case with a bang. 'The subject hasn't come up,' she said. 'I'll say one thing for you, Mum: you're not conventional!'

'That doesn't mean I approve of what you're doing,' Vera said swiftly. 'Well, you'll go your own way, no matter what I say. Do you want Conrad Aylmer to know where you are? Because he was round here looking for you on Saturday.'

'At the moment I don't want to see anyone but Luke. You can tell Conrad that if he calls again.'

When Stephanie arrived at Luke's flat she was still feeling slightly ruffled and she was quick to sense that Luke was not as

213

overjoyed to have her there as she would have liked. She wished that she had not let him go back alone to that cold little flat. He seemed to have become more remote than he had been when they parted. Prue, Stephanie thought fancifully; please don't hang on to him, let me have him now.

Because of this thought she jumped when Luke spoke his dead wife's name.

'Prue's book has come back from the typist,' he said. 'I want to get it to the publisher tomorrow in the hope of getting it read before I leave.'

'Is there a spare copy?' Stephanie asked. 'I'd love to read it.'

'Yes ... of course,' Luke said, just as he had once before and with the same reluctance.

Stephanie went to him and put her arms round his neck.

'Are you pleased I'm here?' she demanded.

'Of course I am!'

He kissed her and the magic was back for both of them. It was going to be all right, Stephanie thought contentedly.

'I hate to ask this,' she said. 'But how much longer do we actually have before your leave is up?'

'I'll know when I've seen the doctor and my London office,' Luke said. 'I think the most I can hope for is another ten days, possibly only a week.'

Stephanie sighed as she leaned against him and Luke said in a troubled voice, 'It's my job. I have to go back to it as soon as I'm fit.'

'I know. I'm not complaining – much!'

In the next few days Stephanie succeeded in changing the atmosphere in the flat. It felt lived in again – and by a living man and woman with no sad ghosts to haunt them. Luke was frequently out during the day, having medical tests and looking up London contacts. Stephanie stayed at home, pottering around the flat, playing at the domestic role which did not come easily to her, and reading Prue's book.

She admired it even more than the first novel and as she read it the thought came to her over and over again – what a film this would make! Could she play the part of the young woman

214

whose story it was? Not easily, Stephanie admitted, because the character was essentially American, but she would not mind taking one of the subsidiary British parts just for the pleasure of being involved in such a strong story.

She was dreaming over it one day when the doorbell rang, which was unusual because callers at the flat had been few. It was Conrad.

'I suppose Mum told you where to find me,' Stephanie said. 'All right, you can come in, but it's no use asking me to do anything that will interfere with this time I'm spending with Luke. We've only got a few days left.'

'All the more reason for you to listen to my suggestion for something to distract your mind after Lindquist has gone,' Conrad said, following her into the living room. 'What's this you're reading? A new script?'

'An unpublished novel by Prue Lindquist,' Stephanie said, gathering up the scattered loose sheets. 'Actually, it could be turned into a marvellous film. Not much in it for me, but a splendid part for you. It's about an American girl in love with an Englishman. She sees war coming and is torn between her own country and wanting to stay with him. I've got some American coffee and I'll give you a cup, but you have to go as soon as you've had it because I don't want you here when Luke gets back.'

'Does he know about our little fling?' Conrad asked.

'I told him in Cairo. He's never mentioned it since, but I don't think he's forgotten about it.'

When she came back from the kitchen carrying a tray Conrad was reading the manuscript.

'You're right,' he said. 'I've only skimmed through a few pages, but the dialogue leaps off the page. The man's role is a gem.'

'Unfortunately, it's difficult to get anything published here at the moment,' Stephanie said. 'Paper shortages and printing restrictions and all sorts of difficulties. Luke may yet have to wait until he can get a copy to America.'

Conrad put the pages down reluctantly and leaned back in his chair, watching Stephanie as she bent over the low table and poured out the coffee.

215

'You're looking breathtakingly lovely,' he remarked. 'Lindquist is a lucky man.'

'I'm the lucky one,' Stephanie said. 'If I'm looking good it must be because I'm so happy.'

'Is it going to last?'

'I shan't change in the way I feel about Luke, if that's what you mean, but of course we've got to part soon.'

Conrad looked away from the grief that clouded her face for a moment. He felt impatient and, if he were truthful, envious.

'You haven't told me what brought you round here,' Stephanie said.

'An invitation to appear at the Stagedoor Canteen.'

'Oh, wonderful! Yes, of course, I'd be delighted, but not until after Luke has gone back to Sicily.'

On a professional basis Stephanie was always in accord with Conrad. They were deep in a discussion of their act for the show when Luke came back. He took in the empty coffee cups, the manuscript – Prue's book – pushed carelessly to one side, and the way Stephanie was looking, pleased and happy and excited. He said nothing, but his dislike of the situation was as obvious as if he had stated it out loud.

'I think we've got everything sorted out, as far as we can without a rehearsal,' Conrad said, getting up. 'Luke, this girl of ours is looking radiant. You must be some sort of magician.'

Something about his graceful movements, and the way he conveyed a subtle amusement, maddened Luke. It was with difficulty that he managed to avoid making any reply at all.

Conrad laughed softly. 'Your late wife's novel is quite excellent,' he said. 'Stephanie is absolutely right in thinking it would make a good film. If you have any difficulty in disposing of the film rights I could probably help. I'd be happy to interest my own studio in it because I want the part of the English lover.'

'Prue wrote a novel and it'll come out in that form,' Luke said. 'I don't want it trivialized into a romance on celluloid.'

His anger was so palpable that Stephanie almost pushed Conrad out of the flat, furious with him because he knew the mischief he had done and was laughing about it.

'Damn you, Conrad,' she said in a fierce whisper in the hall.

'A nasty case of jealousy,' Conrad said, still amused. 'Don't let it stop you doing the show with me, will you? I'll be in touch.'

'I don't want to see you until after Luke has gone,' Stephanie said firmly.

As soon as she went back into the living room Luke said, 'I heard that. Am I in your way? Because, if so, I can take myself off sooner than I'd planned.'

Stephanie quailed. She had not expected Luke to look at her like that, his mouth thin and a nasty glitter in his eyes.

'The last thing I want is for you to go a minute before you have to,' she said. 'I only asked Conrad not to spoil the time we still have together.'

'I'd rather you never saw him again. Would you agree to that?'

For a moment Stephanie hesitated, but what Luke was asking was impossible.

'I couldn't do that,' she said.

Luke's implacably hostile expression was beginning to annoy her as much as it dismayed her.

'You haven't any right to ask it,' she said crossly. 'I have to go on working with Conrad, as you'd realize if you had any understanding of show business. Oh, curses! If only I'd managed to get rid of him before you got home!'

'As you have on previous occasions?' Luke suggested.

'No! He's never been here before and he wouldn't have come now if it hadn't been necessary to talk about an act we have to put together.'

'Aylmer knows all about putting on an act. I only had five minutes with him, but every word, every motion he made was intended to remind me that he'd been your lover. "Our girl" he called you; did you get that?'

'It's just a way of talking,' Stephanie said helplessly.

'A damn funny way! Are you going to take him back again once I'm out of the way?'

'No, I'm not! Luke, how could you even think such a thing after what we've been to one another these last few days? Conrad said you were jealous and I see it's true, but it's not *necessary* ...'

217

'Conrad said! That sleek, lying creep said a whole lot too much. He wants to play the part of the Englishman in Prue's book! Over my dead body!'

'Now we're getting down to the real reason you're so angry,' Stephanie said. 'It's nothing to do with me, it's because he spoke about Prue's book.'

'You showed it to him. Damn it, Stephanie, I thought you understood how I felt about it. I let you read it ...'

'As a concession,' Stephanie said. 'You didn't see any way you could refuse to let the girl you're living with see your dead wife's book, even though you didn't really believe I was fit to turn the sacred pages. Luke, I've had enough of this! It's time you realized that you're alive and I'm alive and Prue is *dead*!'

'I faced up to that long since. You're trying to turn the subject. What I object to is that you showed the manuscript to Aylmer.'

'I went out to make some coffee; when I came back he was reading it.'

It was true, but even as she spoke Stephanie remembered that she had talked about turning the book into a film before she had left Conrad alone with it, and the recollection robbed her words of the force of complete conviction.

'You'd already aroused his curiosity,' Luke guessed. 'And then you sat down and chatted about making a film of it. Let me tell you, if it ever happened neither of you would be my first choice to play in it.'

'Because we haven't led unsullied lives? Oh, Luke, *dear*! If that is what you require you're going to search a long time for any actors who will meet your standard!'

'That wasn't what I meant! I'd never hark back to what's happened in your past ...'

'I should hope not! My God! Even you couldn't be that self-righteous!'

'Self-righteous! That's the last thing I am. It's only Conrad I object to. I do have a right to ask you not to see *him* again.'

'You have no rights at all,' Stephanie said.

She was so hurt and angry that she was having difficulty in breathing and her voice came out in a panting whisper. She was not thinking coherently, but dimly she realized that

218

something was coming up out of her subconscious that she had been suppressing all the time she and Luke had been together. They loved one another and they had been wonderfully happy together. For one miraculous weekend they had been as harmoniously joined as any man and woman could be, but since they had been living in the flat she had sensed something critical in Luke's attitude towards her, and whatever it was she was doing wrong was preventing him from asking her to marry him. She had never admitted it before, but deep inside herself Stephanie was hurt because Luke had never hinted that he wanted her to be his wife.

'You have no rights,' she repeated.

Her words had an effect she had neither expected nor intended.

'In that case, you'd better go,' Luke said.

As soon as he had spoken, he wanted to take it back, to explain that he thought that the love between them gave them both the right to expect a certain standard of behaviour, but before he could speak Stephanie had whirled round and stampeded out of the flat.

She had no money and she had left all her belongings behind. If a taxi had not come into sight she might have repented of her tempestuous flight and gone back, but without giving herself time to think she hailed the taxi and gave the address of her own flat.

Her mother was in when she arrived.

'You'll have to pay for the taxi,' Stephanie said. 'I've left everything behind in Luke's flat.'

'You've quarrelled,' Vera said, looking at her ravaged face.

'Yes. Don't ask me about it. I don't want to discuss it.'

Stephanie waited by the telephone all day, expecting Luke to call her, but no word came from him. She felt cold right through to the bone, sick with disbelief that the wonderful love and trust she had thought was established between them could have disappeared in a quarrel that had blown up in a moment, and ought to have been settled in the same short space of time.

Two

Luke was as stunned as Stephanie by the calamity that had overtaken them. The last thing he had expected when he had flared up and suggested that she should go was that she would immediately take him at his word and walk out. He waited for one moment too long before going after her, and was just in time to see her jump into a taxi and slam the door.

Luke went slowly back into the flat, the impulse to run after Stephanie and implore her to come back beginning to evaporate. His anger at the way she and Conrad had sat and discussed Prue's book stirred in him once more. He was jealous of Conrad, he had to admit that. After all, Conrad and Stephanie had once been lovers and they were still friendly, remarkably friendly considering the way Stephanie said the man had treated her.

He had always disliked Aylmer; yes, and distrusted him, too. Luke remembered his meeting with Ernst von Lynden and the report he had made in Lisbon about it. Had anyone followed that up? Knowing British Intelligence, probably not. There must be someone in London he could contact who would tell him whether Conrad's allegiance had ever been questioned.

His motives were, of course, despicable. Luke admitted that to himself quite frankly. He wanted to show Conrad up as fraud and a Nazi sympathizer so as to give Stephanie a disgust of him. What Luke did not want to admit was that he was using this vendetta as an excuse to avoid facing the real issue between him and Stephanie: her place in his life and whether he wanted her to be his wife. It was something he ought to have faced before he had made love to her, but until that entrancing weekend they had spent together he had not realized how strong the tie between them might become.

The few days they had spent living together in the flat had been a different experience entirely. They had begun to

221

discover that their habits were not entirely compatible. Luke was a natural early riser, while Stephanie, except when she was filming, hardly knew that the morning hours before nine o'clock existed. She was untidy in a way that Luke found exasperating while he, from long years of living out of a suitcase, was almost fanatically precise. They had only talked in the most general terms about the future, but it was obvious that Stephanie wanted to go on acting and Luke, even though he said that he was tired of reporting wars, would be involved in writing in some form or other which was only too likely to keep him moving around the world. Could their lives be fitted into any sort of pattern? There were times when Luke was doubtful.

It was this indecision which kept Luke from following his first impulse and hurrying after Stephanie. That, and his desire to justify his demand that she should separate from Conrad in a decisive way which Luke, in his more reasonable moments, would have admitted would be almost impossible.

He was determined to track down somebody who could tell him whether his Lisbon report had cast any doubts on Conrad's loyalty. Presumably not, since the man was still at large, free to lounge about in other people's flats, drinking their coffee, flattering their girls.

In pursuit of this idea, and to shut out the dismay of knowing that he and Stephanie were at loggerheads, Luke did the round of the Fleet Street pubs, greeting old cronies and throwing out feelers to find someone who could give him information about Conrad.

By the middle of the afternoon, none too sober, he had reached an office in Whitehall and was talking to a middle-aged major who said, 'Luke Lindquist? Yes, we've got a file with your name on it. It was good of you to be so helpful about your sojourn with the Huns.'

'You did get the report then?' Luke said, slightly disappointed to find that the system was more efficient than he had believed.

'Oh, surely! We appreciated your co-operation. What can I do to help you now?'

Luke began to improvise. 'I was thinking of writing another

book, dealing with people who had family connections on both sides,' he said. 'People like Conrad Aylmer, you know, whose loyalties must be sorely tried at times.'

'Interesting idea, but wouldn't it be better left until after the war? You could search out the German angle then.'

'I thought I might make a start while I'm in London, kicking my heels, waiting to go back to Italy. There was nothing in what I told you about meeting Aylmer's cousin that would make it a sensitive matter to approach him?'

'Sensitive from a security angle, you mean? Lord, no!'

The major looked uncomfortable for a moment and then he went on in a dogged way, 'Perhaps not quite in the best of taste, d'you think? I mean, sounding out a man whose mother is living in Germany about how he feels?'

'I'm a tasteless newshound,' Luke said. 'If I think there's a story I'll go and get it.'

'Yes, quite. Well ... that's up to you, of course.'

Luke wandered away, feeling dissatisfied. Everyone insisted that Conrad was above suspicion and yet ... hadn't it been just a bit too easy to get hold of someone who was ready, even eager, to reassure Luke about Conrad's loyalty? Luke was still not totally convinced. There was something in the air, an alertness in official circles when Aylmer's name was mentioned, that made his antennae twitch.

In the meantime, he had had no lunch and he had a raging headache and a pain in his stomach which was all too reminiscent of his past sufferings.

'Damn,' Luke said softly to himself. 'It can't come back again, it just can't. It's only a couple of days since the doc told me I was all clear.'

He got back to the flat just in time to be violently sick. The trouble was, as he was forced to acknowledge, he had got out of the habit of drinking while he had been ill. It was no more than that, he was sure of it, but he felt too wretched to do more than lie down on the bed to recuperate.

Stephanie's clutter was all round him, which did not make him feel any better. He closed his eyes to shut out the sight of a pair of filmy stockings tossed over the back of a chair, and fell into a heavy sleep which lasted for hours.

Luke would have felt less frustrated if he had known that news of his renewed interest in Conrad had filtered through to Claud More and caused him considerable annoyance.

'Damn all curious American reporters,' Claud said. 'Why can't Lindquist leave well alone? The last thing we want is for him to start throwing doubts on Aylmer at this stage. What's Lindquist doing in London anyway?'

'He's been on sick leave. He's due to return to Sicily any day.'

'And things are stirring on that front. As soon as news of the Italian capitulation gets out all the newspapers will be clamouring for their correspondents to join in the landings on the mainland. Why don't we do Lindquist a favour and get him away early?'

When Luke eventually came out of his long sleep he was disgusted to discover that it was after midnight. His first thought was that it was too late now to get in touch with Stephanie and she would think that he was sulking or, even worse, had meant it when he had told her to leave him.

There was not much he could do except go back to bed. Sleep eluded him because he was no longer tired and because thoughts of Stephanie chased round and round in his head. In the early hours of the morning he dropped off once more and again slept longer than he had intended.

By the time he had washed and shaved and had some breakfast – and he was reassured to find that he was ravenously hungry – it was mid-morning. And he was the man who had grumbled because Stephanie had been comatose at nine o'clock! He smiled at the thought, planning to tell her and, he hoped, to make her laugh at his backsliding.

When the telephone rang Luke seized it eagerly, sure that Stephanie had anticipated his own intention to call her, but it was his London office.

'Luke, this is urgent,' his chief said. 'We've been kept in the dark, but Montgomery landed on the toe of Italy some days ago. The Italians have thrown in their hand and landings are taking place at Salerno.'

224

Luke swore briefly but with feeling. The big story had broken and he had not been there.

'Never mind the blasphemy, get cracking,' the head of the bureau said. 'You've got about two hours. There's transport laid on for you, but *keep quiet* about it. Pack and bring your bag with you to the office. I'll give you all the details when I see you.'

He rang off without saying goodbye, leaving Luke looking round him blankly. Two hours and out of that time he had to pack and visit the office and get to wherever his transport was waiting, not to mention settling the affairs he had been dealing with in a leisurely way, thinking he had time to spare. The flat. He had already discussed re-letting it. The agents would have to deal with cleaning it, throwing out odd bits of food and so on. Unless he asked Stephanie and her Mrs Bakewell to deal with it. He had to see Stephanie; whatever else he did he had to see her before he left; but he could hardly offer her a heartfelt apology and throw her the task of clearing out the flat at the same time.

Luke began to pack in a methodical way born of long practice. While he was about it, he packed for Stephanie, too, his hands lingering reminiscently over the soft silky underwear and remembered clothes. It was hell that he was not going to be able to make love to her again before he went.

He tried telephoning her flat, but there was no reply. The only thing he could do was to pile his luggage into a taxi and go round there, and even that brief excursion put a strain on his timetable.

'Don't you go off and leave me,' he warned the taxi driver outside Stephanie's door.

'Not likely to do that, guv, when you haven't paid me,' the driver said.

It was Vera who answered the door.

'Oh, it's you,' she said. 'You might as well save your breath, because Stephanie won't see you. I don't know what you've done, but she's adamant against you.'

'Just tell her I'm here,' Luke asked.

'She's out.'

'When will she be back?'

'Can't say. She's gone off somewhere with Conrad Aylmer.'

There was a hint of triumph in Vera's riposte, a suspicion of a smirk about her expression that rasped Luke's taut nerves. Stephanie had gone straight from him to Conrad. It was the perfect move if she wanted to show him that she valued her independence higher than any wish he might express.

Luke dumped Stephanie's suitcase at Vera's feet.

'Just give her that and tell her I said goodbye,' he said.

Reluctantly, Vera told Stephanie when she got home that Luke had been round.

'He brought your suitcase and all your things,' she said.

Stephanie looked blankly at the suitcase. She had not expected that Luke would do that, just pack her belongings and bring them round to her.

'How did your rehearsal go?' Vera asked.

'Oh ... all right,' Stephanie said. 'Didn't Luke leave a message?'

'Turned round and went without a word. Very rude, I thought.'

As Stephanie unpacked the tears were streaming down her face. What a fool I am, she thought. I've thrown away the best thing I ever had and all for a moment's jealousy and a flash of anger. Why did I agree to start rehearsing with Conrad? If I'd been here when Luke called round we could have talked. That's all it needs, I'm sure of it, just a chance to get together and explain ourselves to one another.

With sudden resolution she dried her eyes and blew her nose.

'I'm going round to see Luke,' she told Vera.

'You look a sight.'

'I know. It doesn't matter.'

Her heart was beating uncomfortably fast as she rang Luke's bell. She had no idea what she was going to say, only the conviction that once they had both admitted they were sorry about their quarrel they would be able to make it up. She rang a second time and then a third, but there was no reply. There really seemed nothing Stephanie could do unless she sat on the stairs and waited for him.

As she turned away disconsolately a man came clattering up the stairs. For one moment Stephanie thought it might be Luke, but it was no one she had ever seen before.

'If you're interested in the flat I'm afraid you're too late,' he said. 'Mr Lindquist put it in my hands this morning and I let it within the hour. I've come round to open it up for the cleaner. The new tenants will be moving in tomorrow.'

'Mr Lindquist has gone away?' Stephanie asked. She heard her voice coming from an immense distance and listened to it with fascinated interest.

'He was sent off abroad sooner than he expected,' the agent said. 'That's the way it is in wartime, isn't it?'

'Yes,' Stephanie said. 'That's the way it is in wartime.'

Three

The blatant happiness between Stephanie and Luke had unsettled Conrad. He had stirred Luke's jealousy because of his own resentment at the easy way they had managed to come together. He assumed Stephanie's misery the next time they met was due to Luke's imminent departure and, since Stephanie did not want to confide in Conrad that she had quarrelled with Luke because of him, he was left feeling envious.

By the time they did their performance at the Stagedoor Canteen Stephanie had learnt to mask the torment of regret that raged inside her. She had never felt so alone in her life, but she still managed to smile and sing, to dance with grace and a touch of sexual abandonment that brought appreciative wolf whistles from the audience of American servicemen for whom the Canteen was run. She was glad when it was over and she could sink back into a routine that dulled her senses and kept her occupied with trivialities.

She stopped reading the newspapers and would have switched off the news on the wireless if Vera had let her. There was hard fighting in Italy; Luke was probably in danger; it was something she just didn't want to think about.

Conrad, on the other hand, read the papers avidly. The unreliable Italians had given in, just as he had always thought they would, but the Germans in Italy were fighting on. Even now they might turn the tide, but Conrad was becoming increasingly convinced that he had backed the wrong side. He was cynical about the value of the reports he compiled for German Intelligence and increasingly impatient with the restrictions his work put on his freedom of movement.

Anton's presence in his house, too, was irksome. In his way he was an admirable servant, but his secret knowledge of Conrad's activities gave him a power which Conrad disliked.

He even dared to sound reproving when Conrad informed him that he was going on a visit to the north of England.

'I thought it had been agreed that your sphere at the present time was to be in the south,' he said.

'I'm going on a private visit,' Conrad said and fumed inwardly at the way Anton pursed his lips.

The atmosphere that had surrounded Stephanie and Luke had aroused a desire in Conrad to prove that he, too, could enjoy the same sort of happiness. None of the pretty women who succumbed so willingly to his advances could give him what he wanted. It had to be Nesta. Conrad had written to her, more unguardedly than he had ever written before, and in return had received an ecstatic reply that she was due for seven days' leave, that she would be in heaven if she could spend it with him.

Conrad met her in Keswick, after a journey which had tried his patience considerably, but all his bad temper dropped away when he saw Nesta, thin, vital and excited, waiting for him. She dropped her kit bag unceremoniously and threw herself into an embrace that had no inhibitions about it and paid no heed to the raised eyebrows of other travellers.

'Why *here?*' she asked as soon as she could draw breath.

'Because I knew someone who would lend me a cottage,' Conrad said. 'I didn't want to go to a hotel.'

He did not say so, but the same thought was at the back of his mind as had haunted Stephanie: he might be recognized.

'Lovely to be on our own,' Nesta said contentedly. 'I'll be able to cook for you.'

'Can you? Cook, I mean?'

'Certainly! My mother saw to that, even though I fought her all the way. Nothing fancy, such as Anton does, but you won't starve.'

'Let's forget about Anton,' Conrad said, putting his arm round her. 'Let's forget about the war. I want to get away from everything.'

The cottage was small and old, crouched in a fold of land with the Lakeland hills rising behind it. It felt chilly when they first went in, but there was an ample supply of dry firewood, and once the fire in the living room was lit the thick stone walls began to take up the heat.

230

'Two bedrooms,' Nesta said. 'Which one would you prefer, sir?'

'The one with the biggest bed. I was told there'd be linen in a cupboard.'

'We'll need to air it,' Nesta said seriously.

'So domesticated!' Conrad mocked her.

He watched as she draped sheets and blankets over a clothes horse in front of the fire, amused by an aspect of her he had never seen before. Nesta looked up and caught his eye and smiled. Her joy at being with him was so intense that Conrad's breath caught in his throat. Even after having known her for years, he was unprepared for the effect that Nesta had on him. She moved him as no other woman had ever done, or possibly ever would.

He held out his arms and Nesta went to him, leaning against him in utter contentment. For the first time for a very long time she felt that Conrad was wholly hers.

'Seven days,' she said. 'Oh, bliss!'

It was the one time when they were able to be together that nothing intruded on them. Stephanie, if she had known about it, would have envied them their isolation. The weather was kind and they were able to go out walking in the crisp autumn air and see the bracken turning gold and the leaves beginning to drift down from the trees. They took the paths into the nearer hills, but they made no great expeditions, content to explore the one small valley which they regarded as their own.

They saw few people and wanted no company but their own. Nesta never questioned their ability to supply one another with all the companionship they needed, but to Conrad it was a revelation. The restless need for entertainment which had driven him to other women in Nesta's absence seemed laughable while he was with the girl who could engage him in fierce argument, or hold him spellbound as she read aloud from one of the few books they found in the cottage.

'Treasure trove!' Nesta exclaimed, holding up a battered *Complete Shakespeare*.

There were pages missing, but often either Conrad or Nesta could supply the speeches from memory. They began to read the plays, haphazardly, in no order, splitting the parts between them as they arose, breaking off to discuss points of interpretation.

There were certain roles which fitted Nesta as if they had been written for her. Conrad had not thought she had a gift for comedy, but she made a delightful Rosalind, boyish and mocking, teasing her Orlando, but still fathoms deep in love.

'Just like I am,' Nesta said, reaching up from her seat on the floor in front of the fire to pull Conrad's head down so that she could kiss him.

To Juliet she brought a youthful gravity, a puzzled acceptance of the deep emotion that welled up in her which Conrad found profoundly moving.

'It's a part you ought to play before you're much older,' he said unthinkingly.

'Oh, if only I could!' Nesta said.

For a moment a shadow hovered over them, but then she laughed and stretched her arms above her head to get rid of the tensions she had brought to her performance.

'This is absolutely my most favourite thing that we've done, reading the plays like this,' she said contentedly.

'Is it indeed!'

Nesta turned to him, laughing. 'Apart from making love to you, my own darling,' she said.

Towards the end of their time together they read *Antony and Cleopatra*.

'This is the best thing we've done so far,' Nesta remarked halfway through. 'I'm surprised.'

'So am I,' Conrad agreed. 'I hadn't thought of myself as Antony, but reading it like this is making me positively ambitious.'

'I'm glad to hear it,' Nesta retorted. 'Darling, I was in despair when I heard you were frittering away your time singing and dancing with Stephanie again. Can't you give it up and get back to real acting?'

'I could try,' Conrad said. 'Come on, let's finish it. "Come, let us have one other gaudy night …" '

She was all the queens of the world and a loving, fearful woman; her beauty took the breath away and yet she was still his small-boned, rough-haired Nesta. After her death scene

Conrad could only just manage to speak Charmian's farewell.

' "Now boast thee, death, in thy possession lies a lass unparalleled ..." ' He broke off. 'Let's leave it there,' he said. 'The rest of the play's an anticlimax.'

'We ought to finish it,' Nesta objected, opening her eyes. 'The last speech by Caesar is a good one about the grave of a pair so famous.'

As always, her rapid transition from high tragedy to practical discussion shook Conrad. How did she do it? Conrad doubted whether even Nesta knew that.

'You're a remarkable actress,' he said, trying to speak lightly.

'We go splendidly together,' Nesta said. 'No, don't make a joke. You know I'm talking about acting.'

He did know it and his silence acknowledged that they had achieved something out of the ordinary that evening.

'After the war ...' Nesta said.

She did not need to say any more. Conrad knew what she was thinking. After the war they must act together, roles such as those they had just read, parts which would stretch their capacities and establish them as leading actors in their field. After the war ... Once again, after having banished his dilemma for the space of a week, Conrad was forced to face up to it. If the Germans won the war Nesta would be torn away from him. He was dedicated to seeing that they did win and for the first time he longed for them to lose.

Wild thoughts of confessing his guilt raced through his mind, to be immediately dismissed. If he did that he would be incarcerated in prison and all hope of a future with Nesta would be lost. Perhaps he could run down his spying activities, fade out of the picture. Even as he thought it he remembered Anton, obsequious and persistent, always enquiring whether there were messages to be transmitted to Germany.

Conrad reached out and caught Nesta to him. She tumbled against him, laughing, and they lost their balance and collapsed on the hearth rug. It was not the first time they had made love in front of the fire, but this time Conrad possessed Nesta with a raging passion that almost frightened her. She thought that it was because they must soon part, and when they finally

233

separated she held him in her arms with a tenderness that had a maternal quality about it.

'My dear one, my dear one,' she murmured softly.

Conrad raised himself on one elbow and looked down at her, wildly dishevelled and naked, her eyes enormous and black in her pale face.

'A lass unparalleled,' he said.

Four

Luke spent a wet, cold, miserable winter battling through Italy with the American troops and then, in the spring of 1944, he was recalled to England.

Everyone knew the invasion of Europe was coming, the only question was – when? Britain was seething with activity, but it was more difficult than ever to get hold of reliable information.

In between endless discussions about the invasion, the other thing that exercised Luke's mind was whether to get in touch with Stephanie? He had heard nothing of her since their last abrupt parting, but now, finding himself in the same country, poor old war-torn England, seeing how shabby and tired the people looked, he thought about her constantly. How had she weathered the months they had been apart? Did she think about him and were her thoughts kind? If they were, it was probably more than he deserved.

He had just got to the point of admitting that it was nothing but stiffnecked pride that was stopping him from approaching her when he was told to report to the American First Army Headquarters, not in Bristol, where it had been housed, but right down on the south-west coast. He went off, grumbling, and found himself trapped behind a barbed-wire cordon. Once inside the sealed off area devoted to the invasion he could not leave nor could he send out any further communiqué until D-Day had arrived.

On the evening of 3 June Luke and a few other privileged journalists were taken aboard Admiral Kirk's flagship the *Augusta* to be briefed by General Omar Bradley on the US First Army's assault plans.

All round them on the choppy grey water off Plymouth the landing craft, packed with assault troops, bobbed and swayed. The smaller LCTs, painted in vivid camouflage colours, were already moving towards the outer harbour, hauling barrage balloons behind them. The larger ships, the LSTs, carrying between 1,600 and 1,900 tons of vehicles or cargo, were a sombre grey.

It had been a fine, sunny day, but General Bradley told the waiting war correspondents that the weather forecast was ominous.

'Choppy water in the Channel with five-foot breakers and a four-foot surf on the beaches. The prospects for tomorrow look bad.'

As Luke had tentatively guessed, the landings were to take place on the Normandy coast. Five beaches had been selected. The British and Canadians were to go in on three to the east, code-named Sword, Juno and Gold, while the American army were assigned the two to the west which had been called Omaha and Utah.

It was Omaha beach which particularly interested Luke. That was the area into which he was to follow the battle-hardened veterans of the US First Infantry Division. He had been into battle with them in North Africa and again in Italy; they were old friends and he was glad to be amongst them once more.

After gaining a toehold on the Normandy coast the Omaha and Utah assault forces were to join up and swing round to cut off the Contentin peninsular, isolating and, it was hoped, capturing the port of Cherbourg. At the same time the British and Canadian armies would be diverting the Germans around the Caen area.

'How soon do you expect to take Cherbourg?' one of the correspondents asked.

General Bradley nodded to the map. 'D-Day plus eight is the estimate, but that's probably better than we can hope to do because Rommel has recently increased his Normandy defences. I'll stick my neck out and say D plus fifteen. I'd even settle for D plus twenty.'

It was a bright moonlit night. Luke did his best to sleep, but it was difficult to settle down, knowing that Operation Overlord was already under way. He fell into a doze, expecting to be awakened at any moment by the news that they were off, but at four o'clock on the morning of 4 June General Eisenhower was

236

forced into taking the decision they had feared: to postpone the invasion for another twenty-four hours.

'Continuing five-foot waves in the Channel and no sign of a break in the overcast conditions until 7 or 8 June,' Luke was told when he woke up.

'If we wait until 8 June the tide won't suit us,' Luke said thoughtfully. 'The halfway high water mark won't be reached until long after daylight. Do you fancy an attack in the middle of the morning? Because I don't!'

'So if Ike wants to go in at dawn and 5 June has already been called off it's 6 June or wait until next month.'

'He won't wait,' Luke said confidently. 'I'll take bets that if there's the slightest break in the weather he'll throw everything in on 6 June.'

By the evening there was a flicker of hope. The wind was slackening and the cloud base was lifting and there was a chance that the better visibility would persist until Tuesday, 6 June. After that it was forecast that the clouds would close in again with the risk of making air and sea support difficult, if not impossible.

No one liked the prospect. GI stomachs were already heaving with seasickness and there were grave worries about the heavy seas swamping the dual drive tanks which were to have been swum ashore straight into action on the beaches.

By four o'clock in the morning of 5 June the decision had been taken. For good or ill, D-Day would be the following day.

At dawn on 6 June Luke stood balancing uneasily in a slow-moving, unwieldy landing craft, looking back towards the land. The sea was churned into a white froth by the wakes of hundreds of ships moving towards France. Packed round him troops in combat gear muttered and grumbled and chewed gum, and some of them hung in despairing misery over the side and heaved up the remains of their last meal.

In the sky ahead of them there was an orange glow as RAF bombers began a massive attack along the coast from the Seine to Cherbourg. Two airborne divisions had already been dropped on the Contentin Peninsular and the German Seventh Army had given out an invasion alarm, but General von Rundstedt, at his headquarters near Paris, still anticipated an

237

Allied attack against the Pas de Calais and insisted that this air drop was only a diversion.

By six o'clock the first wave of landing craft had reached Omaha beach. The soldier nearest to Luke swore with monotonous regularity as they watched the DD tanks attempt to make the landing and founder in the pounding surf.

'We're going to have to go in without our armour,' he said at last.

It felt like chaos at the time, but Luke had been in too many battles not to know that one man's limited view of what was going on could be totally mistaken. It was only later that he pieced together the story and realized how close they had come to disaster. The heavy bombers of the Eighth Air Force, hampered by a mist that was thickened by smoke, and fearing to drop bombs on the men approaching the shore, allowed too great a margin of safety and overshot the target by some three miles. Of thirty-two DD tanks launched off Omaha, twenty-seven were swamped in the heavy seas and became not merely a disappointment but a positive hazard, taking up valuable space in the lanes which had been cleared in the Germans' underwater defences. Where there were gaps landing craft swarmed to get ashore, and on the beachhead there was one almighty jam of troops and equipment.

Luke lay huddled up tight against the sea wall, pinned down with his friends of the First Division by crippling bursts of enemy small-arms fire. Over their heads shells whined from the larger guns further inland which were battering the craft still trying to land.

Sooner or later they were going to have to break out. Either that, or risk being thrown back into the sea.

A sergeant who had been making his way from one group of men to the next under cover of the wall skidded to a halt by Luke's side, his heavy boots grating on the shingle, crouching for cover as bullets rattled past him.

'What gives?' Luke asked.

'We're moving out to take the slopes ahead of us as soon as we get the signal. Of all the lousy luck! Did you hear? Rommel sent one of his crack field divisions to these beaches for an assault exercise! I'll say one thing — they're getting a better work out than they reckoned on.'

Luke did not need telling that he was to stay put. He had been lucky to get in on the first wave ashore, but no one wanted to be hampered by a noncombatant when they went into action. The old familiar question nagged at his mind. Had he done right? Should he have been out there with a gun in his hand, instead of hovering on the fringes observing what other men were doing?

He got a partial answer from the sergeant. He raised his head and looked round and then, as he got cautiously to his feet, he gave Luke a friendly blow on the shoulder.

'Write it up good,' he said. 'The folks back home will want to read about this.'

Luke watched them go in the doubled up run which every advancing soldier he had ever seen adopted, then he turned round to look at the congestion behind him. They were trying to bring bulldozers ashore and not having a lot of success because of the large target the vehicles presented to the German guns. Nevertheless, the waves of men and equipment were still getting onto the beach. The effort it represented, the sheer cost in men and materials, was enough to make you dizzy. What would 'the folks back home' make of it? The anxious mothers and fathers, wives and children and sweethearts in the real Omaha; what possible meaning could it have for them that their menfolk had suffered and died on a beach in France named after their state?

The first line of his report began to form in Luke's mind: 'Today I went to Omaha ...' He would try to put into it something of his pride in his fellow countrymen, the friendly, gregarious, gum chewing youngsters who, even as he lay there on the cluttered beach, were retrieving what might have been a disaster and turning it into a grimly won victory.

Luke's D-Day despatch was the best reporting he had ever done. He knew it and the deep satisfaction he felt as the words moved into order across the page went a long way towards stifling his doubts about the role he was playing. It was worthwhile, this business of standing back from the action in order to tell the world what was going on.

A week later the British had still not succeeded in taking

their objective of Caen and the Americans had not broken through to Cherbourg, but it had become abundantly clear that the Germans had been completely misled about Allied intentions and had concentrated their defences on the Pas de Calais. Luke gave a passing thought to the way this brilliant deception had been carried out and wondered who had been responsible for it. Whoever it was, they must be celebrating their success as the armies penetrated deeper and deeper into their chosen field and the Germans raced to correct their mistake.

Luke took time to have a word with the wounded. Early on only the lightly wounded had been evacuated to England because of the difficulties of carrying the badly hurt men through the crashing surf. Now the beginnings of a prefabricated artificial harbour, contrived by the British, was being assembled and the men were being ferried back to hospitals in England.

In a makeshift ward where the wounded lay awaiting transportation Luke stopped for a word with a youngster with severe wounds to his leg and side.

'Feeling rough?' Luke asked sympathetically.

'Sure am, sir. Still, they say I'll be OK when they've patched me up. My leg ... it is still there, isn't it? The doc swore he hadn't taken it off, but I can't get my head up high enough to see.'

'Can't you feel it?' Luke asked.

'Yeah, but they say you go on feeling a severed limb, like a ghost, long after it's cut off.'

'You've still got two legs,' Luke assured him. 'What do you want me to do? Drop my typewriter on it to prove it's still there?'

'I guess not,' the boy admitted.

There was a picture of a girl pinned to the canvas above his head. Bloodstained and torn, it was still recognizably Stephanie.

'Your pin-up's suffered, too,' Luke remarked, his eyes on the provocative stance and smiling face. There was just the slightest lift to one of Stephanie's eyebrows. As if she had spoken, Luke knew how she felt about the way the photographer had posed her.

'Stephanie Bartram, the film star,' the boy said. 'She's the greatest! I've carried that picture around for months, but I guess it's only fit for the trash can now, like me.'

'Don't say that, soldier! You'll be up on your feet and back in

240

the fighting in a few weeks' time. You'll be sorry then that you didn't appreciate your hospitalization. I know Stephanie Bartram. She's a friend of mine. I'll write and ask her to send you a new picture.'

'A signed photograph?' the soldier asked eagerly. 'Say, that'd be great!'

It was the excuse Luke had been looking for to start writing to Stephanie again. He wanted her to know that he was in France. His reports had been for the American paper, so she wouldn't have seen what he had written, which was a pity. He acknowledged the conceit of it with a wry, inward grin. He wanted her to know that he had been doing some good writing. Never mind the rest of the world, he wanted Stephanie to admire him.

Luke's letter was not long, and it contained no reference to the past, but it did bring him the reply he wanted. She had, as he had known she would, not only sent a photograph to the wounded soldier, but had written him a personal note of sympathy as well. As for her own news, she wrote, 'As you will have heard, we are having a little trouble from the air again and I have gone back to my ambulance driving'.

Nothing more than that, but as he read the words he felt sick. He did indeed know that the British Isles were having trouble from the air. Shortly after the D-Day landings Hitler had unleashed the first of the secret weapons which he was relying on to bring the British and their allies to their knees. Pilotless planes had been sent on their undeviating, purposeful course towards southern England, and their advent had made a lot of people thoughtful about what would have been the outcome if General Eisenhower had not gambled on the hazardous landings of 6 June. The effect of the bomb-laden aircraft on the packed troop concentrations would have been devastating.

Of all the weapons used by the Germans during the war the one Stephanie most disliked was the V-1. Even calling them buzz-bombs or doodlebugs did not alter the fact that they were one of the nastiest things that had happened to the civilian population. They chugged across the sky like maniac toys and even the most hardened Blitz veterans feared the moment when the engine cut out and a nerve-stretching silence preceded the explosion.

In spite of her fear of this new threat, Stephanie went back to her ambulance work with a feeling of relief at doing something useful towards the war effort. She had been involved in a tour of *Spring Cleaning* with Conrad during the winter months, and although the work had kept her mind off the misery of losing Luke, it had not been a happy time.

Conrad's ulcer was giving him bouts of acute pain. He was capricious and difficult to work with. Worse still, with Nesta out of his reach, and plagued by doubts about his work for the Abwehr, Conrad had turned to Stephanie for distraction. Nesta was the woman he wanted, but Stephanie was *there*, and because of his underlying contempt for her Conrad had no doubt that she would respond to his languid, self-confident advances.

Whistle and I'll come to you, my lad, Stephanie thought, torn between exasperation and amusement at his audacity. Not likely!

Aloud she said, 'My dear Conrad, save yourself the trouble! I'm not to be had for the asking, not by you nor by any other man who thinks he can pick me up and put me down as the fancy takes him.'

It was Luke she had in her mind as she spoke, but Conrad did not appear to realize that.

'Have you forgotten how splendid we were together?' he asked, moving closer.

'Let me put it bluntly,' Stephanie said. 'I don't want you. More than that, you revolt me. You're one of those people who've got treachery in their soul. I doubt whether you're capable of being true to anyone, not even Nesta, and I think she's the closest you're ever likely to come to loving any woman. I thought I'd made this clear to you last time you tried it on.'

Conrad shrugged and moved away. 'Darling, I was merely offering a little mutual pleasure,' he complained. 'Everlasting fidelity is *not* my line, I must admit. As for Nesta ... a dear girl, but dreadfully intense. One does need relief from the grand passion occasionally.'

She had angered him more than he chose to reveal. Treachery in the soul ... what a lurid turn of phrase the woman had. He had only one true allegiance, from which not even Nesta could divert him, and to prove it Conrad turned to his espionage activities with more vigour than he had shown for many months.

The details Conrad amassed before D-Day showed that landings were likely to be concentrated on the Normandy coast, but in the skilful hands of the Deception Unit these stories were changed and what was actually transmitted by Anton indicated a quite different area.

Conrad was at first puzzled and then angry when it became obvious that the German forces had been ill-prepared on the Normandy beaches. He even spoke about it to Anton. The tour with Stephanie which had proved a profitable source of news was over and he was back in his house in London, following with mounting disbelief the news of the slow success of the Allied landings.

'I don't know why I bothered with all the reports I've been sending through,' Conrad said, with real bitterness. 'The bloody Abwehr didn't believe them! I slaved my guts out getting information for them and as far as I can see all they've done is stick the notes on a spike and forget about them.'

'Have you given any thought to what you will do if Germany is beaten?' Anton asked.

'Oh ... go to the United States, I suppose. I can find work there, I'm sure.'

'Provided, of course, that no one finds out that you've been spying for the Nazis,' Anton suggested.

Something behind his obsequious manner, some hint of triumph aroused Conrad's suspicions.

'Let me remind you that if I go down, you go down with me,' he said. 'Don't think that you can save yourself by betraying me. If I were to be arrested on evidence from you, you would be a dead man.'

'Do you think you could reach me from prison?'

Conrad smiled. 'You're forgetting something, little man. I

come from a large and powerful family. I don't mean here, I mean in Germany. No matter what happens, some of them will survive. I only have to let it be known that you gave me away and my friends and relatives will know what to do. Do you want to spend the rest of your life as a hunted man?'

Anton tried to hide the shiver that went through him.

'I wasn't serious,' he protested. 'It was you who thought I was talking about betrayal. No such hint ever passed my lips.'

'Keep it that way,' Conrad advised.

The next day the first of the V-1 weapons fell on England and for a time Conrad almost believed that Germany could win the technological war. Then he saw that although the damage was extensive, although the buzz-bombs were intensely disliked, they alone could not bring victory to Germany.

Stephanie, he heard, had gone back to driving an ambulance. Conrad looked back to the early days of the war and found it difficult to believe that he had once agonized over the loss of lives the bombing represented. He had grown harder since then, and more cynical. The Allied air forces had bombed German cities; if the Germans hit back in retaliation what else could they expect? Women were killed, children were killed, the elderly, the helpless, the unfit. It was happening on both sides.

He saw Stephanie occasionally, but he did not seek her out. Her rejection of him had stung, even though he had treated it lightly. With so many troops overseas there were plenty of spare women available. He was lightly and persistently promiscuous, as he had been before the war, but when Nesta came on leave he dropped everything and spent all his spare time with her, even though her growing interest in Zionism was irksome.

'The Jews have a right to their own homeland,' Nesta insisted with passionate intensity.

On this brief leave she was neglecting her own family to move in with Conrad. It was the middle of the afternoon, but they were sprawled across Conrad's large bed, slack and replete with satisfied desire.

'You're only a quarter Jewish by blood and not even that by religion,' Conrad said. 'Why can't you leave them to manage their own affairs?'

'I have to care about people like the Goldstein family,' Nesta protested. 'I've been wondering whether I ought to convert.'

'You! You're a natural pagan, the same as I am.'

Conrad's heavy eyelids drooped over his eyes, but Nesta had nerved herself to have this talk with him and she was not going to be diverted. She propped herself up, leaning on his chest, and tapped him on the cheek.

'Don't go to sleep! I've got things to say to you. Since I've been in London I've had several hints that I'm one of a procession of your loves. Conrad, I have to know – have you been faithful to me since we were last together?'

'Darling, it's a long time between September and July.'

'It wasn't my fault you were on tour the last time I came home on leave,' Nesta said in an even tone, knowing that his light protest was an admission of guilt.

'I'm just saying I don't see you very often.'

'And you can't wait? You have to have a woman, no matter who she may be? Conrad, how *can* you? After the way it was between us on that lovely week together, how can you spoil it by chasing after flimsy little tarts like ... like Dorita Marques?'

She knew by the tautness of his muscles under her hands that Conrad was angry, but he answered in a light, drawling way, 'I don't chase after anyone, darling.'

'No, you look at them with your blue, blue eyes and they tumble into your arms,' Nesta said. She moved away from him, over to the far side of the bed. 'Like I did.'

'I don't love any of them,' Conrad said.

'I know you don't. You love me. Do you think that makes it any easier to bear? You betray yourself and me for a bit of passing excitement.'

Conrad stirred uneasily at that word 'betray', but this time he did not attempt to reply.

'I was a virgin when I first came to you and no other man has touched me since,' Nesta said. She had been determined not to cry, but as she spoke her voice broke.

Conrad reached out to touch her, but she struck his hand away.

'You sicken me,' she said.

'I didn't notice it half an hour ago.'

'Don't taunt me with it! I'm as ashamed of myself as I am of you. If I had any real strength I'd tell you to go to hell and find myself another man who'd really love me. But I don't want anyone else, only you, only you!'

She was crying in earnest now, the sobs racking her slight body, and she no longer resisted as Conrad took her back in his arms.

'Dear girl, don't be so wild,' he whispered. 'You've been listening to gossip and you know how these stories get exaggerated. I may have relaxed in my spare time with a girl or two, but they mean nothing to me. I live under a terrible strain ...'

'Don't we all?' Nesta demanded, but her voice was steadier and she lay quietly in his hold. 'The war is as hard for me to bear as it is for you.'

'Not quite. You have the discipline of being in the army to keep you steady while I'm footloose and drifting.'

'If only we could be together all the time!'

'The war,' Conrad began, but Nesta interrupted him.

'No, not the war! You and your reluctance to be tied down.'

'My way of life was fixed before we met. It's not easy to alter it.'

His excuses were feeble, but the soft voice and the soothing movements of his hands were difficult to resist.

'So I have to forgive you?' Nesta asked.

'Please.'

Nesta sighed, defeated by her desperate love for him and her need to believe that he would continue to love her.

'Will it happen again when I've gone back?' she asked.

'I don't like making you unhappy. I suppose I thought that as long as you didn't know ...'

'I always knew. You told me once that I'd go on loving you after I'd found you out and it would be hell, and you were right, but I thought you would have changed after last autumn.'

He did not answer and Nesta went on in a low voice, 'We could be such a wonderful team, working together, sharing everything.'

'Antony and Cleopatra,' Conrad murmured, teasing her a little now that she had calmed down.

'Why not? You've got money. We could have our own company ...'

'I haven't got that sort of money, darling!'

'If I were you I'd venture *everything* on making my mark on the theatre.'

She had allowed herself to be diverted by her other obsession, but now, looking at the fine profile outlined against the pillow beside her, wistfully tracing the line of his jaw with her finger, Nesta whispered, 'You do love me?'

'Yes. Whatever you may hear about me, always remember that. I love you best of all.'

Half satisfied, and longing to believe in him, Nesta allowed herself to relax. She was worn out by their lovemaking and by the storm that had just passed over them. Her eyes closed and she slept, but Conrad lay wakeful hour after hour and what he thought about was the fighting in Europe and the re-taking of Paris.

Luke was one of a delegation of correspondents sent to see General Bradley to find out his plans for the taking of Paris.

'We'd like to put in a plea for the city to be spared artillery bombardment,' one of them ventured to say.

'My plan is to circle round and pinch out Paris,' General Bradley admitted. 'I don't see any point in attempting to take it by a frontal attack. Once it's isolated we can take it at our leisure.'

'If the Parisians start fighting the German garrison you'll have a battle on your hands whether you want it or not,' another newsman warned. 'From what I've learned, the Resistance is wild for the chance to start picking off Germans.'

'The French army wants the prestige of liberating Paris,' Luke said.

It was difficult to get news out of the beleaguered city, but they heard that there had been sporadic street fighting. They heard, too, that the Germans were preparing to evacuate and that negotiations had been put in hand to arrange for the surrender of the capital. On 24 August the French Second Armoured Division entered Paris and drove to the Hôtel de

247

Ville. The next day General Dietrich von Choltitz formally surrendered Paris to the French.

Luke wandered through the streets, full of laughing, singing people. The tricolour was everywhere. Someone thrust a bottle of wine into his hand and he took a swig at it. Taken like that it tasted thin and sour. An exuberant girl threw her arms round his neck and planted a kiss on his lips. Luke smiled, said '*Vive la France*', and put her away. It was great, it was wonderful; Paris was free again. But they still had one hell of a long way to go.

Five

'I'm being asked to do an ENSA tour of France as soon as the fighting has moved farther east,' Stephanie wrote. 'From which you will gather that everyone here is optimistic about pushing the Germans out of France.'

She paused to think, nibbling the end of her pen. What she had had it in mind to say when she had started that sentence was that she and Luke might run across one another again. Was that what she wanted? This curious, hurtful relationship of theirs, did she really want to keep it going by holding out the hope of a meeting?

With sudden decision she added, 'Perhaps we shall find ourselves in the same town once more. I would be pleased to see you if it works out that way.'

She could have put it more strongly than that. The truth was that she hungered for a sight of Luke again. Through all their separations, the heartbreak and misunderstandings, she had still kept a feeling for him that she had known for no other man.

But even though it might lead to a meeting with Luke, Stephanie was not anxious to do the ENSA tour. The truth was, she was exhausted. The last few weeks, driving her ambulance to incidents caused by the doodlebugs, had been gruelling. Once again Stephanie had seen dead and maimed bodies dug out of the ruins of houses, she had comforted the bereaved, bound up minor injuries, told cheerful lies about the chances of the buried being brought out alive.

She was writing her letter to Luke with a note pad perched on her knee in the ambulance post, waiting for another alert and secretly hoping that nothing more would happen before it was time to go off duty. She pushed her hair back out of her eyes. It needed washing and cutting. She felt scruffy and vaguely unclean, as if the dust of ages, disturbed by the bombs, had seeped into her pores. And tired, deadly tired.

'Cuppa tea, Stephie, love?' another driver called over.

'Mm, lovely, thanks,' Stephanie said. 'Oh, hell! There goes Moaning Minnie again.'

'Here, have the tea quick before anything happens,' the driver said, slopping the hot liquid into a cup.

Stephanie took it and drank it standing up as the mournful sound of the air raid siren faded away. They were all listening and they all heard it coming, the purposeful throb of the pilotless aircraft making for central London.

'Getting louder,' someone remarked unnecessarily.

It seemed as if the doddlebug was right overhead. Was Stephanie imagining it or could she really feel the vibration of its engine? Safest place to be, she reminded herself firmly. If you can hear it above you then it's still on the move and won't come down on top of you.

The engine cut out. It was the most heartstopping thing that Stephanie had ever experienced, and it had been happening over and over again since the second week in June.

Abandoning dignity, the ambulance team threw themselves down on the floor, but the explosion when it came was farther away than they had expected. The doors and windows rattled, the remains of the tea in Stephanie's cup slurped from side to side, but their building was undamaged.

'Near, though,' an ambulance man remarked as they picked themselves up. 'In our sector, I would say.'

'Twenty minutes before we were due off duty,' Stephanie said in disgust. 'Better get ready, I suppose. We're sure to be called out.'

She looked at the tea and decided she might as well finish it; if it was a bad incident it might be a long time before she got another one.

The telephone rang. 'Ninevah Street,' came the laconic message. 'Direct hit on a row of houses. Casualties from flying glass and debris and there'll be a digging out job as well.'

'I know someone who lives in Ninevah Street,' Stephanie said. 'I hope ... oh, well, no use hoping until we see what's happened. Everyone ready?'

As soon as she turned into the Chelsea street she knew that

the flying bomb had landed on the terrace of houses where Conrad lived. The pleasant, narrow houses, three storeys high, had been pulverized by the force of the explosion, and Conrad's house had been close to the point of impact, Stephanie saw that at a glance. Of course, he might not have been at home in the middle of the day, although Anton might have been in the house. Poor Anton, if he had been.

The ambulance was loading up with injured people. A child was carried past Stephanie, conscious but with a white, shocked face, and she saw that one of his feet was almost severed at the ankle, the small white bone sticking out from the mangled flesh.

His mother, streaked with dirt and half demented, was helped into the ambulance with him, still clutching in one hand the duster she had been using when the bomb had fallen.

Then Stephanie saw Conrad. He was being helped out of the debris, covered in dirt, his hair white with crumbled plaster, but apparently unhurt. She was conscious of a feeling of great relief. She wanted to go and speak to him, but an air raid warden held her back.

'No nearer,' he said. 'Can't you see that house is unsafe?'

The inside of Conrad's house had been laid bare. All the frontage had been stripped away. The next door house had been even more completely destroyed, reduced to a pile of rubble. Like a doll's house with the front open all the rooms of Conrad's house had been revealed and on the top floor, trapped by the rafters which had fallen from the roof, Anton lay face downwards on the swaying floor of his room.

'Come on, Steph; we've got to get cracking,' her fellow worker urged, and she had to leave.

By the time Stephanie had unloaded her injured at the hospital the fresh ambulance crew was on duty and she was free to go. Without giving it a second thought she made her way back to Ninevah Street.

'Can't go down there, miss,' a policeman said.

'I was down there in an ambulance a few minutes ago,' Stephanie retorted. 'A friend of mine was in one of those houses. I saw him get out, but I want to know if there's anything I can do for him.'

'The thing is, there's a very nasty bit of demolition going on,' the policeman confided. 'One of the houses is in a very, very dodgy state. Belongs to Conrad Aylmer, the actor, as a matter of fact.'

'That's the man I mean,' Stephanie said. 'I'm Stephanie Bartram.'

'So you are!' the policeman discovered. 'Didn't recognize you, miss, got up like that. Mr Aylmer got out all right, like you said, but his man servant's trapped on the top floor – what's left of it – and at the moment no one can think of a way of bringing him down without the whole wall collapsing. The firemen put a ladder up, but they had to move back when one of them got knocked off it by a lump of stone falling on him – so now *he's* been carted off to hospital. It's risky, very risky.'

In front of his ruined house Conrad was vehemently resisting efforts to send him away.

'I'm perfectly all right,' he said. 'Yes, a bit shaken – who wouldn't be? – but not hurt except for a few grazes, and I'm certainly not going to retire behind a barrier.'

He looked up at the splintered house, to where Anton lay sprawled and helpless. They knew he was alive because they had seen him move. He had even made a pitiful attempt to raise the wooden rafter that lay across his body. It had been beyond his strength and the effort had made the unstable floor sag further towards the empty space beneath.

What Conrad was also looking at was the radio set which Anton had been using when the bomb had landed, exposed for everyone to see if they only had the wits to know what it was.

'A crane?' he suggested.

'We've thought of that,' the demolition man said. 'The trouble is, if we lift the rafter off him he may slide forward and off the edge. And, of course, the whole structure may collapse.'

And a very good thing, too, Conrad thought, with his eyes still on that telltale radio.

'It could be done,' he said slowly. 'If I went in from the back ...'

'Not you sir,' the demolition man said firmly.

'I trained in rescue work at the beginning of the war and made myself useful during the early Blitz. I'll need an

252

expanding ladder that can be operated without leaning it against the wall, rope and an axe.'

Stephanie had been allowed near enough to see Conrad and the rescue team clambering over the tumbled bricks to reach the back of the house. She saw the fire engine being moved, but no one could explain what was happening.

Conrad, in a borrowed tin hat and overalls, was lifted up on the extendable ladder to a window which had remained intact in the inexplicable way such things happened, and which had to be opened with the axe he carried. He hooked the axe back carefully on his belt and climbed in. He was roped to the ladder, which he hoped would save him from tumbling headlong into the fractured bricks below, if the structure gave way beneath him. A second rope was slung over his shoulder.

He got through the window, wincing as he caught his hand on a fragment of glass, but he had underestimated the way the floor inside was sloping, lost his footing and slid helplessly towards the front of the house. It was the rafter which had pinned down Anton that stopped his slide. From the wall above a brick broke loose and fell, then another. Conrad lay on his face and waited.

As soon as it was quiet again he raised his head. Then he inched forward, every movement a hazard, both to himself and to the man who was waiting for him.

The rafter was wedged, but Conrad saw immediately that it could be lifted free. And if Anton had already been secured then he could be slipped out from underneath once the weight that was pinning him down had been removed. Provided, of course, that the floor did not collapse beneath them. Even then he could be rescued, if Conrad had managed to get the rope round him first.

From the moment he had seen that a rescue was feasible Conrad had known that he had to be the one who carried it out. No matter what the outcome, this attempt would make him a hero. If Anton died, in spite of Conrad's heroic effort, that would be a tragedy, but it would not detract from the kudos that would come to Conrad.

It would not be difficult to make sure that Anton died. Conrad would do his part, just as he had said, and God knows

253

that was going to be dangerous enough, but even if he secured the rope round Anton's body that did not necessarily mean that he would be safe.

Conrad looked over the edge. The crane he had suggested was manoeuvring into place in the street below. As soon as he gave the signal they would lift the rafter with all the delicacy they could manage and then … if Anton went down, if the incriminating radio went after him, if they both lay smashed beneath a pile of rubble, Conrad would be free. He had joined the losing side, but there was no reason why he should not survive. He had the axe. He could make sure that the rope holding Anton was severed. Come to that, he could make sure that Anton was dead before he fell. Strange that the idea should suddenly be repugnant to him.

As he crawled towards the other man Conrad saw him lift his head and try to turn.

'Keep still!' Conrad said sharply.

At the sound of his voice, far from obeying that command, Anton lifted his shoulders off the floor and twisted round. Conrad saw quite clearly the look of disbelief and then horror that appeared on his face.

'You!' he said in a hoarse whisper. 'No! No!'

'Who else?' Conrad said. 'We're going to be tied together one more time, my friend.'

Anton made a feeble attempt to shout out to the upturned faces below, but his strength was not equal to it. His body slumped. His expression changed to a resigned and fatalistic acceptance. With the index finger of the hand that lay stretched out helplessly in front of him he did something that made Conrad's hair stir on his scalp. He traced the sign of the cross in the dust.

Anton expected Conrad to kill him. Conrad saw quite clearly that the other man had understood the way he was thinking; might, indeed, have been expected to understand, after the long ordeal of deception they had endured together.

If Anton had fought, even with words, he would have been a dead man, but in his resignation Conrad saw yet one more helpless victim, one more dead child, one more bereaved woman, one more ruined man.

I was better than this once.

The thought came into his head and could not be turned aside.

He had known pity, even shame, when he had first seen the results of war. Now he was so hardened that he could contemplate murder in order to save his own skin. Self-preservation. Everyone was entitled to survive if they could. Even as he told himself that, Conrad knew that the moment for action had passed. He was weaker than he had thought. He would have to rely on Anton keeping his mouth shut as much to retain his own freedom as to protect Conrad. After all, they were on the same side.

Conrad moved again and fed the rope round Anton's inert body. The other man did not seem disposed to help him. Presumably he still thought that he was to die.

'They're going to lift this weight off you,' Conrad said. 'I have to move back out of the way.'

He lifted his hand and waved and then he crawled towards the back of the ruined room.

The grappling arms of the crane descended and groped for the heavy wooden beam. A section of wall fell outwards and the crane was still, as if eveyone was holding their breath. The beam creaked. Conrad heard it scraping against the wall. That was bad. It might bring the whole edifice down. He put his head down and closed his eyes, but he was still conscious of something being lifted and hanging over his head. This was the ticklish part. They had to manoeuvre the crane and its load out through the hole in the roof, then he had to try to drag Anton up the slope of the floor towards the open window and safety.

The rafter was lifted clear. Conrad and Anton were still safe. Conrad put his hands to the rope that held Anton and hauled with all his strength.

'Help me,' he said urgently. 'Damn you, can't you do something to help?'

Anton was injured, that was obvious. At the very least he must have some broken bones. All the same, at Conrad's urging he began to move, with a slow, crawling movement, up the slope of the tilting floor. He was barely conscious by the time Conrad had drawn him level with himself. Conrad seized him,

255

dragged him to the rear of the house, and bundled him unceremoniously half out of the window, regardless of any injuries he might have. There were other hands out there now, ready to take hold of Anton and carry him away. Conrad slumped to the floor inside the window waiting for the ladder to be free.

While he had the time he ought to do something about that radio. It was there, only a few feet away, on a small table. All he had to do was to cut it loose and it would go crashing down into oblivion. He got to his feet, feeling more tired than he had before in his life, and swung the axe against the thin wooden legs of the table.

The radio, heavier than Conrad had realized, crashed to the floor. Suddenly he was having difficulty in standing upright. Everything was sliding, tilting, collapsing, falling. The floor gave way, the wall fell inwards. There was a moment's agonizing pain, a flash of brilliant light, then everything went black and he hung, helpless and unconscious, swinging loosely in the air from the rope still tethered to the ladder, while bricks and masonry battered him from every side.

'I do wish our villains wouldn't turn into popular heroes,' Claud's chief said. He sounded peevish.

'Difficult to handle,' Claud agreed. 'In some ways, of course, it solves our difficulty. We can discontinue the Conrad and Anton network. Now that the stories about Conrad's bravery have got into papers the reason for the silence is sure to filter back to Berlin.'

'They're both in hospital, I take it?'

'Both in St George's,' Claud agreed. 'Anton is likely to be discharged first. He got off comparatively lightly – severe bruising, a broken arm and three broken ribs. I suggest we get him out of London and pay him off as soon as possible.'

'We'll need him to give evidence against Aylmer.'

'If we prosecute,' Claud said.

'Oh, we'll have to,' the head of the department said. 'The trial will have to be held *in camera*, of course, but, damn it, the man's a British national and he's been spying for the other side for years, even if we know that none of his stuff has been getting through. Can't let him get off Scot free.'

'He's hardly going to do that,' Claud said.

He put Conrad's medical notes down on the desk.

'Read that.'

The other man read through the report. When he put it down his face was thoughtful.

'You're right,' he said. 'This is punishment enough for any man.'

Stephanie opened the door of her flat and Nesta walked in.

'Tell me where he is so that I can go and see him,' she said.

'He's in St Geroge's Hospital,' Stephanie said. 'He and Anton.'

'I'm not interested in Anton,' Nesta said scornfully.

She turned, as if to leave immediately, but Stephanie stopped her.

'Nesta, wait! They won't let you in until visiting time. Besides, you must have been travelling for hours. I never expected to see you so soon. When did you last have anything to eat?'

Nesta stared at her. 'I don't remember,' she said. 'It's not important. I hitched a lift part of the way. Food ... I haven't had anything since I left the camp.'

'Then come and sit down. You've got at least two hours before you'll be allowed to see Conrad.'

'It's such a waste of time!'

'Try telling Ward Sister that!'

Nesta allowed herself to sit down at the kitchen table. She even managed to eat Stephanie's one precious egg without apparently appreciating the sacrifice. All her mind was bent towards the hospital bed where Conrad was lying.

'You've seen him?' she asked abruptly.

'Twice,' Stephanie said. 'He was conscious the first time and only just aware that I was there the second. Don't expect too much, Nesta.'

'He's not going to die!' Nesta said fiercely. 'I won't let him!'

'He has bad head injuries, but the doctors are hopeful. The

257

top half of his face is completely bandaged. You'll have to tell him who you are.'

Nesta ladled sugar into her tea and stirred it until it seemed as if the bottom would come out of the cup. Stephanie saw that she was quite unaware of what she was doing.

'Can I stay with you?' she asked. 'I can walk to the hospital from here.'

'Yes, of course you can stay,' Stephanie agreed. 'How much leave have you got?'

Nesta did not reply. Patiently, Stephanie repeated, 'How long will you be able to stay?'

Nesta gave her a quick glance and looked away again.

'I didn't put in for leave. I just walked out,' she said. 'That's why I want to stay with you. I'm not going home, not even telling Mum and Dad I'm in London. If the ATS try to trace me they won't know where I am.'

'Oh, Nesta! Your mother and father will be sick with worry if the Military Police turn up on the doorstep to say you've disappeared.'

For a moment Nesta seemed to waver, then her look of fierce concentration returned.

'The only important thing is to see Conrad,' she said. 'Promise you won't interfere. I'll go back as soon as he's out of danger.'

It occurred to Stephanie, not for the first time, that Nesta's one-track mind could be intensely irritating, but she held her peace.

'Do you realize that I was actually there when Conrad rescued Anton?' she asked.

'No! Tell me ... tell me everything.'

As Stephanie told the story Nesta's tired shoulders straightened and her eyes glowed with pride at the heroic effort Conrad had made, but when it was time to leave for the hospital she said abruptly, 'Come with me.'

'I thought you'd want to see Conrad alone,' Stephanie said.

'It might be easier to have someone else there, especially someone like you who knows us both. You'll think me a fool, but I dread seeing Conrad in pain. I might need you to help me keep control of myself.'

258

They found Conrad looking rather better than the last time Stephanie had seen him. He had been moved from an open ward into a separate room. He was propped up against pillows instead of lying flat, and there was a faint colour in his cheeks, but those disquieting bandages still covered his head and eyes.

'It's Stephanie and I've brought Nesta to see you,' Stephanie said quietly.

Conrad moved one of his hands and Nesta took hold of it and held it tightly.

'Darling ... oh, my darling, I can't bear to see you like this,' she said in a strangled whisper.

'Do I look so repugnant?' Conrad asked.

'No! But you're hurt! I wish it was me instead.'

'I'd hate that,' Conrad said.

His voice was weak, but he sounded amused, almost his old self. Nesta bent over his hand, kissing it, and he passed his other hand over her rough, untidy head.

Stephanie was watching this emotional scene and wishing that she had not agreed to take part in it when the door opened and Anton came in. His right arm was in plaster and he moved stiffly and with obvious difficulty.

'Anton! I'm pleased to see you on your feet,' Stephanie said quickly. She had a twinge of compunction that she had not thought to go and visit the other man on the two occasions that she had been to see Conrad in the hospital.

Anton ignored her, nor did he take any notice of Nesta, still holding Conrad's hand against her cheek.

'Shall I go?' Stephanie asked. 'Conrad isn't allowed more than two visitors at a time.'

She could not understand what it was, but there was something about the atmosphere that she did not like. Anton was staring at Conrad in an avid way, drinking in the sight of him lying there helpless. There was nothing in his manner that showed any gratitude towards the man who had saved his life.

'Don't go,' he said, still without taking his eyes off Conrad. 'What I have to say will not take long and I wish for as many witnesses as possible. So, *mein Herr*, you have played the part of a hero and saved my life. That was not what I expected you to do.'

259

In spite of his weakness, Conrad straightened up and spoke crisply and decisively in German.

'Oh, no!' Anton said. 'We will speak English and then these two charming frauleins will understand what I say. They will not kiss your hand and visit your bed, both of them, when they know that you are a traitor.'

'Be quiet!' Conrad ordered. 'You're demented. One would think that it was you who had had the blow on the head instead of me.'

'You are a traitor,' Anton repeated. 'For years you have been spying for Germany. For many, many years, since long before the war.'

'Conrad's right, you're out of your mind,' Nesta said. 'Stephanie, ring for the nurse!'

Before Stephanie could reach the bell Anton had limped closer to Conrad's bed.

'Stop!' he said. 'If you move I will rip off his bandages.'

Stephanie's hand froze in mid-air.

'That's better. Let me say what I have come to say and then I will go and you, Herr Aylmer, will never see me again.'

'We'll all be pleased to see the back of you,' Nesta said. 'I never liked you, never!'

'And yet you loved this man – this hypocrite. He has deceived you many times, did you know that? With this woman and with others. He is evil, everything about him is saturated in wickedness. He is a Nazi.'

'What utter nonsense,' Stephanie said.

She did not like the way Nesta had turned her head to look at her at Anton's accusation.

She hurried on, 'Conrad made the difficult decision to part with his mother because of her views and his war service has been excellent, quite apart from the way he rescued you.'

'I have been operating a radio transmitter from the top floor of his house since 1940.'

'That's impossible,' Nesta said. 'I've been in the house many, many times ...'

'But never in my room, fraulein.'

'If that were true – if for one moment it was conceivable that it could be true,' Stephanie said, 'then you would be a spy, too.'

Anton's smile was radiant with satisfaction.

'That would be so if I had sent what Herr Aylmer instructed me to send, but I did not do so.'

Conrad stirred. 'Your story becomes more and more unconvincing,' he said. 'I am a spy, but you are innocent. It is impossible. Stephanie, ring the bell and I'll take my chance with the bandages.'

'Perhaps Miss Bartram would like to hear the rest of my story first,' Anton said. 'I must tell you, mein Herr, that I am not Anton Grossmeyer. He, unfortunate man, was captured on the day he landed. I was trained to take his place and you never knew how you had been deceived. Everything I have done has been dictated by British Intelligence.'

'You're mad,' Conrad said.

The small amount of colour he had had when the girls had first arrived had gone. He was worse than white, he was putty coloured and there were small beads of sweat along his upper lip.

'You're making him ill!' Nesta said sharply. 'Oh, there must be a way out of this nightmare!'

Because Anton had moved over close to the bed the way to the door was unguarded. With a swiftness that defeated the injured man she darted for the door, wrenched it open and ran out into the corridor.

Stephanie was watching Conrad.

'Is it true?' she asked.

'Of course not!' Conrad exclaimed.

'It is true,' Anton said. 'Ask your friend Claud More.'

'*Claud*?'

It was Conrad who had spoken, in total disbelief.

Anton laughed, pleased by the sensation he had caused.

'Certainly. The quiet Mr More. Herr More has told me every move I should make. You were surprised were you not, *mein Herr*, that your friends the Germans were so unprepared for the invasion on the Normandy beaches when you had warned them over and over again that this was where they should expect the blow to fall? Not one word of your evidence was ever sent. Instead, every indication showed that the landings would take place in the Pas de Calais.'

261

'Very clever, if it happened to be true,' Conrad said.

'Why are you saying all this?' Stephanie asked.

'Because I am afraid that our friend here will not receive his proper punishment. He should be hanged, did you know that? The punishment for treason is death. I have waited four long years for his trial and the moment when I will see him condemned and now I think I will be cheated.'

'That proves that what you are saying is an invention,' Conrad said quickly. 'No man could be guilty of such a crime and not be brought to trial.'

'Oh, you'll be tried! In secret perhaps, because the British do not want the world to know, not yet, how clever they have been. What I said was that you will not receive the punishment you deserve.'

'What are you saying?' Stephanie asked.

Her voice was no more than a dry whisper because, even though her mind cried out that what Anton was telling them was impossible, she was beginning to find a dreadful conviction in his story.

Four years of hatred lay behind Anton's answer.

'He will live. The British will never hang a blind man.'

Six

The day after the liberation of Paris Luke moved out with the American First Army on the thrust towards the Belgian frontier. To the north the British army was also on the move eastwards, while the Canadians kept the German pinned down in a last ditch stand in the Channel ports. South of Paris the US Third Army under General Patton was making headway towards the Saar, with further French and American contingents moving up from the Mediterranean coast.

For a time the momentum lasted and the Allied armies kept up their dizzying advance across the occupied territories, where the local people went wild with relief at the sight of them, even though the fighting wrecked their homes and sometimes killed people whose only crime was that they were in the way when two great armies clashed.

At every briefing Luke heard the same story: 'We can keep going only for as long as supplies can get through to us', and he remembered the way the fighting had swayed back and forth across the desert because of the same problem.

He heard, as who did not, that General Patton had claimed that his Third Army could win the war if only it could have sufficient gasoline, and Luke knew that there were differences of opinion between the generals as to who should have first call on the dwindling stocks of fuel and ammunition.

By the second week in September the German border had been crossed just south of Aachen. Luke filed his story and then sat back to see what would happen next.

It looked like stalemate: a waiting period on the Siegfried Line until the supply line that stretched back to Cherbourg could be replaced by the recently captured port of Antwerp. And while they were immobile Hitler ordered Field Marshal Walther Model to the Western Front to stiffen the resistance of the demoralized German troops.

There had been talk of a swift crossing of the Rhine and an early defeat for Germany. Luke had always been sceptical, arguing that the Wehrmacht would turn and fight when it was a question of defending German soil.

The news of the daring, imaginative plan for a daylight drop of airborne troops into Holland to outflank the new German lines broke on Sunday, 17 September. Luke begged his way on to transport travelling north and headed for Montgomery's headquarters in Brussels.

It would have been magnificent if it had succeeded, but the resistance was stiffer than had been expected and the weather was atrocious, causing plans for reinforcement missions to miscarry and restricting air support. For a week the British 1st Airborne Division clung to their bridgehead at Arnhem, and then Montgomery ordered their withdrawal and the remnants began to trickle back across the Rhine.

'Gallant is the word, if you happen to be looking for an adjective,' a British officer said to Luke. 'Another great British defeat, almost as good as Dunkirk.'

His bitterness was understandable. Of the 9,000 British troops who had parachuted in, less than two and a half thousand had come out.

'So what happens now?' Luke asked.

'We scour out the Scheldt the hard way. You don't need me to tell you how badly we need those waterways and free access to Antwerp.'

'I've heard that Montgomery believes he could force his way through from the north to Berlin,' Luke said, probing for a reaction.

'Not without being given several US divisions to reinforce the British and Canadian armies. Do you think that's likely?'

'Not likely,' Luke admitted. 'Eisenhower agreed with his generals from the start that US troops would be kept under US command.'

'There you are then.' The British officer was clearing up papers from his makeshift desk as he spoke. He picked up a newspaper, glanced at it and made as if to throw it in the wastepaper basket.

'Is that an English paper?' Luke asked quickly.

'A very out of date one.'

'I'll have it all the same. I've got friends in London and I haven't had news of them for weeks. I'm wondering if they're all right.'

'If you're thinking about the buzz-bombs, I can tell you the attacks have tailed off. The papers are so skimpy these days they're hardly worth reading. The only juicy scandal in that one is about the actor chappy who turned out to be a spy. Conrad Aylmer – you've probably seen his pictures.'

'*What?*'

'True enough,' the British officer said, surprised by Luke's reaction. 'There's only a paragraph or two about it; obviously the powers that be are playing it down; but he's being charged with spying for the Jerries, even though he's in hospital.'

'Bloody hell,' Luke said softly.

He pulled himself together and tried to make light of the news, but inside he was furiously angry. He had warned them; he had gone out of his way to alert the British to the possibility of Conrad not being all he seemed to be, and they had shrugged it off. Now it seemed that he had been right all along. How much damage had Conrad managed to do in the years that had gone by since Luke had put in his report?

He read through the scanty story. Even by British standards it was restrained. In fact, the censorship was obvious in every cagey word. But one passage at the end struck Luke like a blow. 'Mr Aylmer remains in hospital under police guard and no further statement will be issued, said a police spokesman. His only visitors have been his solicitor and his former girl friend, actress Stephanie Bartram.'

So that was why she had not written to him. Or had she sent a letter which had been suppressed? Either way, it seemed that she was standing by Conrad. Didn't she care that the swine had been spying for Germany? Or was she taking the attitude that until he was tried he was innocent?

She was being naive if that was what she thought. The story of Conrad having been charged with espionage would never have been allowed to break if the authorities were not sure of getting a conviction. What would happen to him? Although it was said that he was in hospital, and that he had been injured when a flying bomb had landed on his house, there were no other details. Luke frowned over that item. It was not usual for bomb sites to be revealed and yet this story had gone out of its way to spell out where the buzz bomb had come down. There was something funny going on. He was as sure of it as he had always been that there was something wrong about Conrad.

It seemed that the campaign in France was bogged down until the supply situation could be sorted out. Luke took a trip to Paris, visited Eisenhower's headquarters in Versailles, and sent home a description of his office in an annexe behind the Trianon Palace Hotel, with an amusing comment about the way Ike had had its original grandeur reduced in size until he could feel comfortable in it, which Luke thought would go down well in the States. Then, gambling on nothing dramatic happening in his absence, he hitched a ride on an aeroplane across the Channel and made for London.

There was no difficulty about getting into the hospital nor in identifying Conrad's private ward, guarded by one bored policeman sitting on a chair outside the door. Luke strolled up with his notebook in his hand, studying it as if he were looking at some notes. He had his hand on the door handle when the policeman stopped him.

'Can I see your identity card, sir?'

Luke smiled at him. 'I'm American,' he said. 'I don't have to have British ID.'

The policeman looked baffled, as if he were not quite sure whether this was true, but Luke saw him making up his mind to play safe.

'You can't go in there without authorization,' he said.

'Why not?'

'Orders.'

'But I need to see this patient, officer.'

'Then you bring me a bit o' paper to say so, sir. I don't recollect seeing you before. On the staff here, are you?'

'No, I'm from another neck of the woods,' Luke admitted.

'Ah, that'll explain why you don't know the ropes. You pop along to the office and get your proper authorization and then

266

we'll both be in the clear, won't we?'

He was on his feet and barring the way to the door. There was no way Luke was going to bluff his way past that solid presence. As he turned away he asked, as casually as he had made all his other remarks, 'Is there anyone else with Mr Aylmer at the moment?'

There was a momentary hesitation and then the policeman said with unanswerable good sense, 'You'll see that when you go in, won't you, sir?'

So Conrad had a visitor. If he had been alone the constable would have said so. If a doctor had been with Aylmer he would probably have come out with that. Luke argued that it must be someone else and it would be interesting to see who it was.

There seemed to be only one possible exit. Luke went down the corridor and round the corner. There were one or two people hanging about, waiting to get in to see patients. Luke leaned against the wall and tried to look like one of them.

Inside the guarded room Stephanie was persisting in a visit for which she felt nothing but repugnance. She had been cajoled into it by Claud, who wanted Conrad softened up. In the right frame of mind he might supply useful details about the men who had recruited him to spy for Germany before the war. Unfortunately, Conrad saw through this manoeuvre.

'Dear Stephanie, lovely though it is to see you – though that's not an expression I should use, is it? – this benevolent visit is not going to make me one iota more co-operative,' he said in his most arrogant drawl.

'I wish I could persuade you to take some training to help you cope with your ... your ...'

'My blindness. Don't stumble over saying it, darling. Certainly not! The greater my disability, the more trouble the prison authorities will have in dealing with me,' he said. 'Do you imagine I'm going to make it easier for them?'

Stephanie said nothing in reply to that. With all her heart she longed to get away, but as she had feared, Conrad turned inexorably to his desire to talk to Nesta.

'She owes it to me to hear my side of the story,' he said. 'You've allowed yourself to be used by Conrad and his masters, but at least you've been reasonable enough to come and visit

267

me. Why not Nesta, too?'

'Nesta is not a reasonable person,' Stephanie said wearily. 'And I never loved you in the way she did. You were Nesta's world – next to her acting – and her reaction against you is as violent as her feeling for you once was.'

'She was … she could have been the one woman in my life,' Conrad said.

'You say that now, why couldn't you have lived up to it when you had the chance?'

'One of my many mistakes,' Conrad admitted in an even tone which did not conceal his bitterness. 'Have you heard when my trial is to be?'

'Not for some time and it will be held in secret.'

'Of course. Claud won't want it known how clever he's been until Germany is finally on her knees. I shall plead guilty, of course.'

'I think you ought to put up some sort of defence,' Stephanie said.

'An ally! Dear Stephanie, why did I never realize you were on my side until it was too late?'

'I'm not on your side, but I'm not entirely happy about the way you were manipulated. You might get a lighter sentence if all the circumstances were known.'

'I doubt it, but I'll think about it.'

Stephanie got up to go, but as she had dreaded, Conrad went back to his desire to talk to Nesta.

'She was staying with you, Stephanie,' he said. 'Surely she had something to say you could pass on to me?'

Stephanie shuddered, remembering the awful day when she had had to take Nesta home, the way she had turned on Stephanie, her wild accusations and bitter recriminations.

'Nothing Nesta said that day will bear repeating,' she said. 'Anton's hint that you and I had been lovers set her against me, too. I doubt whether she'll ever speak to me again.'

'That ghastly little man. I should have let him die,' Conrad said reflectively.

In the silence that fell between them Stephanie braced herself to carry out the rest of the errand that Claud had foisted on her.

268

'The International Red Cross have managed to find your mother,' she said.

'I didn't know she was lost,' Conrad said, but his head went up and Stephanie sensed a new alertness in him.

'She's changed her name and left Germany, but they got a message to her and she's written a letter which Claud has asked me to read to you.'

'Why wasn't I told about this immediately?'

'It's not ... perhaps not quite the letter you might have hoped for,' Stephanie said, trying to prepare him.

'Mama was always unpredictable. Go on, read it – if you can, that is. Surely she hasn't written in English?'

'The letter has been opened and translated.'

'Of course; Claud wouldn't be able to resist that. Stop hedging and let me know how Mama has taken the news of my predicament.'

Stephanie began to read, keeping all expression out of her voice.

My darling boy,

I am devastated to hear the terrible news about your poor eyes. Such beautiful eyes, my darling. I can hardly bear to think about it. It is, of course, also very bad news that you will be put in prison. A sad end to all our hopes.

I can write freely now because I have left our unhappy country for a new life. In the end the Führer was not the man I thought him to be. He still talks of ultimate victory, but there are few Germans who believe in it any more. You will have heard that there was an attempt on his life. Perhaps it would have been better if it had succeeded. The bombing has been frightful and I have endured many hardships.

Now I must tell you my news and I hope you will be happy for your old mother. I have married again, such a charming man, a few years older than myself and not, of course, German. I am writing this from Stockholm, but soon we shall be leaving for a new life in South America. My thoughts will be with you always.

Your loving Mama.

Stephanie stopped reading and realized she was holding her breath. Then, to her surprise, Conrad threw back his head and laughed.

'Oh, Mama, Mama!' he said. 'A born survivor! I should have known. I wonder which elderly South American diplomat she has seduced? Not a clue, you'll notice, that would allow me to trace her.'

'The Red Cross have all the details. They can find her again if you want to keep in touch.'

'No, no! I wouldn't for the world intrude on her new life. The besotted husband will be rich, of course – trust Mama for that! No doubt he'll dote on her and she'll have a wonderful time. Good luck to her!'

His laughter did not ring quite true. There was a jeering note in it which made Stephanie wince. Conrad seemed to sense it.

'Did you think I'd mind?' he asked. 'Not at all! Mama and I have grown apart. I'm relieved not to have to worry about her future.'

'That's all right then,' Stephanie said lamely.

As she got up to go, Conrad said, 'Have you got the original letter? The German version?'

Stephanie put it into his hand. His fingers closed round it, crumpling the paper, and once again she wondered whether he was as unmoved by his mother's defection as he wanted her to believe.

When she reached the door Stephanie looked back. Conrad was holding the letter up in front of his sightless eyes and his face was contorted with anger and grief. Stephanie went out, closing the door very quietly behind her.

Outside, the watching constable said to her, 'We've had another newspaper reporter trying to get in. An American this time.'

An American. Stephanie immediately thought of Luke and then reflected how irrational it was to assume that any passing reporter might be him. All the same, because the idea was in her mind, she was able to greet him calmly when she saw him waiting for her.

'You should have worn a white coat and stethoscope,' she said. 'That's the usual ploy.'

270

'I didn't want to be arrested for impersonating a doctor,' Luke said, picking up her light, impersonal lead. 'Can we go somewhere and talk?'

'You can buy me a cup of tea. There's a fairly decent tea shop round the corner.'

She kept her head down and her shoulders hunched, her hands dug deep into her pockets, hoping not to be recognized. Inside the café she led the way to the back of the room, away from the window, even though that window was obscured by strips of paper stuck over it to minimize the danger from flying glass, and then she felt able to relax.

Neither of them had tried to make conversation during the short walk, but now Stephanie asked the obvious question.

'Are you in London for long?'

'I wouldn't be here at all if I hadn't seen a paragraph in an old London newspaper. Conrad Aylmer a spy! I'm so mad I could spit.'

'That's the general reaction. Shock ... horror ... disbelief.'

'I don't disbelieve it,' Luke retorted. 'I warned your British security people, can you believe that? Do you want any of this canary yellow cake?'

'Powdered egg,' Stephanie said. 'No, I don't want any.'

'You don't look as if you've been eating much.'

'Can you wonder? It's been a difficult time.'

'You're standing by him?'

'There's no one else,' Stephanie said. 'Nesta's thrown him over.'

'I don't blame her. I'm surprised you don't feel the same way.'

'Luke, he's blind.'

That had not been in the account Luke had read and it made him pause, but he went on obstinately, 'It's what he did before he lost his sight that bugs me. It seems odd to me, this concern of yours for a traitor. Are you in love with him?'

'I never was.'

'Then how can you defend a man who's betrayed his own side and given away secrets that may have killed hundreds of men?' Luke persisted.

'It's not as straightforward as that. Luke, I'm not supposed

271

to talk about it.' With an attempt at a smile she added, 'Especially not to a newspaper reporter.'

'Whether you talk or not, honey, I'm writing this story and I'll make a damn good try to get it past the censor. I think it ought to be told – one of the biggest security blunders of the war. Conrad went everywhere, saw everything, had friends in high places. He was half German and I told the authorities myself that he'd been sympathetic to the Nazis at one time. There should have been a watch on him.'

'It's not that simple.'

'What about that creepy character who worked for him? I bet he comes into the story.'

An involuntary spasm of disgust distorted Stephanie's mouth. She pretended to drink her tea, hoping Luke had not noticed her reaction.

'Conrad saved Anton's life,' she said, 'Luke, can't we talk about something else?'

'I've got Aylmer on my mind, honey,' Luke drawled. 'Can you wonder at it? He was the reason we parted in anger last time.'

'There was more to it than that,' Stephanie said.

'Not in my book,' Luke said obstinately. 'OK, maybe I was hasty – and so were you! When I started writing to you again it was in the hope of rebuilding our bridges and you seemed to feel the same way. Then wham! dead silence. Was that because of him, too?'

'I suppose so. There was so much I couldn't say. I ... I was pleased when I got your letters, Luke.'

'Sure, but it's Aylmer you're supporting, a lousy war criminal.'

'He's not been tried yet.'

'Oh, come on, Stephanie! Are you trying to kid me you think he's innocent?'

'I know he's guilty.'

'Yeah, and so does everyone else who matters – now that it's too late. I've been watching men die in the last few weeks and in my book the British have a lot to answer for, having a Nazi spy at large and not nailing him.'

'Our people knew all along that Conrad was a spy,'

272

Stephanie said, goaded beyond endurance. 'They put Anton – his name's not really Anton, but I can't think of him as anything else – they put Anton into Conrad's house with his radio and used him to send out false messages to Berlin. Apparently it was a wildly successful operation.'

She was horrified as soon as the words had left her mouth, after all Claud had said about the importance of concealing the double cross, but she had succeeded in silencing Luke.

'My sainted aunt!' he breathed at last, looking dazed. 'What a story! My ... stars! What a story!'

'But you mustn't write it,' Stephanie said in alarm. 'Claud says it mustn't come out until after the war because it might jeopardize other operations.'

'I'm so dumbstruck I don't know what to say. Claud More – he knew?'

'Claud's been in charge of the whole thing from the start.'

'I always thought that smooth b ... beggar was too good to be true.' Luke laughed suddenly. 'I certainly would have egg on my face if I'd written it up the way I wanted to. It's so darn clever it's almost unbelievable. Three cheers for our side!'

'You think they did the right thing?'

'Of course.' Luke stared at her. 'Surely you agree?'

'I have qualms about it.'

'But, Stephanie ... ? It was a great piece of deception. Heaven knows how many lives we may have saved by misleading the Germans. On D-Day, for instance. No wonder they were taken by surprise!'

'I'm all for anything that shortens the war and saves lives,' Stephanie said. 'And I'm not against deceiving the enemy. What I question is whether it was right to use Conrad as they did.'

'He chose his own course.'

'And was kept to it. Inexorably. No matter what he did he couldn't get out of the web that was spun round him.'

'I can't waste a lot of sympathy on a Nazi and I don't understand how you can.'

Stephanie's mouth hardened obstinately. 'Everyone should have a chance to turn back if they get on a wrong path,' she said. 'Conrad should have been arrested early in the war and put in prison.'

273

'That would have destroyed his usefulness,' Luke pointed out. 'I'm sorry, Stephanie, I can't agree with you. With an instrument like that put into their hands British security had to use it.'

'There have been other deceptions, using fictitious agents, Claud admitted as much,' Stephanie said. 'It's the use of a real person I deplore. We're not talking about a machine, we're talking about a man, with a heart and mind and soul. Some attempt should have been made to save him.'

Luke was looking at her oddly. 'You do still care for him,' he said.

'No! Once, a long time ago, I had a brief, silly affair with Conrad, of which I'm heartily ashamed. I've never liked or admired him for anything since except his acting.'

'We've all got to admire that,' Luke agreed. 'He threw dust in everyone's eyes! You may have been sore when he threw you over, but you were as ready as everyone else to kiss and be friends with a Nazi skunk!'

It was more than Stephanie's raw nerves could stand. Her hands were shaking as she pulled on her coat and found her gloves.

'I've had enough of being blamed for Conrad's misdeeds,' she said. 'Thank you for the tea, Luke. I'm glad you're still safe and well. One of these days you may arrive at a better understanding of the way I think about Conrad, but please don't try to get in touch with me. I'm very busy and I'm having to work hard to retrieve some of the damage associating with him has done me. Like you, there are plenty of people who look sideways at me just because I was in a couple of films with him. If you loved me, as you once said you did, if you were even a real friend, you might try to understand my point of view, Goodbye.'

Seven

'Not only are we fighting a desperate battle with the Germans,' Luke wrote, 'but war has broken out between the Allied generals.'

He looked at that sentence, decided it would never get printed and crossed it out. He had fallen into a mood of sour disillusionment which stemmed from his last visit to England and his new quarrel with Stephanie. He had been exasperated by what he saw as Stephanie's misplaced generosity towards Conrad and had let himself give way to a spurt of jealousy that did him no credit at all. On top of that, he was suffering from the frustration of a reporter in possession of a good story which he was unable to make public. Before leaving London he had tried to find a way round the embargo, only to receive a blistering reproof from his chief, who had no wish to get on the wrong side of British Intelligence, coupled with a recommendation that Luke should get back to the battlefield to do the job for which he was being paid.

In December the Germans had mounted a sudden offensive in the Ardennes and the Allied armies were hard pressed to contain it. Luke followed the fighting with growing unease and watched on the map the bulge in the line held by the American forces. Because of the fear of a break in communications between the north and south on either side of the bulge it made sense for command of the two American armies in the north to be handed over to Montgomery. As a temporary measure, it was emphasized; only as a temporary measure. Luke, who knew all the commanders involved, prophesied trouble.

Christmas came with everyone on edge, fearing that the Germans might be across the Meuse before the New Year, but the first Christmas of the liberation was celebrated in France with a gaiety Luke thought misplaced in view of the lives that were still being lost, especially the American lives.

Montgomery opened a fresh attack against the Germans early in the New Year and what some of the US command saw as his offensive against them shortly afterwards. The Germans were on the retreat, the worst of the danger seemed to be over, now the mutual recriminations began.

'The British press isn't helping,' Luke commented irritably to an English reporter. 'All this stuff implying that it was Montgomery who saved the Americans from disaster, trying to get him named commander of all ground forces. It wouldn't *work!*'

A fresh statement from General Bradley emphasized the temporary nature of the change of command, but rumours were circulating amongst the newsmen that both he and Patton had told Eisenhower that they would resign rather than serve under Montgomery. It took a generous tribute from Winston Churchill in the House of Commons on 18 January to calm the troubled waters.

Luke, reading the speech, was forced to admit that the old man had done them proud.

'... the United States troops have done almost all the fighting and have suffered almost all the losses ... the Americans have engaged thirty or forty men for every one we have engaged and lost sixty to eighty men to every one of ours ... we must not forget that it is to American homes that telegrams of personal loss and anxiety have been coming during the past month ... General Omar Bradley was commanding the American forces and so was Field Marshal Montgomery ... all these troops fought in magnificent fashion ...'

'I like the bit at the end about not listening to the shouting of mischief makers,' the English reporter said to Luke. 'I think he means us.'

'Speak for yourself!' Luke retorted. 'If the cap fits ...'

'Perhaps we laid it on a bit too thick,' the other man admitted. 'The trouble is that if you're accredited to one of the armies you're too close to the action to get an overall view, and the briefing at SHAEF in Paris wasn't all it might have been. The main thing is, the Jerries are on the move backwards. Shall we drink to that?'

With the battle of the Ardennes behind them and the

prospect of breaching the Siegfried line in sight, Luke prepared to cover more months of heavy fighting. The prospect did not fill him with any great pleasure. All the same, he was none too pleased to receive orders to report back to England for a talk with the head of the London bureau, nor did the interview do anything to boost his morale.

'I won't pull any punches, Luke,' his chief said. 'Your work for the last few months hasn't been giving satisfaction.'

'Hell! When have I ever failed to meet a deadline?' Luke demanded.

'Hardly ever. That's not the point. It's the content that counts.'

'I've given you the facts.'

'Sure, but where's the extra spark you used to have?'

'It's sort of difficult to sparkle about a few more dead bodies,' Luke said sarcastically.

'I think you've put your finger on the trouble: you're stale.'

'That I'm not!'

'Think about it, Luke. You've been in the war a long time – England, the Western Desert, North Africa, Sicily, France.'

'Are you pulling me out? Is that it?'

'How long is it since you've been home?'

'I haven't got a home.'

'You're losing touch with your roots, Luke. Yes, I'm pulling you out. Not permanently, but as a temporary measure.'

'Now, when we're just about to push into Germany?'

'Germany will still be there in six weeks' time. The war isn't going to end that quickly. I'm giving you a holiday and I'm ordering you to take it in the States.'

'Where I spend my leave is my own concern. I don't want to leave Europe.'

'I know you don't. That's the trouble. You're in danger of forgetting who you're writing for. Go home and talk to some ordinary American people and then come back and file the sort of stories they want to read.'

'Our boys are best and the war would have been over by Christmas if George Patton could have had enough gasoline?' Luke suggested.

'You won't get me riled and you won't get me to change my

mind, no matter how hard you try,' his chief said, unmoved. 'You're booked on a flight to New York tomorrow, you lucky devil, and there's a return sea passage for you at the beginning of March. If you'd been drafted into the army you'd have gone where you were sent. You should be thankful that this is such a pleasant posting.'

With less than twenty-four hours in hand, Luke debated whether it was worth trying to get in touch with Stephanie. Again. They met, they quarrelled, they parted, and every time he swore he would forget her, and every time he remembered. She had told him not to try to see her, and yet ... if he sought her out and apologized, she might yet forgive him.

It was not all that far from Fleet Street to Drury Lane; he had walked it before he realized what he was doing, and there was the ENSA headquarters. Since he was on the doorstep there was no harm in going in and asking whether she was around or not.

'Stephanie Bartram? Doing a tour in France,' Luke was told. 'We can give you her itinerary, if it's important.'

'Don't bother,' Luke said. 'I'll maybe catch her in London on my way back from the States.'

So that was that. No chance of a reconciliation and it was only when it turned out to be impossible that Luke realized how much he had counted on seeing Stephanie.

It was the first time Luke had flown the Atlantic. Not the most comfortable journey he had ever undertaken, but as he shifted in the confined space and the boring hours went by it brought home to him how the world had shrunk in the last few years.

After a few days in New York he hired a car and took off for other parts. The big city was too brash for him in his present mood. The lights were too bright, there were too many people, even the plentiful food and teeming shops affronted him. He would get over it. In his heart he knew that he ought to rejoice that his country was booming: there had been hard years enough before the war. All the same, for the time being the self-congratulatory opulence grated on him and he went off to look for something different.

278

Since it was still early in the year he turned towards the south, looking for the sun. At the end of the second week of his enforced leave he was in California, and he had still not come to terms with the difference between war-torn Europe and peaceful America. True, there were many homes full of anxiety for sons and husbands overseas, there had been plenty of grief for the boy who would not come back, and everyone who learned that Luke had been 'over there' bombarded him with questions, but even though he tried to satisfy their curiosity he still felt that they did not really understand what war was like.

The blue skies and orange groves of California were no more congenial to him than the skyscrapers and traffic of New York. Luke did what he knew he should have done as soon as he arrived and turned his wheels back east to visit Prue's parents in Boston.

They were pleased to see him, but he was appalled by the way Prue's mother had turned the house into a shrine for her dead daughter. Prue's bedroom remained as it had been when she was a young girl, before they had married. Luke had the feeling that her mother would just as soon forget that Prue had been a married woman and pregnant at the time of her death.

Their questions about the fighting he had seen were the most perfunctory he had encountered. Only one thing had any reality for them: the sinking of the *Athenia*. They had all the newspaper cuttings and pictures of survivors preserved in big scrapbooks, together with all the photographs of Prue herself from her first naked appearance on a fur rug to the snapshots of herself she had sent home from the places she had visited in Europe.

Luke was thankful that he was staying no more than a weekend, but he felt lonely when he said goodbye because he had the feeling that he would not go back again and that was one more door closed behind him.

His parents were long dead and there were no brothers or sisters for him to visit. He had a few vague cousins, but he had no intention of looking them up. Being alone in the world had never worried him before, but now he began to realize how rootless he was. He had talked of giving up being a war correspondent, but if he did what would he do, where would he settle? He and Prue had had a rented flat in New York and another in London. At the moment he had no settled base and no necessity for one. He lived out of a suitcase, and a small one at that, and went where the job took him, staying in hotels or cadging a bed with a friend in an army camp, but that was a way of life that could not be sustained in peacetime.

When Luke left Boston he turned south with the idea of making his way back to New York, but because he was in no hurry to arrive he left the main highway and meandered along a subsidiary road until, late in the afternoon, he realized that he was none too sure where he was, although he knew he had left Massachusetts and entered Rhode Island. It amused him to think that he had managed to lose his bearings in the smallest state in the Union.

He had thought of Rhode Island as heavily populated; now he found himself charmed by rolling hills and small lakes. When he stopped for gas he asked the attendant, 'Anywhere round here I could get a bed for the night?'

'Keep travellin' in the direction you're goin' and you'll reach Westerly. Plenty of hotels there.'

'I'd prefer something less formal.'

The attendant was an elderly man, standing in for the youngster who had gone off to join the army. His watering blue eyes considered Luke.

Apparently he decided in Luke's favour because he said, 'Mort an' Edna Cheshunt take in summer visitors. Might be too early in the year for them, though.'

'Can I call them from here to see if they can take me?'

'Could do.' Again there was a long pause. 'Might be better to turn up an' let them get a look at you. Up along the North Road. Farmhouse. Red roof. You can tell 'em I sent you.'

Interpreting this as an assurance that the Cheshunts were unlikely to send him away, Luke set out along the North Road. As he drove through the neat farming country he passed a half finished house which looked as if it had been abandoned. Luke wondered why it had been left in that state.

Another mile brought him to the turn off for the Cheshunt Farm. The house was of a respectable age and solidly built. It had the air of crouching close to the ground, as if to escape the strong winds which blew in from the sea. A red roof, as the garage attendant had said, white painted walls and a thick front door.

The door was opened by a man who gave Luke no greeting, but waited for him to state his business.

'Early in the year for visitors,' he said cautiously. 'I'd have to ask Mrs Cheshunt. You'd best step inside.'

Luke was left standing inside the front door. There was a brass framed mirror on the wall and a braided rug on the floor. He could hear the murmur of voices from the back of the house.

The woman who came through to inspect him was small and neat, with brown hair sprinkled with grey and arranged in a sensible, no-nonsense style. She was wearing a flowered overall, on which she wiped her hands as she looked Luke over.

'How long would you be wanting to stay?' she asked.

'Three nights for certain, possibly the whole week.'

'It's quiet here, nothing to do,' she pointed out.

'Suits me. I'm on leave from Europe and I can do with some peace and quiet.'

'On leave!' For the first time her face showed some animation. 'Are you in the army?'

'No, I'm a newspaper reporter – a war correspondent.'

'Is that so?'

Luke had the feeling that she looked on him as some sort of exotic animal.

He managed to swallow a smile when she went on doubtfully, 'Everyone has to earn their living their own way, I s'pose. I can take you if you're prepared to eat with us. I've no one to wait at table. You'll not be early enough to join us for breakfast, but other meals you can take with us if you've a mind to.'

'That'll be fine.'

They did not get very well acquainted that first night, but the next day Luke went out for a long walk and when he got back he asked, 'Who's building a house just down the valley?'

He felt the stillness that came over the two people, but Mort Cheshunt answered without emotion.

'We started it for our son before he went off to the war. Was to have been our wedding present to him.'

The answer to the question Luke was trying to frame hung in

281

the air, but before he could bring himself to ask, Mort Cheshunt went on, 'He was killed in Normandy.'

'Didn't seem much point in goin' on with the building,' Edna Cheshunt said. 'Though sometimes I think we should finish it. Looks melancholy when you drive by and see the walls half up.'

'I was in Normandy,' Luke said.

It was not easy for them to unbend to a stranger, but by the end of the evening Luke had told them everything he could remember about the way it had been in France in the early days. Everything he thought it was fit for them to hear, that was. He caught Mort looking at him once or twice and guessed that the older man knew that he was censoring his account for Edna's sake.

They showed him their son's photograph and Edna fetched the letter his commanding officer had written to them. While she was out of the room Mort said abruptly, 'I was in the last war. Since we lost Pete I've sometimes thought I could hear the guns in the air again. The sound of war. Nearly cracked your ears open, made your brain spin in your head. I didn't want him to go, but there was no help for it.'

The letter said that Private Peter Cheshunt had died quickly and without pain. Luke doubted whether it was true, but he saw that it helped Edna to believe it and he said nothing to disabuse her of the kindly deception.

By the time he went to bed Luke felt that he had made two new friends. They were simple people, the kind he had forgotten about during his long sojourn overseas. Perhaps his boss had not been so far out after all.

For three quiet days Luke did nothing much but walk on his own and help out with a few chores around the farm. And he did a lot of thinking. The shrine that Prue's parents had built around the memory of their dead daughter had sickened him, but had he not done the same? He had been ready enough to share his bed with Stephanie in the safe haven of a country hotel, but once she had joined him in his London flat he had been on edge because he had felt she was intruding. It had been an additional misfortune that Prue's novel had revived such vivid memories of her. Stephanie had been right in suspecting that their quarrel over Conrad had had far more to do with

Luke's jealousy over Prue's book than over Stephanie's former infatuation for him.

He had been a fool to quarrel with Stephanie a second time over Conrad, especially since he had an uneasy suspicion that there was something admirable in the moral point Stephanie had tried to make. She had been saying that she put people first, even wicked people, and she had gone on saying it in the face of his hostility. The small voice of individual conscience. Wasn't that what they were fighting the war to preserve? And he had let himself get sidetracked into making snide remarks about a physical relationship that was long gone and over. Whatever happened he must see Stephanie again and try to put himself right with her.

When his three days were up Luke asked if he could stay at the farm for the rest of the week.

'Don't see why not,' Edna said. 'You're not hard to have around.'

Luke drove to Newport that day, amusing himself by looking with unenvious eyes at the magnificent summer residences once occupied by multi-millionaires. Very opulent, but not to Luke's taste. He didn't want a mansion, he wanted a home.

On his way back in the evening he stopped and walked up the hill to look at the Cheshunts' unfinished house. It was difficult to visualize it with nothing but the foundations to go on, but the situation was splendid, with a long view down the valley and shelter from the wind from the rising ground behind. Luke sat on a half-built wall and thought.

'Who drew up the plans for your son's house?' he asked Edna over supper.

'My sister Maggie's eldest son is an architect. I'll show you the picture he drew of the way it was meant to be.'

There was nothing spectacular about the planned house, but it was pleasant, commodious and looked as if it would be easy to run.

'I guess we'll have to build it and sell it off,' Mort said. 'The land surrounding it is no great shakes. T'wouldn't be no hardship to part with it.'

'I'm interested,' Luke said. 'Would you consider selling it to me?'

The two Cheshunts looked at one another.

'It'd need thinking about,' Mort said. 'I don't say we might not be as ready to sell it to you as to another.'

'You're a newspaper reporter,' Edna put in. 'Would you only be wanting it for a holiday home?'

'If my plans come to anything I'll make it my base,' Luke said. 'I'm not taking another assignment to cover a war, no matter where it may break out. Following the fighting gets to be too much of a habit. I've known men who couldn't live without the excitement. I don't want to end up like that.'

'It's a lonely place for a man on his own. You're not married, are you, Luke?'

'I was,' Luke said. 'And I might be again.'

He sensed the slight withdrawal and guessed that they were old-fashioned enough to look upon divorce with disapproval. He had better make his position clear.

'My wife was killed on the first day of the war when the *Athenia* was torpedoed,' he said quietly.

'I thought you'd known sorrow,' Edna said.

They had shown him their pictures of their son. Now Luke took out the old scuffed photograph of Prue he still carried in his wallet. It had been taken in 1938, nearly seven years before. Seven years! She looked strangely young, much younger than he remembered.

'A nice face,' Edna said approvingly. 'She will have been a good wife.'

'She was on her way home, expecting our first baby,' Luke said.

Edna put her hand up to her eyes and he was touched by this evidence of emotion from this self-contained woman.

'The girl our son was engaged to married someone else at Christmas,' Edna said. 'I've tried not to blame her. Her husband's in the navy. She didn't want to wait, not a second time.'

'If you came here we might be neighbours a long time,' Mort said abruptly. 'I'm still under fifty and I reckon to carry on farming as long as I'm fit for it. You say you're fixin' on getting married again?'

'I know my mind, but I'm none too sure she'll have me,' Luke admitted. 'She's an English girl.'

284

He hesitated and then decided he'd better come clean.

'You may have heard of her. Stephanie Bartram, the actress.'

'An actress!' Again the faint aura of disapproval was evident.

'She's a very fine person. She drove an ambulance in the Blitz and again when London was bombarded by the flying bombs.'

'Seems like they've got another weapon turned against them now,' Mort said. 'Rockets – V-2s they call them.'

'I hadn't heard that,' Luke said. 'I've been avoiding the news. Rockets? I don't like the sound of that. The buzz-bombs were bad enough, but at least they could see them coming.'

He stowed the photograph of Prue away again. One day he would stop carrying it, but he would never be able to bring himself to destroy it. Stephanie would understand. If they were together, that was. There was a folded scrap of paper in the fold of his wallet where he kept the photograph. Luke took it out and looked at it and then he handed it over to Edna.

'Stephanie wrote that out for me shortly after Prue was killed.'

'You've known her some time then?' she asked with a touch more warmth.

'Since 1939.'

Edna read the lines through in silence.

' "Make wars throughout the world to cease",' she quoted at last. 'We can all say Amen to that.'

She handed the scrap of paper back. 'It must be a comfort to you to be acquainted with such a right thinking young woman, Luke,' she said.

For one moment the image of Stephanie at her most glamorous rose in Luke's mind and he had a wild impulse to laugh, then he suppressed it. She was a right thinking young woman. She was kind, generous, brave and she stuck obstinately to her belief in the value of the individual even when that individual was a German spy. She was everything he wanted and he could hardly see how his life was to go on if he couldn't have her with him permanently.

Nothing was settled, but the Cheshunts promised to think over the offer Luke made them and he gathered that they

285

looked on it favourably. It seemed like a confirmation that he was moving in the right direction when he paid a visit to Providence the next day and ran into an old friend.

'Hey! Where did you spring from?' a voice demanded.

For a moment Luke was at a loss, then he recognized Mike Rothwell, a man he and Prue had known in the early days of their marriage, when they had been based in New York. Prue had kept in touch with him and his wife after they had left, but Luke had let the friendship drop, as he had so many of his old contacts.

They stood around in the street exchanging news until Mike said, 'If you're not in a rush why not come back with me? Lois will be thrilled. I guess you don't want to talk about it even now, but we were sick to the heart about Prue.'

Luke spent the rest of the day with them. Mike was a freelance journalist who seemed to be making a good living for himself. He had a heart condition which stopped him doing any war service and Luke guessed that it was also the reason for living outside any large city.

'We liked your book,' Louis told Luke. 'Are you planning on writing another?'

'I might,' he admitted. 'I've collected a lot of notes and one day I'll get around to putting them together.'

'Great! There are two or three other writers settled in this neighbourhood. You ought to come and join us.'

'I might do that,' Luke said, but he kept his plans to himself, nor did he tell them about Stephanie.

Luke spent the rest of his leave familiarizing himself with the small state he had decided to make his own. He hired a boat and took it up the coast and was pleased to find that he had not forgotten the skill his father and grandfather had taught him as a boy. His Scandinavian blood, he thought in amusement. They'd always told him it was one quarter sea water.

The future looked better and better. A house he liked in surroundings that suited him, good neighbours and congenial friends within easy reach. There was only one thing missing. A wife.

286

Eight

'Nesta Gordon has applied for permission to visit Conrad Aylmer,' Claud More was told. 'Do we let her in?'

'I suppose so. Aylmer wants to see her, I take it?'

'He's asked for her incessantly.'

'He's a lucky man,' Claud said. 'I thought Nesta was totally unyielding, but it seems that, like Stephanie Bartram, she's prepared to be forgiving.'

'Miss Bartram's last visit could hardly be called a success.'

'No,' Claud agreed. 'I hoped that the effect of his mother's desertion would be to make him more co-operative. I made a bad misjudgement there.'

'They're fed up with him in the prison hospital. He has to be watched all the time for fear of what he may do to himself. They talk of moving him to a psychiatric unit.'

'Perhaps this visit will sort him out,' Claud said, not very hopefully. 'Now that the trial is over and he's been sentenced there's not much we can hold out as an inducement to him to give us more information about his pre-war contacts. I might try to persuade Stephanie to see him again at the same time as Nesta. It would pander to his vanity to have two women fawning over him at the same time.'

When Nesta was shown in to Conrad's room he was up and dressed in the prison uniform, but his visitors were taken to him in a small room in the hospital wing, not the interview room where the other prisoners had to talk to their wives and families. Nesta gathered that he was kept segregated, partly because of his disability and partly because of his extreme unpopularity with the other prisoners, who would have treated him far more harshly than the courts had done.

287

It was the first time they had met since the appalling day when Nesta had been forced to believe that the story Anton had poured out was true. She had not seen Conrad before without the bandages which had covered his head and eyes then. As she looked at that beautiful, scarred face and sightless eyes, a spasm of involuntary pity shook Nesta's thin body, a weakening and unwelcome reaction of which she was ashamed.

'Nesta?' Conrad said, and the caressing note in his voice restored her fierce resolve not to show him any compassion. 'Are we alone?'

'The door is hooked open and there's a prison officer sitting on a chair in the corridor outside.'

'Will you come closer? Give me your hand.'

'I'd rather not.'

'You don't sound pleased to see me and yet I understand you asked to come.'

'I had a reason.'

There were two chairs and a small table in the room. Nesta took the unoccupied chair and shifted it so that she was sitting out of the line of sight of the prison officer. Conrad followed her movement with a puzzled look on his face.

'Do you listen to the news?' Nesta asked.

'I know that Germany is beaten, if that's what you mean. I never expected anything else when the invasion was successful.'

'The surrender must come soon,' Nesta agreed. 'But that's not what I'm talking about. Have you heard about the horror camps that have been discovered?'

'Oh ... those. Yes, I know that some atrocities have been uncovered.'

'When the Americans overran Ohrdruf and the news began to leak out I thought perhaps it was an isolated case, a camp where the commandant had run mad, but now we know that there were others – Buchenwald, Erla, Belsen, Dachau. The filth, the degradation, the sheer scale of the slaughter is something that ordinary human beings can hardly take in.'

'It's no use blaming me,' Conrad said. 'I wasn't there.'

'Most of the people in those camps were Jews, Conrad. I've come here today to ask you a question. You loved me once, but you wouldn't marry me. Why not?'

288

'You must realize why not! Because of the double life I was leading.'

'Was that the only reason? If your side had won and you had been able to give up spying, would you have married me then?'

There was no reply.

'You did love me,' Nesta persisted. 'You admired me; you thought I was a fine actress; by my side you could have had a fine career – provided, of course, that I was allowed to go on living and appearing on the stage. Given my Jewish blood, would that have been possible if the Germans had conquered England?'

The reply was wrung out of him, but it was a measure of the hold she still had over him that he gave it at all.

'That might have been ... difficult.'

'Yes, and it would have been equally difficult to explain away a Jewish wife or even a mistress. So you see, you did know. You knew that it was not possible for a good German to lead a normal life with a woman who had Jewish blood in her veins because she was not looked upon as a proper human being. You knew that the Jews were persecuted, you knew that they disappeared, you knew that there were concentration camps.'

'But not that people were treated so badly! Not that!'

'In my eyes you are equally guilty. Once you have decided that some people are superior to others and the sub-humans can be treated like animals, the rest follows.'

'I think you're being grossly unfair to me. When Stephanie comes I wish you'd talk to her. She's the only person who seems to have the slightest understanding of what I've been through.'

'Stephanie's coming here today?' Nesta asked sharply. 'I didn't know that. I must get on with what I came for.'

'Nesta, so far you've managed to stay very calm, but I know that underneath you must be going through the same hell as I am. If only you'd let me tell you my side ...'

'I have to stay calm,' Nesta interrupted him. 'I am an executioner.'

For a moment he did not take it in, then Conrad said questioningly, 'Nesta ...?'

'Keep quite still, Conrad. You can't see and neither can the man outside, but I'm pointing a gun at you.'

He was frozen into immobility, not by her command but by the shock of it.

'How ... how did you manage ...' he said.

'I'm in the army. It's not very difficult to steal a gun. They glanced in my shoulder bag when I arrived here, but there were only men on duty and I suppose they didn't like to feel my body. I carried it strapped to the inside of my thigh. Don't move, Conrad, and don't call out. My finger is on the trigger and the end will only come that much more quickly.'

'You *can't!*' Conrad said with conviction.

'I can. When I saw the walking skeletons at Belsen, when I read about the gas chambers, the mass slaughters, the sickening atrocities, I knew I had to kill a German. I'm calling you to account for the guilt of all your people, Conrad.'

The gun she held was pointed unwaveringly at the marred head of the man she had once loved. All the force of Nesta's unbridled temperament was behind the act she meant to commit. She would have acted then, at the height of her exalted belief in her mission of justice, but for the sight of Conrad's face. His mouth trembled, and he seemed to make an effort to tighten it, but he could not disguise the slow difficult tears that gathered in his blind eyes and ran down his cheeks.

Nesta was sickened at the thought that she had broken him, until he began to speak in a low, hurried voice that barely carried to the other side of the room where she was sitting.

'If you knew how I have longed for death! Nothing you could give me would be more welcome. Why do you think they keep me in hospital? Twice I almost succeeded and they dragged me back. Now, although I look everywhere for an opportunity, the knives are blunt, the windows are barred, there's not even a mirror I could break to cut my veins. From anyone else, I would accept death as a gift, but not from you, not like this, Nesta! I did love you once. I can't let you destroy yourself because of one of your wild impulses.'

'A life for a life.'

'But not your life, Nesta, not yours! What will you do afterwards? You'll be in prison, just as I am now. Confined, fettered, unable to fulfil the destiny you know you have.'

For the first time her resolve wavered and Conrad seemed to

realize it. More than that, his heightened senses had caught something Nesta in her preoccupation had missed, the sound of other footsteps coming along the corridor.

'I am being punished,' Conrad said, with a patience he had never known he possessed. 'I've lost everything – my country, my cause, my freedom, my sight; even my mother has deserted me! I've lost the woman I loved – and I did love you, Nesta – the respect of everyone who matters to me. Terrible things have been done in the name of the people I served. I shall finish my sentence and live the rest of my life shunted from place to place like an unwanted parcel. I'll never appear on the stage again, and neither will you if you do this fearful thing.'

He was talking loudly, to cover the sound of voices in the doorway. He did not know that Nesta, too, had heard them, but he caught the scrape of her chair and guessed that she had stood up. Conrad braced himself. As Stephanie came in he heard her catch her breath and her appalled exclamation: 'Nesta! No, no!'

He launched himself forward. A bullet sang past his ear as his arms closed round Nesta's legs and then she screamed.

'Stephanie! No, no, no! Not you, Stephanie, not you!'

Nesta struggled out of Conrad's grasp. The prison officer had come in and they must both be with Stephanie. Unseen behind them, the blind man's hands sought all over the floor for the thing he coveted beyond all others.

A second shot rang out.

Nine

'There's a big open fireplace,' Luke said. 'We can burn logs on that in the winter. Winters, I have to admit, will be fierce, but we'll keep one another warm.'

Stephanie smiled faintly and her fingers moved in his. That, so far, was the strongest response he had been able to get out of her.

'The house is built on the side of a green hill ...'

Stephanie's cracked lips opened. ' "A green hill far away",' she said in a faint, dry whisper.

'Mrs Cheshunt, our nearest neighbour, thinks very highly of your ability to quote hymns.'

Stephanie owed her life to the fact that she had been wounded in a hospital and a surgeon who ignored red tape had been available. She had been very ill, desperately ill, but the bullet which had penetrated her lung had been removed, the blood she had lost had been replaced, and all within minutes of the shooting.

When they had moved her to a more suitable hospital fever had raged through her body, but now that had subsided. If only he could reach her mind and make her look towards the future, Luke felt sure that she would start to recover.

He only had a few more minutes. Since she had recovered consciousness all his visits had been restricted. While she had been unconscious they had let him sit by her bed for as long as he liked.

He had to get back to Germany. His leave had already been stretched beyond the limit. At least she had spoken and that was a big step forward.

He talked, a little desperately, of the house he had bought in New England. He insisted that they were going to have a life there together, but it did not seem to him that anything he said penetrated the remote region where Stephanie spent her

293

waking hours. Her body was mending, but she was not getting any stronger. The medical people spoke vaguely about recovery taking time, but it seemed to Luke that they were more worried than they admitted.

He almost wished Stephanie had not decided to start talking when her lips parted again and she said, with difficulty, 'Nesta ...?'

'She's all right,' Luke assured her.

'... see her,' Stephanie said.

'No, you can't see her, honey.'

'Must,' Stephanie insisted.

Luke felt himself to be in a quandary, but in the end he decided to tell her the truth.

'Sweetheart, Nesta's having a nervous breakdown. Best thing, really. It means she's being looked after in hospital.'

From the frown on Stephanie's face it seemed that she did not agree with him.

'Not ... punish,' she said in the same difficult whisper. 'Accident.'

'She mustn't be punished, because what she did to you was an accident? Yeah, I guess everyone thinks that. Damn fool girl.'

He braced himself for the next question and, sure enough, it came.

'Conrad?'

Luke's hand tightened. How much of a blow was it going to be when he told her?

'He's dead, my dear.'

Stephanie's eyes closed. Weak tears gathered under her eyelids and ran down her cheeks. The nurse in charge of her came forward with an exclamation which sounded to Luke like annoyance.

Luke bent over Stephanie and kissed her on the forehead.

'I love you,' he said. 'Always remember I love you.'

The words echoed through Stephanie's mind and, underneath them, deeper and sadder, 'Conrad is dead'. She struggled to remember what had happened. Nesta, with a gun in her hand, an explosion and pain, pain. A second shot.

All night she tossed and turned and her temperature rose.

They were sufficiently worried the next day to call her mother into the hospital. Vera looked at the lovely flushed face and unseeing eyes of her daughter and spoke sharply to the medical people who were mishandling her case.

'The thing none of you understands about my daughter is that she's an artist,' she said. 'All this gadding about all over the world, wearing herself out; she was worn to a shadow before she took on the ambulance work again, which I was always against, and the result is, she's got no resistance.'

'It seems to be the news of Conrad Aylmer's death that's distressed her,' the doctor said meekly.

'Who was fool enough to tell her about that?'

'I was,' Luke admitted.

'And you're the man who tells me he wants to marry her! You'll have to learn a thing or two about handling a sensitive woman before that comes to anything.'

'You can't blame me more than I blame myself,' Luke said.

He bent over the bed, in agony because it seemed that he was unable to reach Stephanie in the troubled region to which she had retreated. He had returned to England with all his doubts and worries overcome, determined to lay everything he had at her feet and to win her, no matter how long it took, and was greeted by the news that she was lying in hospital at death's door. He had begged, stormed and insisted and at last had been allowed to see her, waiting patiently until she struggled back to consciousness and now, because of his own damn fool stupidity, she had suffered a setback that had everyone worried.

The hours went by and Stephanie became quieter. Luke sat with her hand lying slackly in his and did not know whether she knew he was there or not.

'Peace is coming soon, sweetheart,' he whispered. 'Peace, my darling. We can be together all the time, living in the house I told you about.'

Stephanie's heavy eyelids fluttered.

'Peace,' she said.

She opened her eyes and looked up at Luke, but then it seemed she remembered what they had been talking about before and the same distress swept over her.

'Nesta,' she said. 'Must see Nesta.'

'But, honey, she's sick.'

Stephanie's hand moved restlessly under his.

'Of course she's ill,' she said. 'She can't live with the knowledge that she killed Conrad. If only I could have stopped her!'

As the meaning of her words sank in, Luke said slowly, 'But Stephanie, my dear girl, it wasn't Nesta who killed Conrad. Her bullet went wide and hit you. She dropped the gun, Conrad found it and turned it on himself.'

Relief and sorrow struggled together in Stephanie's expression and then she said, 'I saw her with a gun and then I was hit and in terrible pain and I couldn't breathe. I heard another shot and I thought ... Luke, I must see Nesta.'

By the time Stephanie got her way and Nesta was brought to see her, Luke had had to tear himself away and return to Germany, still with nothing settled between himself and Stephanie, at least not to his satisfaction. It troubled him, the way she put aside his declarations of love and talk about the future, as if it were something that did not really concern her.

Nesta looked much the same as always except for the way her eyes seemed to have sunk into the deep hollows of her skull, but she had a nurse with her who did not leave her alone with Stephanie.

The sight of Stephanie, out of bed and sitting in an armchair wearing a soft blue dressing gown, seemed to surprise and reassure her.

'How are you, Nesta?' Stephanie asked.

'I still shake and cry for no reason, but they tell me I'm improving,' Nesta said. 'But you ... oh, Stephanie, I didn't mean you to be hurt, truly I didn't!'

'I know. It was a terrible accident. I wanted to see you because I knew you'd be blaming yourself and I thought it might help if I told you there was no need. Come and sit down.'

The nurse retired to the far side of the room, satisfied that there were going to be no hysterical outbursts.

'Can you talk about it?' Stephanie asked cautiously.

'About Conrad? Why not? They've had me talking about it

ever since I started to be coherent. I meant to kill him. They want me to say I feel guilty, but I don't.'

'Why should you, since you didn't, in fact, do it?' Stephanie said coolly.

'I hated him,' Nesta said, as if she had not spoken. 'I can't tell you how much I hated him.'

Her hands were clasped tightly over each forearm. Stephanie saw her fingers arch and she dragged her nails down over her arms as if she were trying to hurt herself.

'My flesh crawls whenever I remember that I let him touch me.'

'He wasn't all bad,' Stephanie said. 'I want to talk about him because I know you and your exaggerated opinions. Conrad had a lot of physical bravery, for one thing. I saw him risk his life more than once to rescue victims of the Blitz. And he saved Anton's life. He was troubled, too, when he saw the suffering caused by the bombing. Looking back, I even think our affair started because he was thrown off balance by a trying interview with a German airman.'

'I felt betrayed twice over when I learned that you and Conrad had been lovers,' Nesta muttered.

'I didn't know about you when it started and I broke it off when I found out,' Stephanie said.

'I suppose taking his own life required courage,' Nesta admitted grudgingly.

'No! There I disagree with you. That was his final selfish act. Yes, selfish! There was no need for him to die. He was getting back his strength, in spite of undermining it by two previous attempts at suicide. He might still have done something with his life.'

'Blind?'

'Other men have been blinded in this war and risen above it, and without Conrad's advantages. He had money. He could have used his wealth to help some of the victims of the war. German victims perhaps, provided he could have got over despising them for losing.'

'You had a low opinion of him and yet you defend him,' Nesta said in puzzlement.

'I wanted him to be ... oh, what's the word I want? ...

297

rehabilitated, perhaps. Yes, I condemned him but, Nesta, have you ever found yourself walking down a path you know to be wrong and yet been unable to turn back? Conrad did that and there were no side turnings for him because they were deliberately blocked off. I feel very strongly that that was wrong.'

'You've jolted me,' Nesta complained. 'I don't know what to think. My head aches.'

She put up her hand to her head and the watchful nurse got to her feet.

'That's enough for today,' she said. 'You've had a nice talk. Say goodbye to your friend and perhaps we'll come again another day.'

Nesta grimaced at Stephanie. 'They talk like that the whole time,' she said. 'Makes you feel about five years old.'

The slight touch of humour encouraged Stephanie.

'You and I deal in words,' she said. 'How well do you know *The Merchant of Venice*?'

'I was going to play Jessica once,' Nesta remembered. 'If you're thinking of "The quality of mercy", you're wasting your breath.'

'There's a passage you might think about. "Therefore, Jew, though justice be thy plea, consider this, that in the course of justice none of us should see salvation – we do pray for mercy". There's one more thing I have to tell you. I think you're strong enough to take it. Conrad made a will while he was in prison and I'm one of his executors. He left all his money to you. I hope you'll take it and use it in the way I wanted Conrad to use it, to help people who've suffered through the war, no matter what nationality they may be.'

The interview exhausted Stephanie rather more than it did Nesta, who went away looking alert and startled.

'You'd make a good therapist,' Stephanie's doctor remarked to her the next day. 'I've heard a very good report of your friend Nesta Gordon since you talked together. What did you do to her?'

'I directed her thoughts away from herself,' Stephanie said. 'Funny, it left me feeling extraordinarily limp.'

'Giving out in that sort of way is tiring. Perhaps we should have put the visit off for a few more days.'

'It fretted my mind until I could do it. What's the news today?'

'The Russians and Americans have made contact on the Elbe,' the doctor said, understanding immediately that it was news of the war she wanted. Automatically, he repeated the phrase that was on everyone's lips, 'It can't be much longer.'

For another two weeks the Germans delayed making their surrender. Stephanie left hospital and went into Sussex to recuperate. Her mother went with her, fussing anxiously.

'Are you going to marry that American reporter?' Vera asked abruptly one day.

'I might,' Stephanie answered.

'He seemed a decent sort and he was half out of his mind when he got back from America and found you in hospital,' Vera said. 'It's not what I wanted for you, but you might do worse. That book of his was quite successful, wasn't it?'

'I believe so,' Stephanie said, suppressing her amusement. 'He's building a house in Rhode Island.'

'Rhode Island! That's where the nobs hang out, or used to in my young day. You could act in a New York theatre and not be too far from home there, couldn't you?'

Stephanie refused to be drawn. She was getting back her strength, but she had fallen into a mood of dreamy acceptance of what each day might bring. Even the end of the war in Europe did not disturb her serenity. It was Vera who broke down and cried.

'I'm sure I don't know why,' she said, wiping her eyes. 'But it's been so long. I felt myself to be a young woman still when it started, but now I feel old.'

'Not yet fifty,' Stephanie pointed out. 'You're tired, as we all are. Old! I feel like something that came out of the Ark.'

'You've got back your looks,' her mother said.

She studied her daughter surreptitiously, not quite understanding the change in her. Stephanie had more than got back her looks; her beauty was radiant and something withdrawn and gentle in her face only enhanced her appeal.

Vera was not the only person to be struck by a new depth to

Stephanie's personality. In response to an appeal from her agent, Stephanie made a brief visit to London.

'You take my breath away,' he said. 'I've got some people I want you to meet. Do you feel up to it?'

'Oh, yes. I'm quite well now. A little tired occasionally and walking up hill makes me puff, but I'm told that will pass.'

She had a pleasant lunch with the agent and a producer and director from New York. Stephanie guessed that she was being sized up for a part. It surprised her that the agent had not told her what it was so that she could have shown an intelligent interest in it, but towards the end of the meal the producer hauled a bulky manuscript out of his briefcase.

'A new play by a new author,' he said. 'I think you'll like it. We need a British actress for the lead. Take it and read it. Rehearsals start late summer for a Broadway opening in October. I'm not making any promises until you've given us a reading and we've talked terms, but I think you could be right for the part.'

Stephanie took the play back to Sussex and read it through in one long gulp lying on a chair in the garden of the cottage she and Vera had rented.

'What's it like?' Vera asked.

'A dream,' Stephanie said. 'The best part I've ever read.'

'That's the most encouraging news I've had in years. Broadway! I always knew you'd have your name up there in lights one day.'

'I've not been offered the part yet,' Stephanie pointed out.

'As good as.' Vera regarded her daughter suspiciously. 'What are you looking doubtful about?'

'Luke.'

'For crying out loud! You're not going to let a half-baked affair with a reporter stop you going to Broadway, are you?'

'I'd like to talk to him before I commit myself.'

A week later Stephanie received a letter and kept the contents from her mother, but she was so restless that it came as no surprise to Vera when her daughter suddenly took it into her head to go out for a walk on the hills at the back of the house.

'Don't overdo it,' she said automatically.

'I'll go up the easy slope,' Stephanie said with an absent-mindedness that she thought must betray her preoccupation to her mother.

She went slowly up the white chalk path and paused to rest at the top, and then realized that for the first time it was not necessary. Her breath came easily and her legs felt strong. If she decided to take on a demanding role she would have the stamina to sustain it.

It was a day in late May, warm and sunny, with big white clouds coming over the hills from the sea. On top of the downs there was a little breeze, but when Stephanie dropped down into a hollow and sat down on the short turf the air was still. An aeroplane passed over and she lay on her back to look at it. An RAF aircraft, but on a peaceful mission. No more bombs, no more killing. Please God that the war in the Far East would be over soon.

Luke found her there, almost asleep. His shadow fell across Stephanie's face and she looked up, blinking at him. She began to sit up, with a smile of lovely welcome on her face, but Luke dropped down by her side and took her in his arms. As they kissed it seemed to Stephanie that she could feel the throb of life coming up from the earth beneath her.

They broke apart and lay looking at one another, smiling and silent, so close that Stephanie could brush Luke's cheek with her eyelashes.

'That's a very teasing thing to do,' he said. 'Well, my lovely girl, are you going to tell me that you love me?'

'So much. Yes, dear Luke, I love you.'

'And you're going to marry me.'

'Yes, but ...'

'There are no buts,' Luke said firmly. 'We're getting married.'

Stephanie disentangled herself and sat up.

'This is the second wonderful thing that's happened today,' she said. 'And we have to understand one another about the first before I can deal with the second. I've been offered a peach of a part in a Broadway play. I don't know how to put this, Luke, except to say quite baldly that I want to take it.'

'Where's the problem? I always expected you to carry on with your career.'

'Even with a career that might take me to both sides of the Atlantic? I'd want to do that if I were offered the chance. Can you understand that after having been through so much with this old country in the last few years I can't just tear up my roots and leave?'

'There's no question of going into permanent exile. I'm keeping the lease of my London flat. If you had work over here we could use it as a base.'

'Would you still feel it belonged to Prue?' Stephanie asked.

'I've put that foolishness behind me. Seeing the way her poor mother clung on to Prue's memory, realizing that it was the last thing Prue would have wanted, finally cured me. As soon as it's possible to get hold of paint and paper I mean to have the flat redecorated. You can chuck out all the furniture and start afresh if you like. I'd like you to feel that you have a home in both countries.'

Stephanie leaned against him, mutely grateful for his understanding.

'What about your lovely house?' she asked. 'How can we be together there if I'm working in New York?'

'You'd have to have an apartment or a hotel room in New York during the week, but if I stood by to pick you up after the performance on Saturday nights we could be home in time for you to have a rest all day Sunday and return to the theatre on Monday. I could get on with the book I plan to write during the week and we could have riotous weekends together.'

'Would you settle for that? It worries me that I wouldn't be making a proper home for you.'

'The play won't run for ever. You might even put a limit on the time you stay in it, though I won't press that idea on you. We can have long periods of domestic bliss and you can learn to milk a cow and make angel cake if that's what you really want to do.'

'And have a family,' Stephanie said quietly.

'Do you want that?'

'I'd like to have your children.'

'Another minute and I'll be in tears,' Luke said, and then he added, under his breath, 'it's a hell of a world to bring them into.'

Stephanie put her arms round him and drew his head down to rest on her breast.

'Have you had a bad time in Germany, my darling?' she asked.

'It's worse than anything you can imagine. I've been feeling sick to the bottom of my soul ever since I went back.'

They lay quietly together until Luke raised his head.

'I used to think you were the most exciting woman I'd ever known,' he said. 'And now you give me comfort just saying nothing and keeping still.'

Stephanie smiled at him and drew her finger down the bridge of his nose.

'I dare say we'll manage to dredge up a bit of excitement once we've married one another,' she said.

'It's just possible,' Luke agreed solemnly. 'Will you listen to me? I've caught the British habit! To hell with understatement. I love you like crazy. I'm mad about you. You're everything I've ever wanted in a woman and then some. I love everything about you from the tipmost hair on your head down to your toes and everything in between – especially everything in between. I'm bursting with pride because you're going to be in a great Broadway success. You're sweet and brave and clever and honourable and the way you look makes my heart turn over. Say something!'

'I quite like you, too,' Stephanie said. 'Oh, Luke, you fool! We'll have our difficulties – darling, let's face that now. Two strong personalities, two demanding careers; there are bound to be clashes. But as long as we love one another it's going to be worth it, I'm quite, quite sure about that!'